BEAU DEATH

BEAU DEATH

A PETER DIAMOND INVESTIGATION

Peter Lovesey

Published by
Soho Press, Inc.
853 Broadway
New York, NY 10003

Library of Congress Cataloging-in-Publication Data

Lovesey, Peter, author.
Beau death / Peter Lovesey.
Series: A Detective Peter Diamond mystery ; 17

ISBN 978-1-61695-974-6
eISBN 978-1-61695-906-7

1. Diamond, Peter (Fictitious character)—Fiction. 2. Police—
England—Bath—Fiction. 3. Murder—Investigation—Fiction. I. Title.
PR6062.O86 B43 2017 823'.914—dc23
LC record available at https://lccn.loc.gov/2017044371

Printed in the United States of America

10 9 8 7 6 5 4 3 2 1

BEAU DEATH

1

The kid was forever asking questions.

"What are those people doing, Dad?"

"I don't know, son. Just looking."

"Why?"

"Why what?"

"Why are they looking?"

"It's some kind of building site. The contractors put those high fences round for safety, but some people like to see what's going on, so they make little windows in the panels."

"What's a contractor, Dad?"

"Never mind."

"Can I look through the little windows?"

"Not now, son. We don't have time."

"Please."

"No."

The kid had been taught the basic courtesies and he was smart enough to use them to get his way. "Please, Dad. Please."

"Only for a moment, then."

They crossed the road to the billboards and of course the observation window was too high for the kid, so the father had to lift him.

"What's that, Dad?"

"I can't see while I'm holding you."

"That big ball."

"What are you talking about? Let's have a look." The father held the kid aside for a moment. "I see what you mean. That's a wrecking ball, son. You don't see them much these days. They're demolishing some old houses." This, he now decided as a caring parent, was not such a waste of time, but should be part of the kid's education. "It's using what we call kinetic energy. The ball is solid steel, really heavy and hanging on a chain from the top of the crane high above the houses. The man in control pulls the ball back towards his cab with another chain and gives it a good swing at the building, like the conkers you and I played with last year. It smashes into the wall and knocks it down." He shouted, "Wow! Just like that."

"Can I see? Let me see, Dad."

"Yeah. I suppose." The destruction was so compelling that he'd forgotten the kid had his nose to the panel and couldn't see a thing. He replaced him at the window.

"Is it going to smash the house down?"

"Not in one go. See if the ball is being hoisted back."

"It is, Dad."

"Good. Watch what happens, son." Shame the peephole wasn't big enough for two to look through at the same time.

"Crrrrrrrrash!" yelled the kid. And then on a disappointed note, "It's still there."

"I told you it takes several goes. Let's see." The kid was thrust aside again. "Yes, he's hauling it back for another try."

"Let me see."

"In a tick."

"Da-a-d."

"Hold on, son."

The ball smacked into the top floor of the end house of the terrace and produced a cloud of dust. Destruction is appealing. All along the barrier, people at the observation windows gave cries of satisfaction.

"Da-a-a-ad."

Like everyone else, the father was waiting for the dust to disperse to see the hole in the masonry.

"Nice one."

Belatedly the kid was given his chance to check the damage.

"Now you know what happens." The show wasn't over, but the father had decided it was time to move on. He lowered the kid to the ground.

"I didn't see."

"Course you did."

"Give me another look. Please."

It was true that the kid had missed the best action. The father peered through again to check that the secondary steel rope was taut in preparation for another smack at the building. "Last time, then." He lifted the kid again.

More shouts greeted another hit from the wrecking ball.

The kid said with delight, "Crrrrrrrrash!"

"Impressive, eh? That's enough, then. We've got to get on."

"Dad, what's that man doing?"

"What man?"

"The man in the house."

"There's nobody in the house, son. It's empty. It's being demolished."

"A man in funny clothes sitting in a chair. Look."

"I've told you before, you mustn't make things up." He shifted the kid from the window and looked for himself. "Oh Christ."

In the attic of the end house, now ripped open, was a crumpled figure in an armchair. The dust from the demolition had coated it liberally and it was a parody of the human form held together by what appeared to be long outmoded garments: olive green frock coat, cravat, grey breeches, wrinkled white stockings. The head, sunk grotesquely into the shoulder bones and partially covered by a long black wig, was a skull and the hands resting on the chair arms were skeletal.

"Can you see the man now, Dad?"

"I can."

"Is he dead?"

Spectacularly, irreversibly, abso-bloody-lutely dead, but you couldn't say that to a small child. "Em, he could be just a dummy like you see in dress shop windows."

"I've never seen a dummy like that. Can I have another look?"

"Definitely not. We're leaving."

In the next hour, the observation windows were more in use than ever on the demolition site in Twerton, the south-westerly suburb of Bath. People were waiting their turn for a look. All work had ceased. The foreman had called the police. A number of patrol cars and vans were lined up on what had once been a narrow road in front of the condemned terrace. But no one had yet started any kind of close examination of the occupant of the attic. Slumped in its chair, exposed to the daylight, the weather and the gaze of everyone, the skeleton was a treat for voyeurs and a rebuke for anyone who believed in respecting the dead. Normally a forensic tent would have been erected by now, giving the deceased some kind of privacy.

The difficulty was that the wrecking ball had rendered the building unsafe. The floor might well give way if anyone tried using a ladder to get near.

"What we need," the senior police officer on the ground said, "is one of those basket cranes they use to inspect street lamps."

"Cherry picker," his assistant said.

"Right. See if you can get one. If nothing else, we'll get a closer look at the poor blighter."

"One is already on its way," someone else spoke up.

"You mean I'm not the first to come up with this brilliant suggestion?" Detective Superintendent Peter Diamond swung around to see who had spoken. "Oh, you," he said to Dr. Higgins, the police surgeon who routinely attended fatal incidents. "Should have guessed you'd be here chucking your weight about."

"That's rich, coming from you," Higgins said, but with a grin. He was about half Diamond's size. "It was my call, so it's my cherry picker and my duty to inspect the corpse and decide whether life is extinct."

"Isn't that obvious?"

"It's the law, Peter, and you know it."

After making a show of another long look, Diamond said, "Unless my eyes are deceiving me, that thing up there is a skeleton. He's been out of it a few years. A few hundred years, if his clothes are anything to go by. No one here is going to report you if you declare him dead without getting close up."

"Sorry. You'll have to take your turn." The doctor meant business. He was already wearing a bright yellow hard hat.

Diamond turned back to his assistant, Keith Halliwell. "What's his game?"

"Dunno, guv. Does he want a ride in the cherry picker? Some people never grow up."

"Where's the site manager?"

"Gone. They all buggered off home."

"Do we know who owns these houses?"

"Some private landlord. There was subsidence reported a couple of years ago and when the borough surveyor was called he declared the whole terrace unfit for habitation. The tenants had to leave and it was boarded up while the legal formalities were gone through."

"That figures," Diamond said. "There's an appeal process."

"Meanwhile some squatters found their way in and occupied it."

"They would."

"Finally a demolition order was made by the council and here we are."

"But a ten-foot fence makes me suspicious. There's more to this than demolition."

"Someone must have paid for the perimeter fence."

"That's what I'm saying. Anywhere in Bath is a prime site. Mark my words, Keith—some sharp dealing has been done here."

"Speculators?"

"They like to call themselves developers. And nobody thought to tell the guy in the attic."

Halliwell had worked with Diamond long enough to treat his deadpan remarks as serious conversation. "No one knew he was there. It's not a proper attic room from what I can see. I'd call it a loft."

The cherry picker trundled in soon after and took up a position in front of the gaping building. Dr. Higgins in his hard hat stepped into the basket as if he was about to lift off from Cape Canaveral, pressed the right buttons on the control panel and was hydraulically raised to the level of what remained of the roof.

"Get your stethoscope out, doc," Diamond shouted up. "We're all watching."

There was no response from above, but the diagnosis didn't take long.

Only after the machine was lowered did Higgins say, "There was no call for sarcasm, Peter. It could have been a plastic skeleton put there by students. Didn't that cross your mind?"

"Actually, no. Are you satisfied he's real?"

"I am now. Real—and well and truly dead."

"Job done, then," Diamond said. "I'll go up and introduce myself. How does this thing work?"

"Haven't you used one before? You'll need the hard hat."

"I'm not going to fall out of the bloody basket."

"Health and safety. I'm a doctor, remember."

"Ridiculous."

With so many witnesses, Diamond was forced reluctantly to comply. Being stubborn, he borrowed a white Avon and Somerset helmet from a police motorcyclist and wore it with the visor up and the straps hanging loose.

The advisability of protective headgear was proved at once. His efforts at the controls were cack-handed. There were smiles all round when the basket made a jerky ascent.

He didn't learn much from his first close look at the skeleton. The figure was well coated in every sense. No doubt it had gathered dust from centuries in the loft, and the latest covering of powdered mortar had spread over that wherever it could settle. Only in a few places did the fabric of the eighteenth-century clothes show through. The skull with its lopsided black wig was at a weird angle, supported by the left shoulder. It was toothless.

As for the chair, it could have been from any period, with sturdy wooden legs, high upholstered back and armrests. There didn't seem to be any other furniture about, but not much of the loft space was visible. Broken tiles were scattered across the floor.

How does a thing like this happen? Diamond asked himself. "I'm just going up into the loft, dear, and I may be some time." Heart attack, stroke, overdose? The poor guy had found some privacy here, for sure, but why hadn't anyone gone looking for him? A missing person must have caused some concern, even a century or more before the police were created.

The big detective gripped the crossbar and leaned as far forward as he dared for a better view. Too far forward.

To his alarm he lost balance and felt himself tipping. His face came within inches of the skull. Only by flexing his legs and hanging on to the bar did he avoid a catastrophic nosedive.

In the middle of this undignified manoeuvre, something flashed.

"Sonofabitch." He knew what it was. Should have expected it. "Keith, grab that camera."

A great picture for the papers, him in his police helmet leaning out of the cherry picker like Narcissus face to face with his reflection, except it was the skeleton. Muttering obscenities, he fiddled with the controls until one swung the boom left and another jerked him savagely to terra firma.

Halliwell had gone in pursuit of the press photographer, but with little chance of success. The age gap was probably twenty years. Presently he returned, panting and apologetic. "None of us spotted him on the site, guv. We were all watching you."

This investigation was off to a bad start.

Little else could be done that afternoon. They ordered scaffolding for the front of the building, but the crew couldn't start for at least an hour and then it wouldn't be simple. A platform for access would have to be constructed and a waterproof canopy rigged over the top.

"This is going to eat into our budget," Diamond complained to Halliwell. "It's already a major operation and it isn't even a crime scene."

"It could be."

"If it is, it's a cold case and they don't come colder than this."

2

Peter Diamond's picture was in close-up in every newspaper next morning, his startled face under the police helmet near enough to kiss the skull. The caption-writers had excelled themselves:

DO YOU KNOW WHY I PULLED YOU OVER?
WHAT DO YOU MEAN—NO COMMENT?
YOU'RE NICKED—300 YEARS TOO LATE
YOU HAVE THE RIGHT TO REMAIN SILENT
RESPONSE TIMES SCANDAL

And some of the reporting was just as barbed. "Veteran detective Peter Diamond . . ." Veteran—an insult to a man still in his prime. ". . . commandeered a cherry picker yesterday to interview a suspicious character lurking in the loft of a half-demolished building in Bath and was surprised to find himself face to face with someone older than himself, a complete skeleton in frock coat and breeches seated in an armchair. It is believed from the style of clothes that the unfortunate victim must have been hidden there for up to three hundred years. Because of the dangerous state of the building it was not possible yesterday to remove the skeleton from the loft. 'We have no idea of his identity,' a police spokesman said, 'and we are unable to speculate on possible causes of death. Detective Superintendent Diamond will issue a statement in due course.'"

Police spokesman, indeed. Total bollocks. No one from

the press had come near the police after the snatched photograph.

Social media had gone viral on the story. The picture was all over Facebook and every other interactive site. Something about Diamond's expression, the staring, drop-jawed alarm in the pudgy, helmeted face, made it a classic.

In his latest workplace, the new CID office in Concorde House, an undistinguished block in Emersons Green on the edge of Bristol, the man himself was under siege. Calls were coming in from press people across the world wanting follow-up interviews. Officially he was unavailable for comment, in meetings all day, dealing with matters of much more importance. In reality he was with Georgina Dallymore, the assistant chief constable, talking about damage limitation.

"Couldn't you have sent up someone else in the cherry picker?" Georgina asked.

"What difference would that have made? The press would still have got their picture. I can't understand what the fuss is about."

"It's you, Peter. Your face."

"What's so special about my face? I'm not one of these celebrities they're always banging on about. The public don't know who I am."

"They do now."

"I don't get it."

"Everyone else does. That's the point. It's comical. You're pop-eyed, like some kid on a rollercoaster."

"I was pop-eyed with panic because I nearly fell out of the basket. I barely managed to save myself. None of the papers mention that."

"Just as well. It wouldn't make it any less amusing."

"It will all be forgotten tomorrow."

"Don't count on it," Georgina said. "Everyone in this place has it on their hand-held device. I've got it on mine. We'll be sharing it for months to come."

His opinion of humanity at large had always been low, and now it took another dive. "Did you call me in about this nonsense, ma'am?"

"If you want a straight answer, yes. I'm trying to restore some dignity to our department. We need to be clear about what happens next in this affair. The eyes of the world are on us. One more episode like yesterday and we might as well all hand in our resignations. What are you doing about the man in the loft?"

"Nothing."

"I beg your pardon."

"It's not a CID matter. There's no crime I'm aware of. Someone from uniform should take over."

"But you promised to report on further developments. It's in the paper."

"I promised nothing. Some pressman made that up. Anyhow, the building's unsafe. Until the scaffolding is in place no one can get at him without dropping through the floor."

"We don't know for certain how he died."

"And we may never know, ma'am. Anyone can see it's an ancient set of bones. It's history, almost archaeology."

"I'm surprised to hear you talk like this, Peter. There are deeply troubling elements in the case. How did the poor man come to be shut in the loft in the first place?"

"I doubt if we'll ever know. He could have gone up there for some peace and quiet, in which case he has my sympathy."

"He was in a wooden armchair, I gather?"

"Probably in the habit of using it as a bolt-hole."

"And died there?"

"It happens. Not a bad way to go, sitting in your favourite chair."

"Was he elderly?"

"Hard to tell from where I was."

"You must have seen his teeth."

"He hasn't got any."

"In that case he must be old. Mind you, 'old' was probably about forty in those days. I can't think how he could
have remained undiscovered so long."

"I expect he lived alone."

"You're not convincing me, Peter. I get the impression
you're doing your best to portray this death as natural so
that you can be shot of it."

"Someone else might enjoy taking it on. As for me I seem
to have made a right balls-up. I only got involved because
it was an unexplained death and now I'm thinking it would
be better from every point of view if I tiptoed away."

Georgina drew herself up in her chair in a way that
brought stress to her silver buttons and Diamond at the
same time. "You've never tiptoed anywhere and you won't
now. I want this death investigated properly and you will be
in charge. Thanks to your tomfoolery we're under intense
scrutiny now. You attracted all this media attention and you
can deal with it. Have the building treated as a crime scene.
See that the remains are collected and given a postmortem.
No shortcuts. Get to it, Peter."

He knew when it was useless to interrupt. "Tomfoolery" was below the belt, but he let it pass. In this mood
Georgina was implacable.

Only one space in Concorde House was suitable for a
private session with the entire CID team. Known as the
meeting room, it was so little used it still smelt of paint,
but nobody complained when they gathered around the
large table. They were pleased to get away from their
computer screens.

Diamond could have taken a seat like the rest of them,
but he chose to stand. His authority had been dented and
he felt the need to remind them who was boss. "I know

what you've got on your mobile phones," he said, getting straight to the source of his indignity. "That photographer shouldn't have been on the site yesterday and if it takes me the rest of this year I'm going to find out who he is and stuff his Nikon where the sun never shines." He paused and switched to a more reasoned tone. "But that's not what this is about. I just came out of a meeting with the ACC and she has instructed us to investigate the death of the skeleton in the loft. If, like me, you're thinking we're about three hundred years too late, then think again. To quote Georgina, the eyes of the world are on us. She wants a result."

"What kind of result?" Halliwell asked. "We're not going to find his name."

Negativity like that from any of them would have been deplorable. From Keith, his deputy, it came as a shock.

"Get with it, all of you," Diamond said, slamming one hand on the table and making a fist of the other. "We're professionals. We've faced bigger challenges than this. Who knows what we might find when we pull out all the stops? We haven't searched his pockets and we haven't sent in the scenes of crime team yet."

"Was there a crime?" John Leaman asked. He was the logic man ever ready to pick holes. Like Halliwell, he needed bringing into line.

"That's what we need to find out."

Leaman raised an eyebrow and said nothing.

Now Sergeant Ingeborg Smith spoke up, and she wasn't entirely unhelpful. "Is the body still in place, guv?"

"Can't call it a body or John will object. Bones is all it is. Yes, it's there, but no longer on public view. Scaffolding and a canopy are being erected as we speak. The trouble is that the whole building is dangerously unstable and they can't work from inside. He'll have to remain there until we find a safe way to remove him."

"A crane?" Leaman said.

"For lifting a skeleton? No way. It would fall apart and leave us with a heap of bones. There must be people who specialise in this kind of recovery exercise. It's delicate work."

"The Velvet Glove Pick-up People," Halliwell said.

"Where are they based?"

"Joke."

"What?"

"I'm trying to lower the tension."

He glared at Halliwell. Maybe that was really the intention. Better give him the benefit of the doubt. "I walked into that, didn't I? Well, I'm dead serious." He switched attention to Ingeborg. "See if you can locate someone capable of taking this on."

She gave a nod and touched the controls on her tablet.

Diamond told Leaman to research the history of the house. "I assume it was built in the eighteenth century. There may be documents in the local records office."

"If it's that old, it must be listed," Leaman said. "I'll try the Preservation Trust." Try them he would, in more ways than one. Nobody was more thorough than Leaman. He'd pester the life out of the people in the records office and the trust.

"Good thinking." Diamond didn't mind giving credit for a positive contribution, the first indication that he might be winning the team over. "Looking ahead, when we succeed in recovering the body, we'll insist on a proper postmortem. Just because the corpse is reduced to bones, I don't want some junior doctor given the job. See that we get the best available, Keith."

It almost went without saying that Halliwell would be the police presence at the autopsy. He regularly stood in for his squeamish boss when the pathologist was at work on a body. "We might be better off with a forensic anthropologist."

"Oh yes?" The big man was wary. He'd taken more than

enough flak from his deputy this morning. "What's that when it's at home?"

"A bones man."

He gave a nod. Halliwell might be trying to redeem himself. "Good thinking. Is there one locally?"

"Must be. I'll make enquiries."

"You can find out a lot from bones," Leaman said.

Ingeborg looked up from her internet search. "You watch far too much TV."

"Then there are the clothes," Diamond said, "what's left of them. A fashion expert can tell you within five years or so when a garment was made. I happen to know someone who can help here."

No one winked or nudged the person next to them, even if the temptation was there. The "someone" was undoubtedly Paloma Kean, Diamond's friend and occasional lover. Paloma owned a successful agency providing costume illustrations for television, film and the stage.

"Has anyone taken photos?" DC Paul Gilbert asked. He was the youngest on the team, eager to be involved, and sometimes forgotten.

Diamond eyed him. Photography was a sore point. But the remark seemed to have been innocent. "Done. A cameraman went up in the cherry picker and got good shots from several angles." He frowned. "Now that I think about it, five or six people went up in that damned contraption for a look yesterday. Why was I the unlucky one who got his picture in the papers?"

Not a question any member of the team was willing to answer. All eyes turned to the windows or the ceiling.

"If you like," Gilbert said, "I could start a display board with the photos, like we have in an incident room."

"Waste of time," Leaman said.

Diamond agreed with him really. The days of whiteboards in incident rooms were over, if they had ever existed except on TV shows, but he didn't like the way clever-clogs had said it. "For this inquiry, seeing as none of us knows much about the eighteenth century, that's not a bad suggestion."

"In here?" Gilbert asked.

"Why not? We'll stake our claim for this as our base. Is there anything I've overlooked?"

"We're getting a big response to your picture in the paper," Ingeborg said.

He bristled again. "Is this another dig at me?"

"Let me rephrase it, guv. There's a lot of interest in the skeleton. People like nothing better than a mystery. Most of what comes in will be no help, but I'm saying all suggestions ought to be examined, just in case."

"Have you looked at any of this stuff yourself?"

"I did this morning. Two or three callers said the skeleton might be that of Beau Nash."

"Beau Nash?" The name was familiar to anyone who had lived in Bath for any length of time, central to the history of the place. Familiar, but hardly a missing person.

Leaman rolled his eyes and said, "Because he's the only eighteenth-century man they've heard of."

"It's indisputable that he lived here."

"In a small terraced house in Twerton? Give me strength."

Ingeborg shot Leaman a look that would have pierced armour plating. "Do you want to hear about this, or not?"

Diamond said, "Go on, Inge."

"The caller said the description of the clothes matched the things Nash usually wore. He had a black wig, which was unusual in those days. Most of them wore white ones. He dared to be different."

"I can't say I know much about the man. He made Bath fashionable, didn't he? The Beau bit turns me off."

"The skeleton was wearing a black wig," Ingeborg said in case the point had been missed.

"It was, I grant you. See what you can bring up on your

tablet about this guy, will you? And, yes, you're right about the public response. We always take an interest in what people have to say."

"What exactly is the ACC expecting us to do?" Halliwell asked.

"What we'd do for any unexplained death," Diamond said. "Investigate and discover whatever we can for the coroner."

"And the media," Leaman murmured.

"Screw the media. I'm not pandering to that lot."

Brave words, but everyone knew that media interest was driving this enquiry.

Ingeborg had been busy on the internet. "Beau Nash was a Welshman, born in Swansea in 1674, and quite a ladies' man, going by this. Sent down from Jesus College, Oxford, for neglecting his studies and getting engaged to one of the local girls."

"Was that against the rules?" Halliwell said.

"He was only sixteen at the time. He tried the army next, liking the idea of a red coat, and that didn't last long either when he found there was more to soldiering than showing off, so he moved to London to study law at the Middle Temple."

"And show off in a wig and gown?"

"I expect so." She was quick to digest the information and rehash it for the team. "Doesn't seem to have spent much time with his law books. Lives beyond his means, buys expensive clothes and gets a reputation as a dandy. You'd think it was a recipe for disaster, but he'd found the thing he excelled at. And when the king—that's William III—makes a visit to the Middle Temple, Nash is the only possible choice to stage a royal pageant. Naturally the show is a stunning success and the king offers him a knighthood, which he declines."

"Why?"

"Hang on," she said, scrolling some more. "You're getting ahead of me."

She didn't take long to catch up.

"He was only twenty at the time and on his beam-ends and you needed funds—a small fortune, in fact—to live the life of a titled man. But his reputation was made and from that time he was a fashion leader and an arbiter of good taste. He seems to have been extremely popular with women and—" she clicked her tongue as she read on—"a big spender of their money. At one time, someone questioned all this high living and said his money must have been acquired dishonestly, so Nash produced a wad of love letters from twenty girls who, basically, were keeping him."

"Unknown to each other?"

"You bet," Halliwell said.

Ingeborg looked up from the tablet. "I don't like saying this about my own sex, but when they're daft they're really daft. He must have broken a lot of hearts."

"I've never thought of him as a letch," Halliwell said. "Anyone with a name like Beau Nash sounds to me like some old queen."

"Please," Ingeborg said with a look she normally reserved for stale bread. "A beau was a good-looking guy who knew how to chat up girls. Do you want me to go on, or have you heard enough?"

"Can we fast forward to when he arrives in Bath?"

She took a moment more to check. "That's 1705, it says here."

"Listen up, people," Diamond said. "We've come to the crunch." He hoped it was the crunch. He'd invited Ingeborg to brief the team, but the chance of any of this stuff being useful to the enquiry was remote.

"Okay," she said. "This is where his life really takes off. Bath was the eighteenth-century equivalent of Vegas. Entertainments of all kinds: music, dances, eating, the theatre, riding in sedan chairs, bathing and drinking the spa water, but the main attraction was the gambling. Gamesters came to the public rooms and huge sums were won and lost at dice games and cards. Nash had got a taste for it and in his first season he had an amazing run of luck at the tables, winning over a thousand pounds."

"How much is that in modern money?" Halliwell asked.

"At least a hundred and fifty grand," Leaman, the walking encyclopedia, informed them.

"From then on he was made," Ingeborg went on. "Everyone wanted to know him. The master of ceremonies, a Captain Webster, invited him to be his ADC."

"What's that?" young Gilbert asked.

"Aide-de-camp. Military term," Leaman said.

"Personal assistant," Ingeborg said. "A massive honour. The MC presided over all the big occasions, so Nash got to see how things were done. And shortly after that there was another extraordinary piece of luck. Captain Webster got into an argument with a man who'd lost heavily to him in a game of cards. He was challenged to a duel that took place by torchlight in Orange Grove and was killed. That was the bad news. The good news was that Beau Nash was the only possible choice as his replacement."

"Convenient," Leaman said.

"Too bloody convenient," Halliwell said. "If the police were any use they'd have wanted to know more about that duel."

"What police?" Leaman said.

"They had watchmen and constables, didn't they?"

"Are you thinking Nash had something to do with it?" Paul Gilbert said.

"Don't you know anything about duelling?" Leaman said. "They always brought along friends as seconds. Nash was Webster's ADC, so it's more than likely he was involved. Webster was a military man and ought to have known how to use a sword, but he was killed. Did Nash have anything to do with it? You bet he did."

"Pure speculation," Halliwell said.

"And we're getting sidetracked," Diamond said, increasingly irritated by all the sniping. He gave Ingeborg the cue to go on. "He gets to be master of ceremonies."

"The king, it says here," she said. "He was known as the King of Bath, and now he was in his element. Under Captain Webster, the management had been slack. Public rooms a disgrace, people drinking to excess and arguments breaking out. The gamblers carried swords for protection and no one could feel safe because there would always be losers. The swords were often drawn as a threat and tore the women's gowns. There were card sharps in plenty, prostitutes, beggars and the rooms stayed open all night. Beau Nash used his authority to change all that. The carrying of swords was banned. Duelling was suppressed. The wearing of riding boots in the public rooms had to stop and women were forbidden from wearing white aprons."

"White aprons?" Leaman said.

"Why?" Diamond asked.

"I'm not sure. Let me read on a bit." She dragged the text down with her finger. "Ah, according to Goldsmith, only Abigails were clothed in aprons."

"Say that again."

"Historical slang for a lady's maid. The aprons were a fashion item our man disapproved of. He once found the Duchess of Queensberry wearing one—a very smart apron made of Brussels lace—in the Assembly Rooms and snatched it from her and threw it to her ladies-in-waiting. He was just as strict with the men. If one appeared in top-boots, the Beau would march up to him and ask him archly if he had 'forgot his horse.'"

"And they tolerated this?" Diamond said.

"From him, yes. He sounds like a tyrant over the dress

code, but he was mostly good-humoured, it says here. That duchess made no fuss. People felt safer after he insisted all dancing should end at eleven. He brought in rules that changed the way everyone behaved, and they were widely agreed to be sensible and needed. The city's reputation improved out of all recognition and there was hardly a VIP in the land who didn't visit. The Prince of Wales, dukes and duchesses, prime ministers, poets and novelists. And they all had to obey the rules. Even when the King's daughter, the young Princess Amelia, only seventeen, pleaded for one more dance after the official closing of a ball at eleven P.M., Nash wouldn't bend his rules. 'But I'm a princess,' she told him. 'Yes, madam,' he answered, 'but I reign here.'"

"Sounds a real bundle of joy," Halliwell said.

"Actually he was admired for it. As time went on and his influence increased, he was more like a mayor than a master of ceremonies. With his young friends Ralph Allen and John Wood he transformed Bath into one of the most beautiful cities in Europe. Many of the great buildings went up during his reign as MC."

"He was the King of Bath," Halliwell said. "We got that. Can we cut to the chase—his sad end?"

"In Twerton," Leaman said with scorn. "I don't think so."

Diamond gave them both a glare and told Ingeborg to keep going.

"He ran into financial problems. He'd never drawn any kind of salary as master of ceremonies. He made his living out of the gaming, which was pretty smart considering how many were unsuccessful at it. He'd been living in style in a large Baroque-style house he'd had built in St. John's Court that's basically still there as the Garrick's Head."

"We've all been there," Leaman said with what sounded like a yawn. "Remember when Georgina insisted we watched her in *Sweeney Todd* and bought the tickets? We all needed a drink after that."

Ingeborg smiled at the memory. "Back to Beau Nash. He dressed in expensive clothes, including a distinctive white three-cornered hat. And when he visited Tunbridge Wells to play the tables he'd travel in a carriage pulled by six greys and surrounded by footmen, outriders and French horn players. He appointed himself master of ceremonies in Tunbridge as well as Bath. His reputation was huge. When the Prince of Wales visited Bath in 1738, it was Nash who acted as host and put up the obelisk in Queen Square to mark the royal visit."

"That whacking great column in the middle?" Gilbert said. "He paid for that?"

"It was even higher originally and surrounded by a pool."

"You were telling us what went wrong," Halliwell reminded her.

She read on. "The rot set in with the government bringing in gaming laws banning some of the most lucrative games like Hazard, Ace of Hearts and Faro."

"This is when?" Diamond asked.

"1739. But the gambling industry hit back. New games were introduced and one of these was EO."

"Say that again."

"EO. The letters E and O, standing for Evens and Odds."

"Do we have to go into all this?" Leaman asked, looking round. There were definite stirrings of impatience.

"Hold on. I must get this right." She switched to another website. "A simple idea that eventually was later developed into Roly Poly, or roulette."

"Roly Poly," Diamond said to lighten the mood. "Love it."

"EO is played with a wheel with forty sections marked even and odd. The wheel is turned and the punters place their bets and win or lose according to which section the ball ends up in. Get the picture, everyone?" She swiped back to the main story. "Nash saw the game being played at Tunbridge Wells and cleverly decided it was the coming thing. It was going to be huge, and he was right. He decided to invest. He made an agreement with the inventor to bring EO to Bath in return for a percentage of the profits. But he soon suspected something was wrong and that the Tunbridge Wells guy had cheated him. He brought a court action, but lost the case. That was bad enough. Worse, he was forced to admit in court that he'd made his living for years by taking a cut from the professional gaming managers."

"Like a protection racket?"

"There was no threat of violence."

"Extortion, then?"

"I suppose you could call it that. He vetted everyone who played at the tables and ruled whether they were suitable. The gambling bosses couldn't stay in business without his support."

"And nobody else knew?"

"It was a massive scandal when the news broke. I don't know where the public thought he got his fortune from, but his reputation went into free fall and so did his income. Eventually he was forced to exist on a handout of ten guineas a month from city funds."

Diamond interrupted again. "Exist where? Where was he living?"

Ingeborg had been speed-reading from some website, summing up the key facts for the others. She was as eager as they were to discover how the story turned out.

"According to this," she said, "he was forced to sell the large house he'd had built for himself in St. John's Court and move into a smaller place nearby in Sawclose. And that's where he"—she clapped her hand to her mouth—"where he died."

An awkward silence followed.

John Leaman didn't hold back for long. "What a fucking letdown. We've listened to you rabbiting on for the past twenty minutes for this? He can't be the skeleton in the loft if he died in Sawclose."

"Hang on a bit, John," Diamond was quick to say. "You can lay off Inge. I was the one who asked her to give us the facts."

Leaman couldn't stop his rant. "She could have saved her breath if you'd listened to what I said at the start—that there was no way Beau Nash ended up dying in a poky terraced house in Twerton without anyone knowing."

Now Halliwell made the mistake of getting involved. "She just told us he fell on hard times."

"Hard times, my arse," Leaman said. "Ten guineas a month wasn't poverty. Scale it up to modern money values and he was well fixed. The so-called smaller house where he ended up wasn't a hovel. It's still there. It's a restaurant, for Christ's sake."

"Next door to the Theatre Royal?" Paul Gilbert said.

"You've got it. Am I exaggerating? Big grand entrance flanked by two stone eagles. The place is called something else now, even if most people still think of it as Popjoy's, and if you've ever been inside you'll know the rooms are big. Fine staircase, plenty of sash windows, nice fireplaces."

"The point is can we be certain he died there?" Gilbert asked. Each of them was doing his best to take the sting out of Leaman's tongue-lashing.

"Ever looked at the plaque outside?" Leaman said.

There was a pause. It seemed that Bath's detective force, trained to miss nothing, didn't read plaques.

"Wait a bit," Leaman said, taking out his iPhone. "There." He brandished the image in triumph. IN THIS HOUSE RESIDED THE CELEBRATED BEAU NASH AND HERE HE DIED FEBY 1761.

From their reaction, you could believe the death had just happened.

"If you knew all along, why didn't you speak up earlier?" Halliwell asked.

"I was waiting for the twist that didn't come."

"John's right," Ingeborg said. She'd been using her tablet again. "He died in that house, aged eighty-six, nursed by his mistress, Juliana Popjoy, and he was given a funeral in the Abbey fit for the King of Bath, paid for by the Corporation. Muffled bells, a procession through the streets with choristers and the town band together with his own bandsmen from the Pump Room and six aldermen carrying the coffin."

If Leaman had been made up to chief constable he couldn't have looked more jubilant. "Enough said?"

3

A summer evening in Paloma's garden on Lyncombe Hill had done much to restore Peter Diamond's spirits. They were seated on patio chairs at a white metal table overlooking the sloping lawn. A bottle of good red was uncorked on the table. The scent of stocks wafted to them from a raised flowerbed. The light was fading fast, but on the roof of the house a blackbird was singing its heart out.

The big detective murmured, "Sanctuary."

Paloma raised her eyebrows.

"A famous scene from *The Hunchback of Notre Dame*," he said. "The 1939 version, with Charles Laughton. He rescues the gipsy girl Esmeralda—that's Maureen O'Hara—from the gallows and scales the front of the cathedral with her in his arms repeatedly shouting, 'Sanctuary!'"

"You and your old films," she said. "What put that in your head?"

"Your garden, a place of sanctuary."

"Still hurting from that stupid picture in the papers, are you?"

She'd seen it, too. The whole world was enjoying the joke. He took a long sip of wine. "Hurting, no. Smarting, possibly."

"What's this talk of sanctuary, then?"

"Escaping from another day at the office."

"Don't you like it where you are now? Bigger than

Manvers Street, isn't it? Better than the custody suite at Keynsham?"

"I'm not on about being relocated, not today. No, it's tensions on the team. We're getting on one another's nerves. They're good detectives, all of them, but there are personality clashes not helped by a case we're not equipped to take up."

"The skeleton?"

"It grins like it's enjoying my frustrations."

"Come on, Peter. They all look like that with the teeth exposed."

"It's got no teeth and it still manages to grin. Jesus, what was that?"

A large explosion had shattered the idyll.

Diamond was out of his chair.

"Fireworks, I expect," Paloma said, still seated, wine glass in hand. "Someone having a party."

Another huge bang rattled the table. She steadied the bottle.

"You're right," Diamond said. "See? Above the trees. Big shower of green and red. And there goes another. It's a bit bloody much when you can't sit in your own garden on a summer evening. Could have been a bomb going off."

Paloma laughed. "Just when you were getting gooey-eyed, talking about sanctuary, too. Shall we go indoors?"

"I think so. This could go on some time. I was in the Met when the IRA bombing campaign came to London. 1990, just before I got the job here. A massive one went off when we were driving past the Stock Exchange. I've been sensitive to sudden blasts ever since." He hunched his shoulders. "There's another."

"You must have been glad to escape to Bath."

"Until now."

"Oh come on." Paloma stood up and collected the wine glasses. "Would you bring the bottle?"

He closed the patio door, still muttering about the fire works. "I've brought some photos with me."

"Photos of what?"

"The skeleton."

"The skeleton and you together?" she said. "I'll try not to laugh."

"Not that damned press picture. The police photographer took these. We always get a record of the scene." He spread them on a coffee table, six shots taken from the cherry picker at various angles.

She faked a disappointed sigh. "I was wondering what you had in the envelope. Could it be a travel brochure, I thought. Venice? Florence? Foolish woman."

"I want your expert opinion on the clothes he's wearing, if you can make out what they are under all the dust and debris."

"Haven't you got him out yet?"

"It's a tricky job, impossible to do without spoiling the integrity of the scene. He's covered with a canopy now. A special crane had to be brought in. We're hoping to lift him out more or less in one piece tomorrow."

She picked up one of the photos. "Mid-eighteenth-century or shortly after, as far as I can tell from the tailoring of the frock coat. The long-skirted, loose-fitting look was on the way out by 1750. Older men might prefer it, but the smart dressers went in for tighter fits like this. I'm interested in the standing collars on the coat and the waistcoat. They would have been called high ton about 1760. This appears to have been a fine brocade once. Rather tattered now. He's definitely a gent. Pity the shoes aren't visible."

"You think the collar makes it more like 1760. That's helpful."

"The dark wig is unusual for the time," Paloma said. "White or off-white wigs were almost universal. They powdered them. This is obviously coated in dust, but I'd say it's black underneath. He may have been eccentric."

"Because of the wig?"

"It's a strong statement, more than shoulder-length. A rug like that wouldn't have disgraced King William the third."

"Did the kings have dark wigs?"

"In the 1760s? No. The Hanover kings went for the short white look, George the second and third, at any rate. The first George did sport a brownish wig, but he was dead by 1730."

"The reason I asked," he said, "is that two or three people called in suggesting our skeleton might be Beau Nash, who was known as the King of Bath."

"The Beau?" she said. "Are you serious?"

"When we get a tip like that, we can't ignore it." He could understand her disbelief.

Paloma laughed. "Forgive me, Pete. You make them sound like informers. Beau Nash is history."

"So we've been checking the history."

She couldn't contain her amusement. "What's the thinking behind this? The wig?"

"That's a factor, yes. I gather Mr. Nash saw himself as a fashion icon who wanted to be seen in his black wig."

"He did. It's no secret. There are plenty of pictures of him. He liked to stand out from the crowd, obviously. He's often pictured in a white tricorne, which I'm sure he chose for dramatic contrast. But none of this means he ended up in a loft space in Twerton."

"Agreed. We made some searches. Well, Ingeborg did, and we found he didn't die there."

"He died in the house next to the theatre, now an Italian restaurant. Didn't you lot know that?"

"We do now."

"Your man is obviously someone else."

"Was he buried in the Abbey?"

She shrugged. "Nobody seems to know. There's a large marble tablet in the south aisle, but it's only a memorial, not a gravestone, and it wasn't put up until about thirty years after his death."

Paloma's grasp of Bath lore always impressed him. She'd know about Nash as the supreme arbiter of fashion in his lifetime.

"So if he wasn't buried in the Abbey, where did they put him?"

"It's rather sad."

He turned to look into Paloma's face and see if she was kidding. She was good at hiding a smile, but her eyes always gave her away. Not this time. "You mean that?"

"There's a strong belief that he was buried in a pauper's grave."

"Get away."

But she was as serious as if she had just come back from the interment.

"After a funeral on the scale he was given?" he said. "A procession to the Abbey? The town band? Muffled bells? The full monty? He was the king. He made the city what it is. Would the people of Bath allow such a star to end up in an unmarked grave?"

"Well, I can't see them removing the corpse from the coffin and parking it in a chair in the loft of some small terraced house in Twerton, if that's what you're suggesting. That's even harder to believe."

Diamond didn't comment. He was weighing all kinds of bizarre possibilities. "Was he officially a pauper?"

"I suppose he was. He must have run up debts. Easy to check. I've got books I can lend you."

"Thanks. I'll look at them. It's all balls, I reckon, but I must make the effort."

"You need to talk to an expert, if only to discover for sure what happened to the body," Paloma said. "Let me think about that. Meanwhile, be an angel and pour me another glass of wine while I track down those books."

The recovery of the remains was fixed for first light when the tricky operation could be done without attracting much attention. A strong police presence controlled who entered the site. If the press came, as they probably would, they'd need to get their pictures from behind the fence. Diamond was there with Keith Halliwell, both in regulation hard hats, and so was Dr. Claude Waghorn, the forensic anthropologist brought in from the university to carry out the postmortem, a small man with a big personality who had already clashed with the manager of the recovery team. He'd insisted on directing the operation himself from the cherry picker at top-floor level and being in radio contact with the crane operator.

"A nit-picker in a cherry picker," Diamond commented to Halliwell.

"No bad thing, guv. We need an expert eye on the job."

Halliwell was right. Only the clothes and the chair were keeping the skeleton together. Waghorn had decided the best strategy was to lift it seated in the chair, a precision assignment. A telescopic truck-mounted crane had been brought in by the contractors and the chair and its fragile occupant would be hoisted from the loft using a sling. But before that, the canopy had to be removed and all the bits of rubble round the base of the chair picked up or there was a serious risk of trapping the feet and legs and parting them from the rest of the skeleton. All this had to be done mechanically.

The task was painstaking and Dr. Waghorn made it more so by personally selecting each chunk of debris to be lifted. From his basket high above everyone else he couldn't have been more animated if he were conducting the last night of

the Proms. He was saying plenty, too, but he had a barely
audible voice and Diamond and Halliwell were spared the
commentary. The crane driver bore the brunt.

Diamond looked at his watch. "Best part of two hours. I
thought we'd be out of here by now. By the time we finally
move him, half of Bath will be watching."

"Ah, but only through the observation windows. They
won't get on the site."

"Who are those two, then—the guys in suits on the other
side? They're not police or workmen."

One of the two he was looking at was squat, overweight
and bald. The head definitely wasn't shaved. His pinstripe
suit looked expensive and his whole demeanour oozed self-
importance. In fact he wasn't doing anything other than
watching Waghorn's performance and making occasional
comments. His brown-suited companion didn't give out the
same aura at all and seemed to be there in a supportive
role, nodding agreement and saying little himself.

"Check 'em out, Keith."

Halliwell went over and approached the sidekick.

When asked, the man in the brown suit said, "What's
it to you?" Seeing the police ID, he quickly added, "I'm
with my boss."

"And who's he?"

"Don't you know him? Sir Edward Paris, Edpari
Properties."

Halliwell had heard of the company, even if he didn't
know the man. Edpari was emblazoned in large letters over
developments across the city. "Does he own this?"

A shrug. "If he wants to, he will before long."

"Do you work for him?"

"Chauffeur mainly."

"Name?"

"Spearman. Jim Spearman."

"The car's nearby, is it?"

"The Range Rover with the others. The clean one. The Bentley is being serviced."

"And how did you get in?"

"Through the gate like you. Nothing gets in Sir Ed's way."

Halliwell returned to Diamond and reported back.

"I've seen the name around. How did he say the last part?"

"Like the French say Paris."

"Makes sense, I suppose, if that's his name: Ed Paris. Is he French?"

"I didn't ask."

"Funny. I would have said it like Campari. That's Italian."

"I know," Halliwell said, and added after a pause, "I do know that much."

"Shouldn't be long now," Diamond said, returning his attention to the work going on in the loft.

How wrong he was. Fitting the huge sling was like herding cats. Each time the straps were swung towards the chair, Dr. Waghorn aborted the attempt. He had his own idea how the job should be done and he wanted perfection. After numerous attempts, he came down from the cherry picker for a consultation with the manager who was nominally in charge.

The two detectives were close enough to hear everything.

"It's not working," Waghorn said in his small, clipped voice.

"You're telling me, mate. It's never going to work with you," he was told.

"It's a disarticulated skeleton. I don't want to end up with bones flying everywhere."

"That floor is going to collapse sometime soon and the whole bloody lot will disarticulate and fall through the hole. Don't hold me responsible if you won't let us do our job. We're not without experience. I've moved a Bechstein grand from the top of a tower block and it didn't take a single scratch."

"This is not a piano."

"It's child's play compared to that."

"Speaking of experience, I have thirty-seven years of recovering bones from difficult locations," Dr. Waghorn said through gritted teeth.

"Can you operate the bloody crane?"

"Of course not. I expect your people to do that."

The manager folded his arms and said nothing. The movement in a telescopic crane is controlled through hydraulics. The boom is made up of many tubes fitted inside each other and the jib at the top works from the tower, swinging the lifting apparatus through wide angles. The hoisting block is heavy and capable of damage if misused.

"Very well," Waghorn said finally. "Attach the sling your way. I'll watch from here—if I can bring myself to look."

Without more fuss the sling was passed under the chair and secured.

The man in the cab had been waiting hours for this. The cables tightened and took the strain and the chair and its fragile burden ascended at a rate that seemed quite shocking after the long wait. There were some cheers and a few laughs at what was quite a comic spectacle.

"Not very dignified," Diamond said. "I don't think the King of Bath is enjoying this."

"He doesn't have much choice," Halliwell said.

Looking uncannily like a rider on a chairoplane, the skeleton was swung clear of the building and out towards the deck of an open lorry, where it was lowered and steadied by a couple of assistants and secured to the sides. The skull had shifted position and some finger bones had to be recovered from the sling, but otherwise everything seemed to be in place.

"Job done," Halliwell said and called out, "Happy, Dr. Waghorn?"

"Hardly the word I'd use," said the anthropologist. "I've aged ten years in the last ten minutes." He marched over for a closer look.

"A coffee would be good after that," Halliwell said, unstrapping his hard hat.

Diamond appeared not to hear.

"Shall we go?" Halliwell said.

His boss was gazing at what was left of the terrace. "The demolition men are going to move in soon and finish the job."

"That's for sure. Delays cost money in the building trade."

"I want one more look inside the loft before they reduce it to rubble."

Halliwell sighed. Coffee would have to wait.

Diamond was pensive. "I wonder if I can do any better with the cherry picker than I did before."

He stepped across and climbed into the basket. Waghorn had controlled the thing like a professional. Diamond needed to remind himself which of the small levers gave upward movement. The one he chose simply caused a judder. Trial and error, he told himself. Another did the job and he was borne smoothly to the height he wanted. Now it was a matter of finding forward movement.

He managed it without mishap and got his aerial view of the space the skeleton and chair had occupied. More of the boards were revealed, some of them splintered and caved in, and he saw just how unstable the flooring was. Nowhere would it be safe to stand.

A little to the left of where the chair had been was what he first took to be some sort of mould. On closer inspection he saw it was a piece of dust-covered fabric.

Curious, he manoeuvred the basket a short way to the side and then forward and leaned over cautiously for a better view.

Now he could see what it was, flat as a dried cowpat but distinctive in shape.

A white three-cornered hat.

The Archway café was the only choice for coffee in Twerton. Located under the railway embankment arches on the Lower Bristol Road, it was more spacious inside than the temporary-looking shopfront suggested. On entering and catching the whiff of fried bacon, the two detectives remembered how hungry they were and ordered the full English.

The place was busy and they were lucky to find a table for three against the wall on the far side. Not wishing anyone to join them, Diamond put a claim on the spare chair with the flattened tricorne belonging to the skeleton. Before leaving the demolition site he had borrowed a useful tool resembling a litter picker and fished the hat out of the loft with that.

"Will it be all right there?" Halliwell said.

"Best place," Diamond said. "I'm not putting it on the floor."

"It's a bit spooky."

"Why?"

"Like Beau Nash left his hat on the chair and is coming back for it."

"Maybe we should order him a breakfast."

"You're freaking me out, guv."

Two mugs of coffee were put in front of them.

They had barely taken a sip when someone from behind Diamond said, "What's your opinion, then, officer? Is it really Beau Nash?"

He didn't recognise the voice. As a film buff, he thought it resembled Alfred Hitchcock's ponderous delivery, trying to sound grand but with a touch of cockney in the vowel sounds. And when he turned, the large-bellied figure

standing over him was not unlike Hitchcock. Sir Edward
Paris, with Spearman the chauffeur a little to the rear.

"Were you listening to our conversation?" Diamond said
without getting up or even making eye contact. He was
annoyed at being waylaid like this and he didn't give a
toss for titled people.

"Not at all," Paris said. "I happen to take an interest in
Beau Nash, that's all."

At the mention of the name, Diamond turned to face
him. "What's your opinion, then?"

"I'm just a humble rate-payer who helps to fund your
salaries," Paris said. "You're the investigators."

"We investigate crime."

"Is that his hat on the chair?"

"I can move it if you want to join us."

"No, we just had our coffee. We're on the way out. I
didn't want you to think we had a guilty conscience and
were trying to avoid you."

"We hadn't even noticed you," Diamond said.

"You noticed us at the demolition site. Bloody trespass-
ers, you thought, what do they want? We got through the
security, no problem. I'm well known for that."

"And for other things, no doubt," Diamond said.

"We won't go into that," Paris said. "But if you have a
decent-sized piece of land you want to sell, I'm your man."
He nodded to his chauffeur and made for the door.

After watching them leave, Diamond said, "Pompous twit.
I'm glad they didn't stay. I've had enough of him already."

"What were they doing at the site?" Halliwell asked.

"I thought you asked the chauffeur that. Getting a close
view, so Paris can boast about it to his friends."

"How would he have known?"

"About the skeleton? Come on, it's in all the papers,
much as I wish it wasn't."

"About Nash."

"He isn't the first to come up with that. People have been calling since yesterday."

"Is the hat the clincher?" Halliwell asked.

"Not unless we can think of a reason why he ended up in that loft. But there are strange coincidences. Nash owned a white hat and wore a black wig. Unusual in both cases. Paloma told me the clothes are right for 1761, the year he died. There were no teeth left in the skull, which is what you'd expect of an old man. He lived to eighty-six. That ticks a lot of boxes."

"They can estimate someone's age at postmortem, but not with much accuracy." No one in CID was better qualified to speak about postmortems than Keith Halliwell.

"We'll see what Waghorn comes up with. He may discover something else that ties in with what we're thinking."

"Would DNA prove it? Can it be extracted from bones?"

"Yes, even old bones. But it's no use having a DNA profile if you've nothing to match it against."

"His descendants?"

"He didn't marry, so there's no official bloodline. I expect there were offspring, because he put himself about, but where do you start? No, I can't see the DNA thing helping us."

"It's new territory for us, trying to work out what happened more than two hundred years ago. What was Twerton like in those days?"

"Before the railway came? Very different. Mainly cloth mills and weaving. The industry went on for centuries. The terraced houses would have been workmen's dwellings. Not the class of place Beau Nash was used to. I doubt if he came here very much at all."

"He was doing his MC bit, lording it over the Assembly Rooms."

"Right. But that's beside the point if he was brought here after his death."

"Is that what you think happened?"

Diamond sighed. He was forced to get serious about the Beau Nash thing. "Someone else would have moved the body here. If they wanted a secret place to put him, Twerton in 1761 was a smart choice."

"But why? Why would they move him?"

"This is just a theory," Diamond said, airing the knowledge he'd gleaned overnight from the books he'd borrowed. "He was a hero for much of his life. He made Bath the most fashionable town in the land. Grand buildings went up, fine streets. You know all this. I don't have to labour it. But in his last years he was a sad case, old and decrepit and running up debts."

"I expect he was still well known."

"For sure. He was master of ceremonies to the end of his life. Visitors wanted to catch a sight of him even while he was being carted about in a sedan chair. The great days were gone, but Beau Nash was a name everyone knew. You only have to read accounts of the funeral procession. People filled the streets, watched from upstairs windows and even the rooftops. After a show like that, every seat taken in the Abbey, can you imagine them burying him in a pauper's grave? I can't."

"Is that true—about the pauper's grave?"

"I heard it from Paloma last night. It's treated as a fact in the books she lent me. Hard to disprove."

"But was it the law?"

"If someone didn't leave enough to pay for his funeral, you mean?"

"Wasn't there something called the Poor Law?" Halliwell said. "The state bears the cost."

"I'm sure you're right and this is my point. Nash had run up debts and was officially a pauper and the law had to be observed."

"You'd think they'd have started a fund."

"Funds take time to organise. They had a body ready for burial. The city paid for the funeral but they weren't going to take on his debts. My theory is this. A few of his friends decided there was no way the great Beau Nash would end up in an unmarked grave, so they secretly took him out of his coffin."

Halliwell's face formed a slack-jawed expression of disbelief.

Diamond wasn't stopping for anything. "The burial went ahead, but without the corpse. The coffin was weighted with sacks of earth. Under cover of darkness the body was moved to the house in Twerton and hidden in the loft."

"Sitting up in a chair?"

"That's weird, I agree. I expect it looked more dignified than laying him out on the floor. Obviously he was going to decompose, so they left him there for nature to take its course, intending to remove what was left of him at a later date and bury him somewhere more fitting. I can't believe they meant the loft to be his final tomb, but in the meantime they would have sealed the access hatch and made the loft appear inaccessible."

"And then what? They forgot about him?"

Diamond shook his head. "Unlikely. We're talking about loyal friends, maybe as few as two or three, who took a big risk for him. Something went badly wrong. There's always a leader in a conspiracy like this. It's possible he was struck down. Sudden illness, or an accident. Anyway, when the main man was out of it, the others couldn't think what to do. They delayed and delayed. In the end they did nothing at all."

"Did you think of all this while we were at the site?" Halliwell asked, impressed, and not for the first time, by his boss's ability to find a rational scenario for extraordinary events.

"It's been a couple of days," Diamond said. "That's just one hypothesis. Do you want to hear another?"

"Not right now, guv. I can see our breakfasts coming this way."

"That was quick," Diamond said to the waiter who put a well-filled plate in front of him. "We're going to enjoy this."

"Is there someone with you?" the waiter asked, seeing the third chair.

"I hope not," Halliwell said. "I do hope not."

"You ordered two breakfasts, I thought."

"And you're right," Diamond said. "Thanks, but our friend Beau didn't show up. He doesn't know what he's missing." When the waiter had left, he said, "Will it put you off eating if I go on?"

Halliwell shook his head.

"The second scenario, then." Diamond was already into his breakfast. "This is unbelievably good bacon. There's a woman involved."

"With the funny name—Popjoy?"

"Juliana Popjoy, yes. All the women liked him, but Popjoy was the one who came back when he was well past it. On his deathbed he told her he was in debt and would die a pauper and he couldn't bear the thought of an unmarked grave. She promised she would never allow it to happen. She was thinking she'd give him a decent burial by selling off bits of his furniture. But she had no conception how much he owed until after he was dead."

"This sounds good," Halliwell said, "and I can see where it's going."

"She'd made a promise, and she kept it," Diamond went on. "She went to the city authorities and did a deal with them. She'd pay off as many of his outstanding debts as he could afford. In return, she'd be given his body to dispose of. Officially, he'd be buried according to the law as a pauper and this would be announced. In reality, she'd find a final resting place for him."

"Definitely more believable."

"What happened after that is not so clear, but it may have gone like this. She was skint herself so she moved into the humble little place in Twerton."

"With the body?"

"Exactly. She hadn't enough left to buy him a burial plot. But it soon became obvious that cohabiting with a corpse isn't practical, so she got someone she trusted to move him up to the loft and seal it. She had every intention of bringing him down later and carrying out his dying wish, but something went wrong. She may have died herself, or turned senile and forgot what she had upstairs. The upshot was that poor old Beau was stuck in the loft until the wrecking ball disturbed him."

"Or how about this?" Halliwell said. "She was a bit of a weirdo and she liked going up to the loft and talking to him."

"You read too many horror stories."

"It's not impossible. People who live alone—"

Diamond stabbed a finger at him. "Don't go there."

"Sorry, guv. My big mouth."

They went back to chewing bacon and mushrooms for a while. This breakfast was as good as any they'd tried in Bath.

Finally, Diamond said, "I'm not lonely. I've got a cat who keeps me sane."

4

Paloma had called Diamond and set up a lunch meeting with a Miss Estella Rockingham, who was researching Beau Nash for a biography.

"Old-fashioned name," he said, picturing a silver-haired lady with half-glasses.

"She's a young and extremely clever West Indian who won an award to fund the project. I'm sure the book will win more prizes."

"Is it written?"

"In outline, I believe. She's constantly going back to original sources. Her research is amazing. She came to me looking for portraits that haven't been used and her knowledge about eighteenth-century costume is awesome."

"Were you able to help?"

Paloma nodded. Her collection of historic illustrations was the best outside the V&A and the British Library.

"Pictures of Beau Nash?"

"And that was a challenge. She wanted him young. The ones you see most often are of a pudgy-faced guy in middle age. Calling him 'Beau' is laughable. But the early ones— drawings, mostly—give some idea why so many women adored him. It takes an exceptional man to look sexy in lace."

"You found what Estella wanted, then?"

"Yes, and she knew exactly which magazines to search.

That was over a year ago. Since then she's been admitted to the Beau Nash Society."

"There's a society?"

"Here in Bath. Haven't you heard of it? Everyone who is anyone is a member. They meet in rooms in the Circus and you can only join by invitation. Estella gave a talk last winter and got the nod—which is more than I did. I talked to them about eighteenth-century costume and all I got for my troubles was a bottle of plonk."

"She probably knows more than they do."

"So do I, but not about Mr. Nash. To be serious, Estella will get invitations from across the world when she publishes her book. She must have found out heaps more about him since. But your discovery is going to amaze her, him being hidden in some attic all these years."

"I don't want to start with that stuff," Diamond said. "We don't know for certain if it's him. You haven't told her what this is about, I hope."

"All she knows is that you're a detective on some kind of investigation that touches on Beau Nash. She'll be so excited."

"Let's soft-pedal on the skeleton in the loft," he said. "Before we reveal any of that I'd rather get her take on where he ended up."

"Do it your way, then. I'll never understand the finer points of interviewing witnesses."

Estella liked Mexican, so the meeting had been set up for Las Iguanas in the courtyard in Seven Dials, reached through a passageway from Westgate Street. Paloma and Diamond got there early and found a table close to the window.

"Are you okay with Mexican food?" Paloma said.

"*Now* you ask."

"Actually I asked Estella and she suggested here. It's not exclusively Mexican. I'd call it Latin American really."

"Fair enough." Diamond was more of a pub food man: pie and chips. "I'm sure I'll survive. What's that monstrosity in the yard?"

"The fountain?"

Whether the rather odd cast-iron structure they could see from the window deserved to be called a fountain any longer was arguable. There was no water spurting from it. The top tier had been adapted for growing plants that overhung three sad black wading birds standing in a stone surround with more vegetation.

"Little egrets?" Diamond said from his limited knowledge of ornithology.

"Glossy ibises, I was told."

"Do they have some significance here?"

"Not to my knowledge. I believe when the developers were creating the yard in the late 1980s they found the piece at Walcot Reclamation and decided it would make a centrepiece. A talking point, if nothing else."

"Why—because it ain't a fountain any longer?"

"Because of all the actors."

"I see no actors."

"Come outside and I'll show you."

They got up from the table with their wine glasses and he was shown a feature he'd never noticed before, Bath's mini version of the forecourt of Grauman's Chinese Theatre in Hollywood—sixteen sets of handprints and signatures cast in bronze and cemented to the top of the low wall around the fountain.

"They all appeared at the Theatre Royal," Paloma said.

He circled it slowly. Derek Jacobi, Peter Ustinov, Susan Hampshire, Edward Fox and twelve others were immortalised there. "Joan Collins—what was she in?"

"*Private Lives*. They all had to press their palms into some orange gunk to make the moulds. It must have seemed a good idea at the time."

"It's a bit lost here."

Paloma's eyes were elsewhere. A young black woman in a pale blue coat with silver frogging had clattered into the yard on the highest heels Diamond had seen in years. "Here's someone who certainly isn't lost. Estella, meet my friend, Peter."

It was the kind of meeting that made him wish he'd chosen a better tie, and, on second thoughts, a better shirt, suit and shoes as well. She was immaculate. They shook hands and she said, "I'm extremely curious to know what you want from me."

"It's no great mystery," he said.

"I thought mystery was your thing. Aren't you in criminal investigation?"

Paloma said, "Peter's head of the murder squad."

Estella's eyes widened. "Murder?"

"And other local pastimes like armed robbery and abduction," he added.

"And you think I can help?"

"Shall we go inside and get you a drink first?"

"A strong one, I think."

In the restaurant, Diamond tried to lower expectations. He hadn't planned to start like this. "You're writing a book about Beau Nash, I'm told."

"And you think he might have murdered someone—my dear old Beau?"

"No, no, not at all. Can we rewind and delete all mention of murder?"

She flashed her small, neat teeth. "You're saving that up for the climax, when you assemble us all in the library and tell us whodunit."

She was being playful when he wanted to get serious. "It doesn't work that way in CID. I borrowed a couple of books about Nash from Paloma. Nicely written, but thin on facts. I gather yours will be more substantial."

"More words for sure. That isn't always a recommendation."

"New material?"

"Every bit I can find. I don't want to pad it out."

"How many biographies are there?"

"Of Beau Nash? I know of seven. The first, and most useful, appeared only a year after his death. That was by Oliver Goldsmith."

"Seven is a lot, but Richard Nash is a fascinating subject, isn't he?" Diamond said, wanting to let her know he'd mastered the basics. "Welsh boy comes from humble origins and survives a series of setbacks to conquer Bath by force of personality."

"His family weren't all that humble," Estella said. "They could afford to send him to Oxford University."

"But he ended up a pauper, didn't he, after becoming one of the most famous men in the land? That's the real fascination for me." It wasn't, but now that they'd started on Beau Nash he was keen to get to the topic of the funeral and what happened after.

Paloma said, "Peter's getting hooked on eighteenth-century history. He'd be enrolling at the university if he wasn't a policeman keeping us safe in our beds."

"Your beds are outside my beat," Diamond said.

"Don't disillusion us, or we won't sleep at nights," Estella said with a smile at Paloma.

The waitress arrived and the next minutes were taken up pointing at things on the menu. They agreed on tapas for starters but the two women's choice of a dish called blazing bird flavoured with flaming hot habañero sauce was a step too far for Diamond. He settled for a Cuban sandwich and asked for a large jug of water and three glasses.

More smiles.

"I don't suppose Beau Nash ever tasted Mexican," he said.

"Boiled chicken and roast mutton were his favourites," Estella said. "They ate mainly meat and not many vegetables. He was partial to potatoes and called them English pine-apples and used to eat them on their own as a separate course. But please let's get to the reason we're here. What is it about the Beau? What do you want to ask me?"

Put suddenly on the spot, Diamond came out with the question he'd planned to slip into the conversation with more subtlety. "Where did he end up?"

"After his death, you mean?" she said. "It's far from certain. Goldsmith doesn't say and everyone since has either ducked the issue or admitted it's a mystery."

"You must have researched it."

She smiled. "Tell me about it! As you probably know, he lay in state for four days and then there was a funeral fit for the King of Bath, with a procession through the streets from his house to the Abbey. It's been assumed by some, including the Dictionary of Welsh Biography and the Oxford DNB, that he was buried there, but like most of his biographers I'm unconvinced. There's a persistent story that he was buried in a pauper's grave."

"That's the one we heard."

She nodded. "He was, of course, massively overspent. Debts of over £1200. Let's say £200,000 in modern currency. So technically, yes, he was a pauper. We know the name of his would-be heir and executor, his nephew, Charles Young, but the disposal of the estate was handled by an agent called Scott."

"Who wanted paying, presumably?"

"Without a doubt. Goldsmith's book tells us the few pathetic items that were left to dispose of: a few books, some family pictures and miniatures, two gold snuffboxes, one presented to him by the Prince of Wales and the other by the dowager princess. They didn't fetch much. The pictures were advertised for sale at five pounds each but finally went for half that amount, and the miniatures as a job lot for three guineas. I'm not sure about the snuffboxes. And of course there were papers, a number of letters and his unfinished manuscript."

"A book?" Paloma said.

"Some pages of a book. A money-making venture that he used to attract subscribers at two guineas a time. The title was *A History of Bath and Tunbridge for these last forty years by Richard Nash, Esquire, with an apology for the Author's Life.* It was nowhere near written. A sprat to catch a mackerel. While he was still alive he hinted that all sorts of secrets would come out—more about other people's private lives than his own. It brought in some funds. Even the city corporation coughed up for twenty-five copies."

"All on spec?" Diamond said.

"A few ineptly written sheets were found after his death and Goldsmith made the best use he could of them. The nephew wasn't happy and complained that Scott had hatched some kind of underhand deal in return for a cut of the profits in Goldsmith's *Life of Beau Nash.*"

"Was he right?"

"He probably was. Nash's scribblings had some value and should have formed part of the estate."

"Did the book sell well?" Diamond asked.

"Goldsmith's? Spectacularly well."

"To all the people fearful of how much would be revealed?"

"Let's be generous. Nash's fame was huge. The first printing sold out in four days."

Paloma said, "Top of the *Sunday Times* bestseller list?"

"Easily. You have to know that Goldsmith was an unknown Irish writer at the start of his career—a hack, really—who in time became one of the greats of English literature, so they did well to get him. It's a fine book and the prime source for us biographers, but Nash's name sold it. A lot of people made themselves rich out of the Beau after his death, selling portraits and poems and tributes, but I don't think his creditors got much."

"Wasn't the house sold?"

"That isn't mentioned in Scott's papers. Almost certainly he'd mortgaged it before his death to offset his debts. He'd sold his coach, his horses, his rings, his watches. He was living off the ten guineas a month voted by the corporation in recognition of his services in better times."

Diamond steered the conversation back towards the matter that interested him most. "But at least he wasn't living alone in those last years."

"No, he had a companion."

"Juliana Popjoy?" A chance to show he'd done his homework.

"Papjoy."

"Excuse me?"

"Papjoy was the name she used. Victorian prudes altered it, thinking it was vulgar."

"Why?"

"Pap," she said. "You wouldn't be asking if you lived in those times. It was a word for a breast, like boob, or tit."

"Got you," he said, trying to think in historical terms. "Papjoy."

"Well"—Estella spread her hands—"I may be out on a limb here, but I'm of the opinion it was a name she took on. She was a courtesan when he first met her and slept with her. To me, Papjoy is just too suggestive to be real. It's in keeping with the names the Restoration comedy writers were using, like Lady Wishfort."

He had to think for a moment. She'd tossed in the name as a scholarly point without a hint of a smile. "Right. Understood."

"And the men's names were just as suggestive," Estella added. "Horner, Pinchwife."

"Coupler," Paloma put in.

"Really?"

"You've heard of *The Country Wife?*" Paloma said to help him out. "*The Relapse?* The National brought *The Beaux' Stratagem* to Bath a year or two ago."

He shook his head. He knew as much about drama as he did about knitting socks.

"Lady Fidget?" Estella said.

"Mrs. Friendall," Paloma said.

"Lovemore? Lady Teazle?"

The two women were definitely enjoying this now.

Estella made an effort to be serious. "It doesn't really matter to you if it wasn't the name she was born with, does it?"

"I suppose not."

"In fact, it matters even less than you think."

"Why?"

"You were saying Juliana was with the Beau at the end but I have to tell you this is untrue."

Frowning, he said, "The books I've been reading claim she was there for him, nursing him through his last illness."

"I know," Estella said. "I've read them. They're wrong."

"Really?" Paloma said. "It's such a nice rounding off, back with his old love."

"Cue the violins," Estella said. "Sorry, guys, but Goldsmith says nothing about Juliana. I don't think he mentions her anywhere in his book, and he's the prime source."

Diamond's best theory about the skeleton and how it came to be hidden in Twerton had just been blown away.

There was a short hiatus while the tapas were put in front of them. Paloma and Estella made noises of appreciation, but Diamond couldn't raise any enthusiasm, even after taking his first bite.

"Are you telling us Juliana Papjoy didn't exist?" he said to Estella, beginning to feel this meeting had been a waste of time. She didn't seem as charming as he'd first thought.

"Not at all. She existed. She was one of a string of mistresses. He was an old goat if you ask me. He once said that wit, flattery and fine clothes were enough to debauch a nunnery. There's independent evidence that Juliana lived with him for some years when they were younger. He bought her a dapple-grey horse and allowed her to have a personal servant and dress in all the latest fashions. She was often seen riding about the streets of Bath and using a distinctive whip like a birch. In fact she was jokingly known as Lady Betty Besom."

Diamond missed the point again. "Besom—another word for breast?"

Paloma laughed. "Who's got a one-track mind round here? It's one of those brooms made of twigs."

Estella said, "In the year of her death a rather cruel cartoon appeared of her on horseback brandishing a besom and wearing one of those enormous Marie-Antoinette-style wigs as she jumps the horse over a barrier labelled the Sacred Boundary of Discretion."

The satire was lost on Diamond. He was trying to pin down the facts that mattered. "If the books have got it wrong about Miss Papjoy, what's the true story?"

"They parted," she said. "Everyone agrees on that."

"Because of the court case, when his income dried up?"

Paloma said, "He couldn't keep her in the style he felt she was entitled to, so he asked her to leave, and she did, for a number of years."

Estella smiled and shook her head. "And came back to nurse him when he was old? That's a sentimental myth invented by the Victorians."

Paloma said with a cry of disappointment. "Are you sure? You know it to be untrue?"

"I've gone into this as deeply as I can. None of the contemporary reports of her death say anything about a reconciliation. I've looked at them all, in the *Gentleman's*

Magazine, the *Universal Magazine* and the *Annual Register,* you name it. The break-up devastated her. She returned to her place of birth, a village called Bishopstrow, just outside Warminster, and vowed she would never again sleep in a bed. And she kept to it. That's how bitter—or heartbroken—she was. She took up residence in the hollowed-out trunk of a huge oak tree and slept on a bale of straw until her death in 1777. Even when she ventured out and visited friends, she'd insist on sleeping rough in some outhouse on straw."

"Poor soul," Paloma murmured. "I did hear this story, but I thought there was a happier ending."

"How long did she live like this?" Diamond asked.

"Thirty or forty years according to the obituaries. If true, that ties in with her relationship with the Beau breaking up sometime between 1737 and 1747, when he was in his prime—socially speaking."

"What year was the court case he lost?"

"1757. Do the maths. She was living in the tree by then."

"And remained there," Paloma said, shaking her head in sympathy.

"So we can't blame the break-up on the litigation," Estella said. "It was something else, a personal issue, I guess. We've all been there, haven't we?"

She fixed them in turn with eyes demanding agreement and Diamond made it appear that he, for one, had been there many times, wherever it was. No use being fainthearted with this young woman.

"For me as his latest biographer, it opened exciting new possibilities," she added. "Have another of the calamares. They're moreish, aren't they?"

"In that case was he alone at the end?" Diamond asked, trying not to sound as deflated as he felt. With Juliana ruled out, his best theory was kiboshed.

Estella shook her head. "He couldn't have coped. He'd

lived to a great age, but he was a wreck by then, in a wheelchair, suffering from gout and leg ulcers. He had intermittent fits and he didn't have a tooth in his head."

A scrap of consolation: the last part checked with the state of the Twerton skeleton.

"Somebody must have acted as carer, then."

"Yes, he had a carer." Her eyes slid upwards. "If you could call her that."

"A woman?"

"Her name emerged in George Scott's correspondence, which only came to light a few years ago in the British Library archive."

"Scott? You mentioned him earlier, the man who administered the estate?"

"Yes. He had all kinds of problems dealing with the creditors and the most persistent and unpleasant was a Mrs. Hill. She really got up his nose."

"He said this?"

"Not in those words. He said it more eloquently, but his anger comes through in letters to a doctor friend written in the year of the Beau's death. This is so crucial to my book that I can quote the exact words Scott used: 'She was of such a fierce disposition that poor Nash had no small degree of punishment in living with this termagant woman. Solomon could not describe a worse.'"

"Solomon?"

"King Solomon. He famously mediated in a quarrel between two women."

"He definitely says Mrs. Hill was *living* with Nash?"

"For the last twenty years of his life."

"Wow."

"Exactly my reaction, except I said something stronger when I read the letter. I don't know what the readers around me in the BL thought."

"So this Mrs. Hill gave George Scott a hard time? Why?"

"She was in possession of a bond for £250 given to her by Nash."

"Big money."

"Mega big."

"A bond being security for a debt?"

Estella nodded. "Nash had no business arranging a bond of that size. He colluded with her to obtain a court judgement for it."

"Who was pulling the strings here—Mrs. Hill?"

"George Scott seemed to think so, and of course after Nash's death the woman was fierce in her demands. He relates in another letter how he was having a conversation with the wife of Charles Young's attorney when Mrs. Hill came in and created a scene. In his words, she 'appeared in full character.' He goes on to say, 'From such a tongue may I ever be delivered. She used me very cruelly.'"

Paloma said, "He sounds paranoid about this woman. What was she on about? She must have known there was no money left in the pot."

"She complained that Nash's possessions had been 'sold for nothing' and should never have been auctioned."

"Hell-bent on getting her £250," Diamond said. "Do you think she treated Nash the same way?"

"Scott said so. It's possible he was biased, but whatever she was like she's gold dust for me. None of the early biographers knew she existed."

"Goldsmith must have known," Paloma said.

"Goldsmith was discreet. He says at one point he could fill a book with anecdotes of the Beau's amours, but he doesn't."

"These days he would," Paloma said. "The first duty of a biographer is to dish the dirt."

"Cynical, Paloma," Estella said with mock reproach.

"Do you want examples?"

"Spare us that. We heard you."

Diamond's spirits had bounced back, his brain fizzing with new possibilities. "I want to know more about Mrs. Hill. What's her first name?"

"I'm still working on that," Estella said. "She's elusive. If I can trace the court documents, I'll find it."

"Any idea where she lived after Nash died?"

"Somewhere in Bath, I expect, at least while she felt her claim ought to be met."

"You don't know much else? Was there a Mr. Hill?"

"There must have been at one stage, but I can't believe he was still around if she'd moved in with the Beau in the 1740s. Have I got you interested?"

A pause, a glance between Diamond and Paloma and then he decided it was time to tell Estella about the skeleton.

She caught her breath a couple of times while he was going over the brain-banging facts. She took a gulp of wine and then another. Paloma reached for the bottle and refilled the glass.

When Diamond finished, Estella stared at him in awed silence.

Paloma said, "Bombshell, isn't it?"

"Nuclear," Estella said. "I'm going to have to rewrite my book."

Another pause to absorb the prospect.

"Don't get me wrong," she said. "I'm not ungrateful. It's a scoop. If this really is the Beau, I don't know what the academic world is going to make of it."

Stuff the academic world, Diamond thought.

"Will it get into the media?" she asked.

He vibrated his lips. "I don't see how we can avoid it, much as I'd like to. They already plastered my picture over the front pages nose-to-nose with the skull, but they haven't yet cottoned on to the fact that it could be Beau Nash. Someone is going to make the connection soon."

"I don't bother with newspapers," Estella said. "I'm

mentally stuck in the eighteenth century. Missed that picture altogether. What's the evidence for this being him? The hat, the wig and the absence of teeth?"

"The clothes he's wearing are right for 1761," Paloma said. "They've deteriorated badly, as you'd expect."

"Can I see them? Did you take a picture?"

"The police photographer did," Diamond said. "He took plenty, but I don't have them on my phone, if that's what you're asking."

"Peter's phone is used for phoning and nothing else," Paloma said.

"Could I get to see the clothes? Where are they now?"

"In a lab with the bones," Diamond said. "A forensic anthropologist is doing the autopsy."

"Right now, as we speak?"

"In his own good time. He's in no hurry."

"I'd love to get some pictures for the book." Understandably she was already thinking ahead.

"I expect it can be arranged after the inquest."

"When will that be?"

"Can't answer that. It's up to the coroner. I'm not deliberately putting barriers in your way, Estella. You've been helpful to us and I'd like to return the compliment. It's just that we have to go through the legal hoops."

"How could he possibly have ended up there?" she said, still grappling with what she'd heard. "I'll have to come up with a theory."

"You and me both," Diamond said. "I thought of one just now when you were talking about the Papjoy woman. It almost made sense of her refusing to sleep in a bed all those years." He outlined the substitution trick with the body to save Beau Nash from being buried as a pauper. "She hid the corpse in Twerton and couldn't find a way to give him a decent burial, so she vowed to sleep on straw as long as he remained above ground. Plausible?"

"Barely," Paloma said.

"Like a penance."

"I know what you mean, but it's unlikely and anyway we know it didn't happen. The woman who was there at the death was a different character altogether."

"The terrifying Mrs. Hill?"

"You need a whole new theory for her."

"More's the pity."

The main course was put in front of them. Suspicious of what he was about to eat, Diamond prised the Cuban sandwich open and discovered layers of ham and roast pork, mustard and pickles in a goo of cooked cheese that formed strings.

"Wishing you'd ordered the blazing bird?" Paloma said.

"This'll see me right." He reached for the jug, his thoughts cascading like the water filling his glass. "How about this for Mrs. Hill? We know the estate owed her money and she wasn't likely to get any preference over all the other creditors. She decided on extreme measures."

Paloma was quick to see the point. "Holding the executors to ransom? She was in a position to do it, I'll grant you."

"The body was lying in state in the house four days," Diamond went on, liking this better than his Papjoy theory, "so she had time to plan. On the evening before the funeral she removed the corpse from where it had been on view and paid a carter to transport it to the secret address at Twerton. She told George Scott she wanted a written undertaking that the £250 bond would be honoured in full or the grand funeral wouldn't take place. She was banking on him paying up to avoid a scandal. But he called her bluff and refused, figuring that she wouldn't want to be exposed as the grasping woman she was. He arranged for the empty coffin to be filled with sand and driven in state to the Abbey."

"So poor Beau Nash was left to rot in the Twerton house?" Paloma said. "This is more believable."

"It would explain why Scott despised her so much," Diamond said. "What do you think, Estella?"

"I'm still coming to terms with the idea that he wasn't buried," she said. "I can't tell you how shocked I am. Years of researching and writing a biography brings you close to your subject and you get emotionally attached to them— even someone as flawed as the Beau."

"He'll be given a decent burial now," Diamond said.

"He would have hated being exposed by the media as some kind of relic. I know I must use the images and publish them, but it feels awfully like a betrayal."

"It's your duty to tell it as it is," Paloma said.

"*If* it is," Diamond said.

5

No one ever asked why he was called Tank. It wasn't the name he was born with. And it wasn't a joke name. You didn't joke with Tank. But that wasn't because he was built for battle and crushed everything in his path. Actually he was a small man. He didn't get into fights at all. The only tank-like qualities he had were to do with his personality. People learned not to oppose him. You didn't want him coming at you because you knew from one look at him that he had plenty of firepower, not often used, but always ready.

He was the leader, no argument.

He must have picked his name for himself. He picked names for everyone else in the squat and they learned to live with them. In most cases they were a good choice. Like Headmistress.

In what she called her dullsville years, Headmistress had never felt comfortable with her given name. She hated all the informal versions of Margaret. In her schooldays she'd been called Marg, Maggie, Meg, Peg or Peggy, so it came as a relief when Tank decided on her first day in the Twerton squat that she was none of these.

"Headmistress."

"D'you mean me?"

"You can share with Joke and Cat."

Simple as that.

He must have discovered she'd done some supply teaching, but it wasn't mentioned. Later she learned that anyone joining the squat was vetted as seriously as if it was the secret service, so he must have found out. Her main concern at the time had been whether Joke and Cat were safe to share a room with. They were fine. Joke snored sometimes and Cat had a thing about fresh air and wanting the window open even on the coldest nights but if that was a hardship, bring it on. In her goosedown sleeping bag Headmistress was laughing.

Altogether, nine people and a dog had shared the Twerton gaff while it was supposed to be empty and condemned. As Tank, the most experienced squatter, had wisely pointed out, demolition orders are never straightforward if landlords are involved. There is always scope for appeals. He'd done his homework as usual, studied the Housing Act, checked the ownership with the Land Registry, and found that more than one foreign owner had an interest in the same terraced block. Good for two years was Tank's prediction and he'd been proved right.

Unfortunately two years soon pass. The notice of demolition had been served and the squatters had hung on until the heavy machinery had rumbled up the street. Then they'd boxed up their belongings and got out. Five of them had heard of a squat in Frome and moved off there. The others pinned their hopes on Tank. He made no promises, but he disappeared for a couple of days. All he would say to the others was that he was making searches. It sounded like the jargon solicitors used to justify themselves when people were buying houses.

Headmistress had a friend in Oldfield Park who took pity and allowed her to bed down in her flat for one night on the strict understanding that it couldn't become a permanent arrangement. She tried to negotiate a second night, but the friend wasn't happy that Headmistress had brought

Tank's dog with her. That night had to be spent squeezed in with Cat in the back of Joke's van. Joke gallantly passed the night in the driver's seat with the greyhound curled up beside him.

Next morning Tank called the three of them for a meeting at the Temple of Minerva in the botanical gardens in Victoria Park. A good choice, because although the building was open on one side it had a roof and they managed to keep dry on a wet summer's day. Evidently Tank had been sleeping on the wooden bench the last two nights.

"Found a place," he told them straight away.

"In Bath?" Cat said.

He nodded.

"Big enough for all of us?" Headmistress asked.

"No problem. You get your own room."

"Cool."

"Thing is, it's non-residential."

Headmistress wasn't sure if this was good news or bad.

But Cat understood. "So we can't be done in the criminal courts."

"What is it—the Pump Room?" Joke said. Just occasionally there was a clue as to how he came by his nickname.

Tank didn't laugh. "Building work has been going on there since January," he said, "and they finish today. Total refit. Gas, electrics, running water, heating, all up and working. Toilets and a shower."

"A shower?" Cat said in a squeak. "Is this heaven, or what?"

"The planning permission is for a centre for oriental medicine."

"Acupuncture and stuff?"

"Much more than that. But what they aim to do in there doesn't concern us because the place hasn't been stocked yet. The owner lives in Beijing."

"One of those Chinese millionaires?" Headmistress said.

"How did you find this pad?" Joke asked.

"By asking around. Bought a few drinks for the foreman and came to an arrangement. Five hundred to borrow a key for twenty minutes."

"Five hundred just to borrow a key?" Cat said in horror. "Where are we getting that much from?"

He didn't tell her. He said, "In the twenty minutes I went down to the key shop and got them to make me a spare."

"Is it really worth that much?" Cat asked.

"You'll see tomorrow morning. We move in before dawn when all the neighbours are asleep. And the move has to be slick, slicker than rifle drill. Joke, you come ready with tools to change the lock on the front door, soon as we're inside. Also a heavy-duty bolt."

"I've done this before."

"That's why you got the job. Get to it straight away. I don't want any of you lot roaming the house deciding which room to bag. We've all got responsibilities. Headmistress, you can write nicely, I hope. We need a notice this big we can pin on the door saying it's a legal squat and we didn't break nothing getting in. The wording is important. I'll give it to you. Have the thing ready, enclosed in a rainproof see-through bag, right?"

Headmistress nodded and Tank turned to Cat.

"You want to use the shower, so you can earn the right. First thing, find the meters and write the reading down. The suppliers are EDF and British Gas. As soon as they open and start taking calls, contact them and set up new accounts. We pay for what we use like anyone else, including water and sewerage. Wessex Water have installed a water meter as well. Don't forget them."

Cat, like the others, was impressed by the planning that had gone into this.

"We're going to be quick and quiet," Tank said, "but let's not kid ourselves. The neighbours will know something's going on. When they come knocking, as they will, we don't open the door."

"We know this," Joke said. "We're not daft. We talk through the letter box."

"Yeah, but be nice. No telling them to piss off."

"I thought it was non-residential," Cat said.

"Our place will be, but the rest isn't. The people either side will have lived there for years. We're part of a large terraced block and they'll very likely panic a bit when they know squatters have moved in next door. Your job—my job, his and hers—is to calm them down. We won't be playing loud music, lighting fires, dealing in scrap metal, doing drugs, throwing all-night raves, any of that shit. We're homeless people through no fault of our own, just wanting a roof over our heads and a quiet life."

Tank had to be serious to make a speech as long as that.

"Look at it this way," Cat said. "I don't suppose the neighbours were too thrilled when they heard about the oriental medicine."

"Right."

"They ought to be glad to get us."

"Yeah."

"So where is this amazing gaff?"

"The best address in Bath. The Royal Crescent."

6

The meeting in Las Iguanas threw everyone off course. Estella was forced to plan a rewrite of her final chapters, and Diamond to examine the role of the fearsome Mrs. Hill. He didn't mind. He was fascinated that in the twenty-first century a case done and dusted more than two hundred years ago was producing twists from hour to hour. There could be no arrests here, no questioning of witnesses, but someone had behaved improperly and quite possibly with criminal intent. The coroner would need to consider the facts before reaching a conclusion on the identity of the skeleton and where, when and how the death occurred.

Dr. Waghorn's findings at the autopsy would be the next piece in the puzzle. All sorts of information can be gleaned from examining bones. Diamond was impatient to get it done, but there was a snag. Anthropologists won't be hurried. Old bones aren't like rotting flesh. They've waited a long time and can easily wait longer. Waghorn was a self-important cuss who'd delay things even more if you tried to hurry him along.

Instead of returning directly to the CID office after the Mexican meal, Diamond drove into Twerton for another look at the demolition site.

It had been levelled.

Any possibility of finding more clues was remote. The

entire row of eighteenth-century terraced dwellings was gone. Hundreds of noisy gulls were wheeling over the rubble. The wrecking ball was already at work on some nearby nineteenth-century houses. "What are the plans for the site?" he asked a foreman.

"Supermarket."

"Haven't we got enough?"

"It's progress, mate."

"Don't know about that. I quite like old buildings."

"These were condemned."

"Who by?"

"Housing inspector, isn't it? Bath's got enough old buildings already and better built than these. You should be wearing a hard hat. Do you have permission to be here?"

No point arguing with him.

Diamond returned to his car and drove off.

In the meeting room at Concorde House, young DC Gilbert had done a good job putting together the information board, except for one thing. Diamond stepped up and unpinned the press picture of himself eye to eye—more accurately eye to eye socket—with the skull. "We don't need this."

Gilbert had turned crimson. He was obviously as surprised as his boss.

"Didn't you put it there?" Diamond said.

"I'd rather not say, guv."

"Someone else did. There's no loyalty any more." He tore the photo in half and stuffed the pieces into the nearest bin. "Is that Beau Nash top right?"

"Yes. It's the one everyone knows."

"Blue eyes with bags under them, double chin, cheeks like mangos. I don't get the 'Beau.' I don't get it at all. Who's the woman with the cleavage?" He was already looking at another portrait, a dark-haired young woman in a ballgown. Unusually for the period she wasn't wearing a wig.

"Juliana Popjoy, his mistress."

"Papjoy."

"I thought—"

"Never mind. We won't go into that." He wouldn't be filling the gaps in Gilbert's sex education. "She's one pin-up we won't be needing. I'll be telling you why when I speak to the team. The one I'd like up there is Mrs. Hill, if we can find a picture. I don't even know her first name yet. She was his last companion—and if you feel sorry for any woman living with a lump of lard like Nash, don't. Mrs. Hill was a toughie who knew what she was taking on." He stood for some seconds more inspecting the rest of the board: shots of the half-demolished house and the skeleton bizarrely seated in the loft space; a map of the Twerton area with the site marked with a red pushpin. None of it necessary, in truth, except to bolster the lad's self-esteem. "It's a fine effort."

"Thanks, guv."

Some inner emotion stirred and it was almost fatherly. "They still treat you as if you're wet behind the ears, don't they?"

"Not all the time."

"I'm guilty of it myself. We've all been through it, but you've taken more than most. In better times we blooded young detectives on a regular basis, but with government cutbacks . . . I don't have to tell you, do I?"

Gilbert smiled faintly.

"Want some advice?"

The young constable couldn't say no to that.

"Fight fire with fire when they try it on. Let them know you're every bit as smart as they are. I did when I was in the Met and making my way."

"Okay."

"Didn't work every time, but they got to know I wasn't a baa-lamb."

Diamond as a baa-lamb was clearly too much for Paul
Gilbert to grasp, but he seemed to appreciate the advice.
"I'll give it a try."

"Good man. Not with me, mind. I'm your guv'nor. But
enough of this. Where's John Leaman?" He needed to
know if Leaman had learned anything useful about the
early history of the now-demolished house.

"In the office."

The murder squad's ace researcher was at his desk in
the CID room wearing earphones. It required some hand-
waving to get him to lift them off.

"What's this? Listening to Beyoncé while on duty?"

Difficult to think of anyone less likely to be listening to
modern pop than Leaman.

"It's an audiobook: Edith Sitwell on Bath."

"Famous poet—bit eccentric?"

"That's her."

"Helpful, is it?"

"Different. In her words, Beau Nash was a magnificent
butterfly."

"All show and no substance?"

"Well . . ." Leaman wouldn't be drawn. He preferred
facts to interpretations.

"A butterfly starts off as a caterpillar. Is that what she
meant? Underneath the finery he was a grub?"

"I wouldn't know. Later she says he was a poor and lov-
able creature who knew pleasure but no happiness."

Diamond shook his head. "I don't know what it is with
this guy. He can charm the ladies even centuries after he
died. What does she say about his last years?"

"I haven't got to that."

"Can't you fast forward?"

"I could, but I wasn't planning to. If I'm reading something, I like to read every word."

Must stop grinding my teeth, Diamond thought. It can't

be good for them. "I know Edith Sitwell might be helpful, but you're doing this in police time and there are heaps of other books about Bath. Have you done the research on the Twerton house?"

"As much as I can. The row of terraces was condemned two years ago and boarded up. Before that it was rented accommodation owned by an offshore company known as Lovemore Holdings."

Echoes of Restoration comedy again, but better not go down that route with Leaman. "And did you discover when it was built?"

"There's no documentation."

"You mean you haven't found it yet. There must have been some legal agreement originally. Purchase of land, deeds or some such."

Leaman sidestepped. "Going by map evidence it was built between 1743 and 1750, a typical row of workmen's dwellings from the early Georgian period. Almost certainly it would have been used by people in the wool trade. They worked from home."

"Cottage industry."

"Carding and spinning went on for centuries."

"I know a bit about that." The team had once worked on a murder that touched on Chaucer's Wife of Bath and Diamond hadn't forgotten that as long ago as the fourteenth century the locals were weaving and making cloth. "Working at home, you say. When did the Twerton mill open?"

"1791."

"Quite a bit later. So in 1761, the year that interests us, the house would still have been an outpost of the cloth trade?"

"The wool was sheared locally and scoured and taken into the houses. They will have had a spinning wheel in the living room and maybe a loom going sixteen hours a day."

"Hell of a life. You'd never escape from work." Diamond glanced around him and shrugged. "And now in our superfast broadband age we'll soon be back to everyone working from home again. Instead of a loom, it's a laptop. Wasn't there any other work in Twerton apart from the cloth business?"

"Farming, but these were typical cloth-workers' dwellings. At the time we're interested in, when Nash died, the house would have been occupied round the clock, and probably by a family sleeping several to a room."

"Making it difficult to cart a corpse upstairs without being noticed. You're not helping, John."

"I'm telling it like it was."

"Are you sure you're not enjoying it? You haven't believed in our working hypothesis from the word go."

"I don't disbelieve the skeleton in the loft."

"Thanks for that," Diamond said with irony.

"But it's not Beau Nash."

"You made that clear from the beginning. Sometimes you might do better to keep your doubts to yourself. I don't think you fully understand the effect it has on the rest of the team when you rubbish their ideas—and mine."

"You want a team of yes-men, then?"

"No, but if you can't say things without suggesting everyone except you is an idiot it's better not to say them at all."

"Is that how it sounds?"

"Quite often, yes."

"Fine. Gag me if you want."

"For Christ's sake, John, don't make a martyr of yourself. Time and again you've been right about things the rest of us got carried away with. You're the cool head I need when everyone else is hyped up and I value you more than I ever say."

Leaman blinked at that.

"It's a matter of tone, of bearing in mind how your words are going to sound to other people." Diamond wasn't best suited to lecturing anyone on tact. Wisely he stopped there.

"You and I are going to differ over Beau Nash, but you're doing the research and I appreciate that. Was Twerton a no-go area for the higher-class types from the city centre?"

"No."

After the heart-to-heart, Leaman appeared unwilling to pick up where they left off. Diamond could almost tap into the conflict going on in his head.

He waited for more, and finally got it.

"They had to drive through if they wanted to visit Bristol. And not all of it was working-class housing. There were pubs."

"But the house we're interested in was essentially a cloth-worker's cottage, right?"

"Yes. Most of them were knocked down by the Victorians and built over, and there was another building boom in the 1950s. Somehow this old terrace survived. Eventually it deteriorated."

"I'd like to know who owned the place in the year Nash died. Some wool merchant, I expect. There must be title deeds."

"I don't think they exist. A change in the law in 1925 meant it was no longer necessary to store deeds going back generations and a lot were destroyed. The best bet is the records office and I contacted them, but they couldn't find anything."

"Is there anything else we can do—apart from reading Edith Sitwell?"

He got a glare for that. "I've compared street maps from the eighteenth century, which is how I fixed on 1743 to 1750. I found a history of Twerton online. Understandably it doesn't go into the kind of detail we're hoping to find."

"Leave it for now, then. I've got some new information myself and I'm about to update everyone in the meeting room—or the incident room, as we'd better call it now Paul Gilbert has done his work on the whiteboard."

* * *

"Are we definitely treating this death as suspicious, then?" Keith Halliwell asked after Diamond had finished updating the team on the role of the mysterious Mrs. Hill in Beau Nash's last years.

"I'm not suggesting she murdered him," Diamond said.

"No? Someone prevented the lawful and decent disposal of a body, and that's an offence under common law."

"You're thinking Mrs. Hill?"

"She's the obvious one."

"Why would she do it?"

"I'll give you one good reason right away," Halliwell said. "She *did* murder him and she didn't want the body examined in a postmortem."

"For crying out loud, Keith," Ingeborg said at once, flushing with outrage. "We've heard nothing but malice about this woman, and all based on what? One man's assessment of her character two hundred and fifty years ago. She stayed with Nash twenty years—and he was old and disgusting by then—so she can't be totally bad. Casting her as his killer is a bit bloody rich. What was her motive?"

Halliwell came back at once. "She couldn't wait to cash in the bond and get her £250. The money was leeching from his household. He'd sold almost everything of value. She couldn't allow it to go on or she'd find herself homeless and with no funds at all when he died."

The reasoning was persuasive, forcing Ingeborg to shift the attack. "How is she supposed to have killed him?"

"Poison, I expect."

"Spare us that."

"They knew about arsenic in the 1760s."

Paul Gilbert said, "In that case, we can find out. Arsenic leaves traces."

Halliwell said without even a glance at the young man,

"After all this time? We're dealing with a skeleton, not a fresh corpse."

Fired up by his recent pep-talk from the boss, Gilbert insisted, "It can be detected in hair and probably in bones."

"Well, let's hope so," Ingeborg said, "if only to get a negative result and prove there's nothing in this crackpot theory. You can bank on it: whenever poisoning is mentioned, the next tired old cliché the sexists come up with is that it's a woman's weapon. She's the carer and the cook, so she's best placed to add the deadly powder to the old man's nightcap."

"The fact that she's a woman doesn't come into it," Halliwell said. "Mrs. Hill is the one with motive and opportunity and there isn't anyone else we know about."

Ingeborg gave a sigh of impatience. "Get real, Keith. Beau Nash died of old age. He was eighty-six, for heaven's sake. That's about a hundred and ten these days. When is the postmortem taking place?"

"It isn't, as yet," Diamond said. "We're waiting to hear from Dr. Waghorn."

"Why the delay?"

"He deals with bones. He would say, 'What's the hurry?' Time pressures are unknown to him."

"Can't we call him and say it's urgent?"

"Having met the old tosser, I don't think that's the way to go."

"What if it came from the coroner?"

"That might work, but in a long career I've found that coroners don't appreciate being pressured either."

"Georgina?"

Diamond pondered the suggestion for a moment. After all, it was the ACC who had called for a full investigation, and no one was better at cracking the whip. "I'll speak to her shortly."

Ingeborg rolled her eyes and said nothing.

* * *

Georgina was staring out of her window at the M4 motorway across the office park. "I miss the view I had in Manvers Street."

"It wasn't that special, was it?" Diamond said. "You overlooked the car park."

"No, but I could see all the comings and goings. You can learn a lot about your staff if you watch their movements. Time of arrival, body language, the company they keep. Here, I look out of the window and all I can think about is escaping over the Severn Crossing and into Wales."

A rare insight into Georgina's secret yearnings.

"You're not Welsh, are you, ma'am?"

"Me? Not in the least. I go there for the music. It's everywhere, even in the accent."

He'd forgotten his boss was a mainstay of the choral society.

"What's your view?" Georgina asked.

"They produce some wonderful rugby players, I'll say that."

"Who are you talking about?"

"The Welsh."

"I meant the view from your window."

"Ah." He grinned. "Couldn't tell you. With all the work that comes in, I don't get time to look out of windows."

She turned to face him. "You never miss a trick, do you? What are you here for?"

"It's the media—the press, TV, radio."

"Where?"

"All around, circling like vultures."

"Here?"

"They will be soon, swooping in."

"I thought they'd gone away after getting that embarrassing picture of you."

"Temporary reprieve," he said. "They haven't yet caught up with our theory that the skeleton might be Beau Nash.

When they do, I don't want to be anywhere near a fan, if you understand me."

"Because it's such a big story?"

"It will go viral, global and galactic."

"Good gracious." Georgina put a hand to her tinted blue curls. "How long have we got?"

"The news could break any time."

"From one of our own?"

He was quick to scotch that suggestion. "My team are discreet. No, the name is already out there. We've had people calling in to ask if the skeleton could be Nash. Actually I'm surprised the press aren't on to it yet."

"We must be ready for them however they approach us. On the telephone, on the internet, in the streets," she said in Churchillian mode.

"A united front," he said.

"United is the word. They're going to push for a press release, and we need to be clear what we say."

Diamond waited for her train of thought to shunt past and return again.

Georgina was frowning. "But we can't be clear without the facts. Why haven't we heard from the pathologist? Hasn't the autopsy been carried out? Without his findings we can't tell them anything of use."

He explained about Dr. Waghorn being a bones man and in no hurry.

"Then he must be told," she said. "Doesn't he understand the urgency? Has anyone told him what we may be dealing with? Do you have his number? Get him on the line and I'll put a rocket under this man."

In the CID room, Diamond was able to announce that the postmortem would be at eight the next morning.

"I'll set my alarm," Keith Halliwell said automatically. Because of Diamond's aversion to blood and gore, every autopsy in the past ten years had been assigned to his deputy.

"Did I say I wanted you there?" the big man said.

There was a general raising of eyebrows.

Halliwell had turned as pale as any of the corpses he'd met on the slab. "You're sending someone else?"

"I'm going myself. What's up with you lot?" Diamond said. "I've never had a problem getting up early."

After a moment to grasp the fact that Diamond could stomach an autopsy on a skeleton, Halliwell produced a wide, relieved grin. "I'll have a lie-in, then."

John Leaman left his chair and asked the boss if he could have a quiet word.

They went into Diamond's office.

"Something personal?"

"No, but you'll want to hear it in private."

"Now you've got me interested."

"It's about Beau Nash."

"Okay."

"And how he's supposed to have ended up in Twerton. I disbelieved it from the start."

"You made that clear to one and all, John."

"But then we discovered this rumour that he was buried in an unmarked grave because of all the debts he ran up."

"It's more than a rumour," Diamond said. "It's widely accepted."

"I know, guv. The biographies, all the guide books, the internet, Wikipedia."

A warning bell sounded in Diamond's head. "I don't rely on the internet for evidence, John. I'm talking about experts, people who've devoted years to the subject. Even the latest biography from America states that nobody knows where he's buried and asks the question whether it was a pauper's grave."

"And I don't rely on modern academics when I can go

to contemporary sources," Leaman said with the stiff-necked bluntness typical of him. "People who write biographies ought to take the trouble to check every detail, but they don't. They repeat what others have already written and mistakes creep in."

"By contemporary sources you mean Goldsmith?"

"Goldsmith? No."

"Come on then, out with it."

"Goldsmith says nothing at all about an unmarked grave—but he isn't my source. I've found newspaper reports of the funeral."

"From 1761?" Diamond said.

"The same week Nash was buried."

"And?"

Leaman was enjoying this. "The Burney collection of eighteenth-century newspapers is a resource these biographers should have consulted if they were any good at their job."

"What are you talking about? Where is this?"

"The British Library."

"You haven't been up to St. Pancras?"

"You can access it. The papers are digitised. I looked at the *London Intelligencer* for 21 February 1761, four days after the funeral. Care to see a printout?" With the air of a magician he opened a folded sheet he'd kept out of sight in his hand.

How could Diamond say no?

"You don't have to read the whole report," Leaman said as he handed it across. "It goes on a bit. The first two lines say it all, really."

Diamond looked at the sentence helpfully highlighted by Leaman in bright yellow: *Laft Tuefday Evening the remains of Richard Nafh, Efq; were interred in the Abbey Church, Bath.*

"Not much doubt about that," the head of CID muttered as everything he had deduced crashed down like the

Twerton terrace, all the work of the past few days suddenly turned to dust and rubble.

"Several other papers carry similar accounts," the human wrecking ball smacked in with another hit. "There's no suggestion anywhere that the coffin was taken after the service to some undisclosed graveyard and buried in the paupers' section. I didn't ever believe that story."

Deeply shaken, Diamond spoke in a voice that sounded— even to himself—a million miles from where he was. "I wonder where it started."

"With some Victorian storyteller professing to write history. They loved wallowing in misery, all the tear-jerking bits like the death of Little Nell and Oliver Twist asking for more. The unmarked grave is horseshit, to put it mildly, just as the stuff about Juliana Papjoy coming back to nurse him in old age was wrong. Sentimental slush."

"You don't need to rub it in, John."

"Shall we tell the others? You can see why I thought you'd like to hear it first."

"Because you want the pleasure of telling it twice over?"

Leaman rolled his eyes upwards, but that was one thing Diamond was right about.

Late in the day, after a dispiriting team meeting when Diamond had left most of the talking to Leaman, the head of CID retired to his office with a book about the history of the Abbey. He'd never been much of a reader, but he felt the need to mug up. After twenty minutes Ingeborg Smith surprised him by bringing in a glass of fizz and a slice of apricot flan. "I thought you might appreciate this, guv. I was saying to the others that we haven't celebrated moving in here."

"Celebrated?"

"Cheered ourselves up, then. So we all chipped in. It's only Prosecco."

"You should have asked me for a contribution," he said, thinking far too late he should have provided drinks himself. The idea hadn't crossed his mind, possibly because the rows of desks in the new CID office reminded him of nothing else but a prison visiting area.

"You've had a lot to deal with."

"I'll come out and join you all."

John Leaman, basking in his latest success, was chatting animatedly with two of the civilian staff.

Unable to stomach any more of that, Diamond chose the other end of the room and was joined there by Paul Gilbert.

"I wanted to ask if I should unpin everything from the board," the young man said.

"Why?"

"Well . . ." He spread his hands as if it was obvious.

"Leave it for now," Diamond said. "We might get some autopsy pictures for you tomorrow."

"I thought if the skeleton isn't Beau Nash—"

"It's still a dead person and we have to try and explain how it got there. You may need to take down the pictures of Nash and his mistress, but I wouldn't do that until we're totally sure."

"But if he was buried in the Abbey like those old newspapers say—"

"Don't believe everything you read in the papers, even eighteenth-century papers."

Gilbert almost choked on a crumb.

"What do you think happened, guv?"

Diamond hadn't given up on the skeleton being Beau Nash. He couldn't banish the image of the dusty old bones in eighteenth-century clothes. He hadn't mentioned his private theory in the meeting. Now he tried it out on the youngest member of the team, youngest but by no means dimmest.

Gilbert heard him out in silence.

"You have to remember we're starting from something

extraordinary," the big man stressed. "If the skeleton in the loft is Beau Nash, then the explanation must be just as extraordinary."

"I see that," Gilbert said. "I can't get my head round the idea that this enormous funeral took place without a body in the coffin."

"It had to, else how did he end up in Twerton?"

That kind of logic was difficult to fault.

7

Late the same evening Georgina was at the wheel of her silver Mercedes coming over Bannerdown, returning to Bath on the Fosse Way northeast of the city. How clever of her sister, Jelly, to have bought a cottage at South Wraxall right beside the arrow-straight Roman road that runs from Exeter to Lincoln—Georgina's favourite road in all of the southwest. The journey home felt like a private drive on evenings such as this.

Or should have done. Tonight her nerves were playing havoc.

Jelly (silly name, but she was stuck with it, being christened Angelica and unable to get her tongue round all the syllables as a child) was seven years younger than Georgina and couldn't be more different in personality. She'd been married three times and the weddings had got more and more extravagant. For the latest, to Wallace, who was "something in the film world," all the guests had been flown out to Bermuda and the ceremony had taken place on a beach. Unfortunately Wallace hadn't lasted any longer than Damian or Jules. Worse, the settlement was taking far too long because of the lawyers. Jelly now said the rest of her life would consist of casual relationships. She was currently using the internet to see what was available.

Georgina had never mentioned Jelly to any of her police colleagues.

Despite the different paths their lives had taken, the sisters got on well and Georgina regularly helped Jelly over her emotional crises. Truth to tell, she enjoyed hearing what some of these oversexed men seemed to think was natural and normal. She didn't even blink, acting the experienced older sister who knew it all, unshockable, sympathetic and never short of advice. Jelly's action-packed private life made a welcome change from reading crushingly dull screeds from the Home Office and trying to apply them at police-station level.

Jelly's latest escapade had been related tearfully over a gin and tonic. She had arranged online to meet a man with an MG Midget. Yesterday he had turned up on time in this dinky red sports car from the 1960s and taken her for a "spin." He hadn't looked anything like his picture and was probably twenty years her senior, but Jelly was willing to compromise, assuming that any owner of a valuable vintage car knew how to treat a lady. Sadly this wasn't the case. Somewhere north of Bristol, Cedric had said he could feel a touch of cramp in his leg. Jelly decided the reason was obvious: he was about six foot six and quite the wrong shape to fit into a car that size. A mile or two further along the road he'd started groaning, so Jelly had suggested they pulled into a layby. Conveniently one appeared almost straight away.

Jelly had expected Cedric to get out and have a stretch, but he'd made even more alarming noises and said he couldn't move and would she massage the muscle, which had seemed to have gone rigid. Tentatively Jelly had put her hand on his thigh only to be told the cramping was lower down, in the calf, and in the other leg. She couldn't bear seeing anyone suffer, so she'd leaned over, reached down and got to work with both hands. For a first date, this Cedric was asking a lot, because Jelly was now face down in his lap. The position wasn't dignified or comfortable. When the muscle seemed to be responding, she'd asked if he was okay and he'd said there was a definite improvement and asked her to keep going. The groaning had given way to a kind of moan that sounded—even to the tender-hearted Jelly—suspiciously like sounds of pleasure.

This was the moment she'd been shocked to hear another voice join in. Someone had said, "So it's you, Cedric. I thought I recognised the car. What's going on here, then?"

Cedric, calm as a horse whisperer, had answered, "No problem, officer. A touch of cramp. The lady is massaging my leg."

Officer? Jelly had caught her breath.

The second voice had said, "Same old game, then? The cramp attack? Does the lady know you're famous for it?"

Jelly, mortified, angry and embarrassed, had stayed face down, not wanting to be recognised, hoping the policeman would go away. He must have driven silently into the layby and turned off his lights and parked and crept up on the car.

Then she'd heard Cedric say, "It's not illegal between consenting adults."

This was too much. Jelly had sat up and said, "I haven't consented to anything. This man got me here under false pretences." After a short, bad-tempered exchange, she'd insisted on being driven home in the police car demanding to know why Cedric hadn't been charged with deception and a whole lot of other things.

Georgina had heard all this with a mixture of outrage and alarm. She could see it mushrooming into a ruinous situation, and not just for Jelly. She could imagine what the media would make of the assistant chief constable's own sister being led astray by this sex pest. Cedric had to be stopped from preying on gullible women. It was a dilemma. You don't want one of your own family put through the ordeal of a court case, yet the man couldn't be allowed to get away with it.

She'd told Jelly firmly to put the whole incident down

to experience and take it as a warning about dating men online.

"Isn't there something in the law about outraging public decency?" Jelly had asked her.

"Leave it," Georgina had warned in the strongest terms. "You could find yourself being charged."

"Me? I'm the victim. I was innocent. He's obviously a predator."

"Yes, and equally obviously known to the police. Leave it to us to deal with him."

It had taken ten minutes and another G&T to make her sister understand what going to court would entail and what damage a clever counsel would do to her reputation. She had finally seen sense.

Georgina had promised—and half meant what she said, because she had to think of a way of keeping Jelly's name out of it—to report the incident to Operation Bluestone, the dedicated rape and sexual offences unit. And now she was trying to put all that out of her mind and concentrate on her driving.

She shouldn't really have been at the wheel. The two drinks were definitely over the limit. At the time, they'd been necessary, as much to control her own emotions as Jelly's. But she'd been unwise to have them. Although she didn't feel the slightest bit drunk, the law allowed no excuses. If she were stopped and breathalysed, her career would be over.

So she kept checking her speed and making sure her steering was faultless. Even on a quiet, safe road like this you could be stopped by some patrol keen to make an arrest. Give nothing away, she told herself. Keep the wheel steady and drive as if you have the lord chief justice in the passenger seat. Twenty minutes and you'll be home.

Two minutes later something new appeared on the display.

A malfunction.

The bulb in her right taillight wasn't working.

Damnation.

Her mouth went dry and her stomach clenched. However carefully she drove, she would now be pulled over by the first police car that came up behind her. She looked in the mirror and saw headlights not far behind.

What next? She could put her foot down and make sure they didn't get close. The temptation was strong. No, no, no. Likely as not, they'd get her for speeding as well.

She saw a space in front of a farm gate and pulled off the road. You had to be careful in the dark. In some places along here there was almost no verge and a sheer drop.

She switched everything off and waited.

The car flashed by. Not a police vehicle.

Could she take the risk of driving down into Bath through built-up streets? It was the only route home. She should have stayed the night at Jelly's. She could easily make a turn and go back, but by now she wasn't far from Batheaston, a lot closer to home than South Wraxall.

For some minutes she agonised over what to do next. She wasn't usually indecisive. Perhaps she'd taken in more alcohol than she thought. Jelly sometimes tipped in as much gin as tonic.

Needing to calm herself, she started going through earlier events, the humdrum routine of work. But of course it hadn't been humdrum today. Anything but, with the Twerton skeleton and the suggestion that it was Beau Nash. When the media caught up with the latest theory there would be mayhem.

Beau Nash.

Ridiculous.

She blamed Peter Diamond, the cuckoo in her nest. Something about that bumptious, exasperating man acted as an attractant to bizarre and sensational cases. He'd deny it, of course. He'd argue that any detective working in a city with Bath's colourful history would find himself investigating extraordinary events, but Beau Nash in a loft was the most extreme example yet.

No doubt there was an explanation. Sanity would prevail.

All Georgina had ever wanted was a low-key existence, free of sensation. Other people achieved it. She knew of assistant chief constables who complained of boredom. Ten minutes in Bath police would cure them of that.

Nothing more had come past. It was after midnight and Bath should be reasonably quiet. She made the decision to drive on.

In the last few minutes a mist had come down—or so she thought until she realised her own hot breath had steamed up the windows.

For God's sake, woman, she told herself, get a grip.

She wiped a space in the windscreen, turned up the air conditioning and got the car back on the road to start the long descent into Batheaston.

Take it slowly. At a sedate speed in low gear she flicked the headlights to full beam. Maybe more power in the electrics would cure the taillight problem.

It didn't. The malfunction notice hadn't gone away.

Again she checked the rearview mirror for headlights. She was alone, thank God.

Not quite.

Ahead, on a stretch with tall trees on either side, her headlights on full beam picked out a figure at the side of the road with one hand raised, maybe to shield his eyes from the glare.

Some optical illusion? A tree stripped of its bark can stand out from the rest and look amazingly lifelike. But she thought she'd seen it move and there wasn't much breeze tonight. It was possible someone was trying to wave her down.

She couldn't stop for anyone.

Anyone.

She dipped her lights.

You never offer a lift at night, she thought. I must drive by.

The few seconds this troubling image had been caught in the glare of the lights had given the impression of a sizeable male with dark, shoulder-length hair. His clothes were strange. The word that popped into Georgina's head was eccentric. Some kind of white jacket or coat and a large white hat. He was either bare-legged or wearing tights.

Come on, be sensible, she told herself. It was only some large item of rubbish caught on a bush and looking life-like. Paper or plastic sheeting that had fallen off a passing vehicle.

She was tempted to flick to full beam again for a longer look, but she didn't. She drove on until the dipped lights briefly caught the figure again.

Definitely a man. He was standing at the end of a driveway to some private house. And definitely waving.

She raced past.

The real shock was the clothes. He'd been dressed in a tricorne hat and frock coat, breeches and buckled shoes. The long hair must have been a wig. It was as if he'd stepped out of the eighteenth century. Or Georgina had travelled back there.

A ghost?

I know who he was, she thought.

The gin has gone to my head and I'm hallucinating. Beau Nash was in my thoughts and my intoxicated brain created this image. He can't have been real.

Whatever the explanation, in this state of panic she wasn't fit to be at the wheel of a car. Half a mile further on she flicked the main beam on again and looked for somewhere to stop. No laybys on this narrow road. But a short way on was a verge wide enough to take most of the car. She slowed, edged the front wheels on to the grass, braked and switched off. A pulse was thumping in her head.

"Please, God," she said. "Please, God, help me."

She'd got the shakes.

DTs?

Surely not.

For some minutes she did nothing. Couldn't even think straight.

Finally she got a measure of control and succeeded in putting some sensible thoughts together. She would drive no more tonight. She'd phone for a taxi, leave the car here at the side of the road and collect it tomorrow when she was sober.

The decision came as a massive relief.

She took out her phone and got through straight away. And what a comfort it was to hear a human voice. It was difficult explaining the section of road where she was, but the woman at the taxi office said they'd find her if she waited by her car with the hazard lights on. "Have you broken down, dear?"

Comprehensively.

"Yes," Georgina said.

"Don't worry. Your driver will be on his way directly."

Profoundly thankful, she sat in the car and for the next few minutes waited for her jangled nerves to calm. Hearing those few words of reassurance had been a comfort and now she needed to restore her equilibrium. She didn't want the driver to see her in the state she was in. She closed her eyes and took some deep breaths. The shaking had almost stopped.

It would take the taxi ten to fifteen minutes.

The pulsing of her hazard lights was making the nearest bushes flash pink. Thinking more like the high-ranking police officer she was, she picked her bag off the passenger seat, stepped out and checked that nothing of value was in the back. Abandoned cars were an easy target for thieves. Then she locked up and stood in a safe position on the verge a short distance away from the car.

The cool night air was helping. She checked her watch a couple of times, but stayed calm. A couple of cars went past. It was too soon for the taxi.

When the arc of light high above the road told her another car was approaching, she didn't get excited. The vehicle was coming from the wrong direction, the way she herself had travelled. She was expecting her taxi to come up from Bath.

The twin beams were too dazzling to stare at, but as they approached, she had the thought that this could, after all, be the taxi. The nearest cab might have been north of the city on another call and got a radio message to pick up a stranded passenger on Bannerdown. It seemed to be slowing. The lights dipped. But it wasn't a taxi.

Or it didn't look like a taxi. You can't always be certain.

It was a four-by-four and it pulled up beside the winking Mercedes.

The nearest window slid down and a woman's voice called out, "Need a lift?"

"Thank you, but I've called a taxi," Georgina said.

"Where are you going?"

"Only into Bath."

"Jump in. I'll take you. You can phone and cancel the taxi."

"I'd better not."

But this was a persuasive lady. "Listen, my darling. They're really busy at this time, after the pubs and clubs close. They tell you they'll take ten minutes and they could be an hour. You never know who's going to drive up and mug you while you're standing here in the open with your handbag."

Put like that, it was a winning argument. Georgina didn't want to be kept waiting and mugged. "Well, thank you."

"Not a problem. I'd never forgive myself if I drove past and read about you in the paper tomorrow."

Georgina opened the door and got into the passenger seat.

"Makes sense." In the darkness of the car the woman was difficult to see apart from a severe blonde fringe, but the voice was friendly and hearty in the way well-heeled Bathonians often are. "I'm Sally Paris."

"Georgina Dallymore."

"Call the taxi people, Georgie, and we'll have you home in two shakes of a lamb's tail."

No one ever called her Georgie, but she was in no position to complain. She made the call and they were okay about it.

"Puncture, was it?" Sally Paris asked as she started up and got the Range Rover in motion.

Georgina didn't want to tell a lie, but neither did she want to admit she was over the limit. "Actually my vision started playing tricks. I knew I shouldn't be driving."

"Responsible of you. I hope I'd do the same." Sally then added in the same amiable tone, "Had a few drinks, have you? I thought I smelt gin on your breath. Where exactly do you live?"

"Bennett Street, if it isn't too far out of your way."

"Top of the town. I know it. Lovely area."

Sociable conversations among people like this well-bred lady tend to follow a script. Any moment it would be "Tell me about yourself. Are you in business?" unless the lines were rewritten, so Georgina asked, "Have you driven far tonight?"

"No distance at all. I was collecting my husband. The chauffeur's night off."

"Oh yes?" Georgina tried to sound as if she, too, had given her chauffeur the evening off.

Sally raised her voice. "Are you awake, Ed?"

There was a grunt from the back, no more.

Georgina hadn't realised there was another passenger.

"Out to the world," Sally said. "One of his cronies invites them to an 'at home' and they all get plastered and the wives and significant others pick up the pieces at the end of the evening."

"Invites them to a what?"

"It's an old-fashioned term for a booze-up. He's the top banana, known as the Beau, so he has to be there. No excuses."

"The Beau?"

"Heard of the Beau Nash Society?"

"I believe I have, but—"

"Fruitcakes, every one. Mostly men, of course. Isn't that right, Ed?"

There was no reply from the fruitcake on the back seat, but Georgina turned her head and caught sight of a pair of chunky knees in white tights and, perched on even chunkier thighs, a three-cornered hat.

A light bulb turned on in her head. The roadside apparition must have been Ed dressed as Beau Nash waiting for his lift home.

"Is he awake?" Sally asked.

"Difficult to see," Georgina said after turning her head as well as she could. The top banana seemed to have got overripe, gone soft and sunk in the seat.

"Try giving him a prod."

Georgina had no desire to prod a strange man. "They dress up for this?"

"It's the committee. Serious stuff," Sally said. "They have rules and rituals and God knows what else. If Ed were awake he'd tell you. He's been the Beau for the best part of twenty years. We get invited to all manner of functions that I try to avoid mostly. I'm forced to put in an appearance at the annual ball as the Belle. Silly, isn't it? I'm sure it all sounds a hoot to anyone who isn't caught up in it."

"Can anyone join?"

"You need to be nominated and vetted. And you have to be well up on the Beau's life story. Some of them write books about him. Between ourselves, I get bored to the back teeth with it all. Like tonight, waiting until after midnight for the phone call. Would I meet him at the roadside at the end of Crispin's driveway? Just when I'm ready for sleep. Have you got one, Georgie?"

"One what?"

"A man."

"Em, no. I live alone."

"Good for you. What do you do—devote yourself to work?"

The topic she was desperate to avoid. "Not entirely. Tonight I was with my sister in South Wraxall."

"Family matters to sort out?"

"Sort of."

"And you both had a few. I don't blame you."

Georgina didn't deny it. As long as Sally didn't learn that her tipsy passenger was the assistant chief constable, the evening wouldn't end in total humiliation. Not far to go now. They were through Walcot and level with the long sweep of the Paragon. "If you'd like to put me down at the Hay Hill turn I can walk the last bit."

"Nonsense. I'll take you all the way. Bennett Street. You must be a high-flyer to be living there."

Georgina fired a fast question. "Where do you and Ed live?"

"Out Charlcombe way, a modern house we had built, a frightful let-down when we entertain because everyone expects the Beau to be housed in Georgian splendour."

"I expect it's more comfortable than an old building."

"It has a few redeeming features. You must come and

visit and we'll get to know each other better. Do you have a business card?"

"Not with me," Georgina lied.

"Look in the side pocket. We always have a few of ours in the car."

"Thanks."

"Found one? Give me a call next week. I'd like you to meet Ed when his eyes are open. Hey-ho. This looks like Bennett Street. Which end, Georgie?"

"This end will do."

The Range Rover came to a halt. "He's not even capable of saying goodnight," Sally said. "He could be dead for all I know."

8

The postmortem examination of the Twerton skeleton, as it was known, was to be conducted in the university anthropology department. Peter Diamond wasn't expecting anything that would turn his stomach, but he still took the precaution of starting the day with a lighter breakfast than usual. He told himself he was apprehensive, and that was a reasonable human reaction. It was nowhere near cowardice. Driving up Widcombe Hill to the main campus, he raised morale by whistling the old song "Dem Bones."

He knew where to park and where to find the department. Human remains might intimidate him, but academia didn't. University lecturers and students are as likely as anyone else to feature as suspects in serious crime and he'd interviewed several over the years. When he'd left grammar school at sixteen to join the Met, his form master—a sarcastic old tosser—had told the class, "Today, Diamond is leaving us. Most of you will soon be entering the sixth form and preparing for Oxford, Cambridge or some other place of higher learning. Diamond is enrolling in the university of law and order, where his familiarity with detention and punishment will no doubt stand him in good stead. As you bid him farewell, be warned. It may not be the last time you see him. If any of you in your ivory towers fail to live up to the high moral standards this school has endeavoured to teach you, it's quite possible you'll wake up early one morning to the sound of your front door being kicked in by your old chum Diamond."

The cheap laughs no longer hurt, but the idea of the university of law and order had stuck in Diamond's memory. Policing as higher education was not so far-fetched. The campus left a lot to be desired and the tutorials could get rough and bloody and the only qualification on offer was the third degree, but they were learning experiences and he reckoned he'd graduated with honours.

So he strode the cloisters of Bath University—walkways, to be realistic—with no sense of inferiority. He found the right room with ten minutes to spare. Rather to his surprise it was a lecture theatre with tiered seating and about a dozen students already in there using their phones, doing their hair and chatting about anything except anthropology. A huge plasma screen was mounted high on the wall to the left. A still image of the skeleton was displayed slumped in the chair in situ in the Twerton roof space.

He hadn't expected the autopsy to take the form of a lecture. He'd pictured three or four people at most gathered around a table to observe Dr. Waghorn holding forth as he picked at the bones. But there was no question this was the right room. The skeleton had been removed from the chair, stripped of clothes and was in pieces arranged tidily but ignominiously on a table at the front. None of the students seemed to be taking any interest.

The Beau isn't happy about this, Diamond thought, clinging to his belief that the bones were those of Richard Nash. John Leaman's discovery that the burial had taken place in the Abbey had shaken him, but not enough to change his opinion. He would not be budged from his suspicion that some trickery had taken place enabling the body to end up in the loft in Twerton.

So he was troubled to see the remains already stripped and laid out as if for an anatomy lecture. Usually an autopsy starts with the corpse in the clothes it was found in. The pathologist removes them in the presence of the witnesses.

He stepped closer and took stock in his own inexpert way. Bones are said to reveal all sorts of clues about the life of an individual, but there was little to go on except some arthritic distortions of the joints that you would expect to see in an elderly person. The skull looked to Diamond like any other except for the absence of teeth. No vestiges of hair, which was a shame because if there had been any question of poisoning by arsenic, as Keith Halliwell had suggested, it would have been detectable in hair like layers of sedimentary rock. However, as arsenic had often been taken medicinally in the eighteenth century, notably by people infected by syphilis, the presence of the poison may not have been a sure sign of murder. A man as sexually experienced as Nash would have been at risk of venereal disease.

Little goes undiscovered on the autopsy table, but would a dissolute life be evident from these old bones?

More students arrived, so Diamond made sure he had a seat in the front row, and presently a young woman in a white lab coat came in pushing a steel clothes rack on wheels that looked as if it had been borrowed from some dress shop. The remnants of the clothes, presumably. Under the plastic cover the shapes of several hangers could be made out. Then a photographer came in and arranged two cameras on stands. A third assistant had a video camera and close-ups of the skeleton soon started appearing on the large screen. Maybe after all the Beau would get the attention he deserved.

Claude Waghorn made his entrance wearing surgeon's scrubs, cap and mask as if he was about to conduct a full postmortem on a fresh corpse. All he lacked was the rubber boots. Much to Diamond's disgust, he was wearing sandals.

The room had filled and the students still hadn't all got

seated. Although Waghorn must have noted Diamond's presence, there was no meeting of eyes. The anthropologist stood in front of the bones, gazed up to the top tier and addressed his audience in the mincing voice familiar from the demolition site. "Today you are privileged to be present at a medico-legal investigation of human remains and I must ask you to treat the occasion with respect. Kindly find a place and have the good manners to remain seated until the autopsy is complete."

He waited with folded arms.

When everyone was settled, he said, "I must also insist on total silence."

Only then did he take a pair of surgical gloves from his pocket and make a performance of putting them on, magnified on the screen like a TV commercial. At last he said with a lack of volume that almost dared anyone to breathe, "The skeleton was discovered just under a week ago during the demolition of an eighteenth-century house in Twerton."

Shots of the building site now appeared on screen in a short PowerPoint presentation. If *that* picture appeared, Diamond would feel like pulling his jacket over his head. But he need not have worried. This was all about Waghorn.

The star of the show was saying, "I was called to the scene at an early stage and took command. Fortunately the demolition had been halted before irreparable damage was done to our subject. You will know that when decomposition has taken place the bones become disarticulated because the tendons and ligaments that bind them together are lost. Unless the subject is horizontal at death, you end up with a heap of two hundred and six bones. Unusually, this skeleton was more or less intact in a seated position, supported by a combination of its clothes and a wooden armchair. As you saw on screen it was clothed in the vestiges of an eighteenth-century male costume typical of the upper class including jacket, waistcoat, shirt, breeches, stockings, buckled shoes and a long black wig. Under my close supervision the seated figure and the chair were eventually lifted from the loft space and transported to a laboratory here.

"Removing the clothes from a skeleton is a painstaking process taking several hours at the best of times but is even more laborious when the garments have mostly rotted and there is a generous coating of dust. Each item of dress can contain clues to the time since death, the subject's identity and, more importantly, the cause of death. It's all evidence and is treated with the utmost respect. That particular process would have taken far too long to perform in front of you. In fact, it was a two-day job. Strictly speaking, it was part of the autopsy and you must take it as a given. The remnants of the clothes are on the rack which my assistant will uncover later. Shall we begin?"

He's milking this, Diamond thought. It's an act.

"One takes nothing for granted," Dr. Waghorn continued, ignoring the fact that he was asking his audience to take the undressing for granted, "so let's start by confirming the sex of the deceased. What is the most obvious indicator of the gender?"

A voice from the back said, "The pelvis."

"Who spoke?"

Everyone turned to see. A hand was up in the second row from the back and it belonged to a shaven-headed male in a football shirt.

Waghorn gave the offender a look as if he was next for dissection. "Do you understand English?"

"Yes."

"You're not deaf?"

"No."

"My question about gender was rhetorical. Didn't I ask everyone just now to remain silent?"

For a short interval that must have seemed unbearably long to the hapless student, Waghorn stood in silence, as if the entire procedure had been ruined. Finally he resumed in that thin, strangled voice. "A female pelvis is typically broader than that of a male and this is most apparent in the anterior area known as the pubis. The lower section of the pubis is wider in the female to facilitate birth. Our subject is definitely male. I won't prolong this by going into the several other signs of gender.

"To save time, I measured each of the bones already, starting with the calcaneus at the heel and progressing to the top of the skull. In total he is 1.705 metres, a fraction over five foot seven, but beware. This will not be the height of the living body. A variability factor needs to be added. My calculation is five foot eight at death. Our height diminishes with ageing after reaching a maximum in our late teens or twenties. Let us now deal with what we have in front of us, starting from the top."

The magnified image of the skull was on the big screen.

Waghorn was using a pointer. "In passing, note the prominence of supraorbital ridges characteristic of the male. And now you are—or should be—speculating as to racial identity. Difficult, always difficult, because of the continuum of variation among the races. I would normally look first at teeth, but we have none here. The recessive cheekbones and the narrowness of the palate suggest he was white or Caucasoid in racial type, but this can be deceptive. Of more interest is the tendency of the palate to be triangular rather than the deeper U-shape of the typical African skull. It's a fine judgement, best left to the expert." He bent over the skull as if he hadn't seen it before, looked up at his audience and said, "Caucasoid."

No question who he meant by the expert.

"The absence of any hair is to be expected, although we all know of cases of hair surviving thousands of years under favourable conditions. Of more interest in the present subject is the absence of teeth. This may lead us to make an assumption about age, but of course some people lose all their teeth early in life, so I shall look for more reliable indications of age presently when we examine the vertebrae."

The head bone connected to the neck bone. How laborious was this going to be?

"Had the teeth been intact they would have yielded more information about age. Can we have the camera on the mandible, please?"

Diamond's knowledge of anatomy was scant, but he knew the mandible had something to do with the jaw. Still with the head bone, then.

How long was this likely to take, and what would come out of it? Waghorn was hedging on almost every decision. Okay, the skeleton was male and Caucasian and average in height, but little of use to the investigation had emerged.

The process continued in the same formal manner for the next twenty minutes, more of an anatomy lecture than an autopsy. Diamond was peeved by what seemed like a deliberate move to sideline him. The whole performance was designed to stifle comment. In a small group he wouldn't have hesitated to ask questions. Here any interruption would undermine the teaching. Stuff that. He'd still speak up if there was cause.

"And so we come to the ribcage."

The neck bone connected to the chest bone.

"I would like the camera to display each side in turn, in no particular hurry." Waghorn stepped to one side and took a drink of water.

"Has everybody had a chance to form an opinion? I hope so, because there's something of note here that I wouldn't want any of you to overlook, and by the expressions on your faces I can see that most, if not all, of you have missed it.

Once more, please," he instructed the assistant filming the event, "and can we zoom in?"

The image on the screen got unpleasantly large, more like venetian blinds than ribs.

"I want to speak about the phenomenon known as green bone response, green bone being living bone still mostly covered with soft tissue. Do you notice the shape of the left fifth rib compared to its counterpart on the right side? Compared also to the other ribs? Green bone when damaged perimortem can react to trauma by bending or twisting in a characteristic way that you wouldn't observe if the injury were inflicted after death, when the flesh has deteriorated. Look." He used the pointer again.

Diamond sat forward, prompted by the mention of injury. He was close enough to the skeleton almost to touch the rib, but it was clearer to see magnified on screen, and if there was a difference it was easy to miss. He still wasn't certain he could see it.

If Waghorn had found something of importance, all the posturing could be forgiven. He was in full flow again. "The bending of the green bone may not be obvious to most of you. When you get a full incision it shows better by curling inwards and if the cut is made in a way that exposes only a thin slice of bone then that piece will usually bend outwards. However, that hasn't happened here. To the trained eye there is evidence of a thrust with a sharp instrument." His pointer showed a tiny chip in the bone. "An instrument that damaged the rib as well as penetrating the soft tissue and inflicting a fatal injury. However . . ." He let the word stand on its own for a few dramatic seconds before adding, "It is not impossible that a separate thrust did the serious damage to vital cardiovascular structures."

Diamond couldn't contain himself. "Are you saying he was stabbed?"

"Did someone speak?"

Reproach spread through the room like gas.

Everyone waited, expecting the autopsy to be suspended.

Waghorn stood transparently deciding how to deal with the offence. He took a deep breath, tilted his chin and announced to the room in general, "I had better explain that it is customary for the police to send a representative to witness a postmortem where foul play is suspected. The interruption came from . . . Would you remind me of your name, officer?"

Bloody insulting. He was well aware of the name.

The obvious response was to counterpunch. "Diamond, Detective Superintendent Diamond. You're seriously suggesting one small blemish on a rib shows he was murdered? I've cracked my own ribs several times over playing rugby."

"Other people's ribs, too, by the size of you."

There was amusement.

"It doesn't mean I died."

"We'll take your word for that, Mr. Diamond." Waghorn's tongue was as sharp as any stand-up comedian's.

"I'm making a serious point. I'm saying the injury could have happened earlier in the man's life."

"And I can say what I wish in my own lecture theatre unless you propose to take over. I gave my expert opinion, subject to the limitations I am working under. If you were listening, I spoke of a probability, not a certainty."

"All on the basis of a chipped rib?"

"On the basis of severe blood loss. Haven't you seen the staining on the clothes?" Waghorn beckoned to the assistant who had been standing beside the clothes rack looking bored.

She unzipped the plastic cover to reveal a few garments looking as sad as the unsold remnants of a sale. They were in large transparent evidence bags on hangers. She lifted off the almost threadbare eighteenth-century frock coat and displayed it to the students like an item up for auction, followed by the waistcoat in slightly better condition and, finally, the remains of the shirt. Each had a plate-sized brown stain on the left side. None of this had been visible at the scene, where dust had covered everything.

"I took the precaution of sending some threads for testing," Waghorn said. "Definitely blood."

Diamond let fly. "Why didn't you inform me at once?"

"What's the hurry?" came back the response.

It broke the tension and earned a cheap laugh.

Waghorn rubbed it in. "Anthropologists are used to working with a timescale of centuries or millennia, not what happened yesterday or the day before."

Diamond had heard enough from this wannabe comic and was out of his seat looking at the clothing. There were stains in plenty caused by putrefaction, but the large dark patch from blood loss was unmistakable. He searched for the point of entry. Unfortunately the fabric was so tattered he couldn't tell where the knife had penetrated.

"May I resume, or am I under arrest for failing to report a crime?" Waghorn asked, still playing to his audience.

"Were there any defensive wounds?" Diamond asked.

"I was coming to that. Would you care to return to your seat? Everything comes to him who waits."

Diamond remained where he was.

But Waghorn had the advantage and knew it. "Is this harassment, or what? I can't be comfortable with you so close, as if at any minute you'll be feeling my collar."

More laughter.

Only in the interest of getting more information, Diamond returned to his seat.

"Thank you." Waghorn turned back to face his audience. "I was about to examine the vertebrae, another source of useful information about age, but perhaps I may be excused for pandering to the police and dealing first with the arms or, to be precise, the hands."

The camera zoomed in and the pointer came into play again, indicating the finger bones of the right hand. They were clearly incomplete. The forefinger ended at the knuckle.

Was this the defensive wound Waghorn had said he was coming to—an entire joint severed? Picturing the struggle, Diamond was finding it difficult to contain himself. But he was glad he'd kept silent when Waghorn resumed.

"Don't be deceived by the absence of the top two sections of phalanx from the forefinger. The recovery of the skeleton from a partly demolished building was, to say the least, a difficult operation. Ideally I would have supervised the attachment of the sling we used to lift out the remains, but I was compelled to hand over to a team said to be experienced in such things. In consequence, several small bones were dislodged. The majority were recovered from the sling. Not all, unfortunately. Although I personally searched the loft space and the sling I didn't find these tiny pieces of bone. All things considered, we were fortunate that this was the only loss. But the left hand is far more interesting."

To Diamond's eye, the image that now flashed on screen was less interesting than what they had just seen. The bones appeared to be complete.

Waghorn said, "Observe the middle phalanx of the little finger, or pinky, as our American cousins term it."

The camera operator zoomed in on the piece of bone between joints.

"Can you see a tiny nick?"

The magnified end of the pointer looked the size of an ingot as it hovered over the bone. The indentation Waghorn was talking about was clear.

"This, I suggest, is evidence of what interests Mr. Diamond, an apparent attempt to parry an attack." He took a few steps away and punctuated his remarks by improvising a reconstruction of the scene with the pointer in his right hand jabbing at his left. "So we can posit a sequence of events. Our man is under threat from somebody with a sharp instrument. He raises his left arm to ward off the attack and is cut on the finger. A second thrust hits him in the chest, splintering bone, penetrates the flesh and ruptures a vital organ."

Diamond hadn't needed the histrionics from the pathologist. He'd pictured the attack as soon as the damage to the finger was shown. Conflicting emotions gripped him: contempt for Waghorn's behaviour and excitement at being presented with what promised to be the most sensational murder case of his career. Nobody else in the room knew that the victim could actually be Beau Nash and he had no intention of telling them his theory as to how and why the body had been removed to Twerton.

Waghorn was back on script and talking about outgrowths on vertebrae. Diamond didn't pay attention. His brain was mapping a procedure of his own. How do you deal with a murder two hundred and fifty-odd years ago when all potential witnesses and suspects are dead?

If the killing of Beau Nash was the overriding issue, there was still the secondary mystery to be explored: why had the body been found in the loft in Twerton? Was that where the murder had taken place or had he been stabbed to death at his home in Sawclose and moved there? Find the answer and you might unmask the murderer. An encouraging amount of information had already been unearthed, but there was more to come, he felt confident. He'd need to enlist more help from historians like Estella.

How would his employers react to him spending time on an eighteenth-century murder case? Headquarters wouldn't be thrilled if twenty-first-century crimes were put on the back burner. He'd have to make clear that this wasn't happening. But the beauty of the Beau Nash case was that

Georgina had insisted he did the job. He could quote her own words back to her if necessary. "I want this death investigated properly and you will be in charge. You attracted all this media attention and you can deal with it." The media interest wasn't going away. Once the press learned the identity of the skeleton and the cause of death the phone lines at Concorde House would go into meltdown. In fairness to everyone at the new police office, he'd better give advance notice of what they should expect. He'd have another session with Georgina as soon as this autopsy was over.

You'd think a murder from so long ago could be dealt with at leisure.

Not so.

But the urgency that now gripped Peter Diamond wasn't shared by Dr. Waghorn. His painstaking journey across the arid landscape of the bones continued into a second hour and seemed to be heading for a third. Most of the students had a glazed look and certainly Peter Diamond did. He was strongly tempted to make his exit now that the cause of death had been established. Anything else of interest would surely appear in the report for the coroner. But he was here as the police witness and he had a duty to see it through. If something else of interest showed up he'd kick himself for jumping ship.

The usual sequence in dealing with an unexplained death requires identification of the body before the autopsy takes place. The first duty of the coroner is to find out who the deceased was. When it is obvious that no one can say for certain, then the autopsy goes ahead in the hope that it will provide information about age, racial type and physical appearance, including any disfigurements. The coroner will then carry out an investigation as the first stage of the inquest.

Of course Diamond had his own opinion who the skeleton was, but legal proof was another thing altogether, and this suited him. No need for Waghorn to know. Better all-round if the autopsy took place without prejudice. So the big detective was comfortable, not to say cocky, at being the only person in the room who could name the victim.

Yet he was under no illusion. Any time now the news would break that the skeleton of Beau Nash had been found. Once that was known, it was inevitable that one of the students in this room would tell the press about the fatal stabbing.

His secret was helping him sit this thing out.

The hip bone connected to the thigh bone. His own thigh bone needed stretching. Two hours gone. A coffee would be good.

And so it continued from thigh bone to knee bone to shin bone to ankle bone to heel bone to foot bone to toe bone when he felt like chorusing in relief, "Now hear the word of the Lord."

"In summary," Waghorn said, dashing Diamond's hope that this marathon was over, "the deceased was an elderly male, probably over seventy, about five foot eight in height, toothless, but otherwise intact, who would appear to have met a violent death by some sharp instrument that marked his fifth rib on the left side and the middle phalanx of the small finger of his left hand. The latter is of significance because a defensive injury would suggest he was the victim of an attack, rather than inflicting damage on himself. The staining of the left upper part of the clothes leads me to presume that the likely cause of death was the business end of the sharp instrument penetrating the thoracic cavity and severing a vital organ. This will, of course, go into my report. Are there any questions?"

The students were already closing their notebooks and preparing to leave. Pity anyone so obtuse as to prolong the session.

"You may speak," he said.

It happened.

The offender was the same student in the football shirt who had spoken at the beginning. Perhaps he hoped to redeem himself. Anyway, he had his hand raised.

"Please," Waghorn said to the room in general. "There is a question."

Groans.

"Have the courtesy to remain in your seats." Then to the questioner, "Yes?"

"Could it have been a sword?"

"Could what have been a sword?"

"The sharp instrument."

After a moment, Waghorn said, "Conceivably. Why do you ask?"

"Didn't they carry swords in those days?"

"In which days?"

"I don't know—the eighteen-hundreds?"

Somebody else said, "The seventeen-hundreds, dumbo. The clothes are definitely seventeen-hundreds."

Diamond said, "I have it on good authority that the frock coat is typical of about 1760."

"There you have it from the police," Waghorn said. "Far be it from me to question their information. However . . ." He walked to the clothes rack and lifted a smaller evidence bag from the rail and held it high for all to see the pair of once-white underpants inside. "I don't believe they wore Y-fronts in 1760, not with the Marks and Spencer label."

9

Clenching and unclenching his fists, Diamond remained in the lecture theatre with Dr. Waghorn. All the audience had left and so had the technicians.

"Is it some kind of student hoax?"

"The pants?" Waghorn said. "I don't see how it can be. They were under the breeches, in position around the pelvis when I separated the clothing from the bones—and must have been when the skeleton was first revealed in the loft."

"You don't think they could have been put on afterwards?"

A shake of the head. "Impossible. Haven't I made clear already that a skeleton without flesh is disarticulated? This one was only held in place by what remained of the clothes. Any idiot trying to dress it in pants would need to strip off the breeches first and the whole structure would disintegrate."

"All right. What would an eighteenth-century man be wearing? Some kind of drawers?"

"For pity's sake, superintendent. I'm a forensic anthropologist."

"The clothes don't interest you?"

"That's an impertinence. Didn't I make a point of bringing them all to the autopsy and showing everyone the bloodstaining?"

"You just said you're an anthropologist. Let's say

ninety-five percent of your attention was on the bones.
What the victim was wearing was secondary. I'm not blam-
ing you."

"It sounds suspiciously like it."

"You took off the pants and put them aside." Picturing
the scene, Diamond had a new thought. "Did you have an
assistant working with you?"

"I did. It's normal."

"The young woman with the clothes rack?"

"Becky. But I trust her absolutely. She wouldn't stoop
to the sort of trick you're suggesting."

"She put the clothes in evidence bags and hung them
on the rack? Yes? And where was the rack kept overnight?"

"This is absurd."

"I'm serious. The pants must have been introduced by
some joker."

For that, Diamond was given a look as if he'd messed
the floor. "The lab is kept locked. I am scrupulous about
security."

"I need to speak to Becky."

"She's worked with me for three years."

"I don't care how long. I must get to the bottom of this."

Waghorn smirked. "The bottom decomposed a long
time ago."

"Where can I speak to Becky?"

"She's at her break now. I don't want her interrogated."

"It's got to be done. You've uncovered a murder and it's
going to be investigated whether it took place fifty years
ago or two hundred and fifty."

He sighed like a slashed tyre. "Very well, but I hope
you'll treat her with more civility than you're treating me."

"You haven't gone out of your way to be helpful."

"It's not my job to come up with an explanation." The
smug little man had no idea how close he was to being
thumped.

"You must have known days ago about the Marks and Spencer label and you said bugger all about it until it was forced from you by that student asking a question."

"Today I was conducting an autopsy, superintendent, a serious procedure. Can you imagine the reaction from a roomful of students if I showed them the pants at the beginning?"

"I'm not talking about today. It was bloody obvious something was wrong, yet you didn't pick up the phone."

Waghorn shrugged as if such obligations were beneath him. "I was preparing the skeleton for the autopsy table. You have no idea how demanding that is."

Diamond shook his head. "The press are going to make us look like clowns. Right now your students are spreading it about on social media."

"I can't help that. It's public knowledge now."

An alarming possibility had hammered Diamond's brain ever since the autopsy ended. "Suppose this isn't a stunt. We've all assumed up to now—or at least I did and so did my team—that the skeleton is a piece of history from 1760 or thereabouts. Could we be mistaken?"

"Of course." Waghorn gave a sniff that was the nearest thing to an apology he would concede.

"Not good enough," Diamond told him. "I need your advice here. How old are these bones? Is this a modern man?"

"By modern, you mean since Y-fronts were invented? When was that?" Waghorn took out his smartphone and worked it rapidly with his latex-covered thumb. "Chicago, 1935. I don't know when they got into M&S, but it wouldn't have been long after. We could be speaking of sometime in the last eighty years, then."

"This is ludicrous," Diamond said. "Can't you tell?"

"It's not easy determining the time since death. I can't say merely from looking at bones whether they go back twenty years or two hundred."

"There are tests, aren't there? Carbon dating?"

"That's an archaeological measure in thousands of years. It wouldn't help us. The best hope would be to look at the levels of nitrogen and amino acids remaining. This would be an indication of how far the bones have deteriorated. They lose proteins as time passes."

"Are we talking decades, hundreds of years, or what?"

"Decades, possibly, but the test is still far from accurate. Other factors come into play."

"It's a skeleton, for God's sake. How long does it take for a corpse to be reduced to bones?"

Waghorn lifted his shoulders and pulled a face. He didn't like being pinned down. "In our climate, and if it isn't buried or in water, as little as one to two years. But let's not forget where it was. A loft space can get exceedingly hot in the summer months and that would accelerate the process. The clothing may delay it a bit."

"So we could even be dealing with a twenty-first century murder?"

"Except for the style of clothes."

"He could have liked dressing up in eighteenth-century gear. I've heard of stranger things."

"This is getting beyond me," Waghorn said.

"Me, too," Diamond said. "But it can't be ignored. Those tests you were talking about. We'd better get them under way."

"They're not cheap."

"My gaffer will have to worry about that."

"There is one test we can run quite soon, using ultra-violet light. Fresh bones fluoresce. Under UV a cross-cut of one of the long bones will glow pale blue around the hollow part and the thickness of the ring of colour is a good indication of the timespan. The fresher the bone, the thicker the band of light."

"Go for it, then," Diamond said. "How soon can we get results?"

"That isn't up to me."

"Somehow, I thought that was what you'd say."

"And did you interview the technician?" Georgina asked Diamond when he reported back. She'd come in late to work after taking an early taxi to Bannerdown to collect the car and drive it to the Mercedes garage to get the lamp bulb replaced. Needing a trouble-free, quiet morning today of all days, she'd walked into a hornets' nest in CID.

"Becky?" The big detective was mired in gloom. All his theories were shafted. The failure was the most galling in his long career.

He forced himself to speak about Becky. "I was impressed with her. Waghorn was so taken up with his damned bones that he failed to see there was anything wrong with the clothing. Becky knew straight away that they were Y-fronts and found the Marks and Spencer label."

"This was when they were preparing the skeleton for the autopsy table?"

"Yes."

"And she drew the label to his attention?"

"She did. Takes her job seriously. I can't see her as the weak link. She's well drilled in continuity of evidence."

"You said Dr. Waghorn was preoccupied with the bones?"

"He doesn't see the pants as his problem."

"He's right. The problem is ours, God help us," Georgina said. "It's been mayhem here. The press have been demanding a statement since the autopsy finished this morning. Some mischief maker tipped them off."

"That's no surprise," he said. "The autopsy room was full of students with their smartphones."

She wasn't listening. "So I've called a press conference for five this afternoon for you to update our media friends."

Just when he was thinking his life couldn't get any worse. "A press conference? Today?"

"Give them the facts, Peter. Better than having them make things up—which they're well capable of doing. And they want a picture of the pants. It'll be all over the newspapers tomorrow and it won't be pretty."

He'd never thought of Y-fronts as pretty.

"I see the look on your face," Georgina went on. "We can't duck this. Long experience has taught me not to make enemies of that lot. They're already annoyed that they weren't allowed on site when the skeleton was hoisted from the loft."

"They still got their pictures."

"Once they get a sniff of a story they don't go away. Prepare a statement. I don't want you doing this off the cuff."

"The problem with a statement is knowing what to state," he said. "My first thought was that the pants were a stunt."

"University students?"

"Highly likely. But Dr. Waghorn won't have it. He insists the skeleton would have fallen to bits if anyone tried putting the pants on it. If he's right, we've got a totally different case on our hands."

"He can't be right, or the whole thing is nonsense."

"That was my first thought, ma'am."

She eyed him warily. "But you've had a second one?"

"I have."

"Go on, then."

"I'm now regarding it as a case of murder."

"That's no surprise. The stab marks and the bloodstains."

"The pants could make it much more recent than we were led to believe. A twenty-first-century job."

Georgina took a sharp breath and said nothing.

"Waghorn says he can't tell from the state of the bones how long it is since the victim died."

"It's a skeleton, for God's sake. It can't be all that recent."

"Above ground, the soft flesh breaks down quite quickly.

Even in our climate we could be talking about as little as two years. Hot air trapped in the loft."

"I need a paracetamol," she said, reaching for her handbag. "I've had a headache all morning and you've made it a whole lot worse." She dipped her hand in and came out with the packet of painkillers and the visiting card she'd been given by Sally Paris. She'd dismissed the card from her mind because she had no intention of following up the chance meeting of the evening before. She hoped Diamond hadn't noticed.

"The speed of decomposition came as a shock to me," he was saying.

"Do you honestly believe this?"

"I'm trying to keep an open mind. He's arranging tests."

"At our expense, no doubt." Georgina took a bottle of water from her desk drawer and poured some into a cup. No one should see the ACC drinking from a bottle. She swallowed two tablets and washed them down.

"The tests will tell us," Diamond said. "We need to know."

"But if they prove the bones are modern we have to explain why a modern man was wearing old-fashioned clothes."

"It's a mystery."

"What's happening with the clothes? Are they still up at the university?"

"I've arranged for them to be collected."

"Good."

"We can run our own tests."

"Peter, you keep talking about tests."

He could almost hear the calculator working in Georgina's head. "We need answers."

"Surely if this is a modern crime there's a more cost-effective way of dating it."

"What's that?"

"The Y-fronts. I can't say I have much experience of

men's undergarments," she said. "Are they worn much these days?"

He'd rather be walking on red-hot coals than talking underwear to the assistant chief constable. "They may not be as popular as they once were, but they've never gone away. It's the support."

"I'll take your word for that. Will it help the case if we show them to the media?"

His eyes doubled in size. "Help the case? How?"

"Somebody may see a picture in the paper and recognise them."

"With respect, ma'am, I don't think this is a good idea. Everyone knows what Y-fronts look like."

"Not everyone," she said in a pious tone.

"These are in poor condition," he said. "Holes and stains."

"I see." She thought about that for a while before saying, "What we do is show the press a similar pair."

This was catastrophic. "You want me to appear at a press conference and hold up a pair of pants? Don't you think I've suffered enough?"

She was indifferent to his pain. "What's your problem, Peter?"

"This whole damned case has been a gift to the gutter press from the start," he said. "They won't treat it seriously."

She raised her forefinger as if she'd seen the light. "Well, why don't we get hold of one of those mannequins? I don't mean a person. The fibreglass things they use in the underwear department in Jolly's."

She'd got this idea and she had to be dissuaded—fast.

Desperation was driving him now. "I suggest we offer them a press kit with some official photos."

"Will that be enough?"

"Photos of the real pants. Much better."

"As you wish," she said. "Just get it done as soon as possible and make sure I get a copy."

She wanted her own picture of the pants. Wisely he passed no comment.

John Wigfull, the civilian press officer, had been tasked with notifying everyone that a statement about the Twerton skeleton would be made at 5 P.M., reasonable timing for the morning papers and the late evening newscasts.

Diamond gave Leaman the job of putting together the press kit including photos.

"Have we given up on Beau Nash?" Leaman asked.

Diamond wasn't giving him the satisfaction of saying, "I told you so."

"Not entirely."

"But you definitely want a picture of the actual Y-fronts in the press kit?"

A tight-lipped, "Yes."

"With respect—"

"When anyone uses that phrase to me, John, I know they mean the opposite. Just get it done."

"No problem."

Thanks to the paracetamol, Georgina's headache was gone. Surely it hadn't been a hangover? She preferred to think the stress of the past twenty-four hours was responsible. Dealing with Diamond on a daily basis was stressful enough and the added worry of leaving the car on a public road overnight had been too much. Thank goodness no one here at Bath Central knew what had happened.

She picked the visiting card from her desk and was about to bin it when she saw something that made her hesitate.

The name on the card was Lady Sally Paris.

Lady?

How easy it is to make assumptions. In her wildest dreams she wouldn't have supposed the Good Samaritan of the night before had been a titled person. She'd introduced herself as Sally, which had sounded friendly and informal. But she *had* said something about the chauffeur having the night off. Georgina wasn't used to mingling with the aristocracy, but now it had happened she was already having second thoughts about throwing away the card. People like that can be helpful contacts. Networking was the way to get on these days.

The embarrassment of last night needed to be put in a new context. Nobody of Lady Sally's status in society was going to think a couple of G&Ts were grounds for dismissal from the police. Lords and ladies were knocking them back all the time. What had seemed a potential scandal a few hours ago was laughable now. After all, Georgina reflected, elevating herself to the level these people operated from, one had done the responsible thing and stopped driving. Any alcohol was out of one's system by now.

One would take up Sally's invitation and arrange to visit her at Charlcombe.

Shortly after 4 P.M. came a call from Dr. Waghorn.

"Something new?" Diamond said, trying not to sound too eager. He'd learned to play his cards cannily with this smart alec.

"I think you'll be interested. We discussed PMI tests on the skeleton in the hope of learning the time since his death."

"PMI?"

"Postmortem interval. Well, here at the university we have the facilities to run one of the tests straight away. Did I say? I got it under way shortly after you left."

"The ultraviolet?"

"Yes, but a word of caution here. UV isn't much more than a crude indication of bone age. The test should be used in conjunction with the other tests I mentioned and they take longer."

"What did you find?"

"If these had been old bones—say two hundred years—I would have expected them to show yellow. They fluoresced blue."

He felt himself fluorescing bright pink. "Meaning they're fresh?"

"Relatively so. All I can say at this stage is that they are not more than a hundred years old. For your purposes, the age of the bones doesn't match the style of clothes the subject was wearing."

"Apart from the pants?"

"That's true. The Y-fronts may well be his own."

"You'll let me know the minute the other tests come back?"

"That is a promise, but don't call me. I hate being pestered."

Diamond wasn't listening. His brain was in overdrive. He'd just been handed a twentieth-century murder case, if not a twenty-first. All the theorising about Beau Nash and how he had ended up could safely be forgotten. This was a new mystery with challenges of its own.

He didn't make any new friends at the press conference, but he wasn't feeling sociable. This duty had been foisted on him at a time when he wanted to be up and running. With Keith Halliwell at his side—all the friction between them forgotten—he went through the motions in front of a batch of microphones, some TV cameras and a smallish gathering of reporters and photographers who had come at short notice.

"You all have a press kit and I won't waste time telling you what you can read yourselves. The newsworthy bit is that this man appears to be a murder victim and the stabbing could have taken place more recently than anyone at first supposed. We're just at the start of our enquiries. We haven't identified the victim yet and this is where you can help. We're interested in hearing from the public about any elderly male without teeth who went missing in the past seventy years."

"And had a thing about dressing in old-fashioned clothes?" the man from the *Sun* asked.

"Possibly."

"An actor?"

"We're not ruling anything out."

"Are the clothes authentic eighteenth-century—apart from the Y-fronts?"

"Tests are being done on them. We don't know yet."

"How long had he been in the loft?" the *Bath Chronicle* woman wanted to know.

"We can't say with any accuracy yet."

"A long time, surely, to have turned into a skeleton?"

"Could be as short as two years according to the experts, but the likelihood is longer."

"How much longer, do you reckon?"

"I'm not reckoning."

"As long as Y-fronts have been available?" someone from the back put in.

"That would be the absolute beginning of the timespan. Which I'm told is just before the Second World War."

"Can't they be dated from the style?"

"Good point. We've taken that up with the manufacturers."

"Some of us keep our underwear going until the elastic goes."

Diamond took that as a joke, not a question. It got a few laughs and somebody at the back made a remark he didn't catch that sparked another bout of laughter. Most of these press people knew each other well.

The big-mouth continued with the backchat and there was an edge to the amusement—more like forced laughter—that Diamond didn't care for. Difficult to see who this troublemaker was because his view was blocked by two TV cameramen. The glimpse he got when one of them moved was of shoulder-length dark hair and a fancy jacket, but the voice was definitely a man's. A hippy with a grudge against the police? It would be worth checking whether this person actually had a press pass.

The questioning from the others was rapid-fire, so Diamond soon got distracted and when he next looked, the joker had changed position, or vanished.

He was relieved when the focus moved away from the Y-fronts. "How will you handle the murder element of this case?"

His answer came almost automatically. He wanted to get this over and start on the real work. "We have an experienced team in Bath CID and no effort will be spared in establishing the facts."

"Have you found anything else at the site?"

"Nothing I haven't told you already."

"The house is demolished, isn't it? Will you be searching through the debris?"

"Most of it has gone to landfill. If necessary we'll do a fingertip search."

"'If necessary'? Don't you think it's worth doing?"

"Identifying the victim is our priority. The few details we have about height and so on are in the press kit."

"It was a fatal stabbing?"

"So it appears."

"Did you find the weapon?"

"No."

"Have you traced the owner of the house in Twerton?"

"That's a separate line of enquiry. For some years the house has been condemned and occupied only by squatters."

"Haven't you forgotten someone?"

"Who's that?"

"The skeleton—or does he count as a squatter?"

More laughter that Diamond didn't join in. He sensed the unwelcome presence had moved to the opposite side. Those with cameras didn't stay long in one place. He wasn't giving the barracker the satisfaction of a proper look.

"Was the loft sealed off from the rest of the house?"

"We don't know. The demolition took place before we could check."

"Presumably it was, or someone would have looked in there at some point and had a nasty surprise."

More amusement and laughter that lingered too long. And this time Diamond did catch a glimpse of someone he didn't know to be a journalist and the long hair looked uncannily like a wig. The face was old, the figure portly and the clothing . . . well, it was old-fashioned in style. But then in the blink of an eye it was gone. The trick of an overactive brain, obviously. The demands of this case weren't good for his mental well-being.

Getting a grip on himself, he issued a warning. "I hope none of you make the mistake of reporting this in a light-hearted way. We're dealing with the apparent murder of an elderly man." He stopped himself from adding, "It could come back to haunt you," but the cliché almost tumbled out. The presence at the back of the room must have brought the words to mind.

He continued. "Whatever his story is, it had a tragic outcome that will have affected several lives, people who may not even know it yet. He could be someone's husband, father or grandfather." And now despite his best intentions the homily got personal. "Believe me, the moment of learning about a violent death is hell. Anyone unfortunate enough to have known a murder victim will tell you about the pain, the grief, the black despair that won't go away. You people are the message bringers. Don't forget the living when you report on the dead." At risk of being overwhelmed by his own memories, he took refuge in another cliché: "We'll be pursuing every line of enquiry and as always we look to you to pass on any new information that may come your way."

When they were well away from all the microphones, he put on a show of bravado for Halliwell. "Buggers. They'll take no notice. They'll play it for laughs, some of them, anyway, giving the skeleton a stupid nickname, Bony, or some such."

"If it catches people's interest, does it matter?" Halliwell said. "We want all the publicity we can get."

"Publicity is double-edged. The public gave us Beau Nash's name. We spent the best part of a week on a wild goose chase thanks to that useless tip-off."

"He *was* dressed like Nash," Halliwell said. "The stuff we learned could still come in useful."

"Yeah? Convince me." He thought about asking Halliwell if he'd noticed anyone unusual at the back, but he couldn't be sure how much of it he'd imagined.

"Pity," Paloma said.

"Why?"

"I was thinking this was a case I could help with, something we could work on together. I even had visions of getting you into a frock coat and breeches and going to one of those costume balls they put on at the Assembly Rooms."

He almost choked on his coffee. "Give me a break."

"I'll have to, won't I?"

They were in his front room in Weston after a meal at his local. These days the Old Crown called itself a gastro pub and had a chef and served dauphinoise potato with some of the dishes, but you could still get the classic fish and chips he always ordered there. Paloma had settled for the Cornish hake fillet with wild mushrooms, wild garlic and Jersey royals, so both of them had been catered for.

Raffles padded into the room and tried jumping on to

Paloma's lap, but needed scooping up. His rear legs weren't as strong as they'd once been. Once in place, he started purring—as if he knew who had provided the gourmet salmon and whole shrimps he had just enjoyed. Normally he subsisted on a diet of Whiskas and dry food.

"You spoil him," Diamond told her.

"He needed fussing up." She smoothed her hand gently over the warm fur. "He's rather thin these days."

"It's his age."

"How old is he now?"

"I don't speak of it in his presence. All I know is he costs me a fortune at the vet's."

"He was Steph's cat, wasn't he?"

He nodded. "A stray kitten who just walked in when we first moved into this place. That was the year I was dealing with a bunch of oddballs who met in the crypt at St. Michael's to discuss crime stories. Crime experts—the Bloodhounds, they called themselves—and would you believe they didn't know a real murderer was among them? Anyway, Steph was here holding the fort as usual, trying to unpack cardboard boxes and suddenly became aware of this little tabby exploring them. She was captivated but did the decent thing and asked around and eventually took him up to the place for strays at Claverton."

"I think I know the rest."

"Yes, she kept asking if anyone had claimed him and they hadn't. He settled in here as if it was meant to be."

"He's smart."

"He helped me through the worst time of my life. I'll be gutted when he goes."

"Don't think about it. Enjoy him while you've got him."

"We're all going to go sometime."

"Snap out of it, Peter. You're getting morbid."

"One of those newspapers called me a veteran. 'Veteran detective Peter Diamond.' That was a first."

She laughed. "Did you take that to heart? Treat it as a compliment. They might as well have called you a safe pair of hands or a mastermind."

"Not if they'd seen me flipflopping over this damned case. Even my own team are losing patience."

"There's always a low point, isn't there? You've passed it now. Onwards and upwards."

In truth, it felt to him like backwards and downwards. The Beau Nash enquiry had been progressing nicely, with a named victim, a place and time of death and a potential suspect. Now he was back to an anonymous set of bones. "I still need your help."

"How exactly?"

"With the clothes. We've got them at the police office now. Would you come and give an expert opinion?"

"Tomorrow?"

"Please."

"There you are, then," Paloma said. "Already moving on."

"The things the victim was wearing look authentic, being in such a bad state, but I wonder if it's fancy dress. I've got to assume he liked dressing up."

"In which case the garments are unlikely to be genuine eighteenth-century. The real things are museum pieces. We don't let anyone try them on."

"You're talking about the Fashion Museum?"

"Of course." The collection in the Assembly Rooms in Bennett Street was almost Paloma's second home.

"Where would anyone go if they wanted to hire an outfit for one of those balls you mentioned? A fancy-dress shop?"

"There are three or four in the area, but I'm not sure if that's what you mean. Those places stock a whole range of things for hen and stag parties and the like. Gorilla suits, Frankenstein outfits."

"Cheap and vulgar."

"Not all of it. They have some better-made clothes. But

the class of people who attend the balls tend to go to theatrical costumiers or specialist suppliers. You can hire some gorgeous things and if what you want is not in stock you get it handmade."

"Probably in the Far East."

She smiled.

"Wigs?"

"They supply those, too. All the gear. Where's your laptop? I'll show you."

"You won't. It's not here."

"You're incorrigible. How do you manage your life, paying bills and checking bank statements?"

"The post mostly."

"Take my word for it, then. For well-made clothes you'd go to one of the firms I'm talking about. Tomorrow I'll look at the stitching and see if I can tell you some more."

"There's quite a bit of this dressing-up going on, is there?"

"More than you'd think. I've heard of several annual balls at the Assembly Rooms and the Guildhall with more than three hundred guests immaculately dressed. Admittedly there's some licence over which period is represented. An early Georgian gown might be seen at a Regency ball."

"Is that a sin?"

"It's about a hundred years different. Fashion is always changing. As well as the balls there are private parties going on all the time and charity dos and civic occasions when the town lashes out and goes all Jane Austen."

"The costume firms do good business, then?"

"Their stock would amaze you."

"It would depress me. But it's an obvious line of enquiry. Nobody has yet explained how an old guy in eighteenth-century clothes ends up in a loft in Twerton. Do you get old men attending these affairs at the Assembly Rooms?"

"Certainly. They're often the ones who can afford to

be there. It's not just dancing. There's usually supper and card games. Gambling."

"Have you been?"

"No, but I wouldn't mind," Paloma said. "Would you?"

"Not my scene."

"There's drinking."

"Not beer-drinking, I bet. And I don't suppose the dancing is jive."

"It's all in period, as it should be. Before a ball they offer classes for people to learn the steps. You'd be all right."

"I didn't think we were talking about me."

10

Next morning the murder squad was in session.

"We'll get nowhere until we identify the victim," Diamond told the team. The intent in his voice was obvious to all. He was in no mood for sarcasm from anyone. "Male, elderly, five-eight in height. And toothless. Must have had a reason to be dressed in eighteenth-century costume and wig. The marks of interest on the bones are the damage to the ribs and hand and the indications that he was old. Have I missed anything?"

"The absence of hair," Ingeborg said.

He hadn't seen this as significant, so he waited for her to explain.

"We seem to be assuming he was bald and we could be wrong about that."

"I'm not assuming anything."

"What I mean is that we should look for hair. Hair survives longer than anything except the bones."

"Dr. Waghorn didn't find any on the scalp," Diamond said. "He's painstaking and he'd know the importance. But you're right, Ingeborg. We won't give up on this."

"If we can find a single hair there's information to be got from it. Will Waghorn have searched the clothes for hairs when he was undressing the skeleton?"

Paul Gilbert chipped in with, "And the inside of the wig?"

"He's extremely thorough and he had an experienced assistant. They used evidence bags, so I suppose there could be the odd hair lurking inside. Forensics will do their own check. I'm having the clothes examined by an expert today to see if they're genuine eighteenth-century—which has now been thrown into doubt."

"If they're not old, we can find out who made them and maybe where they were bought," John Leaman said.

"You can hire costumes," Paul Gilbert said.

"What's your point?" Leaman said.

"They weren't necessarily bought."

"Fine. That's good," Diamond said at once, not allowing the session to be undermined by old antagonisms in the team. "As soon as anything is confirmed, we'll start making enquiries with the manufacturers."

"Are the pants being checked to see when they were made?" Leaman asked.

"That's already in hand. Marks and Spencer have a company archive up at Leeds. It's vast. They do heritage tours and lectures. I've spoken to the lady in charge and emailed her pictures of the back and front and the label. She promised to get back to me shortly. If we can focus on just a few years, we'll be in a far better position."

"To check missing persons?" Gilbert said.

"Right—and that won't be easy. The numbers who go missing every week never fail to amaze me and a high proportion of those are elderly, but it's got to be done. That's going to be your task, Paul."

"Okay, guv."

"Then there's the Twerton connection. John, you were checking the deeds of the house."

"I did," Leaman said, emphasising that it was a job completed. "I spent a day and a half at the records office."

"Getting the ancient history of the terrace? That's no help now. We've homed in on the past fifty years."

In this business-like session even Leaman resisted the urge to complain. He'd save his moan for later.

Diamond asked, "Did you root out anything at all about who lived there?"

"In recent years? The place was condemned and became a squat. Before that, the owner lived abroad and did the letting through an agency that went bust. I can't tell you any more because like everyone else I thought the skeleton had been shut in the loft for hundreds of years."

"You'll make enquiries now?"

"Can do."

"Will do. Directly, this morning."

Leaman swivelled his chair from side to side and said nothing.

"Don't just rely on official records," Diamond added. "Knock on doors. Visit local shops. Talk to the postman."

Knocking on doors wouldn't come easily to Leaman. Tapping on a keyboard was more to his liking.

Ingeborg asked, "Is anything being done about the crime scene? I know it's been levelled, but the murder weapon could be buried in the rubble."

The same point had come up at the press conference. "I drove past last night," Diamond informed them. "Unfortunately, the developers were quick off the mark. All the loose stuff has been loaded on to lorries and driven away to some landfill site. You wouldn't know a building had been there. I'm not optimistic about finding anything at this late stage, but I'll ask uniform to do a fingertip search."

"Uniform are doing massive overtime already this week," Leaman said.

"What for?"

"The fireworks. Haven't you heard them going off? The World Fireworks Championships."

"Here in Bath?"

"Two nations put on a display each evening. It has to be policed."

So that was why his quiet evening in Paloma's garden had been ruined. "I did hear something. Bugger it, if I want plods for a search, I'll get them, fireworks or no fireworks."

Halliwell added, "To be fair to Dr. Waghorn, he spent a lot of time sifting through the rubble around the skeleton before it was hoisted out."

"Yeah, and missed the hat." Diamond felt no need to be fair to Waghorn. "He wasn't doing a search. He was moving bits of slate and masonry from around the chair. He wanted to get the sling in place and lift the whole thing out in one piece."

Ingeborg said, "The clothes must be our best lead, and not only the pants. Could the frock coat and breeches come from the theatre? They've done a few period dramas in recent years."

"Restoration comedies. *The Beaux' Stratagem* with the National," Diamond threw in, surprising everyone.

Some looks were exchanged.

He wasn't telling them he'd pulled this plum from his earlier meeting with Estella. "Would you ask them? I'm sure their wardrobe mistress keeps a record of the costumes they make over the years."

"It does seem the victim was dressed as Beau Nash and not just any man from that time," Ingeborg said. "If there was a play that featured him as a character . . ." She turned to Diamond as the newly revealed theatre buff. "Any thoughts?"

"Can't say it rings a bell," he said. "Is anyone else a theatre-goer?"

It seemed unlikely and so it proved.

"Check with them anyway, Inge. Go to it, people. We can crack this."

* * *

With the team as usefully deployed as the few hard facts allowed, he went to the entrance to meet Paloma. His new workplace didn't run to a front desk and a helpful sergeant. Anyone who wanted that sort of service went to the One Stop Shop in Manvers Street, where the guardians of law and order were now slotted in with waste and recycling, Age UK, housing benefits, Shopmobility, healthy lifestyle and even a small café. The days of the blue lamp and a central police station were over.

Paloma was in the building already, business-like in glasses and with her hair back from her face in a French twist, distinctly different from the look Diamond was used to. She was in a grey trouser suit and carrying a leather bag.

"Heck of a way from Bath," was the first thing she said.

"You're telling me."

"It's like a foreign country out here. I stopped to ask where the police building is, and the locals didn't have a clue."

"I'm responsible for Bristol and South Gloucestershire as well now," he said. "It's a bigger empire."

"Does the emperor get paid more? I can see from the look on your face that he doesn't."

"What's in the bag?"

"My inspection kit. Things you won't have here."

He took her to the section at the back of the building where the evidence sergeants zealously guarded their collection of exhibits waiting to be produced in court. Even though Diamond vouched for Paloma, the Cerberus behind the desk insisted she produced her driving licence and a business card.

As a riposte she requested two sets of PPE.

Flummoxed by initials as always, Diamond was too proud to ask.

The clothes rack with its cover was wheeled out. They were shown into a small room containing an inspection table, shelving and little else.

"The lighting isn't great," Diamond said.

"I came prepared." Paloma took out a torch.

She emptied her bag completely and like a surgeon arranged the things she would use in a row along the shelf: magnifiers, torch, tweezers, calipers, tape measure, camera, pen and paper.

Overshoes and protective suits contained in plastic film covers had been supplied by the sergeant and one mystery was solved: PPE was personal protective equipment. The protection wasn't for the people, but the exhibits.

"Face-mask first," Paloma said when Diamond unwrapped the paper suit and prepared to step into it. "There's a sequence."

How did she know this? She didn't routinely handle evidence. He could only surmise that she'd checked the drill before starting out.

The complete professional.

They did the dressing. Mobcap (and hairnet in Paloma's case), pair of latex gloves, suit, overshoes and a second pair of gloves for disposal after handling items and before touching others.

Looking the part, however weird they appeared, they set to work.

"This looks awfully like the real thing," Paloma said as she eased the thin, heavily stained shirt from the bag with as much respect as you'd give to one of Shakespeare's first folios. She arranged it on the table and a pungent smell came from it, dust, death and rotting fabric. "It's in a pitiful state."

She began a commentary almost as if she was the voice-over at a fashion show and the shirt was crisp and spotless. "Plainwoven Holland linen, rather than silk. Never silk for shirts. And the design is spot on. Can't fault it. Men pulled shirts over their heads rather than buttoning them all the way down. There's just this slit ending at the mid-chest area and the only buttons are high up to fasten the collar at the neck. See how high it is on the throat? Full, generous sleeves, pleated and forming cuffs at the wrists with ruffs. Gussets under the arms and on the shoulders. All hand-stitched."

She reached for an LED magnifier from her bag and examined a seam under the intense white light. "With linen thread, which is right."

"Rather than cotton?"

"If this is the work of a modern seamstress, she knows her fashion history. Have you noticed the length of the shirt, Peter? The men of the time used it as an all-in-one garment with the tails tucked into the breeches and functioning as underwear."

"All frock coats and no pants."

She may have smiled behind the mask.

"Is it the real deal?" Diamond asked.

"I was ninety-five percent sure until I saw these."

He looked. She was pointing to the two buttons under the dusty ruff on the collar.

"Pearl buttons?"

"They can't be right," Paloma said.

"Didn't they have them?"

She shook her head. "The history of mother-of-pearl goes back to ancient Persia, but buttons like these weren't available in the west until the 1890s in America. Then everyone fell in love with them and it was mass production."

"Proof the shirt isn't genuine?"

"I don't know about 'genuine.' It's expertly made. But the buttons of a gentleman's shirt would be fabric-covered, Dorset-style, needle-woven, and these aren't. I guess they wouldn't be visible under the ruff. The lace on the collar hides them. Just a detail really."

"But a giveaway?"

Paloma had so admired the tailoring of the shirt that

she clearly felt almost disloyal about exposing the flaw. "If you want to call it that, yes. The bloodstain is real enough, isn't it?"

"What you can see of it." Much of the shirt front had deteriorated to threads. Those that remained had a definite brown tinge on the right side—the victim's left.

"Will you get DNA?"

"I hope so. Some bloodstained threads went off to the lab. Now that we're talking about a more modern murder, DNA could be the game changer. When we believed the killing was in 1761, I couldn't see it helping us because even if we got a result there was nothing to compare it with."

"So even genetic science has its limitations."

"And I have a bad habit of running into them. The point of entry of the murder weapon may be clearer on the waistcoat. Shall we look?"

"I'd like to admire this for a moment longer," Paloma said. "The workmanship. Exquisite."

"But it's not the full ticket?"

She inhaled sharply and audibly, as if she'd burnt herself. "Didn't I just say? Everything except the buttons is genuine. The construction, the materials, the finishing. All the work was handmade then, and there must have been some wonderful shirtmakers in business."

"No other modern stuff? Machine stitching?"

Her eyes opened wide. "Absolutely not."

They returned the shirt to its bag and put on fresh gloves before starting to examine the other stained and threadbare things.

The search became almost as protracted as Waghorn's autopsy. Paloma confirmed that the waistcoat and frock coat had been made with the same level of skill as the shirt. "Look at the embroidery on the waistcoat. Beautiful work."

"What is it, floral?" he asked.

"Oak leaves and acorns, by the look of it. Pity so much has rotted away."

When they examined the breeches, she gave a cry of delight at finding fabric-covered buttons of the sort she'd been talking about earlier. "What's more, you can see where adjustments have been made. They let out the waist at some stage."

While she was admiring the workmanship, Diamond continued to look closely for hairs and other fibres, but found none.

"I'm certain now. This is mid-eighteenth-century, what's left of it," Paloma told him. "Those buttons must have come later, much later, but the clothes are original."

He couldn't share her delight, although he tried to appear interested. She'd given another twist to the tourniquet this case had become.

"The white tricorne was a rare item," Paloma said when they took the still-flattened and far from white hat from its bag. Where part of the crown had been torn it flapped open when she turned it over. "Most well-to-do men favoured dark hats and white wigs, but Beau Nash bucked the trend."

"We've ditched the Nash theory. He's out of it as far as I'm concerned, and good riddance."

"Hold on, Pete. You can't ignore him altogether. Isn't it obvious this man was a Nash impersonator?"

Another angle. After the episode of the Y-fronts, Diamond wouldn't care if he never heard of the Beau again.

"Get with it, man," Paloma added, surprising him with the force of the words. She'd become fractious and he didn't understand why.

With the job completed, he took her to the self-service kitchen everyone shared. Spotlessly clean. Good lighting. Cheerful green and white plastic tables and chairs. He hated it.

He made her a coffee.

"There wasn't much you didn't know already," she said when he thanked her for coming in.

"The pearl buttons."

"Those—yes."

"Lighten up, Paloma. You helped enormously. They change everything."

She seemed unmoved. "Because they were sewn on later? The shirt was genuine eighteenth-century and some modern person did a repair job?"

"The buttons are evidence that the skeleton isn't Beau Nash or any other man of his time."

"It appalls me," she said, and the reason for her annoyance became clear. "An eighteenth-century shirt is fantastically rare, a museum piece, not fancy dress for some rich yuppie to ponce around in."

"It didn't do him much good."

She dredged up a faint smile.

"Maybe the owner wasn't a rich yuppie," he added, "but the last in line of an old Bath family, a good man who'd fallen on hard times and the costume was all he had left, the heirloom he wouldn't be parted from."

"Why do you say that?"

"Because I don't want you losing sleep over it."

She didn't seem impressed.

He said, "I can think of better ways of losing sleep."

She gave him a kick under the table.

"What I was about to say," he said, "is that I learned today that the fireworks we heard the other evening were part of an ongoing event, the world championships, would you believe?"

"I heard about that, too. I checked the internet after the bangs all started again the next night. Two cities go head to head each evening and at the end of the week the judges decide the winner."

"Would you like to go?"

"I thought you hated bangers."

"Not if I'm expecting them."

"Righty," she said, raising her thumb. "I'm up for it if you are. Tomorrow night, the grand finale?"

"Where?"

"The lawn in front of the Royal Crescent. Should be spectacular."

Back in the CID room, he sat on the edge of Keith Halliwell's desk and updated him on Paloma's findings. "At one point she called the victim a Beau Nash impersonator. That's another angle. Why would anyone want to dress up as Nash?"

"People enjoy dressing up."

"Yes, but what for?"

"Fancy-dress parties."

A shake of the head. "This wasn't fancy dress. Paloma is sure it was an authentic eighteenth-century outfit with some modern alterations. Pearl buttons, the breeches let out a bit. An antique costume is worth serious money. I can tell you I wouldn't wear it to a party and run the risk of beer being spilled on it."

"Or the breeches splitting when you danced," Halliwell said.

There were times when Diamond thought his deputy would benefit from a course on respect in the workplace. "I might wear it for a more serious occasion, a ceremony, let's say."

"A wedding? They do weddings in costume, don't they?"

"Something bigger, a national celebration like the millennium, or the golden jubilee when the city needs to put on a show."

"And did it?"

"That's what I'm asking. Do you remember?"

"All I can recall about the millennium was the hoo-ha over the new spa bath not being finished on time. And even when it finally opened six years late I don't think Beau Nash was part of it. Jumping in for the first swim? No, I don't see it."

"What did we do for the Queen's jubilee?"

"I'm not the best person to ask, guv. I'm more interested in football."

"Think of another key year. When was Nash born?"

Halliwell shook his head.

"Paul Gilbert wrote it on his noticeboard. Go and check?"

"Right now?"

"We need to know."

With a shrug, Halliwell got up and headed for the meeting room. He was back in a short time to find Diamond had taken over his chair. "1674, in Glamorgan."

"Okay. Was anything special laid on three hundred years later in 1974—a street procession, a commemoration ball, an exhibition? I can't believe the year went by unnoticed."

"Are you thinking our skeleton was playing the Beau? They wouldn't want an old man as the main character, would they? They'd want some young fellow."

"They might feature both. All the pictures you see are of him as an old guy. I'm simply trying to make sense of this person going to all the trouble of kitting himself out in a real frock coat and breeches from the eighteenth century. Where would he have got them? Can you buy them?"

"You can buy anything on the internet."

"Come on. The bloody internet had barely started in 1974."

Halliwell was unimpressed. "Antique clothes have been bought and sold for much longer than the internet. If you had a load of money and really wanted to impress your friends, you might decide to pick something up at auction."

"Money comes into it for sure. But then this rich old guy ends up dead in a small terraced house in Twerton."

"Lured there by his killer."

"In costume? I can't begin to explain it, Keith. Maybe we'll get some answers as the day goes on. Check the *Chronicle* archive for those key years we're talking about. 1974, 2000 and 2002."

He liked 1974 now he'd thought of it. The tricentenary of the Beau's birth couldn't have passed unnoticed by the city.

The first of the team to report back was Ingeborg. "I went to see the wardrobe mistress at the Theatre Royal, guv, and you were right about *The Beaux' Stratagem*."

"Of course I was right. Did you doubt me?"

"The National Theatre brought it here on tour in 1989, with Brenda Blethyn playing Mrs. Sullen."

"Never mind Mrs. Sullen. Is there a character called Beau Nash?"

She gave him a suspicious look. "I thought you'd seen it. There was another production in 2015."

"Did I say I'd seen it?"

"You gave that impression. Obviously I got the wrong end of the stick. To answer your question, he's not in it. The play was written in 1707, before he got famous."

He'd already skated over any mild embarrassment. "Another production in 2015, you said?"

"The National again. This is the problem. They provide their own costumes."

"They count them out and they count them in again?"

She nodded. "They would have noticed if one went missing."

He wasn't troubled. The "problem" wasn't a problem any longer. The case had moved on in the short time since he'd asked Ingeborg to contact the theatre. Now that Paloma had decided the clothes on the skeleton were eighteenth-century originals, the theatre wardrobe had ceased to be of interest. He didn't like disappointing his most dedicated detective, but she had to be told.

She took it well.

After he'd explained, she said, "The wardrobe mistress was telling me there's a big demand in Bath for historical costumes."

"When you say 'historical,' you mean old-style, right?"

"Of course."

"Not originals?"

"They'd be too valuable to wear to Regency balls and things. Someone spills a glass of red wine and it's goodbye to a piece of history."

"And several thousand quid."

"You might get away with it at some more serious function where food and drink don't come into it. I expect it's more sober at the Beau Nash Society."

Alert to every possibility as always, Ingeborg spoke of the society as if they both knew all about it. In reality they hadn't discussed it. The only information Diamond had got had come from Paloma's friend Estella.

"Funny you should mention this. Are you thinking of joining?"

Ingeborg laughed nervously. "No way. Not my scene at all."

"You're well qualified with all your knowledge about Nash."

"You're joking, I hope. If you're talking about my potted biography the other day, that was a cyber rush, in my head and out of it."

"You don't retain that stuff?"

"No chance. I was summarising from various websites."

"I met one of the members. Her name is Estella and she's writing a book about Nash. She's your age or younger."

After a moment's thought her eyes widened in alarm. "I

don't know if I'm reading you right, guv, but they'd know I was a stoolie in the first two minutes."

He smiled. Putting her forward as a member wasn't part of his planning. "Pity. I'd like to see you in a wig and long frock."

"Can we be serious?"

"Fair enough. What else do you know about this society?"

"It's for plugged-in people like your friend," Ingeborg said. "They have rules. Everyone dresses the part, even for regular meetings when they have speakers or listen to music. They're mostly members of the glitterati, so they prefer to buy their outfits rather than hire and they don't like to wear the same thing too often, which makes good business for anyone who deals in period costumes."

"The glitterati? Here in Bath?"

"Fat cats. Call them what you like."

He couldn't see Estella as a fat cat, but the glitterati tag might apply.

"How long has this society been in existence?"

"Couldn't tell you, guv."

"Worth finding out, isn't it? Don't panic, I'll do it myself. However . . . someone must have made those alterations to the original costume and I expect they were local. They let the breeches out and sewed pearl buttons on the collar. It was done to a high standard, Paloma says."

"A long time ago."

"They could still be around. If we could trace them, they'd be a key witness."

"I'm with you. It's worth a try."

John Leaman was the next to enter the office, back from several hours of doorstepping in Twerton. One look told Diamond all he needed to know.

"Look on the bright side, man. You got out of the office for a change, didn't you?"

"Much good it did me," Leaman said as if the whole thing had been devised to frustrate him. "The terrace has been a slum for years. It's hopeless trying to get the names of people who lived there before the squatters moved in. Tenants came and went: students, illegals, street musicians, runaway spouses."

"Who was the landlord?"

"Some letting agency called Up Your Street had it last, known locally as Up Yours."

"Where did it operate from?"

"Oldfield Park. They charged fees upfront, over and above the rent. This is standard practice and it's out of control because of the demand for cheap housing. Anyone can set up as a letting agency and there's hardly any regulation."

"I know it's tough out there."

"Horrendous. With the housing shortage any number of scams have grown up. You find your tenancy agreement was only for six months and they demand another fee to renew. This lot got reported and did a runner overnight."

"For keeps?"

Leaman nodded. "I feel sorry for these people scraping a fee together and being ripped off. I've had bad experiences myself renting in Bath. Right now I've got a landlord I can rely on, I think, but you can never be certain."

"Tell me about it," Diamond said. "I rented in London in the eighties. Got suckered more than once. It's a minefield."

"These days it's a whole lot worse because of internet scams," Leaman said. "You'd think it would be easier making a search for a place online than flogging around from agency to agency, but there are crooks who pose as landlords and ask you to pay a fee in advance for a property that doesn't exist or is already rented. They catch a lot of overseas applicants that way."

"Any idea who the actual owner of the terrace was?"

"Lived abroad is all anyone seems to know. I'm not sure if there was one owner or a string of them."

"The council must have dealt with someone when they condemned the place. You can't knock down a whole terrace without consultation."

"I've been concentrating on the tenants."

"Get the name of the owner and we might get a handle on it. We might also do well to talk to some of the local housing charities. They may have dealt with some of the people who rented."

"When you say 'we' . . . ?"

"I mean you, John."

"Thought so. I'm going to need help. This is a pig of a job you've handed me."

"It ain't all glamour. I'll see if I can spare another plod."

"What do you mean, *another* plod? It's me working on this."

"Sorry. Another super-sleuth."

Leaman muttered something inaudible.

"Speaking of plods, was the fingertip search in progress out at Twerton?" Diamond asked.

"Waste of time. They don't know what they're looking for."

"Anything, tell them anything, but best of all would be the murder weapon," Diamond said. "What Dr. Waghorn insists on describing as a sharp implement. Could be some sort of dagger or a kitchen knife or a chisel, I suppose."

"Sword?"

"That was suggested at the autopsy, but not by Waghorn."

"By you?"

"One of the students. There's always one."

"Is it so far-fetched?"

"In a poky loft in Twerton? You couldn't draw a sword, let alone use it."

"Doesn't Waghorn have an opinion about what was used?"

Diamond shook his head slowly. "He's leaving it to us to find out. And he's right."

"Well, nothing sharp has surfaced at the building site yet, not even a cocktail stick."

"I doubt if the good people of Twerton are into cocktails."

They were joined by Keith Halliwell looking as if he'd won the lottery. "Significant dates, guv."

"What about them?"

"Those years you and I were talking about—1974, 2000 and 2002. There's another one: 1909."

"Too far back for us."

"Hold on. I've been checking the papers. 1909 was huge in Bath. Don't ask me why, but they put on a pageant, and not just a few people dressing up, but three thousand of them, with acting, music and dancing, all in costume. It went on for a week and was the biggest blast the city has ever seen."

"Where did you find this?"

"It was all over the papers at the time. There are books, postcards, lantern-slides. Visitors came from across the world. Every city called Bath wanted to be there. That's twelve in the US and two in Canada. The Lord Mayor of London in his coach. The king couldn't be there because his health was failing by then, but he sent his brother, the Duke of Connaught. Every building along the procession route was decorated."

"Was Beau Nash part of this shindig?"

"As a main character, yes. They covered the entire history of Bath from Prince Bladud and his pigs to the modern age of tourism, and Nash was the star performer in one big scene depicting a royal visit that really took place in the 1750s. A big procession, a gun salute, music, singing and dancing. Nash comes on and greets the princess."

"Are there pictures of this?"

"I can show you some online. Better still, I can tell you the name of the guy who played Nash."

"Really? A name at last."

"A local doctor, Leslie Herbert Walsh. I'm sure he's our man." Halliwell had taken out his phone. Up came a shot of a good-looking man in frock coat, brocade breeches, white silk stockings and black buckled shoes and holding a white tricorne.

"Are you sure?" Diamond said. "The wig's wrong. This is white. Beau Nash wore black."

Halliwell shifted the picture a fraction and some writing came into view: *Beau Nash, Episode VII.* "So they got the wig wrong. Doesn't matter, does it?"

"It matters to us. The skeleton was wearing a black wig. And I'm not sure the coat is right, either."

John Leaman was still in the room and now he joined in. "There's a bigger problem with this."

"What's that?" Halliwell asked, irritated.

"Like the boss said, he can't be our man because 1909 is too far back. Nobody in your pageant could have been wearing Y-fronts."

"Not *my* pageant."

"Y-fronts weren't invented."

Halliwell refused to be downed. "Ingeborg just did an internet search on Dr. Walsh."

"Ingeborg is supposed to be working on something else."

"She was at her desk so I told her what I found and she was excited and got the facts straight away. Leslie Walsh was born in Croydon in 1867 and came to Bath after he qualified as a doctor, a single man living first in Walcot, then Gay Street, and later Great Pulteney Street. At the time of the pageant he was 42, but—here's the bottom line—he didn't die until 1949, when he was 82 and Y-fronts definitely *were* around." He didn't actually push Leaman in the chest and say, "So there," but the message was clear.

Leaman said with barely disguised sarcasm, "And he didn't have a tooth in his head. Is that on the internet as well?"

Halliwell snapped back, "It's perfectly possible at his age."

Diamond was weighing the hard information. "Do we know where this doctor was living at the time of his death? Twerton is quite a comedown."

"He must have retired there."

"Pure supposition," Leaman said.

Halliwell wasn't quitting now. "Private doctors have always had rooms in Great Pulteney Street, but they don't live there after they stop working. They move out."

"To a two-up, two-down in Twerton? A doctor? Give me a break."

"He could have fallen on hard times. Too fond of the bottle. Or the horses."

Now Diamond shook his head. "We haven't mentioned the biggest problem of all, Keith. You said he died in 1949, right?"

"What's wrong with that? He was old, like our skeleton. He could have kept the costume all those years and dressed up in it for old time's sake. Maybe took the trouble to get himself a more authentic wig. I reckon the pageant had been the biggest moment in his life."

"It's not that."

"What is it, then?"

"How could anyone know he died in 1949 when his body wasn't found until now?"

11

Dr. Walsh ceased to be a serious candidate when further enquiries revealed he had died on a precise date in 1949 at an address in Okehampton, Devonshire, and probate had been granted to a firm of solicitors.

Halliwell looked like the goalkeeper who'd dived the wrong way and lost the penalty shoot-out in the World Cup.

"Don't take it to heart, Keith," Diamond told him. "You did well to find him. In my career I've wandered up more blind alleys than I care to remember. I don't know who writes my script but if I ever find out, he's mincemeat."

"I even told Paul Gilbert to put the name on his incident board."

"It can stay there for a bit. Keep the lad happy. Nobody looks at the bloody board anyway. I was thinking of pinning a pair of Y-fronts on it to get some attention."

Halliwell didn't want his mistake on public exhibition for a moment longer. "I'm going to speak to him now."

Diamond returned to his office. Truth to tell, he was as disappointed as his deputy. To progress in any investigation you need suspects and they were unlikely to emerge until the victim was named. He sat in his chair and pondered what it was that people liked about dressing up. Personally, he'd made strenuous efforts all his life to avoid wearing fancy dress. As a kid he'd once been persuaded by his parents to go to a friend's birthday party dressed as a chicken, but through some misunderstanding the party wasn't fancy dress. Every other kid had been in everyday clothes. The mockery still rankled. He was a plain clothes man, through and through. He'd been only too happy to get out of police uniform when the chance came to join CID.

Yet the Twerton victim had chosen to put on the Beau Nash outfit. Why?

If nothing else, Halliwell's theory about Dr. Leslie Walsh had provided a possible answer. The handsome medic was supposed to have got a taste for strutting about and being the centre of attention. If he'd kept the clothes and the wig for years, the theory went, he must have had a reason and his secret fix was recapturing his triumph of July, 1909. Too bad it was another blind alley.

What other reason could there be for dressing the part?

The theatre, obviously. Parts were written for people of all ages so it was not impossible that the victim had been cast in one of those Restoration comedies Paloma had talked about. If so, it seemed likely that the actor had been a professional. Amateurs tended to go for "safe" plays. When they did comedy it was usually farce.

Suppose a professional actor was deeply serious about getting into his role as a Restoration beau and made a thing of dressing in a genuine eighteenth-century frock coat and breeches. Far-fetched? Method actors went to extraordinary lengths to immerse themselves in the parts they were playing. If one really wanted to inhabit the role he might go to the trouble of kitting himself in clothes from the 1760s.

The house in Twerton wasn't known locally as a theatrical boarding house, but so what? An elderly method actor playing a minor role, and still doggedly trying to "become" the character couldn't be ruled out.

The only other reason Diamond could think of for

dressing up was the need to conform. If you attended some event where everyone wore the gear, you'd do it, however stupid you looked.

A re-enactment?

Or the Beau Nash Society?

He arranged to meet Estella again, this time at the Podium, the oddly named place that isn't a platform in a concert hall but two floors of shops he'd never used and, upstairs, the Central Library. Estella had said on the phone she was doing research there.

They met at the top of the escalator inside the glazed atrium. She was in purple and red today, still making a fashion statement. Platform heels, trailing scarf, plenty of bling. She must have stood out in the library reference section.

"Will it take long?" she asked at once. "I bagged a place at a table in there and I don't want to lose it."

"Everyone needs a break at some point," he said without answering the question. "Let me get you a coffee."

They settled for one of the covered tables in the street outside, set back far enough from the noise of traffic. "I'm hoping you've got something even more sensational to tell me," she said when they both had cappuccinos in front of them.

"About what?"

"The Beau, of course."

"I don't know about sensational," he said. "Where did we leave him?"

"In the roof of an eighteenth-century house in Twerton. The revelation that's going to turn my book into a bestseller."

Gulp.

He felt an uprush of guilt. He'd been so preoccupied with this maddening mystery that he'd failed until this minute to inform Estella about the latest findings. He lowered his eyes and found himself staring at the image overlaid on his coffee. The outline of a heart had turned into the letter Y.

She would be devastated.

"I'm afraid there's a problem."

She started to laugh, but the amusement soon went out of it. Her eyes narrowed and her fingertips drummed the edge of the table. "Tell me."

"We believe the skeleton can't be Richard Nash after all." Without interruption he explained about the autopsy and the Y-fronts and the bone that had fluoresced blue. Deciding it was more merciful to release the full force of this bombshell as one impact, he added Leaman's discovery in the *London Intelligencer* that Beau Nash had been buried in the Abbey.

Her first reaction was denial. "It can't be true. Can't be. We all know what newspapers are like."

"It's in several. Even if they all got it wrong, the Y-fronts and the forensic tests tell us the Twerton victim is someone modern."

The traffic noise provided its own grating soundtrack whilst Estella struggled to come to terms with the loss of the sensational story that would have transformed her book and her career. Finally she said in a voice devoid of vitality, "I feel such a fool."

Anything he said would sound like empty words.

"I should have checked for myself," she added. "So much is online now that it's a blessing and a curse. No disrespect, but when some policeman finds out more than someone like me who has invested years of study, it's humiliating."

"My team catch me out on a regular basis."

"I've been doing my research chronologically, leaving the death until last. I'm still plodding through primary sources about his earlier life."

"You would have got to the funeral eventually."

"Yes, and the discovery would have been even more heartbreaking. I can't in all honesty say I feel grateful for this, but I should be."

"It staggered me, too."

"You still don't know who the skeleton is?"

"From a police point of view it's vital that we find out. The autopsy suggested he died from a stabbing."

"In the Beau Nash clothes?"

"They were bloodstained."

"How ghastly."

He took her concern for the victim as encouragement to move on to the real reason for contacting her. "So we're trying to find an explanation for the clothes, working through several lines of inquiry."

She didn't seem to have listened.

He tried a more direct approach. "I'm told the Beau Nash Society dress up in period costume and you're a member."

"A very junior member," she said from a million miles away.

"Do you mind talking about it?"

"I made my promises sometime last year."

"Promises?"

"First you attend as a novice to see if you like it and if the members approve of you. If all goes well, you're invited to an initiation ceremony when you promise to abide by the rules."

"Like a nun taking her vows?"

"No," she said with a click of her tongue. She was getting her confidence back with this change of topic. "Not a bit like that. There's nothing quasi-religious about the society. We have a mutual interest in the Beau, that's all. He drew up a list of rules for the proper conduct of people using the Assembly Rooms, and the society did the same. Simple as that."

"Dressing up for meetings and suchlike?"

"That's in the rules, yes."

"But you don't dance and gamble like the Beau?"

"Sometimes at the annual ball we do. Mostly we invite speakers to address us on aspects of eighteenth-century life in Bath and Tunbridge Wells, where the Beau was MC. And we do all we can to safeguard his reputation."

His eyebrows shot up. "Is that at risk?"

She raised a faint smile. "Between ourselves, it wasn't all that good in his lifetime. We stand firm against anyone who takes liberties. His name is a brand in Bath. There used to be a Beau Nash cinema in Westgate Street and a Beau Nash pub at the top of Milsom Street. They both have new identities now."

"Did your society have something to do with that?"

"They like to think they did. The Beau would have hated his name being used to sell things."

"Difficult to control."

"Of course."

"In the eighties there was a Beau Nash nightclub behind the Abbey in Kingston Parade." He realised as he spoke that she wasn't even born in the eighties. "Long before I arrived here. But I was treated once to a Beau Nash brunch in the Pump Room."

"In the *Pump Room*?"

"He wouldn't have known what a brunch is."

"How ridiculous. Are you kidding?"

"No. It struck me as funny at the time."

"I think you'll find it's no longer advertised," she said. "Those Pump Room people should be ashamed of themselves. Anyway, the Pump Room didn't exist in his day."

"The Beau Nash bedroom in the Royal Crescent Hotel?"

"The society knows about that. I don't think anyone is so misguided as to believe he ever slept there. Like the Pump Room, the Royal Crescent wasn't built until after his death."

"A bedroom isn't so stupid-sounding as a brunch. Would he have objected? I thought he was in his element in bedrooms."

She didn't comment.

"Is that your main activity?" Immediately he turned the colour of a ripe Worcester apple. "Stop. I'd better rephrase that. Is that the society's main object, suppressing the use of his name?"

"Not at all. It's not even in the rules. Simply something we keep an eye on."

"Your members must have some clout."

"Some of them do. It's regarded as an honour to be invited to join."

"Councillors, local gentry, peers of the realm?"

"All of those."

"How many altogether?"

"I'm not sure. They aren't all active."

"This is what interests me. One of them may be not active. Inactive, in fact."

"The skeleton?" she said, eyes enormous. "One of our members?"

"I have to ask."

"You're seriously suggesting the skeleton could have been one of us?"

"It's a man in a frock coat and breeches with a Beau Nash hat and wig. We have to explore every possibility. Do the men all dress like that for the meetings?"

Estella shook her head. "The president. Only the president wears the white tricorne and black wig. We call him the Beau. It's like a badge of office."

"Passed down from one president to the next?"

"I couldn't tell you that. I've never asked. The rest of us all supply our own costumes, so I would imagine they do the same."

"Must be expensive."

"It is. I had to get a gown made specially. Fortunately my parents helped out with the cost. Some of the ladies wear something different each time. I can't possibly keep up with that, so I change the accessories—the hat and wig and necklaces. It's a challenge. As the only black woman I stand out."

"Do the men change their costumes?"

"Those who can afford to."

"How long has the society been in existence?"

"I don't know. Like I said, I'm one of the newest members."

"Who's the current president?"

"Sir Edward Paris, who built half of modern Bath as far as I can make out."

"I met him only this week." Tempted to add "pompous ass," Diamond chose for once to be tactful.

"Funnily enough," Estella said, "he looks rather like the real Beau when he was about the same age."

"Is that a factor in choosing the president?"

"No. He can be anyone approved by the members."

"Anyone who owns half of Bath?"

"I guess that helps."

"How is he chosen? By election?"

"I'm not sure. Ed was already in office when I joined."

He noted the "Ed" and was pleased he'd been discreet. "It's a bit sexist, isn't it, just having men for president? Aren't the lady members eligible?"

She smiled. "I don't think the society is ready for a cross-dressing Beau. But let's give them credit. They're not racists. They welcomed me to their ranks."

"I'm sure you know more about the real Beau than the rest of them put together."

"I thought I did. I'm so glad I didn't speak to anyone about this nonsense." She finished her coffee. "I'd better get back."

"I'm truly sorry for the disappointment," he said.

"I needed to know. If the skeleton had gone into the book, illustrations and all, that would have screwed up my reputation as a scholar. And I have learned something every other biographer has missed—the reports of his burial inside the Abbey. No one has nailed that before."

For some minutes after Estella had left, Diamond remained at the table reflecting on what he'd heard. Then the call signal on his mobile jerked him back to the here and now.

He fumbled with the thing and almost dropped it. "Yes?"

"Am I speaking to Mr. Diamond of the Bath police?"

"You are."

"Janice Bale."

He was usually good with voices and hopeless with names. He couldn't place this lady.

"Marks in Time."

He still didn't get it, but he said, "Right," in the expectation that she would fill him in and she did.

"The Marks and Spencer company archive at Leeds. Your undergarment."

"The Y-fronts? Do you have a date for me?"

"We studied all the pictures you sent and we can confirm that this particular design in pure white cotton with the elasticised leg opening has been widely retailed for a very long time, since at least 1952."

"As early as that?"

"It was always popular. However, the selvedge is more modern, no earlier than 1970."

"That helps."

"And the St. Michael label in that particular design wasn't introduced until 1989."

"Excellent. Was this line of pants replaced at some point?"

"No, but the label changed in 1995."

"Brilliant. We're looking at a six-year interval, then."

"You are and you aren't. That's when they were on sale. This particular variety was hard-wearing and would survive many washes. Our product research tells us that some gentlemen keep the same underwear until the elastic goes and they're forced to buy more."

"Deplorable," he said, trying not to think about his own.

"Our briefs are bought in sets of three usually."

"I know."

"So the same pair won't be worn daily. You can multiply the average life of one garment by three. Or by six if he bought two sets. If it doesn't get washed every day a garment has a longer life, obviously."

"I'm with you."

"And the method of washing and drying makes a difference. Tumble dryers have improved, but the earlier machines could overheat and damage the fabric. I don't suppose you know if your man dried his on a washing line?"

"I don't know who my man is, let alone how he did his laundry."

"The label says he wore the large size, if that's any help."

Diamond wore XL, which he'd always considered normal. "It's not large really, is it? What are we talking about here—36 to 39 inches?"

"Not necessarily. Our block sizes have got tweaked over the years to fit the average physique. The tendency is for waist sizes to increase. In 1989, large could have been more like a 35 to 38."

"Not large in the sense of a sumo wrestler, then? Getting back to that timespan when they were on sale in your branches . . ."

"1989 to 1995."

"You were saying that should be elastic, also?"

"I don't follow you."

"I'm talking about the timespan, ma'am. The average life of a pair of pants. You were saying it needs to be stretched."

"For the reasons I mentioned, yes. I suggest you spread the six-year interval to at least fifteen."

12

"This will impress you," John Leaman said when Diamond returned to the police office.

"Try me."

"The Twerton squatters. The last people to live in the terrace, right?"

"Go on."

"I had a call from the owner of the nearest corner shop and he told me one came in today and said they'd gone upmarket. They're currently in the best squat ever, in the Royal Crescent."

"Never."

"It's true. Some Chinese millionaire bought a house last year as an investment and had the interior upgraded and redecorated with a view to making it a centre for oriental medicine. On the day after the decorators moved out last week, the Twerton mob arrived in a van with their sleeping bags. Nobody knows how many. They've been moving more stuff in ever since and all the neighbours are going spare."

"How did they get in?"

"Nothing forced. It seems they had a key or knew the combination. Probably paid a wedge to the decorators."

"They won't be easy to shift. Were we officially informed?"

"Uniform were told at once by the people next door, but you know how it is."

"Nobody wants a repeat of Stokes Croft."

In 2011, Avon and Somerset police had attempted to evict squatters from a shop undergoing refurbishment in the Stokes Croft district of Bristol and the protest soon became a riot lasting most of the night and involving three hundred protestors. Several officers and members of the public were injured and the police were criticised for being too heavy-handed.

"So it's softly softly, is it?"

"It's a case of 'police aware.'"

"Aware, but staying away."

"Rightly so," Leaman said. "The 2012 act doesn't apply because the planned use of the house is non-residential. It becomes a civil matter. The owner will need a court order."

"Are you sure these squatters are the Twerton people?" Diamond asked.

"Positive. It's no secret."

"The guy the shopkeeper spoke to—do we know his name?"

"He's known as Tank."

"We must talk to him. He'll be suspicious of our motives, but by the sound of it he's proud of what they've done. We'll let him know we're not plotting to evict him."

"Won't wash, guv. In their eyes we're all fuzz."

Diamond nodded. "Or worse. You're right, John."

"And I can't see uniform agreeing to us making contact."

"They don't have to know."

Leaman could still be shocked by his boss.

"Which house is it?" Diamond asked.

He'd already decided to drive up to the Royal Crescent and see for himself. The chance of making contact with the people who had actually lived in the Twerton property was too good to pass up.

Whichever way he approached the Grade I listed building in its elevated, open position, the grandeur of the concept never failed to move him. In the afternoon sunshine against a cloudless sky the sweep of the palatial terrace—actually more of a half-ellipse than a true crescent—stood for all that was best about the city he seldom praised but secretly loved.

He'd asked Ingeborg to come with him.

They stopped the car outside number one and walked the cobbled road to check the occupied house. The frontage behind the railings was less than twenty feet, so they could get close to the doors and windows without appearing too obvious. But there was no need for subterfuge because in front of the occupied house a notice in large, bold lettering was displayed on a board screwed to a post anchored in a planter:

We the present occupiers hereby assert our rights under Section 6 of the Criminal Law Act, 1977 and will prosecute anyone who threatens violence for the purpose of gaining entry to this house. There is someone in occupation at all times who opposes unauthorised entry.

We caused no damage and did not break anything when first entering and we have video evidence to support this. We will continue to respect the property until such time as the owner serves us with a legal notice to quit in the form of a written statement authorised by the county court or the High Court.

"They're not new to this," Ingeborg said.

"And they're not inarticulate," Diamond said. "Let's see if we can speak to anyone."

He rang the bell.

A dog barked from somewhere inside.

After a few seconds there was a squeak from the flap on the letterbox and it was pushed open a fraction. A woman's voice said, "Yes?"

"Just enquiring if Tank is at home," Diamond said, bending low.

"What do you want with Tank?"

"Tell him it could be payday."

"Does he know you, then?"

"He wouldn't remember us. My name is Peter and Inge-borg is with me. Can we come in?"

"You're joking. First rule of the house. Residents only. Are you media people?"

"Don't insult me. Would Tank care to come out to collect his handout, then? We're not trying to con our way inside."

"How come you know him?"

"He was in Twerton. Look I'd love to talk about old times, but not bent double and through a letterbox. My back is starting to ache. Tell him we'll meet him for a bite to eat." He turned and asked Ingeborg, "Somewhere nearby?"

She was quick with a suggestion. "The Green Bird."

He knew exactly where she meant. "The Green Bird, round the corner in Margaret's Buildings." To make the invitation more persuasive he added, "Famous for its food. Join us, if you like. What's your name?"

"They call me Headmistress."

"Should I remember you? Were you in the Twerton place that got levelled?"

"For a short while."

"Come too, then, Headmistress. Say in about twenty minutes. You'll find us at one of the tables outside. I'm the big guy in the dark suit. Inge is the blonde in a beige jacket and black trousers."

"You'd better not serve us with a writ, mister."

"We're not bailiffs, my love. What you'll get served is a plate of delicious cooked food. I bet you don't get much of that where you are."

When they'd left the crescent and were in Brock Street, he said, "The Green Bird is good. The table outside gives them a chance to look at us without feeling trapped. And if the other customers object to crusties, we'll be in the fresh air."

"Why should anyone object?"

"This isn't Twerton. Unwashed people in striped woolly hats and dreadlocks may not be all that welcome."

"You have a mental picture already, do you?"

"Don't you?"

"In the place they're living they'll have better showers and bathrooms than you and I do."

"But do they use them?"

"We'll find out," she said coolly.

"Did I say something wrong?"

Ingeborg said, "If you really want to know, guv, you did."

"What was that?"

"The only thing we know about these people is that they're squatters. It doesn't mean they stink. They're probably forced into desperate measures."

"Okay. Point taken."

"And there's another thing. I don't wear beige. Beige is a turn-off."

"What colour's your jacket, then?"

"Tan."

"They'll know what I mean."

"That's beside the point. You tell anyone the woman with you is wearing beige and they'll think boring."

Chastened, he did his ham-fisted best to make up for being so crass. "Whatever you are—and you can be a pain—you're never boring, Inge. In future I'll say tan."

The Green Bird café was only a short walk from the Royal Crescent, in a paved pedestrian-only street. The boards outside spoke of breakfast, lunch, cakes, tea and coffee. "Let's get something on the table before they come," he said after a look in the window. "Fancy some cake?"

"Is this on expenses?"

"It's work, isn't it?"

"I'll have the polenta cake and a coffee, then. Should we have a Plan B?"

"Why?"

"In case they don't like the look of us. It works both ways."

She was right. He'd made crude assumptions about Tank and the Headmistress. The job sometimes drained him of humanity. More than most, he ought to have sympathy for the homeless, particularly the young unemployed. His own grandfather, once a prisoner-of-war forced to work on the Burma railway, had returned to civilian life in 1946, a pathetic shadow of the strong man he'd been. The bomb-damaged home his wife and children were in was due for demolition and they were forced to join the nationwide squatters' movement. Tens of thousands of ex-servicemen and their families made desperate by the shortage of housing occupied army camps and any empty properties they could find. That generation of the Diamond family had moved into a block of so-called luxury flats in Kensington sharing rooms with others. Someone made the mistake of forcing the locks and all the occupiers were brought to court, but the judge took a lenient view and bound them over "to keep the peace"—an irony that didn't escape the ex-servicemen who had spent six years fighting to restore the peace. Eventually the family were given a prefab. The fact that it was constructed of asbestos-cement sheeting was another story. They had survived.

So Ingeborg was justified in reminding him that squatters were people driven to desperate measures. This lot had been turfed out of Twerton. It was immaterial that they'd ended up in the finest address in Bath. You went where you heard of a place that was empty and where there was a way in without forcing the locks.

Two coffees and two slices of cake later, Ingeborg asked him, "Could that be them, do you think?"

A couple with a black greyhound were staring into the window of an art gallery across the street. Both looked about forty and were dressed casually, but not scruffily. No dreadlocks and no striped woolly hat. The woman was about six inches taller than the man.

"I doubt it," Diamond said.

"They're not looking at the artwork. They're studying our reflection."

"Can't see why anyone would call him Tank."

"For a joke. Like some big men get called Shorty. She doesn't look to me like a headmistress. Anyway, they're deciding whether to come over."

The right decision was made.

"Try not to show surprise at anything I say," Diamond said without moving his lips.

The couple arrived at the table and it was definitely the voice of Headmistress that said, "You must be Peter and Ingeborg."

Diamond was on his feet, hand outstretched, but Tank didn't offer his. He didn't look friendly either. "You told her you knew me. I've never seen either of you before."

"Didn't I make it clear?" Diamond said. "I know *of* you. You lived in the place at Twerton that got demolished and now you're at a much better address. Why don't you join us and have something to eat? It's a good menu."

"What do you want?" Tank said. "We don't have any spare rooms."

He thought they were homeless.

Diamond managed to keep a straight face by not looking at Ingeborg. In her fashionable tan jacket this would test her social conscience. "We're not asking for rooms. It's not about the Royal Crescent. We're interested in the Twerton gaff and what happened there. I'll pay good money." Diamond felt in his back pocket and placed a twenty-pound note on the table.

Tank eyed the money as indifferently as if he was playing poker.

"Buy the dog some food," Diamond said.

With nice timing, the greyhound sniffed at his leg and he offered the back of his hand to a warm, wet tongue. Deciding they were friendly, the dog rested its long jaw on Diamond's thigh and eyed him beguilingly.

People and their pets. The squatters exchanged a look and sat down.

"They do an all-day breakfast," Diamond said.

Headmistress said, "He'll have one. A sandwich will do me. Coffee for both. I'll go in and see what they have. Would you keep an eye on the dog? I don't trust Tank." She handed Diamond the greyhound's lead.

"Order a breakfast for me, too," Diamond called after her. "We're paying."

She asked Ingeborg, "How about you?"

Ingeborg said she was okay with the cake she'd already got.

"What do you want from us?" Tank asked for the second time. He looked even smaller when seated, olive-skinned, probably of mixed race, with a smooth, neat-featured face that gave nothing away.

Diamond shrugged. "I told you already."

"What is it about Twerton?"

"You must have heard about the skeleton."

"Nothing to do with us."

"You never looked in the loft all the time you were there?"

"There was no way in. If there ever had been, someone must have sealed it and done a good job of rendering. You're police, aren't you?"

Diamond didn't deny it. "Dealing with a bigger matter than your squat. I was hoping you might help us identify the guy."

Tank stared back at Diamond with calculation. "He was dressed in old-fashioned clothes, wasn't he?"

"Not entirely. The underwear was modern."

"Has that been in the papers?"

A nod.

"We don't read them. You're not seriously suggesting we knew him?"

"I'll take you at your word, you didn't. How long were you occupying the house?"

"Two years and a bit."

"How many of you?"

"People came and went, maybe fifteen or twenty in all that time. They found somewhere they liked better and moved on."

"Were you there from the beginning?"

"I was, yes. The whole terrace was declared unfit for human habitation. There's always a delay before the bulldozers move in. We were in the same day the previous tenant moved out."

"Did you know who it was?"

"I didn't meet him, if that's what you're asking. He was Polish or something. Letters arrived with names we couldn't speak."

"No family?"

"No kids. There was a woman and an old guy who slept downstairs. He could have been the father of one of them."

"Do you know how long they lived there?"

"Couldn't tell you."

Headmistress returned from placing the order. She'd brought a tray with coffees and a dog bowl filled with water. "We should come here more often."

Tank said to her, "Before you say anything else, these people are dicks."

"What the fuck . . . ?"

"Avon and Somerset's finest," Diamond said, untroubled, "but as I keep saying we're looking for information about the Twerton gaff. The Royal Crescent will be someone else's problem." He asked Ingeborg if she had a paper tissue. His trouser leg was damp where the dog had rested its muzzle.

He mopped up and turned back to Tank. "The old guy you mentioned. Did you actually see him?"

The ghost of a smile crossed Tank's lips. "Are you thinking they left him behind in the loft?"

"It's worth asking."

"He died. There was a funeral. They carried him out in a box."

"You kept an eye on them, then?"

"On the house, while we waited for them to move out. Getting a squat is all in the timing."

"Was anything left behind?"

"What do you mean—curtains, carpets and fittings? We didn't sign a contract."

"Any idea what the man did for a living?"

"He was in the building trade. Had a rusty white van parked outside."

"Did the woman go out to work?"

"Yes. Don't know where, though."

Headmistress said, "School meals service. I used to see her in the kitchen at Oldfield Park when we collected the lunches for our kids."

"So you really are a headmistress?"

She laughed. "Supply teacher. That's just a name the others call me."

"You said you 'used to' see her."

"She left before he did. Probably made the money she wanted and went back to Warsaw or wherever. A lot of the East Europeans come here just for the wages. It's big bucks compared to what they can earn back home."

"And you said the man was a builder." Diamond was thinking about the expert job that had been done to seal off the loft. "Did he leave the country as well?"

"Must have," Tank said tight-lipped.

"I don't think so," Headmistress said. "I see his van around still. I saw it in Manvers Street yesterday turning into the old police station. I reckon he's found work there. The university took over the building and they're having all sorts of work done on it."

Manvers Street.

Diamond glanced at Ingeborg, who had raised an eyebrow.

Their former workplace, much derided in its day but regarded now as a lost home-sweet-home. What a cruel twist of fate if a murder suspect was employed there knocking the guts out of the old place.

"How do you know the van?" Diamond asked Headmistress.

She was getting looks like guided missiles from Tank, but she wouldn't be silenced. "By the rust marks. He's bumped it a few times. There's no writing on the side, if that's what you're asking. With a name as long as his, you'd need a van twice the size to get it all on."

"You wouldn't remember the name?"

"You're joking. It began with a W and ended with a Z with about fifty letters in between."

"She's making this up," Tank said.

"Slight exaggeration," Headmistress said. "It was more like fifteen. And his first name was easy to remember. Jerzy."

Tank turned towards her accusingly. "How do you know that?"

"It was on the letters that came for him. Jerzy, kind of warm and cuddly, I thought." She gave him a mocking smile.

Diamond said, "I'm thinking you knew these people better than you've made out. Was there an arrangement when you took it over as a squat? Did you get a copy made of the front-door key?"

She was about to respond when Tank gave her such a nudge that she slopped coffee over the twenty-pound note still on the table. She picked it up, shook it and handed it to Tank.

"Shouldn't have asked," Diamond said. "I'm not the least

bit interested in how you got in, believe me. Whatever you did is history now."

Ingeborg said, "I think the food is arriving."

"And when we've eaten," Diamond said, "we'll walk the dog. I'd like you to come with me to Manvers Street and see if Jerzy is there."

13

It was a well-fed but far from friendly party that progressed down the sloping streets towards the former police station. Diamond, at Tank's side, was remarking on changes to the city scenery he'd noticed over the years he'd served there, but the squatter didn't join in. To him new buildings were opportunities. A short way behind, Ingeborg and Headmistress were in debate about the rubbish problem in the streets. Only the dog was at ease, loping ahead with the light-footed agility of the breed.

Billboards had been erected around the decommissioned police station.

"It wasn't a bad old place," Diamond said with an upsurge of nostalgia. "Do you know how much Bath University paid for this prime site? A mere seven million. I hope they're not demolishing it entirely."

"Why?" Headmistress asked.

"It was twenty years of my life."

"Move on," she said.

"We have. We moved on to Emersons Green and I flog thirteen miles along boring roads each time I drive there."

Ingeborg cut short the rant by asking the others, "Where did you see Jerzy's van go in?"

"The site entrance up ahead."

"Let's check."

No one was on the gate but there was a sign about

unauthorised persons and hard hats that the quartet ignored. Headmistress did take the precaution of using the braking mechanism on the dog lead to put the greyhound on a shorter leash.

Two large skips loaded with rubble stood as objects of reproach in front of the old police station.

"Even the asphalt has gone from the forecourt," Diamond said in a hurt voice.

"Contractors' parking up ahead," Ingeborg said. "Is that where the van might be?"

A row of vehicles included two silver vans, but no white ones with rust marks and dents. A man was sitting inside the cab of a small truck, so Diamond asked him if a Polish guy called Jerzy was on site.

"What's his trade?"

"Some kind of builder. Drives an old white van."

"Never heard of no Jerzys here."

Ingeborg said, "You might know him as Yurek."

"Yurek? Why didn't you say? A sparky called Yurek is round the south side working on the lift. He was when I last looked, anyway."

They were already moving on when the man called after them, "Are you lot supposed to be on site?"

They ignored him.

"Where did that come from?" Diamond asked Ingeborg.

"Yurek? It's a nickname for people called Jerzy."

"How do you know?"

"Friend of a friend."

"I thought you said Yorick."

"Oh yes?"

"The skull in the gravedigger scene."

She smiled. "What is it with you and skulls, guv?"

Headmistress added, "You should get out more."

The staircase Diamond had used daily for twenty years had gone and was replaced by an external lift shaft. He gave it the sort of look a polar bear gives a snowmobile. "They wouldn't want the students getting tired climbing all those stairs."

One side of the shaft was open. Two men in hard hats and overalls were at work on the looped cables below the lift car.

"We're looking for Yurek," Diamond called out.

One of them turned his head. "What for?"

"Are you Yurek?"

"I'm busy right now, mate." A trace of East Europe came through.

"We're police."

"All of you?"

"Two of us. Step outside and I'll tell you what it's about. You're not in trouble."

"I will be if we don't finish job tonight." He said something to the other man and emerged from the space. "Make it quick, mate."

Diamond showed his ID.

Yurek, or Jerzy, was a slight man in his fifties with flecks of grey in his eyebrows. The eyes were blue, deep-set and intelligent. He looked at Tank and said, "Twerton, three years ago, right?"

Tank nodded.

Diamond and Ingeborg needed to speak privately to Jerzy. Tank and Headmistress took the dog to look at the other side of the building.

"I know what this is about," Jerzy said. "Saw it on news. Skeleton in loft. Same fucking house."

"We're trying to trace all the previous tenants," Diamond said. "You were there until it was condemned and the council took over."

"Whole sodding terrace condemned. Nothing wrong with it. Someone saw chance to turn profit. Walls would have stood for years. I was forced out."

"That's you and your family?"

"Just me."

"I thought there were others."

"You mean my woman and her old father? He died. And she pissed off back to Poznan."

"How long were you living in the house?"

"Ten, eleven years, easy. Low rent suit us fine. Wasn't luxury. Toilet in back yard."

"Do you know who owned the terrace?"

"Some company. I deal with agency in Oldfield Park. Up Your Street. Fucking useless, they were. Not there any more."

"While you were living in the house, did you do any work on it?"

He hesitated, becoming wary. "What you saying? Anything needed doing, agency supposed to fix."

"Yes, but you're a professional. You can fix things yourself."

"Like change light bulbs? I did that, sure. Anything else—their responsibility. Supposed to be."

"I was thinking of the roof. An old building like that. Tiles must have needed replacing."

Jerzy looked at him as if he knew where this was leading. "Never went up there. Well built. Workmen's houses, but well built."

"You wouldn't have needed to go in the loft?"

"No access."

"Wasn't there a water tank up there?"

"Water was from spring into catchment chamber outside. Storage tank in kitchen. No upstairs plumbing. We use old tin bath."

"So you lived there all that time without knowing what was in the loft?"

"My woman wouldn't stay one minute if she knew."

The answers Diamond was getting may have been brief,

but they sounded convincing. The real problem was that nothing new had emerged. "Who lived there before you did?"

"Some guy on his own. Never met him. House was empty six weeks before we started renting."

"Lived alone, did he? How long had he been there?"

"How would I know?"

"Was he old?" Diamond was thinking back to the few things he'd learned about the skeleton in the loft.

Showing his contempt, Jerzy vibrated his lips softly and looked away.

Diamond was starting to understand the difficulties John Leaman had faced when trying to compile a record of the tenancy. "Didn't anyone mention this man's name?"

"Did once. Didn't mean much to me."

"What was it?"

"I forget."

"Try and remember."

"Something English, like Harry."

"Harry who?"

"Or Bert."

Ingeborg smiled. You had to, or you'd weep. Jerzy was the witness to make you think about jacking in the job.

"So whatever his name was, he was probably English. Any clues what he did for a living?"

"What do you mean?"

"If Harry or Bert had a trade, like you, he might have left some of his bits and pieces around the house."

"Bits and pieces?"

"In your case, it might have been fuses, or cable-cutters or pliers."

Bad example. Jerzy stared at Diamond in reproach. "I don't leave nothing lying about. I have tool box. Each pair of pliers has slot in box. I take with me when I move to new place. My living, get it?"

Patience, Diamond told himself. This isn't good for the hypertension. "What I'm getting at is this. Whenever I move into a new place there are signs of the people who were there before me. Small things, maybe, down the back of the sofa or between the floorboards. A receipt, a button, a few coins if you're lucky. You come across some little item and it's a link with the previous tenants."

Jerzy frowned and shook his head. As well as having a poor memory he lacked curiosity, let alone observation skills.

"You said you heard the guy's name once, so you must have talked to somebody about him. The agency?"

"No."

"A neighbour, then, or someone who called at the house, like the postman or a meter reader."

"You think so?" It sounded like a challenge Diamond wasn't going to accept.

"And they didn't say any more about him, whoever he was?"

"They could have talked to my woman."

"Ah."

"Her English better than mine."

"And she's back in Poland now?"

A nod.

"She didn't learn anything else about those tenants?"

"Don't know. Wasn't interested."

"Are you still in touch with her?"

"No, mate. Don't I say already?"

"Say it again."

"Back in Poland."

Through gritted teeth, Diamond said, "Why? Why did she leave?"

"She dump me, don't she, after her dad die? I put up with smelly old man sleeping in my living room all those years. Soon as he is gone, so is she. Fucking fated, that house. Bad."

Ingeborg immediately picked up on the last remark. "What did the house have to do with it?"

"Dead man in loft."

"But you didn't know that."

"Do now. Makes sense, don't it, all the shit that went wrong? Rows we had. Old man and his bronchitis. Her leaving. It was house. Everyone touched by evil."

This had strayed into the realm of gothic horror and Ingeborg wasn't having it. "You can't say that. Just because you had some bad experiences—"

"Wasn't just me. What about guy who lived there before me?"

Diamond butted in again. "This is who we've been on about for the past ten minutes. What about him? Go on."

"His woman left him, just like mine did."

"You didn't tell us that."

"You don't ask."

"For Christ's sake," Diamond said.

Ingeborg, staying cool, said, "Tell us what you know, Jerzy."

"Well, we hear there is woman living with him and she can't stick it so she walk."

"You can't say who told you this?"

"My woman, I expect. And she's—"

"Back in Poland. You told us."

Jerzy grinned. He had a sense of humour.

"But you still can't tell us who they were, these people, or anything else about them?"

"I told you name."

"You told me two names, Harry or Bert."

"Harry is more like. I think Harry."

"Okay, we'll go with Harry. Did he keep the house nice?"

"It was okay."

"The little garden at the back? Did he grow anything?"

"Forget-me-nots."

There was a pause while Diamond and Ingeborg decided whether this annoying man was winding them up. It seemed he wasn't.

"Bloody things came up each spring. Like weeds, aren't they? I take spade, get rid of fuckers."

That figured, Diamond thought.

"Then I grow potatoes."

At this point Diamond decided he didn't want to hear about the potatoes and it was unlikely anything else would emerge. The unwanted forget-me-nots had summed up the interview. "We're leaving now," he told Ingeborg.

On the walk back to the car after they'd left Tank and Headmistress exercising the dog in Queen Square, Ingeborg said, "What did you make of all that, guv?"

"Not much," Diamond said. "There wasn't much."

"A wasted afternoon?"

"You never know. Some of it could be helpful."

"Like what?"

"Like the two women who lived in the house both walking out on their men. Didn't that strike you as strange?"

"Not in the least," she said. "A tin bath in the kitchen? I wouldn't have stuck it for love nor money."

He grinned. "A hundred years ago most of the population scrubbed up in front of the kitchen sink. Bath night was a luxury."

"This wasn't a hundred years ago. It was in living memory. It's primitive."

"One ended up in Posnan," Diamond said, still thinking about the two fugitive women. "I wonder what became of the other?"

"Living with Harry?"

"Or Bert."

"Are you thinking she's dead?"

Some thoughts need time to mature. The tenants before

Jerzy may well have been there during the crucial 1989 to 1995 slot and may have known the dead man. "Put it this way: I'd like to be reassured that she's still alive."

"He couldn't be sure about names so how would we find out?"

"By digging."

"Digging in the backyard?"

"I don't mean literally."

"Why not?" she said in all seriousness. "It wouldn't be the first time an unfortunate woman has gone missing and been killed and buried by her so-called lover."

He weighed the suggestion. Typical of Ingeborg to come up with the wronged-woman scenario. They'd only just heard of the existence of this lady and already she was cast as a murder victim. Yet Inge's intuitions were never wholly unfounded. The house was already a murder location.

Stay within the bounds of reason, he told himself. The corpse found at the address hadn't been buried. The fact that an unknown woman had lived there at one time and then left was a far cry from proving she was murdered and buried there. People walk out on their partners every day of the week. Stronger evidence would be needed to justify the man-hours expended on a dig. Headquarters wouldn't wear it.

And yet . . .

"It's a building site now," he said.

"A crime scene," Ingeborg said.

"Technically, yes, but it's been levelled. Loads of stuff has been taken away."

"The ground could still be holding evidence," she pointed out. "All we've done up to now is a fingertip search. If we leave it to the builders, they could be laying foundations any time, spreading concrete or driving in piles. We'd need to move fast."

"This is too speculative," he said.

"Okay, forget about the woman if you want to," Ingeborg said. "Think about your crime scene. Isn't that what you taught me to treat as hallowed ground? That small piece of garden is all we have left to explain a really bizarre case of murder."

"It was ruined before we knew we were dealing with murder. It's flattened now."

"Under the surface. Who knows what may be buried there? Is it still cordoned off?"

A chill of guilt went through him. He couldn't answer. He hadn't been back. He stood still, lost for words.

Ingeborg wasn't sparing him. "We don't have any idea who the killer of the man in the loft was except he used the place to hide the body. Chances are he lived there as a tenant. You can't live in a place without leaving evidence of yourself. Who knows what might turn up if we do a dig?"

"You seriously think there's a body there?"

"Aren't you listening, guv? I'm talking about stuff he may have discarded. An empty cigarette packet, a lottery ticket, a teaspoon, a glove, a hairclip, a foreign coin. It helps build a picture of who was living there. I don't need to tell you this."

She was right. His mindset was all wrong. He'd given so much mental energy to learning about Beau bloody Nash that basic procedures had been neglected.

"I'll clear it with Georgina."

"As soon as we get back?"

"Soon as."

But Georgina wasn't in Concorde House. She was visiting some people in Charlcombe, Diamond was told by her personal assistant.

"Is she expected back today?"

"She didn't say. She wasn't in uniform."

"Unusual."

"Yes, she was looking really smart in the sort of blue the Queen sometimes wears. Heels, too. And she'd had her hair done again."

"I'm sorry I missed that."

He asked to be informed if Georgina returned that day, but it sounded unlikely. In her absence he couldn't authorise the dig, so he asked Ingeborg to drive out to Twerton and make sure the builders weren't already corrupting the crime scene. "If it isn't already sealed off, get it done. With luck, we'll have a busload of bobbies out in the morning with spades and sieves."

He called Halliwell and Leaman to his office. "Thanks to the Marks and Spencer lady we have a time frame. The Y-fronts first went on sale in 1989 and were replaced by another line in 1995. Allowing that some guys keep their underwear going for several years, we agreed that the outside limit is 2005."

"Too big," Leaman said with his customary plain speaking.

"What do you mean—too big? The Y-fronts?"

"The time frame. Sixteen years in a place where lodgers came and went like tube trains. Can't we cut it down more?"

"How do you propose to do that?"

"A probability graph."

"A *what?*"

"The early nineties, when pants like that were on sale everywhere, must be more likely than 2000 or after."

"Okay," he said, dazed by the reasoning.

"As the time goes on, the probability declines. It's a distribution curve and it falls away after 2000."

"I get it now, John."

"But can we agree on it?" Leaman insisted. He could be so exacting.

"No argument." Diamond said to shut him up. "You were looking at dates, Keith."

"Was I?" From the frown on his face, Halliwell was trying to picture a distribution curve.

"Come on. Dates when the city may have put on some kind of event involving Beau Nash."

"Right. 1974, three hundred years after he was born."

"Too far back. The pants weren't in production then."

"The other likely dates were the millennium and the Queen's jubilee."

"Unlikely," Leaman said.

"What?"

"We just agreed 2000 and 2002 are both towards the end of our time frame, so you can't call them likely. To my recollection nobody dressed as Nash for either."

The blood pressure was rising. "All right," Diamond said. "Here's a better suggestion. The Beau Nash Society was meeting regularly right through those years and the president always dresses the part. He's known as the Beau."

"You think our victim was one of their presidents? Wouldn't they have noticed if he suddenly went missing?"

"In the suit," Halliwell added.

"It's a line of enquiry," Diamond said, undermined by the reactions of his colleagues. "Don't stamp on it before we even get it running. These people meet regularly and some of them are pretty high-powered. The current Beau is Sir Edward Paris, the property tycoon. You and I met him in the Archway café."

"*Him?*"

"Him."

"He looked in good health when we saw him."

"Be serious, Keith."

"Why would anyone as well-off as that end up dead in a loft in a Twerton terraced house?"

"If I knew the answer to that," Diamond said, "this case would be done and dusted. Let's investigate and find out. I've met one member, Estella Rockingham, a writer. She's been helpful but she only joined recently. She wouldn't know what was going on in the 1990s."

"Who would?"

"Our friend Sir Edward, for one."

"Where does he hang out?"

"The society meets at a place in the Circus, but unless either of you fancies dressing up in a frock coat and breeches, we won't get past the door."

"They can't bar us," Leaman said.

"I don't want to muscle our way in. It's no basis for an interview. I'd rather speak to him in his home."

"Where's that?"

"I'm told it's a large modern house out at Charlcombe." He stopped and slapped his hand to his forehead. "Did I just say Charlcombe?"

14

Georgina was admiring the infinity pool.

She'd never seen anything like the sheet of still water reflecting the setting sun and forming this private horizon, with the purple blur of the Cotswold Hills making a theatrical backdrop on the other side of the valley. She and her new friend, Lady Sally Paris, were on sun loungers on the patio. Each had her own small table with a tall glass of chilled white grape juice and elderflower and bowls of pistachios and salted almonds. Sally had offered Pimm's, but Georgina had been firm about staying free of alcohol. She didn't want a repeat of the Bannerdown experience, or worse. Driving along the narrow, serpentine lane looking for the house had been a test of her nerve when sober.

"Bliss," Georgina said.

"Do you think so?" Sally said. "I insisted we had the pool built without realising what an engineering challenge it was. We endured stroppy workmen for months and months before it was signed off."

Their previous meeting in the dark hadn't given Georgina much idea how Sally looked. She was as elegant as her voice, blonde hair expensively cut in a classic fringed bob, a neat, small face with beautifully formed lips. Age? Closer to fifty than forty. Clothes with top designer labels, no question.

"Do you swim in it?"

"Not at all. I don't enjoy swimming and Ed won't go near the water. He can't even do a doggie paddle and he's terrified of drowning, poor old darling. The only one who uses the damned pool is Spearman, our chauffeur. He's like a member of the family. Been with us years."

"It's a stunning feature to have with that view as well," Georgina said. "You don't have to swim in it to enjoy it."

"Exactly how Ed puts it. He's going to like you. We'll join him shortly. He won't come outside."

One uncertainty was removed. The last Georgina had seen of Ed on the back seat of the Range Rover had left some doubt whether he was still alive.

"Was the house your own design?"

"Ed's, you mean? Yes. We had our usual long-suffering architect who put up with me and my maddening changes of mind. He's already at work on our next property."

"Won't you be staying here?"

"Georgie, we're forever on the move. I don't think we've had more than five years in one place all our married life. Ed's a nomad."

A rich one, Georgina thought. "Are your houses always modern in style?"

"Without exception. We're currently on a steel and glass kick, as you see. He adores glass. I can put up with living in a goldfish bowl, especially as we're in the middle of nowhere, but some of my clients are uncomfortable with it."

"You're in business? I didn't realise."

"Wasn't it on the card I gave you? I wouldn't call it business. More like a service for ladies of a certain age. Holistic beauty treatments. Massage is a vital part of it so the glass walls aren't ideal. I had to have blinds installed. Are you feeling chilly?"

"No. I'm fine."

"You drew your arms across your chest."

"It's the thought of being massaged in front of an open window."

"Exactly the point I was making."

"And do you do facials?"

"Much else besides. Botox, dermal fillers, hair removal. Our lovely city has more than its share of rich ladies wishing they were prettier than they are. You know the old saying: time is a great healer and a lousy beautician."

"But how satisfying to be in a job that leaves people feeling better about themselves."

"Charming thought. What do *you* do for a living, Georgie?"

Georgina didn't hold back this time. She'd already decided to be truthful. She wasn't ashamed of her job. It was just the other evening after the G&Ts that she'd chosen to be secretive. "I'm a rather senior police officer."

"Ooh. How senior? Stripes on your sleeve?"

"No stripes."

"Crowns?"

"A silver wreath with crossed tipstaves."

"God help us. You must be the chief cop."

"Almost."

"Well, paint me green and call me a cucumber. I never thought I'd have anyone as high-powered as you sitting on my patio. Do you ride a horse?"

"That isn't necessary. I'm behind a desk most of the time seeing that things run smoothly."

"I bet they do with a woman in charge. I must tell Ed. He gets worried reading in the *Chronicle* about crimes in Bath. We'll both sleep easier now we've met you."

"I'd rather you told him later, after I've gone," Georgina said. "Most men seem intimidated when I tell them what I do."

In another fifteen minutes darkness was descending and the moon was up, reflected in stepped bars down the centre of the pool.

"It's so lovely."

"Sometimes I sit here in the evening and the bats put on an aerobatic display for me. I don't know whether they'll treat us tonight."

Georgina gazed upwards and tried not to see bats. They gave her the creeps, but she wouldn't be saying so to her titled friend.

"Oh *Himmel*," Sally said. "There they go again."

"The bats?"

"The fireworks. Didn't you hear? It's too much, every night this week. I'm told it's some sort of competition and Bath ought to be proud of staging it, but I can't agree. You heard that one, I'm sure."

"Yes, I did," Georgina said. "Ooooh."

An amazing eruption of light spread across the sky and lit up the pool. Plumes of gold and silver sparks soared and tipped in wonderful parabolas mirrored in the water.

"Exciting."

"Not for me," Sally said. "We'll see no bats tonight. Stay here and watch if you want. I'm going indoors."

Georgina felt she had no other option than to follow.

They got up and moved towards the floodlit house. To Georgina's eye, the ultra-modern building was a monstrosity, a three-storey structure with a twist, thrust into the hillside like a massive corkscrew and completely out of sympathy with the natural contours of the Charlcombe valley. Enormous sheets of reinforced glass formed the walls. Bright red exterior steel staircases to some of the rooms gave the ultimate lie to any concept of symmetry. It could have been a giant pylon after an earthquake.

At the top of the main staircase, Sally said, "I know what you're thinking about the house. Everyone thinks the same when they visit. Personally, I'd be willing to live in the lodge, which is altogether more humble and homely, but Spearman is installed there with his wife and son so I can't. No matter. Tell Ed this aberration gets your juices going and he'll be in ecstasy."

Georgina had no intention of telling Ed any such thing. Ed in ecstasy wasn't a prospect she wished to experience. But Sally was stimulating company, outspoken and so disarming. You would never have known she was Lady Sally.

"Believe me, Ed's going to be impressed by you. He's really turned on by powerful women. Be sure to keep out of the bedroom when he shows you round the house."

Georgina nearly choked on a nut she was chewing.

"Joke," Sally said. "He's a pussycat really, whatever may be going on inside his head. Now that I've given him this build-up, I mustn't keep you in suspense any longer. Shall we join him?"

Their steps echoed on white oak floorboards. They were in a large living room, larger than it appeared through the glass outside. The leather sofa looked so low that Georgina wondered if she'd ever be able to get up from it. Otherwise the room was sparsely furnished with matching armchairs, low tables and bowls of flowers that may have been silk but so well made you would scarcely have known.

"Take a seat and I'll see if the master of the house is respectable," Sally said. "He's been having a nap."

In as dignified a fashion as she could, Georgina lowered herself into the sofa and pulled the hem of her skirt over her knees. Left alone, she decided on a strategy for meeting Ed. Better not talk about architecture. She'd be at odds with him there. It would be hypocritical, not to say dangerous, to give the impression she liked the steel and glass. The Beau Nash Society ought to be a safer topic. She'd learned things about the real Beau Nash in recent days.

If she survived this test, her next meeting with Peter Diamond would be something to relish when she tossed in the titbit that she'd recently visited the current Beau. The look on that seen-it-all-and-bought-the-T-shirt face would be priceless.

The boards creaked again. More than one person for sure. Every move in this house was telegraphed.

"Don't get up, Georgie," Sally said. "No need to stand on ceremony. You two have met already."

The barrel-shaped man with her was in a white bathrobe and leather flip-flops and festooned with gold jewellery. He grinned and raised a limp hand in the way Roman emperors do in films. At a guess he was fifteen to twenty years older than Sally, but the face, being pudgy, was well preserved—probably improved by Sally's anti-wrinkle treatment. He was completely hairless except for a triangle of white fuzz on his chest showing above the bathrobe.

Without being asked, Sally helped lower her husband into one of the chairs. "So," he said to Georgina, "you're a cop."

"A top cop," Sally said.

"Funny we haven't met before at some civic bunfight," Ed said. "Don't you have to do the glad-handing like me?"

"Not much," Georgina said. "I'm overseeing operations mostly." She shifted the interest away from herself in a way she thought rather neat. "But as president of the Beau Nash Society you must know just about everyone of importance in the county."

"Who told you that?"

"Little me." Sally had spoken from across the room where she was gazing out at the fringes of the city, ribbons of light linking building developments very likely put there by her husband's company. "Someone needed to explain why you were wearing your Beau costume."

"When was this?"

"In the car the night before last, when we gave Georgie a lift."

Ed looked blank. "I can't remember fuck about the night before last."

"Honey," Sally said with a click of her tongue.

"It's a fact."

"I wish I could say you were tired and emotional but it wouldn't be true. You were paralytic."

"Take a word of advice from a man who knows," he said to Georgina. "Never drink anyone else's homemade wine. Do you know anything about Beau Nash, Georgie?"

"The basics," Georgina said. She was already resigned to being addressed as Georgie in this house, but she would make damn sure nobody at work ever took such a liberty. "I've lived here long enough to call myself a Bathonian and as he was our most famous son it's splendid that you keep his name alive."

"Famous son, my arse."

Sally shot him down. "Ed, that was uncalled for."

"But true. He was a Taffy, born in Swansea and raised on leeks and seaweed."

"Now you're being ridiculous."

"Laverbread is made from seaweed."

Good thing he didn't know Georgina's idea of happiness was visiting Wales. She would keep that to herself.

"There's worse I could say about the Taffies."

Sally said, "And we don't wish to hear it."

"I'm not wearing the costume now. I can say what I like in my own gaff. I'll tell you this for nothing, Georgie. After the best part of twenty years being the Beau, I've honoured the old poser long enough. I've learned the dances, worn the wig, played the card games, rolled the dice, eaten the food and listened to more bum-numbing lectures than Einstein ever did and now I deserve a break. I'm a builder ferchrisssake. What am I doing poncing about in a frock coat?"

"It's the honour," Sally said. "They respect you."

"They did at the beginning. The glamour fades."

Georgina wasn't sure how to proceed. She hadn't expected this tirade.

"How did you get involved?" she asked.

"When I was thinking about expanding into restoration work, doing up old buildings, I went to this slide lecture in the Guildhall. Got chatting to the geezer in the next seat and it turned out he was from the Beau Nash Society. He's dead now. Anyway, he asked me to be his guest at the annual dinner and ball and I thought it would be a bit of a laugh so I agreed. Forgot about it until a card with a gold edge arrived and I found out what I'd let myself in for, like hiring a costume and learning to dance before I even got to the dinner. This was before I met Sally. Blow me if I didn't enjoy myself. Took to the dancing lessons like a duck to water."

Sally said, "The fact that several gorgeous young women were learning with him had nothing to do with it."

"Minuets, cotillions, you name it. Looking at me, Georgie, you may not think so, but I'm light on my feet. Twinkle-toes. I can chassée with the best."

Certainly it took some believing.

"To cut the story short, they took to me in a big way at the ball and persuaded me to join. Inside three months I got my own tailor-made coat and breeches. That's another story, the fittings—"

"Oh for God's sake, get on with it," Sally said.

"I'm getting there. Next thing was the Beau dropped dead. Professor from the university. He hadn't been in the position long. Overwork, they said. A case of high Beau pressure, I say."

"Give us a break," Sally said.

"Nobody wanted the job and for a while it looked like the society might fold. So they asked me. I wasn't keen at the time. I'm not a Nash scholar. Then the bait was offered. Lunch with the lord lieutenant and stuff like that, useful contacts for my corporate empire, so I took it on. And if I say so myself, I've done them proud, unselfishly giving my time to the cause for no reward."

"Apart from all the extra contracts," Sally said.

"Such as?"

"Kelston, Norton St. Philip, Westbury."

"We put in our bids in the usual way."

"And always came out the winner. How strange."

"You extended well beyond Bath?" Georgina said, to put a stop to the bickering. It was making her nervous.

"No scope for development in this city," Ed said. "Wherever you turn there are preservation orders."

"Ed's company only takes on large-scale projects," Sally said. "Anything under five hundred houses doesn't interest them."

"Between ourselves, house building isn't the way to go any more," Ed said. "Too much government interference. I told them what they can do with their affordable housing. We take on big commercial builds."

"Police stations?" Georgina said on a sudden impulse.

"What?"

They both stared at her.

"We were forced to sell our building in Manvers Street."

"To the university. I know about that," Ed said.

"And since then we've been moved from pillar to post. We have to lease buildings. We're currently in Concorde House, out at Emersons Green, and the lease runs out in a few years. A new purpose-built police station would be wonderful."

"For you, maybe," Ed said.

"For the community."

"Stuff that."

"Ed does a lot for the community already," Sally said. She was clearly used to smoothing the way when her husband came out with such putdowns. "New supermarkets make a difference to people's lives. He builds schools. A church once."

The mention of supermarkets had triggered something

in Georgina's brain. "You wouldn't be speaking about the site at Twerton, by any chance?"

"Twerton?" Ed said. "No, that's one of my rivals. He's a cheapskate. Did you read in the paper about the skeleton? They were using a wrecking ball, would you believe? Everyone uses hydraulic excavators these days. If they'd brought one in for the demolition the damned skeleton would never have been found and I'd have been saved no end of grief."

"Grief? Why?"

"The Beau Nash suit and Y-fronts. Guess who's known for wearing both. Old flames I hadn't heard from for years got in touch to see if I was dead. My ex told her solicitor to put in a claim for a slice of my estate."

"The whole thing was weird," Sally said. "Are you any closer to knowing who the man was?"

"We have some ideas about his age and appearance, but it's still a mystery," Georgina said. "It may be one of those cases that never gets solved."

"He was murdered, wasn't he?" Ed said.

"Apparently, and I have our top detective working on it."

"He hasn't spoken to me."

"If you can throw any light, I'm sure he'd be only too pleased to meet you."

"When did the murder happen?"

"Anything up to twenty-five years ago going by the style of the victim's underwear."

"Too far back. I didn't join the society until 2000. I'm the millennium Beau. I can't tell you much about what happened before then."

"Professor Plum," Sally said.

"Is that a joke?" Georgina asked.

"Only between Ed and me," Sally said. "Silly private joke. He was the previous Beau, the one Ed took over from. Professor Orville Duff. You must have heard of plum duff."

"Do you know what happened to him?"

"Well, he isn't your skeleton, if that's what you're thinking," Ed said. "He was cremated. I went to the funeral along with most of the society. One of them spoke the eulogy and we all went back for a drink to his memory at the Garrick's Head, our favourite watering place. You know why?"

"I can't say I do."

"It was where the Beau lived. The real Beau. The original."

"I see. And who was the president before Professor Duff?"

"Offhand, I couldn't tell you. Before my time. I could find out. Some of our older members were around then."

"Ideally, my SIO should speak to them. I'm sure Detective Superintendent Diamond would find it helpful."

"Send him along. We have a meeting a week Wednesday in our rooms in the Circus. I'll introduce him to the old-timers."

"What a good idea. We'll certainly take you up on it." Then she had another thought, a rather subversive one. "But don't you insist on eighteenth-century costume?"

"For the meeting, yes. It's one of the rules."

Georgina tried to picture Diamond in lace and satin. "And if there's one thing Beau Nash demanded it was observance of the rules."

"Silly arse, yes. Listen, Georgie, there's no need for your fellow to dress up. He can catch us after we finish."

"But if he wants to see you in session?"

"That's another thing. He can come as my guest."

"But not in a lounge suit?"

"For that, he'll need to hire the kit."

15

A voice from behind said, "D'you mind, dude?"
Diamond swung around. He was about to step into
Georgina's office next morning to ask her to authorise the
dig at the Twerton site. No one in Bath Central had ever
called him "dude."

He was looking at a young man who was clearly not
police. Hair to his shoulders, white bucket hat covered
in badges. Black T-shirt with the word FIXER across it in
yellow, faded blue jeans and trainers.

"Talking to me?" Diamond said.

"I need two minutes, max." He winked. "Pig of a day
coming up."

You couldn't say he was charming or persuasive, but
something about the wink and the voice caused Diamond
to shrug and say, "Go ahead then."

Georgina's visitor went in. And if it wasn't two minutes,
it was still pretty quick.

The Fixer came out and raised a thumb. "No probs,
dude."

Diamond said, "Cool," and sounded cool and got the satisfaction of a double-take before he stepped inside the office
himself.

Georgina greeted him with a wide, unexpected smile.

"Peter, I'm glad you looked in."

"Are you, ma'am?" he said, puzzled.

"It's high time we made some progress on the Twerton murder. What is it, a week since we found the skeleton?"

"Six days actually."

"Six days too long." She still looked pleased.

"I wouldn't say that, considering we had no reason to suspect it was a murder."

"Until the postmortem, you mean?"

"In the two days since, we've achieved plenty. We're better informed than we were at the start."

"'Better informed' isn't exactly naming names."

"This isn't simple," he said. "The more we investigate, the more intricate it gets. That's why I'm here."

"It's defeated you?"

"No."

"You want my advice?"

"We're checking the previous tenants of the house—which is a tough nut to crack because the letting agency closed down and there's no documentation anywhere. We're having to rely on hearsay, but we can't afford to ignore it."

"And?"

"We traced the squatters who were in the place and they led us to the last paying tenant, who is an electrician, Polish. He was there ten or eleven years, most of the time with a partner, also Polish, and her elderly father. And in case you're suspecting what I did, the old man was given a proper funeral and cremated. He isn't the skeleton."

"Who is it, then?"

He frowned. The smile was lingering on Georgina's face. Clearly she knew something he didn't. "I can't tell yet, but the Polish guy remembered who was living in the same house before him. A couple."

"Did he say who they were?"

"He didn't meet them. His partner heard about them from the locals."

"When would this have been?"

"The time slot we're interested in. The late nineties."

"About the time the murder was done?"

He nodded.

"Excellent," Georgina said rubbing her hands. "We must find other sources, get descriptions, names."

"That's proving difficult. But the Pole did know something else. The woman walked out at some stage."

"They argued?"

"He doesn't have the details. She left one day and wasn't seen again."

"Ah."

"And with my suspicious mind I'm thinking if her man was the killer, did he also murder the woman?"

"A double killing? You said she walked out."

"The Pole said that. It's what other people would assume if she vanished from the house. I'm thinking perhaps she never left."

"What would he have done with the body? It wasn't in the loft."

"The small back garden."

"Buried her?"

"Under the forget-me-nots."

"Peter, there's a lot of supposition here."

He wasn't going to admit he'd been influenced by Ingeborg. When you hit a brick wall, intuition might get you over it. "Ma'am, you asked me to investigate and this is where it's led me. That's why I'm here. I need bobbies with spades and sieves."

"Hasn't the garden been gone over already?"

"Not dug for human remains. After the terrace was demolished the contractors removed the rubble and now they want to start work on their supermarket as soon as possible, putting down foundations. I'm trying to preserve it as a crime scene, what there is of it. To them it's days lost. Time is money."

"You're asking me to conjure up a working party?"

"Please."

She took a deep breath. "You couldn't have asked at a worse time. Uniform are fully stretched this week."

"There's never a good time, ma'am. We're under-resourced. We both know that."

"Just about everyone is on overtime with these fireworks displays each night. They can be dangerous events if they're not policed properly."

"Half a dozen officers could do the job."

"What? Patrol the World Fireworks Championships?"

"Dig up the Twerton garden."

"We can't spare them," she said, shaking her head.

"The digging has to be in daylight. I won't take them away from the fireworks."

"That isn't the point. These men and women are working their socks off day and night."

He tried flattery. It sometimes worked with Georgina. "We in CID have confidence in you. When the pressure is on, we always know we can count on you."

"Really?"

"In all honesty, ma'am."

She sighed. "Between ourselves, I enjoy fireworks as much as anyone, but I'm not best pleased about the way this was foisted on us. Did you see the young man who was leaving as you came in?"

"The dude with badges on his hat?"

"Dude?" She gave him a look that let him know he would never make chief superintendent while she was in charge. "He's the organiser. As far as I can tell, he's a self-appointed impresario who offered Bath as a venue. The event is usually in Blackpool when it's in Britain. He put in a bid and they were only too pleased to take him up on it. He goes by the—to me—alarming name of Perry the Pyro."

"Pyromaniac?"

"My thought exactly, but apparently it means he's a pyro-technics expert. He must have some influence with the council and the rugby club because he managed to get the Rec for the shows. I'm assured they all worked well so far and tonight will be the end of it."

"That's all right, then. He can get by with fewer bobbies."

"No, no. Quite the reverse. Tonight's finale will be on the lawn in front of the Royal Crescent."

"On the *lawn*?" Diamond was doing his best to look surprised. Better not tell Georgina he and Paloma planned to be there. She might decide he could help with the policing.

"God knows how he persuaded the residents it was a good idea."

The occupants of the crescent zealously guarded their exclusive rights of use of the patch of turf in front of their building.

"Where will the audience be? Below the ha-ha, I sup-pose. Open ground."

"That's my concern. It's a free show. Anyone can turn up, so we'll need a big police presence."

"You can't spare a few men for my dig?"

She didn't answer. She drew herself up in her chair and looked as if she was about to announce the host city of the next Olympics. "Peter, listen to this. I have some important information for you. I—personally—have been working behind the scenes."

"Oh yes?"

"I became interested in the costume the skeleton was found in—the frock coat and breeches that led us all to believe he could have been Beau Nash. My thoughts turned to occasions where such clothes are worn, even in the twenty-first century."

"Balls."

"I beg your pardon."

"They're worn at costume balls at the Guildhall and the Assembly Rooms. Large annual events."

"You've done some research of your own, then?"

"Covered every angle we can think of."

"In that case, you may have come across the Beau Nash Society."

Couldn't deny it. He'd been homing in on the society in recent days. But he was cautious. "I interviewed a member, yes."

"You have already?" She sounded slightly deflated.

"They meet at a house in the Circus. And they all dress up, bloody fools. Fine if you have the time and money. It's mostly for the idle rich."

"Do I detect a note of envy?"

"No. It wouldn't appeal to me."

"But if you've spoken to a member you must believe they could help the investigation?"

"No stone unturned, as they say."

"Well,"—she brought her fingertips together—"I may be able to help. I won't bore you with the details, but I recently met some people who know more about the Beau Nash Society than you and I could learn in a lifetime. Sir Edward has been president ever since the year 2000. He is known to the members as the Beau. You may have heard of him as a property developer."

"You're speaking of Sir Edward Paris," he said. He could have said a tosspot called Sir Edward Paris. That was what he was thinking.

"Ed, as I know him." With a superior smile, Georgina said, "Over a drink at their ultra-modern home in Charlcombe last night, the subject of your investigation came up."

He frowned, not liking this. "How was that?"

"No need to get hot under the collar. Only three of us were there—Sir Edward, Lady Sally and me. I ventured to suggest it might be helpful for you to meet Ed."

"Did you?"

"And he agreed. No one is better placed to tell you what goes on."

He bit back his annoyance.

"Better than that," Georgina went on, "Ed himself suggested you come to their next meeting, a chance to rub shoulders with the members. Isn't that a splendid offer?"

"Bit of a problem there," Diamond said straight away.

"Oh?"

"Like I said, they dress up. I'd stand out like a sore thumb."

"Of course you will if you go in the kind of thing you're wearing. Hire a costume."

His hands flew up like a kick-boxer under attack. "I'm not dressing up."

Georgina was unmoved. "I knew you'd say that. Take a moment to let the idea sink in, Peter. This is your chance to watch the society in session. Ed is offering to introduce you to some elderly members who were around at the time of the murder. It's not for me to say that they know who the victim was and who did it, but you'll look awfully silly if they do and you turn down this invitation."

"I don't need to see them at their meeting. I can go to their houses."

"That won't do."

"Why not?"

"I promised Ed you'd be there."

"Jesus."

"He'll make sure they talk. He's very persuasive."

Diamond shook his head. "I'll feel a total wuss."

"It's not about you, Peter. It's about bringing a killer to justice."

"I know, but—"

"It's an order. I'll tell you what. Do this for Avon and

Somerset and I'll guarantee you get your six bobbies with spades and sieves."

Clobbered.

He said nothing in the CID room about the dressing up. He simply announced that the dig would get under way the same afternoon.

"Anyone heard of a dude called Perry the Pyro?" he asked.

Looks were exchanged.

"Perry Morgan." Ingeborg said at once. "The man behind the fireworks."

"That's him. Is he local?"

"He's been around sometime, staging events. Not long ago it was the balloon fest. And I think he was behind the pop festival in Prior Park. He's only a young guy in his twenties and I believe he lives above the pet shop in Union Passage. They let him hang posters in the windows."

"I met him briefly this morning."

"He's all over the social media."

"So he's not really a fireworks expert?"

"Not an expert on anything except working the crowds. Are we interested in him?"

"Just checking. He seems to have got Georgina in a tizzy. She's bothered about the fireworks moving to the Royal Crescent tonight. It's too open, she thinks."

"The organisers must know about safety. They've done several evenings already."

"What really bothers her is the residents. They're not people you mess with. They don't take kindly to events like this. They have to move their cars from in front of the crescent."

Leaman said, "My heart bleeds."

"And they're picky about the use of the lawn. They have a society that looks after the upkeep. I assume Perry the Pyro has cleared it with them."

"Don't count on it," Ingeborg said. "People like him take a lot for granted." She was working her iPhone. "Here's one of his tweets." She handed him the phone.

The tweet said: *Must-see amazing free world fireworx finale Royal Crescent tonite. Be there.*

"How does he make his money if it's free?"

"It's been going on all week at the Rec. He'll already have made a killing in gate money. Are you thinking of going?"

"Paloma wants to see it, so we'll go along."

"I might do the same."

"I'm going for sure," Paul Gilbert said.

"There you are," Ingeborg said. "If we're typical, most of Bath will be there."

The dig that afternoon was started in hot sunshine. Five male constables and one female arrived at the site in a van and were met by Diamond. "It's not a huge area, as you can see," he said. "That's the good news."

"What's the bad news?" one of them asked.

"I want to go down six feet."

Something was said that he pretended not to hear. They got out the spades and made a start. After an hour most of the surface rubble had been removed and it looked more like the garden it had once been. You could even see the remains of some forget-me-nots. He handed out bottles of water.

Someone said, "I felt spots of rain."

They all looked skywards. A bank of dark cloud was moving in. "Should cool you down," Diamond said.

"Haven't we done enough for today?" someone asked.

One of the diggers said, "All the buried bodies I've ever read about were in shallow graves."

Nobody else said anything, so the man made his point again. "Shallow, not six feet under."

"They're the ones we hear about," Diamond said. "Think of the ones that never got discovered."

By the end of the afternoon the sum of their finds was a horseshoe, a triangle of chalk, some crushed beer cans, half a rubber ball and nine inches of tape measure. The rain hadn't stopped and the conditions had become impossible. The diggers were hip-deep in a trench that was fast filling with water.

In the minivan, the shallow grave man said, "Here's the story so far. The people who lived in that house kept a horse, but there wasn't much grass for it to eat, so it survived on chalk, beer and rubber balls. In the winter it needed to keep warm so they measured it up for a coat, but it was hungry and ate most of the tape measure."

"You're nuts," one of the others said.

"Tomorrow we'll try and get the real story," Diamond said. "Why the long faces? The ground should be softer after the rain."

16

Parking was a problem. Every space in the nearby roads had been taken and Charlotte Street car park was teeming. In the end Paloma had to leave the car at Green Park.

"Worse than a football match," Diamond said.

"These last few evenings of fireworks were all publicity," Paloma said. "It's going to be crowded. I thought all that rain might have put people off, but it stopped before dark, like they said in the forecast."

"Shame. I was banking on staying indoors and watching from your bedroom."

"Less of that, please."

It was dark by the time they reached Royal Victoria Park and got a sense of the size of the crowd, surely the biggest since the Three Tenors attracted more than thirty thousand in 2003. The difference was that this time no seating was provided. Those who wanted to be close to the action had arrived early and stood shoulder to shoulder below the ha-ha, the sunken six-foot barrier between the performance area and the crowd. A few yards back some brave souls had spread blankets for picnics at the risk of getting trampled. Vendors of drinks and snacks were doing good business where they could weave their way in.

As was the custom for big events, every light in the Royal Crescent was switched on—notably in the squatters' house as well as all the others—making a memorable spectacle in itself. The residents' lawn above the ha-ha was reserved for the fireworks teams and scaffolding was in place.

"Should be starting soon," Diamond said when he and Paloma had chosen a place to stand in front of the trees in Royal Avenue. "The finalists are France and China, and Bath is putting on some kind of extra display at the end."

"I don't know if I'll last that long," Paloma said. "I should have brought ear plugs. I've got some at home."

The public-address system was already pumping out high-decibel canned music. Presently it stopped and after some painful audio feedback a human voice was heard imploring the crowd to take some steps backwards for the safety of people at the front. The appeal seemed to be heeded.

"Seen any police yet?" Diamond asked Paloma. "Most of Bath Central is here."

"On duty?"

"They'll be in high-vis jackets."

She shook her head. "I wouldn't want their job."

A new voice welcomed everyone to the World Fireworks Championships and explained about the rules for competition and the earlier rounds at the Rec.

"This'll be Perry the Pyro," Diamond said. "Can you spot him? White hat, long dark hair."

"No chance from this distance. I wish they'd stop talking and get on with it."

The national anthems of France and China blared from the amplifiers but no one at the back took much notice. A man to Diamond's left offered him the use of binoculars. He was able to pick out Perry with a hand-held microphone strutting along the edge of the ha-ha like Mick Jagger. "And now, dudes," he was saying, "it's over to the teams. First up is France. As you know, the French do three things better than anyone else: wine, cheese and sex. Now let's see if they can make it four. Put your hands together for our cousins from across the Channel."

If anyone actually clapped it wasn't heard because a volley of mortar blasts got the French programme under way. Finally all attention focused on the fireworks. Patriotic red, white and blue in cascades lit up the night, multiplied into millions of sparks curving outwards over the crescent. The crowd responded with the obligatory oooooghs and aaaaaghs. There was stirring synchronised music from Bizet as well, but the real treats were in the sky.

"Worth coming for?" Diamond said.

If Paloma answered it was lost in the next explosions.

The French display took almost half an hour, but seemed longer, such was the intensity. Everyone seemed to agree the show was worthy of the finale and better than anything seen on previous nights.

Smoke could be seen along the length of the lawn and teams were at work rigging the next display. The smell of sulphur spread across the park.

The interval was welcome and the drinks vendors did a good trade.

"The Chinese should give us something special considering they invented fireworks," Diamond said. "Are you up for it?"

"I am, but my ears aren't," Paloma said. "I think I'll be deaf for the next twenty-four hours."

At the front, Perry was working the crowd, asking them how amazing the French display had been and whether China could top it.

"He's good at this," Diamond said. "It's a rare talent."

Paloma didn't seem to have heard. He took out a tube of mints and handed it to her.

Huge aerial shells announced the start of China's effort. This time the sky turned red as lithium atoms showered over the crescent. What followed was exceptional. How the effect of a silver brocade waterfall was achieved was a mystery and that was just the start of a programme that had the crowd gasping between cries of appreciation. When it finished there was little doubt that China was the winner, but the announcement was delayed. Instead, *Greensleeves* suddenly boomed from the public address system. Could there be a dispute over the result? Perry the Pyro was nowhere to be seen. It transpired that in the hiatus the city of Bath was about to make its own contribution to the evening.

"Can your eardrums stand any more?" Diamond asked Paloma.

"If we start walking now, we might escape the worst of it," she said.

"Good idea."

But they hadn't got far before a fusillade of mortars shook the ground. Diamond looked over his shoulder. "How do they follow that?"

"With an anticlimax," she said. "Just look at it."

Somewhere in front of the scaffolding, a set piece tableau outlined in fizzing light had appeared. The figure of a woman in Georgian costume appeared to be curtseying to a bowing man in frock coat and wig.

"If I'm not mistaken that's Jane Austen and bloody Beau Nash," he said. "The bugger follows me everywhere."

17

Diamond had uncorked a French wine in Paloma's sitting room and was pouring it when his phone buzzed. "At *this* hour?"

"Better answer it," Paloma said.

"Ten to one it's a cold call." But he recognised the number on the display.

Ingeborg's voice was charged with tension. "Guv, where are you exactly?"

"Paloma's house. Why?"

"You'd better get back to the crescent. There was a shooting. A man is dead."

"What?" Stupid reaction. He'd heard what she said. Troubling images invaded his brain. The size of that crowd at the show. Some idiot loosing off a gun. Panic and mayhem. It was likely others had been injured as well. He needed to get there fast. "Are you there now, Inge?"

"On the residents' lawn where the fireworks were. The show finished a while ago. We've sealed it off. There's no shortage of manpower."

That was a first. On reflection, most of Bath Central had been on duty.

"Well, you know the drill. Witnesses. Detain anyone who saw anything. Call the police surgeon, scene of crime unit and pathologist. I'll see if I can get to you before they do."

He told Paloma and apologised. "God knows what can

be done at this time of night, but it must be dealt with." He thought of the difficulty of a crime scene littered with firework debris and witnesses who spoke Chinese and French. Don't meet trouble halfway, he told himself.

His preference was always to drive well inside the speed limit, but this called for a change in behaviour. He put his foot down. Not much was moving into town, but unending headlights dazzled him, almost certainly people coming away from the fireworks.

He parked behind a police minivan on the cobbles in front of the Royal Crescent. Some of the lights at the windows were now turned off. At ground level a few of the inevitable gawpers watched from behind the railings, but everyone else seemed to have left except the display teams and the strong contingent of police in their high-visibility jackets.

He crossed the lawn to where he was confident he would find Ingeborg with Keith Halliwell. Fireworks require darkness, so the building's floodlighting had been turned off. Shadowy figures were moving about with flashlights and hand torches, their voices raised as if to compensate for the difficulty of seeing.

Compelled to take notice of things he'd not really taken in during the show, he made out from the languages being loudly used that the rival teams from France and China had worked from separate ends of the crescent lawn. The standing structures erected for Bath's rather cheesy effort occupied the no-man's land in the middle.

Bits of both figures were still smouldering. The fumes of burnt chemicals made his nostrils tingle.

A flashlight had been lashed to the railings with the beam showing the reason for all the extra activity—the victim of the shooting, face down behind the charred remains of the Beau Nash figure. It seemed only one person had been hit.

"Are we certain he's had it?" Diamond asked no one in particular.

A voice in a French accent said, "'Ad it?"

"Is that you, guv?" Ingeborg came from nowhere and shone a torch at him. "You got here fast. Yes, no question he's dead."

"Any witnesses?"

"If there were, we haven't found them yet."

"In all that crowd? Tens of thousands. Surely when the gun was fired . . ." He stopped. Common sense kicked in. "The sound was masked by the bloody fireworks."

"Seems so."

"Where was he hit? Head? Chest?"

"Both. He took several shots."

"Anyone know who he is?"

"Didn't I say? It's Perry the Pyro."

Spikes thrust through his veins.

"Give me the torch."

Suddenly ice-cold, he confirmed what she'd said. Death is difficult to accept at any time. Here the shock was extreme. The go-getting young guy had been the personification of vitality. Only a short time earlier he had been the main man of the entire show, working the crowd like an evangelist preacher raising the expectations of everyone present. Now the long, dark hair was fanned across the turf, almost covering that white hat, except that there was more red than white. Some of the badges glinted moistly.

Speculating why the killing had taken place was pointless when so little was known about the man and his contacts, but Diamond's job was to go beyond speculation and find logical reasons. People like Perry, the movers and shakers of this world, can be ruthless in getting what they want. Witness that "D'you mind, dude?" moment. Who could say what enemies he'd made on the journey here?

Another car bumped over the cobbles. The police surgeon. All he would do would be to declare life to be extinct. Most times it's screamingly obvious, as now. Nice little earner for a local GP. But of course it can involve unsocial hours.

He was the same Dr. Higgins who had used the cherry picker to declare the skeleton dead. "What are you doing here?" the sarcastic little man asked Diamond. "Hoping to make the front page of the *Sun* again?"

Too shocked to trade insults with this jobsworth, Diamond turned to Ingeborg and said loudly, "Did you call a real pathologist? We need an expert here."

She confirmed that Jim Middleton was expected, an assurance that did nothing for Diamond's state of mind. Fifteen years before, his beloved wife Steph had been gunned down only a short distance from here, on the lowest stretch of the sloping lawn below the crescent, and Middleton had attended the murder scene and afterwards carried out the autopsy. No reason to blame Inge or the pathologist. His own raw emotion made the memory painful.

The scene of crime team arrived in two vans. Their first task would be to fix some temporary lighting.

Asked when anyone had first noticed Perry was missing, a short man in a tracksuit, one of the event organisers, said there had been some confusion after the Chinese display. Perry had been expected to step forward and inform the huge audience that while the judges were coming to a decision the city of Bath would present a show of its own, but he hadn't appeared, so Bath's set-piece figures had been activated without any announcement. And after the five-minute show was over and Beau Nash and Jane Austen had fizzled out, Perry still couldn't be found, so one of the judges had been forced to take over and declare the result. The Chinese *chef de mission* had been handed the trophy and the crowd was unaware that anything unplanned had happened. It was only after people were starting to disperse that one of the riggers had stumbled on the body on the turf.

"Did anyone touch him?"

"Several of us—to see if he needed help. But it was obvious he'd been shot and was dead, poor guy. We told the nearest policeman."

He spoke to Ingeborg, "Take the names of that rigger and everyone who handled the body." Then he asked the tracksuited man, "How could he have been shot without anyone noticing?" The question came out like an accusation of negligence. Diamond wasn't in a mood to spare people's feelings.

"No one had any reason to go round the back of the figures."

"Why not?"

"We don't go near for safety reasons," the man said. "The things are ignited remotely using infrared signals."

"There were plenty of people involved in setting off the fireworks. Someone must have seen what was going on."

"Don't count on it. The guys up here all had their own jobs to do and there weren't many of us."

"Yes, but someone fired a gun."

"If you'd been here—"

"I was."

"Then you must have heard the mortars the Chinese were firing. Even with ear muffs on, they were deafening. Rapid, too. And of course everyone looks to the sky to see the effect."

He'd done the same. He wouldn't have witnessed the shooting even if he'd been at the front.

A sudden flash of light transformed the scene. A police photographer was taking shots of the corpse.

Another thought occurred. "Some of the flashes from the fireworks lit up everything brighter than daylight."

"I can only speak for myself and I wasn't looking for a gunman."

Diamond gazed up at the huge mass of the crescent. Now that midnight had come and gone, most of the lights were out. "People in there would have had the best view of the firing area. Some of them must have been watching from the windows."

"Yes, but, like I say, would they have noticed what was going on down here?"

He had to concede that the man had a point. Most of Bath had watched the free show, but finding even one witness to the shooting would be a challenge.

He stepped over to where the Chinese team were uprooting hundreds of racks and tubes used to fire the mortar shells that had made such an impression. "Anyone speak English?"

Apparently not. This was the worst start to an investigation he could remember.

More of them were loading a truck. By repeating the same question several times over he found someone who appeared to understand what he asked.

"Good. Did any of your guys see the man get shot?"

A shrug.

"Would you ask them?"

Another shrug, but the man did at least say something to his colleagues. No one appeared interested. The speaker of English shook his head and said, "See nothing."

The French, when Diamond tried them, were more animated. He got a "Zut alors!" and much gesticulating, but nobody admitted to witnessing the murder.

"So who was the rigger who found the body?" he asked Ingeborg.

"He's local. His name is Dave Bateson. I'll call him over."

Dave Bateson was one of the Bath team and he looked like a coal miner coming off shift. It seemed his responsibility had been to make sure the two figures stayed fully ignited and in motion for as long as possible.

"I thought it was all remote," Diamond said.

"Yes, but once they were alight, things could go wrong.

We were confident Beau Nash would keep bowing, but Jane Austen was more complicated and could easily have gone belly up."

Jane Austen belly up would not have enhanced her reputation or the city's.

"How do they work?" Diamond asked. "Like the moving signs in Piccadilly Circus?"

"Not really. It's all down to the lancework."

"What's that when it's at home?"

"Set-piece pictures like you saw—they're powered by multiple firework fountains known as lances mounted on a wood or metal frame and connected by a fuse. The manufacturers are perfecting new systems all the time. These things were automatons. It's very high-tech."

"Oh yes? So high-tech that you had to be ready with a box of matches if they failed?"

Bateson gave a nervous laugh. "It's not like that."

"When did you actually find the body?" Diamond asked.

"Only after the show was over. I must have been close to him when the figures were set off. I was keeping behind the frames so as not to be obvious. I wouldn't have noticed anything on the ground while I was on duty. That's pressure, that is. Imagine if I failed."

"Jane Austen fizzing out?"

"Or the other one."

The whole concept of Jane Austen and Beau Nash appearing together was fatuous anyway. They were born a hundred years apart. The Beau had been dead nearly forty years when Jane arrived in Bath.

"So can we be confident the body was lying there all the time?"

"I suppose. Horrible shock I had, almost falling over it like that. Soon as I did, I called my mates over and we made sure it wasn't some drunk. When we saw the blood we called your lot."

"My lot?"

"The police."

"Right." Diamond's mind was on other things. "The layout for the show must have been planned some time ahead. Did you have anything to do with it?"

"No, each team planned its own."

"I'm talking about the areas the teams were given to set up their displays."

"Got you. That was fixed a few weeks ahead, but it was obvious, really. You had to give the finalists separate stations and it made sense to keep them apart with our bit standing between."

"It's becoming clearer to me now," Diamond said. "If the shooting was pre-planned, the killer must have known his best opportunity was to do it behind all the action while the show was in progress."

"I can't argue with that."

"He could be reasonably confident Perry the Pyro would be standing behind your figures. Where else would he go when he wasn't out front giving his pitch to the audience? He wouldn't want to spoil their view so he'd go round the back."

It had made sense for Perry to retire into the shadows between announcements. Having watched the show from the front, Diamond had needed to understand how the event had been handled up here on the residents' lawn. Little more could be learned from this witness so he let Bateson go.

Detectives are taught at police college that the first twenty-four hours after a murder are the most productive of vital information. You shouldn't expect much sleep. Diamond had never followed the rules. He called Keith Halliwell over. "One of us should be here when old motor-mouth arrives to look at the body. Is there any word from him?"

"Jim Middleton? Last I heard, he was on the road."

"Which road?"

"He's coming in from Devizes. If you want to get away, guv, I'll do the honours with Jim. At this time of night he might be less talkative than usual."

"I wouldn't count on it."

This earned a grin, but both men knew the real reason Diamond didn't want to meet Middleton. Halliwell had been with his boss on that dreadful morning in February 2001 when Steph Diamond's body was found.

"I'm going to take you up on it," Diamond said. "If I've had some shut-eye, I'll be firing on all cylinders in the morning. I'll tell Inge to stand down as well. And most of the plods. There isn't a lot they can do at this stage."

"It's down to us as usual."

"But I wouldn't call this usual, Keith. Everything I've seen and heard so far makes me think this death is unusual. Highly unusual."

18

"First job: next of kin."

Nobody spoke.

"You know my view on this," Diamond said. "I don't believe in asking uniform to knock on someone's door and give them the bad news. It's our duty."

It didn't surprise him that no eyes locked with his when he looked around the room. The entire CID team apart from Keith Halliwell had assembled next morning for instructions.

"I'm asking one of you to take this on."

Ingeborg broke the silence. "We don't know who it is, do we?"

"We should get an idea after we enter the victim's flat. He lives over the pet shop in Union Passage. If there's someone sharing it with him, a wife or partner, be ready to break the news sympathetically."

"And if no one is at home?" Ingeborg said.

"Talk to the neighbours, look at the address book, files, letters or whatever, and get names. It could be his parents in this case. He was in his mid-twenties by the look of him."

"They will have heard already, won't they?" John Leaman said. "His name is all over the media this morning."

"We still speak to his people. Whoever breaks the bad news will then become the family liaison officer."

"Job like that needs the woman's touch," Leaman said.

Ingeborg snapped back: "Sexist. I was waiting for you to say that. What's wrong with a man supplying the TLC for a change?"

"Enough," Diamond said. "This is a job for you, Paul."

Paul Gilbert nearly bit the end off the pen he was chewing. "Me?"

"You can handle it."

"I'm not even married. Comforting some widow—I wouldn't know how to start."

"May not be a widow," Leaman said. "Think about that."

"May be his parents, like the boss says," Ingeborg added. All too obviously she and Leaman were relieved to be spared one of the hardest of all duties a police officer has to perform.

Diamond hadn't picked Gilbert randomly. The young man had been the junior member of the team for longer than was good for him, yet he was probably the same age as Perry had been, if not older. In more affluent times new recruits would have joined the team. Cuts in police numbers by successive governments produced this strange effect that a DC in his twenties was treated as the permanent new boy.

"So," Leaman said, sitting taller now there was no need to keep his head down, "who gets to look inside Perry's flat?"

"Not you," Diamond said. "We have another operation underway in case any of you are forgetting. I need a senior officer to take charge while I deal with the shooting."

"The skeleton?" The chance of an executive role had instant appeal for Leaman. "I don't mind taking over if that's what you're saying."

"It's exactly what I'm saying, John."

The unexpected honour brought a glow to Leaman's cheeks. He'd long considered himself capable of heading a murder investigation. "Thanks, guv."

"I mean taking over at Twerton."

"Understood."

"I'm not sure if you do understand. I'm talking about the dig."

"Dig?"

"At the scene. I spent yesterday afternoon there. Didn't Inge tell you?"

Ingeborg shook her head. "It was a busy time."

"Six PCs with spades are out at Twerton searching for another body, a woman who went missing in the late nineties. They got down four feet in the first trench. Found a few household objects, but no human remains as yet."

Most of the colour drained from Leaman's face. "You want me out there?"

Diamond checked his watch. "They'll be making a start about now. I told them to be there early."

"It's raining," Leaman said looking towards the window. "Bucketing down."

"That shouldn't hold them up. They come prepared with wellies. It rained when I was there. Quite a cloudburst at one stage. Some water collected in the trench, but after it drains it's easier to find things."

Ingeborg said in an aside to Gilbert, "Suddenly the job of family liaison officer sounds quite appealing, eh, Paul?"

"What am I supposed to do?" Leaman asked. "Oversee the digging?"

"You said you don't mind taking over. Take wellies with you. Waterproofs. An umbrella might not be such a good idea. The diggers could get stroppy if they see you under cover."

"How deep are they supposed to go?"

"About another foot, but the going is slow at the level they are."

"And if there's nothing down there do I call it off?"

"No."

"No?"

"You start another trench. Don't look like that. It's only a small garden."

Others in the room were given jobs collecting information online. The autopsy wouldn't be before next day, when Keith Halliwell would be back. As Diamond's deputy he would attend. Normal service resumed.

Three of them drove into the city in Ingeborg's small car. Because Union Passage is in a pedestrianised area, they were forced to park in the Podium and walk some distance through the downpour sharing one small pink umbrella. Things could have been worse. At about the same time John Leaman was squelching through mud at the building site. Nothing was said, but he was in their thoughts.

The narrow thoroughfare, twelve feet across, medieval in origin, appeared in early maps as Cockles Lane and Slaughterhouse Lane, and was rebuilt late in the eighteenth century by the city architect, Thomas Baldwin, who also designed the Pump Room and much else of note until he was sacked for refusing to let the corporation inspect his accounts. Close up—and you are forcibly close up in this congested walkway—the modern shopfronts make it appear much the same as any other twenty-first-century street. This morning its period charms had no appeal to the three detectives.

"Where's this pet shop? I'm getting soaked," Diamond said.

"You're holding the umbrella," Ingeborg pointed out. "Look at Paul."

"There's more of me. Do we know the name?"

"Fur All That's Wonderful," Gilbert said.

"Did you say *fur*?"

"Groan," Ingeborg said.

They found it halfway along, close to the intersection with Northumberland Place. A poster for the fireworks was still in the window.

"Strange," Ingeborg said. "I thought pets were upset by fireworks."

"Let's get in the dry," Diamond said, pushing open the door.

The shopkeeper, a large blonde woman with owl-like eyes behind red-framed glasses, must have wondered what this trio had come to buy. They didn't have the look of customers wanting to buy a kitten. In the state they were in, a sack of dry straw bedding might have been more to the point.

Diamond introduced himself and learned that he was addressing Deirdre Divine, the owner of the shop and the flat upstairs as well.

She'd heard about the shooting. "It's tragic," she said with all the sensitivity of someone reading the shipping forecast. "If I wasn't dealing with life and death all the time, as I am in this line of work, I'd be crying my eyes out. Who would want to shoot Perry? He was a delightful man and a perfect tenant, the best I've ever had."

Alert to his new responsibility as family liaison man, DC Gilbert asked, "Did he live alone?"

"Sadly, yes," she said. "I offered to let him have a parrot or a budgie for company or even a small reptile. He wasn't persuaded. Perry always said he was too busy to care for a pet."

"Didn't he have anyone else in his life? We need to find his next of kin."

"Who would that be?"

"Parents? Family?"

"Not to my knowledge."

"Visitors, then?"

"I can't say I've ever noticed anyone. He had his own front door, and I don't believe in prying. Most of his business was done on the phone or the computer as far as I could tell. He was a busy man."

"Did he ever speak of any worries?" Diamond asked her.

"To me? Lord, no. He kept up with the rent, so I had no complaints."

They were getting the impression Perry didn't confide much about his private life to his landlady.

"We need to see inside. Do you have a spare key?"

"It's a smart lock."

"Smart in what way?"

Ingeborg murmured, "Digital, guv."

Miss Divine explained with a cryptic smile, "You have to know the combination for the push buttons."

"And do you know it?"

"Of course I do. It's my property. I thought it up." She may indeed have thought it up, but she wasn't ready to volunteer it. The smile hadn't shifted.

"And?"

"There's no point in having a security code if you give it away the first time you're asked."

"We *are* police officers, ma'am."

"Hamsters."

Diamond didn't take offence. He'd been called worse, a lot worse. She was being playful, he decided. He indulged her with a grin. "We do have a job to do. I'm trying to save you the bother of going out in the rain to let us in."

She was persuaded. "One ate one, one ate two. There's no room for sentiment among pet-shop owners. All kinds of animals consume their young, hamsters especially. Do you follow me?"

"I do now."

Outside in the rain, in front of Perry's door, they ignored sentiment, thought of cannibal hamsters, and punched in 181182 and it worked. Facing them on the other side of the door was a flight of stairs. All the way up were posters of events Perry must have arranged: pop concerts, more fireworks, a fashion show and a celebrity football match.

The flat was open plan, with a double bed at the end

farthest from the street and a separate area for lounging, with twin sofas, plasma TV and sound system. The computer shared a white desk with a printer, some local papers, neatly stacked, and a range of reference books including *Who's Who, The Good Hotel Guide* and the *Complete Book of the British Charts*. The cooking area looked as if it wasn't much used. In fact, the entire flat was so tidy it was hard to believe anyone lived there.

"You'd better check the computer, Inge. Paul, I suggest you start opening drawers. Letters, notes, addresses, like I said. I'll see if there are phone messages. This guy shouldn't be a mystery much longer."

Having assigned the duties, Diamond started searching for a phone. Not obvious. He'd assumed there would be a landline. Now he supposed it would be a mobile. He tried the bedside table and the desk.

Gilbert was going through a chest of drawers. "He looks after his clothes well. So carefully folded they look new."

"Maybe they are," Ingeborg said. "He can afford it."

"It's almost obsessive," Diamond said after looking into cupboards with the contents lined up like little soldiers. "And there isn't much you can call personal."

"I need a password," Ingeborg said. "He's strong on security."

"Try Fixer."

It didn't work.

"Pyro."

She used the keyboard again. "No joy. We may have to take the computer back to the office and get an expert working on it."

Frustration was starting to set in. Diamond's confident claim that Perry wouldn't be a mystery much longer was looking threadbare already. "You'd think a man as active as he was would have an address book or a calendar," the big man said.

"Phone," Ingeborg said. "He'll keep that stuff on his phone." She didn't add that it was high time Peter Diamond moved into the twenty-first century, but it was implicit in the way she spoke.

"That's my point," he said, rattled. "I've spent the last ten minutes trying to find it."

"He'll have had it with him. Wasn't there a mobile on the body?"

"We made a point of respecting the integrity of the scene. If there was one, it will either have been picked up by the SOCOs or gone to the mortuary."

"Or taken by the killer."

"You can trace a stolen phone."

"If we knew the number, we might be able to."

"People he was doing business with will know it."

"Let me do some checking." Ingeborg took out her own phone.

Diamond was already thinking the crucial facts about Perry wouldn't be found here in the flat. "And I expect he owned a car and we need to find that," he said to Gilbert. "He probably drove to the crescent and left it somewhere near. Parking was a nightmare on the night, but he will have got there early enough to go anywhere he wanted."

"Charlotte Street car park was nearest," Gilbert said. "Just a short walk away."

"On second thoughts he may have used a taxi. Living here in the centre of town, where would you keep a private car?"

"I can ask Miss Divine."

"Do that."

With his two assistants occupied, Diamond returned to the unpromising job of searching the flat. He was puzzled by the absence of any obvious affluence. Perry had made a name for himself staging major entertainment events.

Where there is mass participation there is money. Yet the wardrobe, when he looked in, had only two suits and some casual jackets, none of them with expensive labels. The four pairs of shoes or trainers looked more useful than fashionable.

If the money didn't go on material luxuries, where was it spent?

He was getting an idea.

Beyond the bedroom was an open door to a shower room. To one side was a hand basin and above it a mirror and a glass shelf with brush and comb, aftershave, deodorant, electric toothbrush and floss sticks. Opposite was a wall-mounted medicine cabinet.

People's pills and potions are almost always instructive but, once again, Perry seemed to have the basics and little else. Ibuprofen, indigestion pills, antihistamine, throat lozenges, sun oil, nail scissors and Band-aids.

He shut the door, disappointed. Tried a chest that contained bed linen, each item folded and stacked tidily, though not after Diamond had been through it.

Ingeborg was still on the phone.

He started opening the drawers of the desk where she was seated. Pens, Post-its, unused paper, envelopes, a stapler. Not the stuff he was looking for.

Well hidden, he decided. Perry would have realised Miss Divine knew the combination and could look inside the flat at any time.

If you didn't want your landlady to find something, where would you keep it?

The kitchen area? He'd already concluded that the guy existed mainly on meals he microwaved. There wasn't a toaster, a blender or a crockpot. The saucepans on the hob looked squeaky clean. The pedal bin was empty. There was little in the cupboard above the microwave except two mugs and several plates of different sizes, a packet of cornflakes, a cut loaf and teabags. The coffee was in a packet inside the fridge—which also contained milk, apple juice and two cartons of spread that Diamond opened, just to be certain.

Perry appeared to have achieved the ultimate in lean cuisine. He didn't buy pasta, potatoes or eggs. Even Diamond, who lived a low-maintenance life when at home, sometimes cooked himself bacon and eggs. Two slices of back and two extra large ones. Actually with tomatoes. Throw in some mushrooms. And a sausage or two, not forgetting a slice of fried bread.

In fact, you would have wondered if anyone lived here at all were it not for the freezer below the fridge, stuffed with pre-cooked meals from Waitrose. He lifted them out and made sure nothing else was underneath. Then he ripped the packaging off each one and made sure it was what the label claimed before tossing them all back. They'd be no use to Perry now. No use to anyone, for who would want a dead man's unused food?

He opened the microwave and ran his finger along the side. Definitely used on a regular basis.

A sigh was his private show of disappointment. It seemed his theory was unfounded. He couldn't think where else to look. Back of the wardrobe, under the bed, behind the curtains? All checked.

Ingeborg finished her call. "Guv."

"Mm?"

"The SOCOs found a smartphone clipped to his belt. An iPhone 7 plus. Top of the range."

"Where is it now?"

"With the MDE."

"Have a heart, Inge."

"Mobile device examiner. The crime scene team put it in an evidence bag and handed it in."

"Who is this—anyone I know?"

"A young guy called Hector seconded from Bristol. I doubt whether any of us knows him."

"He'd better be good. Soon as we get back we'll look him up. I'm thinking we've done all we can in this place."

"What were you searching for when I was phoning?"

"I had a thought, that's all. There isn't much evidence of heavy spending here, but he would have got large payouts for the events he arranged. Crossed my mind that most of it could have gone on drugs."

"Why not?" Ingeborg said, eyes widening. "Worth checking, for sure. He was living a life on the edge. Setting up these shows had to be stressful. And he didn't eat much, going by what's in the fridge and the food cupboard. He was painfully thin and that's often a sign."

"Yep, but I made my search and found nothing."

"What would he have used? Not heroin, surely? He wouldn't want to get drowsy."

"Coke, I expect. Supposed to make you alert and confident."

"Where would he store it?"

"I'm no expert. I think they use plastic bags or containers. The main thing with cocaine is to keep it from getting moist, so it needs airtight storage in a cool place."

"The freezer?"

"Not in this case. You saw me going through the packs of macaroni cheese and cottage pie. All innocent. My theory had better be put on hold. What's that?"

Both of them turned at the sound of the door clicking.

"Me," Gilbert said, freshly returned from downstairs. "I had to wait my turn. Someone had brought in a stray dog."

"It's a shop, not a dog pound."

"Tell that to the lady who found the dog."

"What does Miss Divine say?"

"She put down some food and water and phoned the RSPCA."

Diamond rolled his eyes. "I meant what did she say about Perry?"

"He didn't have a car. Like you thought, he used taxis to get about."

"Okay, we're done. Let's go. We haven't learned as much as I hoped."

Ingeborg asked Gilbert to help her carry the computer downstairs. It was an all-in-one machine, twenty-three inches, not particularly heavy, but awkward. They wrapped it in a bed sheet from the linen chest.

"This could be our best bet," she said.

"Our only bet," Gilbert said.

"No, the SOCOs found his phone."

They started the careful descent of the stairs, Diamond leading.

Halfway downstairs, he changed his mind, stopped and almost sent the three of them and the pc crashing to the bottom. "Thought of something."

"The umbrella?" Ingeborg held it out to show she hadn't forgotten it.

"No. Excuse me." He pushed past them both and up to the top. Straight to the cupboard over the microwave. Reached for the cornflakes.

The carton had been opened but felt full, and heavier than it should. The flap at the top was fastened. He flicked it up and looked at the cornflakes inside. Pulled out the inner bag.

Secreted underneath was a plastic box used to store 35mm slides—except that there were no slides in there.

When he lifted the lid he found it was packed with layers of folded paper. He took one out, unwrapped it and found a small quantity of white powder.

What next? In movies and TV, the detective dips a finger—always the small finger—into the substance and tastes it. Diamond was far too experienced to risk poisoning himself.

"Good find, guv," Ingeborg said with real admiration. "Is that what I think it is—wraps of some drug?"

"I'll be surprised if it isn't."

"What made you think of the cornflakes?"

"The crockery. He had plates and mugs, but no bowl. How would he eat his cornflakes on a flat plate?"

19

Georgina was pacing the CID room, lioness-like, when they returned. Gilbert entered first holding the computer still wrapped in the bed sheet. Diamond and Ingeborg followed. All of them were drenched.

"Still tipping it down," Diamond said unnecessarily.

Georgina was eyeing the small object he was carrying wrapped in a pillow case. "What's that?"

"We're not certain, ma'am. I've kept it covered."

"Is it alive?"

"I hope not. It may be cocaine. I need to get it analysed."

"Cocaine from Perry's flat?"

He nodded. "If I'm right, he's more than just a pyro."

Her face went through a series of rapid reactions, from interest to shock to guilt, and Diamond knew why. A suspected cocaine user had been given police permission—her permission—to stage the biggest firework display ever seen in Bath. "Does he have a record?"

"We haven't checked yet. We're treating him as a victim, not a suspect."

She'd gone from Post Office red to Kleenex white. "I took him to be a competent young man. I ought to have checked with the PNC. Things could have gone disastrously wrong."

Could have gone wrong? Diamond was tempted to say that a fatal shooting was worse than wrong, but he spared Georgina's feelings. No doubt she was thinking in terms of mortars smashing through windows in the Royal Crescent and creating an inferno of Bath's most glorious building. "If it's all the same with you, ma'am, we'll get out of our wet things and take these items to someone who can deal with them."

"Do that," she said, her eyes glazed.

Diamond started to walk away, but Georgina's powers of recovery were legend.

"And then come and see me in my office, Peter. There are urgent matters on my mind."

While Ingeborg and Gilbert went to seek out a computer forensics expert, Diamond headed for the drugs unit. When he handed across the plastic box, the two sergeants in there asked what he thought was inside.

"I'm keeping an open mind, but I wouldn't have come to you if I wasn't suspicious. It was well hidden."

"Have you tasted it, sir?"

"No way. Is that what you do?"

He got a pained look from the one who appeared to be in charge. "We're not amateurs."

"How long will you take?"

"About five seconds. Marley will know. Put the box on the floor. You can leave the lid on."

Five seconds was an overestimate. Marley was a brown and white springer spaniel who confirmed cocaine as soon as he was brought in. There was no barking, no yelping even. He went straight to the box, stood quite still and focused intently with eyes and nose.

"That's coke," the sergeant said. "He's been on more busts than any of us. The street value of the finds he's made runs into millions. It's the large nose and long muzzle of the breed. Good dog, Marley." He took a plastic container from a shelf and rattled it. "Want to give him his reward?"

"Will he take it from me?"

"He will when he's off duty. He's a different dog then. He's waiting for you to take the box away."

Diamond didn't like that look in Marley's eyes. "I'd rather you did that."

Georgina was behaving as if the entire population of Bath was on its way out to Emersons Green to lynch her.

"It's a bad, bad day, Peter."

"Why is that, ma'am?" he asked, feeling chirpy again.

"Can't you see? If this isn't handled right, the media will portray us as incompetent. A shooting in front of the Royal Crescent when almost our entire strength was on duty there. And now this—a drug user in charge of a fireworks show."

"He didn't personally light the fireworks."

"He was the front man and probably high on cocaine at the time."

"What do you want me to do—hush it up?"

"No, no. It will leak anyway. But if questioned, you don't need to go into detail about whom he approached."

He enjoyed the "whom." She was a stickler for correct grammar.

"I'll do my best to cover up for whomsoever you mean, ma'am."

She twitched and looked towards the window. The lynch mob couldn't be far off. "It's not a case of covering up for anybody. You can give a vague answer, can't you?"

"If pressed."

"This is our reputation at stake. God knows we've had more than our share of scandals in recent years. How do you propose to handle this murder?"

"In the usual way, ma'am," he said in a fine demonstration of vagueness.

"Meaning what?"

"We'll gather all the evidence we can and decide on possible motives and draw up a list of suspects."

"When you say 'we' . . . ?"

"Me and my team."

"Is that wise?"

He frowned, not liking this. "We're CID. That's what we do."

"But you're already at full stretch on the Twerton murder. You can't be in two places at once."

He got it. She wanted to hand the Beau Nash case to someone else. "We can, between us. We're an experienced team. DI Leaman is currently out at Twerton on the dig you and I discussed the other day."

"They're digging—in weather like this?"

"In waterproofs and wellies. I made sure they went prepared."

"Has he found anything?"

"I haven't heard from him this morning."

"Drowned, I shouldn't wonder."

He gratified her with a grin. "He's unsinkable, is John Leaman."

"I hope so, for his sake."

"Not forgetting the six diggers, ma'am."

"Absolutely not." But the six diggers weren't high in Georgina's thoughts. She beat a short tattoo with her fingers on the arms of her chair. "This new case will require more resources. It's not as if it happened twenty-odd years ago, like the Twerton murder."

"More resources would be good," he said, ignoring the last low punch. "We can always use help. Where from?"

She didn't exactly answer. "There's a drug element and we both know how dangerous that can be. I want you leading the team. Peter."

"Well, I am."

"Fully engaged, I mean, with all your senior people involved, including Inspector Leaman."

Now the warning light had gone from amber to red.

"Then what's going to happen about Twerton? We can't just fold our tents and walk away. The press are on at us all the time for updates. It's an active case, a headline story."

"Credit me with some intelligence, Peter. I'm bringing in a team from Bristol."

"What?"

"You heard me."

This was beyond all. "You can't do that. It's my patch."

"It's what the government keeps telling us about: maximising resources. Bristol are overmanned just now. We're all Avon and Somerset, aren't we? I've discussed it with senior colleagues at Bristol Central. They'll relieve you of the Twerton case. Detective Chief Inspector Crocker will take over."

"Crocker?" He could barely get the word out. "Charlie Crocker. He can't do it. He's all wind and piss."

"Please. That's no way to speak to me, and no way to speak of a colleague."

"No colleague of mine. He'd ruin everything, destroy all the work we've put in. You can't honestly think a goon like that—"

"Before you go on, Charlie Crocker earned a chief constable's commendation for the way he dealt with the neo-Nazis at College Green last year. He's a valued officer clearly destined for higher things."

"So they jump at the chance of unloading him on us. The man's a walking disaster area." But insults wouldn't win this contest. He had to think of something that would make an impact on Georgina. He thought hard and, as so often when the adrenalin was pumping, a bold idea came. "Can you imagine him interacting with your friends from Charlcombe?"

She blinked. "The Parises?"

"I wonder how Sir Edward and Lady Sally will take it when he wades in, bragging about kicking shit out of the neo-Nazis. Could be okay, I guess. For all I know, they may hold ultra-right-wing views themselves."

"I think not. My impression is that they're liberal-minded about most things."

"So they won't mind Charlie's effing and blinding. Fine."

The worry lines were multiplying by the second. "Is he like that?"

"Only when he gets on one of his hobbyhorses, like the class system. Abolish the House of Lords and string them all up from Westminster Bridge, Charlie says. But that's okay if your friends are liberal-minded. The problem as I see it lies elsewhere."

"What do you mean?"

"The Beau Nash Society. When he visits there, he'll come up against a few of the filthy rich, as he calls them. Sure to."

"Oh my God."

"I may be wrong. He could choose to remain silent. He won't have much to talk about except his politics. He doesn't know the first thing about Beau Nash."

"Does he need to go there?"

"It's arranged, isn't it? Sir Edward is expecting a senior detective. You had me in mind when you promised to send your man to the next meeting."

"Oh dear, yes."

"That's why I've been doing a crash course on the Beau and his fifty years of life in Bath: the houses he lived in, his mistresses, his circle of friends. And his rules for the Pump Room. I'm so well briefed I could go on *Mastermind*, I was told. The reason I'm doing so much homework is to blend in with the members. Simply wearing the frock coat and the wig isn't going to fool anybody."

"I'd forgotten about the costume. Have you hired it already?"

He hadn't, but he wasn't going to say so. "Paloma is looking after that. You expressly told me to get one, if you remember. Funny, I can't picture Charlie in the gear. Have you told him?"

She coughed as if she had a bone stuck in her throat. "I haven't spoken to him. His name came up when I phoned my opposite number at Bristol."

"It would," Diamond said. "The first name they'd think of."

A pause for reflection.

"Do we really need to have someone attending the Beau Nash Society?" Georgina said.

"I'm sorry, ma'am. I'm confused. You told me I should go there and mingle with the elderly members who were around at the time of the murder. You said you'd done me a good turn and arranged it with Sir Edward. 'Hire a costume' were the words you used."

"So I did."

"We can see if it fits Charlie Crocker, but I doubt it somehow. He must be six inches taller than me and built like a super-heavyweight. Mingling with the elderly members will be a challenge. I hope he doesn't knock any of them over."

Georgina caught her breath and covered her eyes. "Say no more. I've made a ghastly mistake. This man mustn't be allowed within a mile of the Beau Nash Society."

"How can we put him off?"

"You say you're well prepared. We'll go back to Plan A."

"With me in charge?"

She nodded and he could see the full consequence of the decision struggling to emerge on her beleaguered face, so he helped with a suggestion.

"You'll speak to Bristol and tell them we don't need reinforcements after all? We can cope?"

"If you're confident we can."

"Not a problem, ma'am."

He came out of the office pumped up—until he realised he'd just talked himself into dressing in the damned frock coat and breeches and enduring a deeply embarrassing night. Up to this minute he'd promised himself it wouldn't happen because he'd conjure up some excuse. No escape now.

Towards midday Keith Halliwell appeared in the CID room looking like a piece of twine chewed by Marley the sniffer dog.

"Caught up on your sleep, then," Diamond said and didn't wait for a reaction. "Did the crime-scene guys make any more discoveries?"

"They made a preliminary check and put up a forensic tent and then decided to wait for daylight before doing the fingertip search."

"Sensible."

"But Jim Middleton arrived and made an inspection of the body by flashlamp. After an hour and a half he stopped for a cup of tea from his thermos."

"Tea and conversation, knowing him."

"I wouldn't call it that. He did all the talking. It was more of a monologue than conversation."

"What about?"

"Fishing. He's an angler. So there we were at three in the morning talking about something called the perfection loop which had nothing to do with the killing. It's a knot they use in fly fishing. Finally he got back to the job and did another hour."

"What did he have to say about the shooting?"

"Bullet to the head would have been fatal whether it was the first shot or not. He wasn't willing to say the range it was fired from except it wasn't a contact wound. There was another through the chest. He ruled out suicide."

"That hadn't even crossed my mind."

"Nor mine. We finally got away about four A.M. He arranged for the body to be removed at first light and he wants to do the autopsy this afternoon if we can get someone to make the identification. Is there a next of kin?"

"We haven't found one. We could ask his landlady, Miss Divine."

"Will she be okay with that?"

"I'm sure she will. The first thing she said to me was that she's dealing with life and death all the time. Can you be the police presence?"

"I always am."

"Untrue," Diamond said, hackles rising. "I did the last one myself."

Halliwell grinned. "The bones. So you did, guv. So you did."

"But with two investigations to oversee—"

"Say no more."

He asked Ingeborg to drive him back to the Royal Crescent. Although the rain had eased off, the turf was squelchy to walk over. Below the ha-ha, council workmen were clearing rubbish left by last night's spectators. On the residents' lawn, the crime scene area was marked with do-not-enter tape. High above it like a rebuke the charred figure of Beau Nash was outlined against the louring sky, Jane Austen having been dismantled.

The forensic tent, too, had gone. The body had been removed to the mortuary. Bright yellow evidence markers had been placed on the surface where items of possible interest had been found.

"How many bullets?" he asked the senior man.

"Five for sure."

"Are you thinking a revolver?"

"We're not thinking anything, Mr. Diamond. We're just collecting and marking at this stage."

"Any footprints?"

"Shoeprints, unless you were expecting Man Friday. So

many, it's ridiculous. The world and his wife came by for
a look. And where the surface turned to mud, all that rain
has spoilt our chance of some nice prints. I wouldn't pin
any hope on a result."

"DNA?"

"You're joking."

"Why is it never like it is in the training sessions?"

"You tell me."

Diamond doubted whether there was any value in
remaining there and said so to Ingeborg. "I'm going to
speak to the drugs squad again."

"You think that's behind this?"

"With guns in play? Got to be, hasn't it? Perry must
have upset someone big time. Our lot have the latest intelligence. They'll know what's happening on the street and
who's really dangerous."

"His phone may have some names."

"The phone and the computer. But I'm not confident,
Inge. You don't store your supplier's contact details unless
you're daft, and Perry wasn't that."

"I don't get it," she said. "He was a user, right?"

"Fair assumption."

"Why would he get shot when he's a paying customer?
The drugs barons wouldn't want him dead. They'd want
him to go on depending on the stuff."

"Maybe he changed his supplier."

"Hadn't thought of that."

"Or he complained about the quality or threatened to
name names. The main thing that came across to me in
my short encounter with him was that he didn't kowtow
to anyone."

"Dangerous."

"The barons may have thought so. Obviously it wasn't
a casual killing. There was planning behind this. They
would have known where he would be and what a fine

opportunity it was to gun him down when the fireworks were blasting out."

"When you say 'they,' are you thinking there were other people involved?"

"Not in the shooting. A job will be given to a single gunman, but others will have made the call. We're likely to be dealing with hard professionals."

"Can we handle that?"

"Of course. Let's go."

In this assertive mode, Diamond turned abruptly and felt a contact of something against his arm. A sudden movement above his head caused him to duck and sheer away. He lost his balance on the slippery turf and fell.

Only after he was dumped on his backside in the mud and felt the damp seeping through his trousers did he see what had happened. He'd bumped against the lancework figure of Beau Nash. Even as he lay shocked and humbled, there was a whirring noise and the mechanism gave one more twirl. The Beau performed an elegant bow.

"Bloody thing."

Two of the crime scene people helped him up. Not Ingeborg. She was looking away with her hand over her mouth.

The SOCOs asked if he was all right.

"All right except for my suit ruined. I only got it back from the cleaner's the day before yesterday." He raised his voice for Ingeborg's benefit. "I saw you smirking, Sergeant Smith. It's your car I'm going to be sitting in."

On the drive back, Ingeborg offered to make a detour to Diamond's house in Weston so that he could change. A helpful suggestion, a peace offering he huffily accepted.

While he was upstairs, she gave Raffles an unexpected serving of beef in jelly.

"You weren't feeding that cat, I hope," he said when he came down in his second-best suit and saw Raffles licking his lips beside an empty dish. "He gets fed morning and night. Those are his times."

They decided to get some lunch themselves since they were so convenient for Diamond's local, the Old Crown. Over ham, egg and chips and with a pint of strong bitter in front of him, he was more forgiving, even confessing to feeling vulnerable.

"How, exactly?" Ingeborg asked.

He took a long sip of beer. "This is in confidence, right? Have you ever thought of me as superstitious?"

She shook her head.

"Feet firmly on the ground, right?"

He could see her struggling to avoid more laughter. "All right. Unfortunate choice of words. You know what I mean."

She managed a nod, not a solemn nod, but a definite attempt to be solemn.

He continued. "Ever since that ridiculous photo of me and the skeleton got in the papers, I've felt as if I'm being picked on."

"Who by?"

"The fates, I suppose." He drank some beer. "Well, Beau Nash, if you want to know. You saw what happened this morning. I brushed against the thing and went arse over tip. It had to be bloody Beau Nash, didn't it? If it had been Jane Austen messing me up I wouldn't have thought anything of it. Pure accident."

"That's all it was, guv."

"I don't know. It's a series of embarrassing events, like revenge or something. I refused to believe he's buried in the Abbey when he plainly was. Even after Leaman found the newspaper accounts I was thinking Mrs. Hill had fooled everyone and secretly moved the corpse to Twerton. I went to that autopsy in the belief they were Nash's bones and got my comeuppance with a pair of pants."

"You shouldn't take it personally."

"So who was it who had to hold a press conference and show a picture of the Y-fronts to the media? Muggins. How can I avoid taking it personally? Originally Georgina wanted me to go in front of them and hold up the pants myself. Imagine the captions they'd have thought up for that picture."

Ingeborg was forced to cover her mouth again.

"Next, Georgina gets friendly with the president of the Beau Nash Society and volunteers me for their meeting. Great—except it involves dressing up in white tights and breeches, frock coat and wig."

She started shaking uncontrollably. "You didn't tell me."

"I haven't told anyone. I walked into it. She was threatening to hand the case over to Charlie Crocker from Bristol. I wasn't having that."

The mention of Crocker came as a shock to Ingeborg. The Bristol police hadn't got a good word to say for the man. Suddenly Diamond's misfortunes weren't so funny. "Why? What's her reason?"

"We're overstretched."

"We can manage."

"I told her—and to show commitment talked myself into wearing the fancy dress. Is it any wonder Beau Nash is getting to me?"

"But did she say any more about Charlie Crocker taking over?"

"The threat was withdrawn."

"Thank God for that."

"No, you can thank me."

"I do. I do. It's an opportunity, guv. Look at it that way."

"Now you're talking like Georgina."

She continued to talk like Georgina. "We've spent a lot of man-hours trying to identify the skeleton. This is a real chance to crack it—a bunch of people who dress up regularly in eighteenth-century costume. One of them may have the answer. This is about attitude. If you go there feeling like a victim you'll get nothing out of it. Tell yourself you look terrific in the outfit and you will."

He frowned. On second thoughts, she was talking more like Paloma than Georgina and she was making sense.

She hadn't finished. "You probably know more about Beau Nash by now than most of their members. After all, we spent days digging out the true facts of his life, exposing the myth about Juliana Papjoy. You're a Beau Nash expert."

"I wouldn't say that."

"You'd better start saying it and believing. By showing confidence you can make your visit a triumph. If you don't, you'll lay yourself open to more embarrassments. When is this meeting?"

He tried to sound enthusiastic. "Wednesday night."

"Have you got the costume?"

"Not yet."

"Better get one fast, guv. You want it to fit."

"I was thinking of asking Paloma to hire one for me. She's got contacts in the historical costume world."

"Call her now. Please, guv. For all our sakes."

The autopsy on Perry Morgan was conducted the same afternoon in the mortuary at the Royal United Hospital after Miss Divine had viewed the body and confirmed the identity of her former tenant. Old motormouth, as Diamond called Jim Middleton, provided a running commentary through-out interspersed with fly-fishing anecdotes whenever he stepped back to allow his assistant to clean up. The sole police witness and captive audience was Keith Halliwell. When it was over, he called Diamond from the hospital.

"All done, guv."

"What did you learn?"

"A lot. You wouldn't believe how many knots they have in fishing. I made the mistake of mentioning the perfection loop to show I'd paid attention last time and he was away. There's the Albright, the grinner, also known as the uni, the clinch, the nail, the double surgeon—"

"What's that for?"

"It connects the leader to the tippet."

He didn't want to know any more. There were more urgent things. "Tell me about the autopsy."

"The killer wasn't too accurate. Only two shots entered the body, one in the chest and the other in the head."

"He was firing in difficult conditions."

"That's true, I guess. Anyway, the one through the cranium is what killed Perry, in case you hadn't worked it out."

"Sounds like the *coup de grâce* after the first one knocked him down."

"Wasn't mentioned."

"Only me speculating. I suppose we have to wait for test results to find out if he was high on cocaine that night?"

"I told Jim our suspicions and he sent blood, urine and vitreous fluid for analysis as well as hair samples. The lab will probably confirm he was a user, but the coke metabolises quickly, so I don't know what we're likely to find out about his state that evening. Is the drug use important when we know a bullet killed him?"

"It's early days, Keith. I want all the information we can get."

"He did remark on Perry's skinny physique. Cocaine suppresses the appetite, and the latest research suggests it actually prevents fat from being stored by the body. Won't be long before it's marketed as a slimming aid in this crazy world. He also took swabs from each nostril and looked inside the nose for signs of cartilage erosion from the snorting, but that was inconclusive."

"Inconclusive sums it up."

"If there was more, I'd tell you."

"I know. I'm not ungrateful."

"I was wondering, guv."

"Wondering what?"

"If I might knock off duty for the rest of the day. I'm still weary from last night."

"Okay, we'll see you tomorrow. Going fishing, are you?"

Late in the afternoon came a call from John Leaman—a man who hadn't been much on Diamond's mind. A rapid recap was needed: Twerton, the demolished terrace and the six diggers.

"John? How's it going there?"

"It wasn't the best day I ever spent," Leaman said in an accusing tone.

"I didn't send you there to have a ball. Are you through yet?"

"Just about. The weather slightly improved this afternoon."

"Yes, that rain early on was the worst I remember. I was out in it."

The last remark wasn't appreciated. "I don't suppose you were ankle-deep in mud at the time."

"I told you to dress for the conditions. Didn't you run for cover when it came down hard?"

"Yes."

From the clipped way the word was spoken it was obvious there was more to come, but Leaman felt entitled to a prompt, so Diamond provided it. "And?"

"I ordered a halt when it got really impossible, but there was nowhere nearby to shelter except my car. The minibus that dropped them was on another job. They piled in somehow, all six of them, mud all over them and all over the inside of my car, the seats, the floor, even the windows."

"It's known as a bonding experience."

"What?"

He didn't push it any more. He knew how the messed-up car would play on the mind of an obsessive-compulsive.

"Never mind, John. Take your motor to a garage that offers a valet service and charge it up to CID expenses. Did you find anything when you finally got back to the dig?"

"We did. That's the reason I called."

"So the day wasn't a complete write-off?"

As a consolation for all the misery Leaman was about to have the last word. "I think you may be interested."

"Go on, then. I'm all ears."

"We found some bones."

20

It occurred to Diamond as he was driving down to Twerton to see the bones that the timing wasn't the best. Right now, a third corpse might shock Georgina into changing her mind. There was still a real danger of Charlie Crocker muscling in. There had to be a smart way to handle this.

What was that bit of twisted wisdom he had once heard?

When in charge, direct; when in trouble, delegate.

John Leaman had turned up a crucial bit of evidence, so why shouldn't he be given the chance to follow it up? If Ingeborg's hunch was right and it emerged that the remains were those of the wife or partner who had gone missing in the 1990s, then inevitably it wouldn't be long before the male tenant known loosely as Harry came under suspicion of killing both the woman buried in the garden and the man found in the loft. The two enquiries would fuse as one.

Made sense.

Meanwhile, he would be in no hurry to tell Georgina about the find. The remains would need to be examined before anyone took them seriously.

At the site, Diamond drove over the rutted remains of the road and parked behind the Honda Civic hatchback owned by Leaman. How six men and a woman had squeezed into that small car to get out of the rain wasn't nice to imagine.

Leaman was standing alone, arms folded, barely recognisable in mud-coated overalls and wellies. The king of spades, as Diamond now privately dubbed him, didn't summon up as much as a nod. If he was jubilant at making the find, any joy was internalised.

"You sent the others home, then?"

"The minivan came for them. They had a hard day. We all did." He looked and sounded terribly down. Browned off in every sense.

"Your car doesn't look too mucky standing beside mine."

"You think so? It's a disgrace. Want to see inside?" Leaman's striving for perfection was often helpful to the team, but made life difficult for himself.

"I'll take your word for it. Where are these bones?"

"At the far end. You're going to ruin your shoes."

"It's why I'm here."

Every part of the small garden seemed to have been turned over. Leaman led a snaking route around heaps of soil and deep trenches to the farthest end where yet another excavation had been started.

"Not far down, then?" Diamond said, looking in. "The typical shallow grave."

Leaman took that as criticism. "It's only shallow because I ordered a halt to the dig once we'd decided the first piece was definitely bone."

"I can't see anything."

"What do you expect? It's not the full skeleton." He crouched and pointed. "They're quite small pieces, broken up by some of the heavy machinery that was here, no doubt." You would think from Leaman's tone that the bulldozers had been sent in specially to spite him.

With difficulty, Diamond made out some greyish-brown scraps that could just as easily have been stones. "Is one of these the piece you examined?"

"No."

Leaman stood again, dipped a grimy hand into the pocket of his overalls and brought out a chunk of bulbous material almost the size of a golf ball, but emphatically bone, irregular on one side as if it had snapped off. "It's the top of a femur where it joins the hip."

"May I?"

Diamond took the object in his hand, felt the weight, looked closely at the surface and turned it over.

He whistled.

"Good find, John. And there's obviously more."

"You can see pieces of the shaft. There ought to be other bones lower down. We only had spades and trowels to work with, which is why we stopped digging. We need finer tools and an expert now."

"I know exactly who to ask."

"Jim Middleton?"

"No. Our bones man."

"Dr. Waghorn? I thought you didn't get on with him."

"He's a sarcastic old git and if this turns out to be animal bone he'll give us hell, but I'm willing to risk it. You've opened a whole new line of enquiry."

The ridges of resentment on Leaman's mud-spattered face vanished like ripples in a puddle. He didn't raise a smile, but he appeared less likely to offer his resignation. "What made you so sure there was someone buried here?"

"I can't take credit for that," Diamond said. "The possibility crossed my mind when I heard about a missing woman, but it was Ingeborg who convinced me we must dig. She won't like me saying it was feminine intuition."

"Personally I don't believe in that."

"Neither does she, but she has an uncanny way of pointing me in the right direction. Right now I'm interested in *your* abilities. How would you feel about taking on this side of the investigation?"

At first, Leaman was wary. He wasn't going to be caught twice over. "I don't want to spend any more time in this quagmire."

"John, I'm offering you the chance to head the enquiry."

The voice changed. His entire manner underwent a transformation like a long-term convict at the moment he was told he'd been reprieved. "You want me in charge?"

"You've got the experience."

"I know, but—"

"No false modesty, John. You can handle this, right?" He pressed the piece of bone back into Leaman's palm like a badge of office.

The hours of misery were as nothing now. "Right. Where do I start?"

"First, you go and see Claude Waghorn at the university and ask him to confirm that this bone is human. Then you bring in the scenes of crime team to search for more clues. They're professionals. You don't have to stand over them. You can safely leave them to dig for days on end while you get on with the detective work."

"What should I be doing?"

Typical Leaman. "Where do I start?" "What should I be doing?" He'd do the job as well as anyone on the team and he probably knew the answers to his questions, but he was programmed to work to instructions.

"Redouble your efforts to find who these tenants were. You know I met a Polish guy called Jerzy, don't you, known to his mates as Yurek? Electrician working on the Manvers Street site. He and his partner were the last official tenants here before the squatters took over. They had the place eleven years. He didn't meet the previous tenant, but he was told there had been a woman living in the house for a time. She left one day and wasn't seen again."

"This is her?" Leaman opened the hand containing the bit of bone.

"A piece of her, possibly. You may get more clues as other bones are recovered. But your main line of enquiry has to be naming and tracing the main suspect."

"Her partner? What else do we know about him?"

"Jerzy was vague. He said he'd been told the guy was a Brit and he suggested he was called Harry. Don't place too much reliance on that. I couldn't be sure if he was guessing."

"Probably was, then."

"The thing about these two is that they were firmly in the time frame when the skeleton was killed and hidden in the loft. Like I said, Jerzy was here eleven years and the squatters for over two after the place was condemned—two and a bit, they said. That's thirteen since our mysterious couple were here, which checks neatly with our other point in time, the period when that particular pattern of Y-fronts was still in use."

"So how do you see it? Harry murders the man in the frock coat and the woman finds out and gets murdered herself?" Leaman's confidence was growing by the minute. He was sounding more like Diamond's partner in the case.

"I can think of a dozen scenarios. She was asking too many awkward questions. Or he was afraid she'd talk. Or he caught her trying to get into the loft. Or she was a good Christian soul with a conscience who wanted to go to the police. Or they did the killing together and fell out and he couldn't risk a break-up. Or she demanded money in return for her silence. But it's too soon to speculate. We're at the stage of collecting information."

"How long was Harry living here alone?"

"After the woman vanished? I got the impression it was a few years. Shall we move? I can feel the damp coming through my socks."

"I warned you, my friend," Leaman said. "You should have brought wellies."

Diamond quietly noted "my friend" and was amused. The two senior investigators wound their way through the heaps of earth and back to the cars.

"The SOCOs aren't going to be too pleased that we dug the site over already," Leaman said.

"You did the heavy work for them. They've got the beauty part now, disinterring the bones."

Paloma hadn't wasted any time. She wanted Diamond for a fitting that evening at her house in Lyncombe.

"Isn't it gorgeous?" she said when she took the rented outfit from its cover and showed it to him.

"It's pink," he said in alarm.

"Pinkish-mauve. A soft shade like this shows off the embroidery."

"Flowers."

"Leaves and flowers. That was the style. You need to look authentic."

"Like the sugar-plum fairy. I can't believe this is happening," he said. "Have you ever had that dream when you arrive at some posh event like a wedding and discover you're naked? That's how I'm going to feel."

"You'd feel far more embarrassed if you turned up in your day clothes. Try the breeches first. I got the largest size they had, but there's room for adjustment. I can reposition the buttons if need be."

"I'm not *that* enormous. What's in this packet?"

"White stockings. I had to buy those. They don't come with the costume."

Grumbling to himself, he went behind a Chinese screen she had thoughtfully provided. The fit was pretty good. The breeches fastened over the stockings. He put on the linen shirt and tucked the flaps under the waistband. Apart from some tightness on the shoulders when he tried the frock coat, the costume would pass muster.

"Better than I hoped," Paloma said when he emerged.

"The jacket may be a size too small. I don't want to burst a seam."

She told him the armholes were cut high to achieve an erect posture. "Actually it's a very nice fit. Be glad you're not a woman and wearing stays."

"Have you got a mirror?"

"Hey ho." She smiled. "I think someone rather fancies himself as an eighteenth-century gent."

"I need it for the wig."

She held up an oval hand mirror. "Line it up with your forehead and pull it backwards over your head. Had to be white, I'm afraid. Only the Beau is allowed to wear black."

"Like this? Is it straight?"

"Perfect. There's a full-length mirror on the far wall."

He went over and stared at his reflection. Pink or pink-mauve, the colour was still hard to accept. "I was thinking the coat would be dark grey or black."

"That wouldn't be right. You'd look like an extra out of *Pirates of the Caribbean.* Take my word for it, Peter, this is what the others will be wearing."

"I can't believe I'm doing this."

"Actors do it and think nothing of it." She reached for her phone. "Can I get a picture?"

"Absolutely not. I'm getting out of this now."

"But you must practise the walk. You're wearing something special and you need to flaunt it."

"I think you're enjoying this."

"Someone has to. You made it very clear you aren't. A prop might help. I've got a silver-handled cane somewhere. Try the walk while I'm out of the room."

In truth, Paloma was right. He knew he must be convincing. Her advice chimed in with what Ingeborg had said earlier. This was about an attitude of mind. He'd need to banish the embarrassment.

He took a couple of hesitant steps and then lengthened his stride, puffed out his chest and walked the walk. I can do it when no one is watching, he told himself. Now I must have the guts to do it in public.

"You don't have to overdo it," came Paloma's voice from behind. She'd returned unnoticed and was watching from the doorway. "That's a little too much swagger. They'll be comfortable in their costumes. They're used to it. All you have to do is feel comfortable in yours. Now try with the stick."

The stick definitely helped.

"I like the look," she said. "Does wonders for your figure."

"Hides the pot belly, you mean?"

"Beau Nash would approve. How are the shoes?"

"They'll do nicely." They were black with large silver buckles. In reality they were a size too large and slipped a bit, but he could pad them with paper tissue.

"I could have got matching pink. Men wore all colours."

"Black is good."

"Why is this meeting important?" she asked.

"I'm hoping these people can help me put a name to the skeleton. Some of the older members were around at the time we think the murder was committed."

"They may put a name to your killer as well. Wouldn't that make it all worthwhile?"

"Just about."

His first action next morning was to visit the drugs unit. Neither of the two sergeants was there. He knew he was in for a battle when he saw the man in charge. Inspector Don Tate was notorious for giving little away about the unit's activities. Tate had left Scotland twenty years before but was as dour as any Aberdeen fish-filleter. Moreover he still had a brogue so broad that it took a while to tune in.

"You know why I'm here?" Diamond began.

"The Peruvian marching powder?"

Diamond didn't know the expression and not a word of it was understandable to him. "Excuse me?"

"Cocaine."

"Got you. The stuff I brought in yesterday. Has it been analysed yet?"

Tate nodded and kept his mouth shut. Probably he felt he'd said too much already.

It was ridiculous to Diamond that the drugs unit couldn't fully confide in CID, and the reticence wasn't entirely down to Tate's personality. He'd come up against this brick wall before. Everyone in the policing of drug offenders would talk of ongoing operations requiring secrecy, as if no other section worked on the basis of confidence. As Diamond saw it, all sections of the police were on the same side. This would not be simple. "How was the quality?"

"Better than most."

"Pure cocaine?"

"You don't get pure cocaine here. It's twenty to twenty-five percent at best."

"Not crack, anyway?"

"Aye."

"Did your guys tell you who it came from?"

"The laddie who put on the fireworks show, I was told."

"Correct."

"And now you're going to ask me who his dealer was. I can't tell you."

"I didn't expect it from you, Don. But you can point me in the right direction."

Tate pulled a face as if someone was trying to throttle him. "Sensitive information."

Unmoved, Diamond told him, "I won't share your precious secrets with anyone outside my team. We're professionals, same as you."

"We have several ongoing enquiries."

"Is there ever a time when you don't? That's how you work."

"Aye, but I can't have the work of many months compromised by your lot pulling in people under surveillance by my teams."

"This was murder, Don. I'll pull in whoever I believe has information."

"You have your job." Tate glared. "I have mine."

"And you're about to give me the tired old line about a conflict of interests. I'm looking for some cooperation here. Have you ever stopped to look at the name of this building when you come in each day? It's Concorde House. Not a lot of concord in here this morning."

"Whose fault is that?" Tate said.

Diamond rolled his eyes. "I brought the cocaine straight to your team. Don't you owe me something in return?"

"It may seem a big deal to you, Peter, but having a user ID'd is no help to us when he's already dead. We're interested in the big boys."

"So am I, ultimately. The boys who order the shooting of dopers they want eliminated." Diamond had known it would be like this but being forewarned hadn't made him any less irritated. "For now, I'll settle for the name of his supplier. You don't want me making wholesale arrests, you say. Better name someone, so I can get the job done with minimal damage to your stings."

Tate gave him a level look. "Nice try."

"What do you suggest, then—that I get out on the streets and run it my way, putting the fear of God into all the coke-heads we can find so that they cough up the names of these people you're unwilling to identify?"

"You wouldn't do that."

"Try me."

"Perry Morgan wasn't on our radar. I'd tell you if he was. So how could I know who supplied him?"

"You said it was good quality cocaine."

A nod.

"And you saw the wraps. Plain white paper. Was there any indication from the way it was folded who might have made them?"

"We had a look."

"Got any prints?"

"From what?"

"Give me a break, Don. The wraps, folds, bindles or whatever the current term is. You don't have to be obtuse as well as tight-lipped."

"Nothing definite was found."

"But you have your suspicions? You're not going to let a chance like this go begging."

Tate sneered. "And you're not going to stop trying, are you?"

"Why would I? The signs are that Morgan was addicted and using a large part of his income to keep stocking up. He must have become a nuisance or a threat to his killer. Is there anyone in your sights who would resort to murder?"

"That would be unusual."

"But not unknown?"

"The barons are into other crimes." Sensing he was on safer ground, Don Tate expanded a little. "Money-laundering more than anything. That's how we get on to many of them in the first place. They have cash-flow problems, but not the sort you and I would have. They have to find ways of hiding their dirty money in offshore accounts or in businesses that routinely handle large amounts of cash."

"I understand that. One way of disposing of hot cash is to pay a gunman to take out someone you don't like."

"In which case," Tate said, looking away, out of the window, "first find your gunman."

"There were no witnesses."

"Ballistics?"

"May identify the weapon. Not the man. If I don't get names from you, Don, I'm serious about taking to the streets."

"You'd set us back months of patient work if you do. And you'd get nothing. The guy you want doesn't do street dealing."

This sounded awfully like confirmation that a particular individual was in the frame, teased out of the wily Scot through sheer persistence. Long experience of questioning tight-lipped criminals might be about to pay off. "So you do have someone in mind."

"I wouldn't say that."

"Of course you wouldn't if you could avoid it, but you just did. He doesn't do street dealing, so he must be selling at a higher level to better-off celebrities and the like. Am I right?"

Rattled, Tate pointed a finger and said, "Lay off, Peter." He rolled the final "r" like a motorbike revving up.

"Touched a raw nerve, did I?" Diamond said. "If you won't tell me, there are big-name people in this city who can. I see it in your eyes, Don. And your white knuckles. Where shall I go looking for these snow birds—the racecourse, the Pump Room, the theatre, or can you suggest a top hotel?"

"You could blow an entire operation."

"Sorry," Diamond said with irony. "You can't say I didn't inform you first." He got up from the chair. "I must get started."

Tate gave him a murderous look. "The wraps would appear to have been made by a dealer we already have under surveillance. He folds them in a particular way we recognise. He will have bought the cocaine from someone higher up the chain who imported it, someone outside our authority. We're working closely with the National Crime Agency."

The mention of the all-powerful NCA was supposed to spook Diamond. It didn't.

"Name?"

Tate flapped his hand in derision.

"I'm asking for the name of the local man."

"He's small time, not likely to possess a firearm or think of hiring a gunman. We don't regard him as dangerous in that sense."

"So you can safely tell me who he is."

"I canna."

There is an old proverb about using a sprat to catch a mackerel. This was the moment Diamond reversed the process.

"Someone else will."

"Who do you mean?"

"Don, we both know who I mean. His distributor."

If Tate had been tasered he couldn't have twitched more. "You don't . . ."

"But I do. Albanian and dangerous."

A moment of silence before a rare smile dawned. "Albanian? Who are you kidding? Newburn doesn't buy from an Albanian."

Diamond smiled back. He'd caught his sprat.

"Thanks. And where do I find Newburn?"

Don Tate sighed heavily. "He's a gallery owner."

"Which gallery?"

"Upmarket."

"I'm sure. But what's it called?"

"I told you—Upmarket."

"That's the name of the shop?"

"The top of Broad Street. If you question him, for Christ's sake don't give him any hint that he's already on our radar."

"Relax," Diamond said. "We'll make it clear we're investigating Perry's death and checking everything on his phone."

"You'll keep me informed what happens? Now I've told you this, I'm insisting on cooperation."

"That's rich," Diamond said.

"You gave your word."

"All right. You're in the loop, don't worry. We got there in the end. You know, Don, you could take lessons from one of your team."

"Who do you mean?"

"He doesn't believe in faffing about. I've seen him in action. He's straight to it."

Tate reddened. "Who the fuck are you talking about?"

"Marley the sniffer dog."

Paul Gilbert had hit a problem with the task Diamond had given him as family liaison officer: there wasn't any family to liaise with. The dead man Perry Morgan seemed to have been without a living relative. Miss Divine from the toy shop had performed the macabre duty of identifying the corpse before the autopsy and up to now she was the main authority on his life.

"Have you discovered anything at all from public records?" Diamond asked when he returned to the CID room.

"He's a Bathonian, born in Dolemeads in 1990."

"Where exactly?"

"One of the cottages opposite the Baptist church."

"Prepare to meet your God."

Gilbert blinked and stared back at Diamond, who wasn't known to quote the Bible or utter death threats.

A nice moment this, watching the changes in the young man's face as the penny dropped. "The writing on the roof?"

"Spooky, eh, in view of what happened to him?"

"As it turned out, yes."

Widcombe Baptist Church, formerly the Ebenezer Chapel, on Pulteney Road, is distinguished by the sobering texts emblazoned in huge white letters on the four sides of its roof (the others being "Christ died for our sins"; "We have redemption through his blood"; and "You must be born again"). When the district known originally as "mud island" changed over the decades from a slum to a new council estate to a gentrified locality where the average price of property rose to over half a million, requests were made by aspiring Widcombe residents to have the texts erased, but they remained and as part of a Grade II listed building their survival passed into the safe hands of English Heritage. For Peter Diamond, they were a feature of the city worth keeping, particularly as he didn't live within view and see the messages each morning when he pulled back the curtain.

"So you have the birth certificate, do you? Who were his parents?"

"Henry Morgan, taxi driver, and Fiona Glynn, unemployed."

"Unmarried by the sound of it. Aren't they still around?"

"Both dead," Gilbert said. "I got the certificates. She went first, of cancer, in 2002, and he was killed in a car crash five years later. He was only forty-three."

"Perry would have been eleven or twelve when his mother died. Bloody hard for a kid that age."

"Really tough. I found the notice of her death in the *Chronicle* and he's mentioned as her much-loved son."

"You've been busy. Was an address included?"

"Not in the paper. On her death certificate. Oldfield Road."

"Anything in the report about her partner the taxi driver?"

"They seem to have separated at an early stage. Not even sure if they ever lived together. His fatal accident gets a write-up in 2007 with a photo of his wrecked taxi. He broke down at night on the M4 coming back from Heathrow and was stationary on the hard shoulder when a transporter ploughed into the back. Pure bad luck."

"Not all that uncommon, sadly. Does Perry get a mention?"

"In the paper? Briefly, as a son, living with him at Larkhall. But he's named on his father's death certificate as the informant."

"Same address as his father?"

"Doesn't tell you. It just says Perry Morgan, son."

"I'm getting the picture," Diamond said, more for his own benefit than Gilbert's. "Brought up by mum until her death, when he goes to live with dad in Larkhall. After the crash he's alone in the world at sixteen or seventeen. I wonder what he did next. The shock of being orphaned must have taken a while to get over. Can't see him running the sixth-form disco. Yet in a few short years he becomes the local impresario staging everything from wrestling to the world fireworks competition."

"Where would he get the confidence?"

"Cocaine helped."

"Yes, but . . ."

"I know. There has to be some kind of grounding in event management. He didn't leave Bath, it seems. These are the years we need to concentrate on. Make a list of all the shows he organised and start contacting the people he would have dealt with. How did they hear about him and what do they know? Find out who he mixed with."

"Miss Divine said he didn't get visitors."

"Doesn't mean he didn't make contacts outside. He knew how the world works, so he must have rubbed shoulders with all sorts. He was capable of thinking big and persuading people he was the real deal. They call it chutzpah, but where did Perry get it from at such an early age? My first thought is some kind of training in art."

"Art? Why?"

"Artists carry conviction. Tell you a row of bricks is a masterpiece and you look at it and believe them."

"Sometimes you do," Gilbert said in a tone suggesting he, for one, would take some convincing.

"It's all about persuasion. Where would he go to study art?"

"The university?"

"Why not? The art courses are all based at Newton Park these days, aren't they? At one time it was the Academy of Art at Corsham Court and then it was Sion Hill and then it was all taken over by the university. See if there's any record of him on their courses. He could have been a dropout."

"How about the cocaine angle?" Gilbert asked, not wholly sold on the art college theory. "Does he have form?"

"Nothing was known to the drugs unit until I mentioned it, but he seems to have bought his wraps from a supplier called Newburn." Diamond snapped his fingers. "And Newburn is a gallery owner. Must be why the art popped into my head."

"Want me to visit him, guv?"

"I'd better go myself. DI Tate in drugs is pissing his pants about us interfering. You've done a useful job already. Now fill in the missing years."

Paul Gilbert was proving to be a vital member of the team, growing in self-confidence. The best detectives have an inner fire. Motivation. A sense of justice. Commitment to the cause. Whatever it was that made a good cop, the young man had it in large measure.

Ingeborg had her hand raised to get Diamond's attention. She, too, had proved her worth many times over. He crossed to her desk, tidy as always. A see-and-store book of 8 x 10 photos of the crime scene. Phone, notepad, pen neatly positioned.

"The first ballistics report is in, guv."

"Quicker than usual."

"I've been giving them a hard time. I mean, when they've

got bullets that impacted with soft turf, as they have, it shouldn't be difficult getting the striation pattern."

He was eager to hear this. The markings on the bullets—as individual as fingerprints—would have been compared with a huge bank of gunshot data to see if there was a match with any other crime. A positive result would very likely confirm that they were dealing with a contract killing. "So what are they telling us?"

"There were no casings recovered, meaning almost certainly that the shots were fired from a revolver rather than an automatic. The shell casing stays in the chambers until it's manually removed. They're 9mm, which is nothing unusual. They checked the pattern with the national database and got a nil return."

He frowned. "This isn't helpful, Inge. You're telling me the gun hasn't been used before in any recorded crime."

"I'm just reporting what they told me."

"So what are we to make of it? Either the killer isn't a professional gunman or he is—because he's smart enough to arm himself with a new weapon."

"That's devious thinking. You're ahead of me."

"Doesn't help us, though."

"I wonder if we're dealing with an amateur," she said.

"Who keeps a revolver in his sock drawer? This isn't America."

"It happens. There are guns in private hands. A one-off shooting by someone driven to desperation."

"By drugs, you mean?"

"Possibly. Or some personal issue."

"People with personal issues mostly make a poor job of murder and it's often spur-of-the-moment. There was definitely premeditation here. The killer chose the time and the place. The gunfire was masked by the fireworks and everyone except him was staring up at the sky."

"He wasn't all that accurate."

"Two hits out of five? That isn't bad. Anyone who has used a handgun knows it's a crude weapon compared to a rifle. Didn't we learn anything else from ballistics?"

"That's it in a nutshell. We'll get some detail later."

Ingeborg never showed much in her expression, but he thought he saw some disbelief.

"I heard what you said, Inge, about an amateur. They aren't all hotheads, I have to say. I may be influenced by the drug element. Perry was pretty successful at what he did and that can lead to all sorts of jealousies by less talented people. Let's keep an open mind about motives. We don't know enough about his contacts yet."

"Are you going to make a call on his supplier?"

"Newburn? He's next."

21

For all Diamond knew, Upmarket may have been in business as an art gallery for months, if not years. He wouldn't have noticed. His idea of art was the framed film posters from the 1940s that adorned the hallway and stairs of his house in Weston. *Build My Gallows High*, with Robert Mitchum, old sleepy-eyes, cigarette drooping from his lips; *Casablanca*, showing Bergman and Bogart cheek to cheek; and a favourite that never failed to raise a smile, *Payment on Demand*, with a vengeful Bette Davis in a red strapless gown standing over a kissing couple and the plot summary, "The one sin no woman ever forgives. He strayed and he paid! She saw to that!"

Images as obvious as his treasured posters would not be offered for sale at any gallery in Bath. Typically an overpriced item that was more eyesore than art (in Diamond's estimation) would be displayed in the window against a black background that blocked the view of the gallery interior.

The current offering in Upmarket—when he got there—was a large carriage clock without hands or numbers. The face was a human face with a large Salvador Dali moustache that might have been meant to stand in for the hands of the clock. But then a peculiar thing happened. Diamond moved his head a fraction and was surprised to see the moustache jerk to a new position.

Instead of 9:15, it showed 10:20. He moved again and it was 11:25 and he realised he was looking at some kind of hologram. Novel, but grotesque. He wouldn't have given it house room if it was offered as a gift. He turned his back on it. Of much more interest was the fourth-floor window of the building across the street, the obvious place for a police CCTV camera to have been secreted to film everyone who entered Upmarket. He could imagine Don Tate going through the footage later and saying, "I knew that Sassenach fucker would compromise our investigation."

Before going in, the Sassenach fucker glanced up at that window and touched the brim of his trilby.

The interior of the gallery was narrow but extended further back than he appreciated from the street. He pretended to take an interest in the works on display, all evidently created by the same hand. A theme was apparent. More hologram faces stared out at him from household objects: a birdcage, a fan heater, a saucepan and a food processor. They opened and closed their eyes, grinned and scowled. Personally he found them creepy. They might appeal to someone's sense of humour, he supposed. Not his.

At the far end he caught sight of a living face, a young woman at a desk behind a computer, so he touched the hat again and said, "Just taking a look, if I may."

"Please do," she said in a voice that would have got her the best table in the Pump Room. "Are you interested in surrealism?"

"Not specially."

"Don't hesitate to ask if anything interests you."

Ask the price was what she meant, because nothing was tagged.

"I was hoping to see Mr. Newburn," he said.

For this he was rewarded with a sigh, a knowing look and

the abandonment of all charm. She reached for a phone. "Who shall I say is calling?"

"Peter." Buyers of cocaine—and at the beginning he meant to pass himself off as one—wouldn't give much away, least of all their surnames.

She spoke something into the phone that wasn't meant for Diamond's ears and then looked up. "He'll be down shortly."

"Good."

If it hadn't been so transparent that the head of CID wasn't a man of culture, he might have asked politely who the featured artist was. Equally, if the gallery assistant had thought Diamond was a potential buyer he might have been offered a glass of wine.

Neither occurred.

Presently she got up and reached behind for her coat and Diamond guessed what was going on. Newburn's arrival would be the cue for his assistant to leave the shop for a time. The drug dealing was conducted in private.

Now he'd made clear he wasn't there for the art, Diamond stood by the window looking out at the traffic until a voice behind him said, "Have we met?"

He turned and faced five-foot-nothing of cultivated innocence in a pink velvet jacket, striped shirt and lavender-coloured trousers. Tinted blond hair fluffed to candyfloss consistency over a boyish complexion. Small soft hands that had clearly never gripped anything rougher than an emery board. Tiny feet in crocodile-skin shoes.

Have we met? If we had, I'd remember you, matey, Diamond thought. "This is the first time." He didn't offer his hand. He wasn't taken in by the fragile appearance. Dealers in drugs were hard men.

The assistant glided past them both and left the gallery.

"I believe I'm in the right place," Diamond added.

"The right place for what?"

"For the art."

"Art?" Newburn said with raised eyebrows, as if he sold compost. "Oh, you mean the holograms."

"No."

"What, then?"

"The origami."

This was met with a frown.

"The art of paper folding."

"Ho, ho, ho." The joke wasn't appreciated.

"If you know what I mean."

Newburn plainly knew what he meant, and was not ready to trade. "Peter, you told my assistant. Peter who?"

"Diamond." Nothing to be gained by keeping up this pretence, so he took out his warrant card. "CID."

The gallery owner turned a shade pinker than his jacket. For a moment he looked as if he would take flight like a Michelangelo cherub. He glanced left and right and then ahead at the door, probably checking to see how many other burly policemen had come to arrest him. No doubt he'd mentally rehearsed this personal Armageddon many times over.

Diamond was the next to speak. "Making enquiries into the sudden death of Perry Morgan."

"Who?"

"Don't mess with me, Newburn. You know about the shooting."

"Shooting?"

"At the fireworks Saturday night."

"I can't help you. I wasn't there."

"But you knew the victim." Having given the sharp shock, Diamond offered some reassurance, the possibility that this might not be a drug bust after all. "We're speaking to everyone he came into contact with. He was a client of yours."

"What makes you say that?" The little man was stalling.

"We searched his flat and found some wraps. Your

handiwork, I'm reliably informed. Before you say another word, I'm not here to pull you in. I'm investigating murder, not the dealing."

Newburn swallowed hard, getting over the first shock and deciding how to react. It seemed he was ready to talk. "What do you want to know?"

"Did he come here to buy?"

A nod.

"On a regular basis?"

"It was occasional, after a payday, I suppose. His work wasn't regular."

"Did he buy in bulk, then?"

"He preferred it that way and so did I."

"How did he find you?"

"Through a recommendation, he said. He came in one morning."

"With a large amount of cash?"

"Of course."

"A recommendation from another user? Did he say who?"

"No."

"When would this first visit have been?"

"Towards the middle of last year. I haven't known him long."

"Did you get the impression he'd moved on from another seller?"

"I've no idea."

"That's not good enough. You must have formed an opinion."

"All right. I suppose he had. Why do you ask?"

"Another supplier may have felt he was justified in killing him."

"Oh, I doubt that. Not in Bath."

"It's all very civilised here, is it? A shake of the hands and a fond goodbye. Was Perry Morgan already an experienced user? Did he know about quality and prices?"

"He wasn't a beginner."

"He's quite well known in Bath. Did you recognise him?"

"Not when he first came in. Later I saw his picture in the press, but I didn't let on. My better-known clients prefer it that way."

"Did he ever reveal anything about his situation?"

"You mean his finances? Never. They don't like you knowing what they can afford."

"Or you raise the price?"

He was tight-lipped.

"Actually I meant his personal life. He had a flat above a shop in Union Passage and lived alone there."

"He never spoke of anyone else. I wouldn't expect him to."

This wasn't stonewalling, Diamond decided. If the land-lady, Miss Divine, was to be believed, Perry had guarded his privacy. Newburn was scum, but his account so far rang true.

"Is there anyone in the drug community who may have wished him dead?"

"Not to my knowledge. Why should they? It's the middle-men like me who are most at risk of violence."

Indisputably true, but if this toerag wanted sympathy from Peter Diamond he wouldn't get any.

"How do you protect yourself? Do you have a gun?"

Newburn didn't say anything. The change in his skin colour was the giveaway.

"So you do."

"I told you I wasn't there when he was shot. Besides, I had no reason to wish him dead."

"Where's it kept?"

"I've never used it." His right hand moved towards the inner pocket of his jacket.

"Don't."

"I was about to show you."

"I'll see for myself." Diamond stepped forward, pulled

open the front of the pink jacket and removed a small black gun. Going by the weight, it was loaded. "Dinky."

But it was an automatic and they eject the casings at the scene. This couldn't have been the weapon used in the murder.

"Self-defence," Newburn said. "I meet some unpleasant people in the course of my work."

"Snap," Diamond said.

"Are you going to charge me?"

"What with—possession of an unlicensed weapon? Not at this minute. I have more important things to do. You'll hear from us."

He pocketed the gun and left soon after.

Georgina had warned him that taking on a new case of murder when he was already dealing with the Twerton skeleton would stretch him and she was right. This evening he was due to attend the Beau Nash Society meeting wearing the rented costume—a challenge that required a different mindset from dealing with pond life like Newburn. He needed time to prepare, so instead of returning to Concorde House, he decided to knock off early. First, he phoned Keith Halliwell.

All the key people in CID were usefully occupied, Halliwell told him. Leaman had informed everyone he was in charge of a third investigation. He was currently waiting for news from Dr. Waghorn about the bone dug up at Twerton. A team of crime scene examiners was already on site lifting more fragments. Five DCs were knocking on doors making yet more enquiries about the earlier tenants of the terrace. Ingeborg was with Hector, the mobile device examiner, checking the contents of Perry Morgan's phone. Paul Gilbert was at the university going through enrolment records to see if Morgan had ever been a student there.

"And how about you?" Diamond asked Halliwell.

"Standing in for you, guv."

"Standing or sitting?"

"Doing what you would normally do if you were here. Someone has to oversee it all. How did it go with the gallery owner?"

Diamond updated him and then said, "I won't be back tonight. It's the Beau Nash bunfight and I need to get ready."

"Rather you than me."

He drove home and phoned Paloma. She had already offered to help him get into the costume before driving him to the house in the Circus where the meeting was to take place. She suggested he came about 5:30, which left time to freshen up.

But not before he'd fed the cat. Raffles made sure of that with some heart-rending mewing. The years had taken their toll of some of the wily old tabby's abilities, but he was more vocal than ever.

Rarely had Diamond looked forward to a shower so much. Visiting Newburn had left him feeling dirty. There were no marks for the soap and water to remove. It was all in the mind, yet the act of cleansing felt as necessary as if he'd been back to the crime scene and jumped into one of Leaman's trenches.

He'd always found showering a sure way of relieving mental stress. He didn't go to the extreme of the James Bond method, starting with warm water and turning it down to finish stone cold. The Peter Diamond shower was hot, strong, steady and unchanging, a perfect recipe for fresh thinking.

He'd need to be sharp for his appearance at the Beau Nash Society.

When Georgina had threatened to remove him from the case and bring in Charlie Crocker he'd been forced into some wild claims. He wasn't anywhere near Mastermind level on Beau Nash. Even so, the prospect of an evening with all those keenos and academics had influenced his bedtime reading. Instead of the latest final sensational who-would-have-thought-it unmasking of Jack the Ripper, he'd been working through a small stack of books about the Beau and the extraordinary way one charismatic Welshman had taken over and made Bath his own. Admittedly the conquest was on a lower scale than many people believe. Most of the buildings that define the modern city were simply not there when Nash arrived in 1705. No Royal Crescent, no Queen Square, no Circus, no Theatre Royal, no Assembly Rooms. Even the Great Bath had not been excavated. To call it a one-horse town might not be fair to a cathedral city, but it was largely given over to slums. The transformation from small spa to one of the architectural glories of Europe took place in the years of Nash's supremacy and after.

While the jets of warm water were reviving him, Diamond mused on how Perry Morgan must have had some of the Nash attitude, the strength of personality that persuaded people of influence to allow a young man to stage major public events. Would a modern-day Nash have laid on the world fireworks competition and marched into the assistant chief constable's office to demand adequate policing? Without a doubt. Such people weren't put off by authority. Would some mean-minded person have shot him dead? Possibly, human nature being what it is. Remarkable enterprise can spawn remarkable jealousy.

Better put Perry out of his mind for this evening, he decided. He finished showering, dried himself and changed. In ten minutes he was on his way to Lyncombe.

Paloma had a pizza supper and salad ready when he arrived. "I know you're not over-keen on salad," she said, "but it balances the meal, I think. Shall I open a can of beer?"

"I could break the abstinence of a lifetime and allow myself one," he said.

"I phoned Estella earlier. She's going to be there tonight, so there's at least one person you'll have met."

"Did she say what happens at these meetings?"

"The welcoming of strangers, of course."

"What's that?"

"Anyone who hasn't been before gets put in a sedan chair and is carried into the presence of the president and made to recite Nash's rules for the Pump Room. Nothing to worry about. He speaks them first and you repeat them."

He didn't like the sound of that at all. "A sedan chair? Really?"

She laughed. "No. I made it up to see the look on your face. It's just a social get-together. Sometimes they have a speaker, Estella said, but there isn't one tonight."

"Pity. That would have taken some of the heat off."

"And at some stage they discuss business."

"What kind of business? Seriously. I want to know."

"Like the arrangements for the annual ball, which dances they need to learn. Stuff like that. All quite harmless. Brace up, Peter. I shouldn't have teased you."

"I need another beer."

"You don't. You need to be on top of your game—and I'm serious about that."

He knew she was right. The evening was his opportunity to learn things vital to the case. Unless his theory was rubbish, he was going to meet people who had known the skeleton when it was a living, breathing individual.

He'd cleared his plate and he couldn't have told you whether the pizza had been a Margherita or a Four Seasons.

"Let's get you into the clothes," Paloma said.

He was glad he'd tried them on before. This time they didn't feel quite so freakish. By the time he was in white stockings, breeches and floral waistcoat, it felt almost normal to put on the frock coat.

"Fine," Paloma said. "Just the shoes and the wig now."

"What time is it?" She'd persuaded him to remove his wristwatch.

"Almost time to go."

22

"You won't forget to pick me up at the end of the evening?"

"And leave you to walk home dressed as you are? It's tempting, but I'm not completely heartless."

"If you don't mind, I'll sit here a moment until I see someone else go in."

"In case it turns out to be one gigantic hoax? Peter, it can't be."

Paloma had slotted into a space in front of the north side of the Wood family's masterpiece, the three-storey Romanesque creation known originally as the King's Circus. The terraced building formed a circle broken only by the three roads that led into it. Romanesque? Imperial Rome had certainly been in John Wood the Elder's mind when he wrote the proposal announcing that the space in the middle would be used for "the exhibition of sports." Whether lions and Christians featured in his plan is less certain. He laid the foundation in 1754 and died the same year, after which his son, John Wood the Younger, oversaw the construction. Completion was 1767, so Beau Nash didn't live to see it. But the cream of society moved in, among them the prime minister William Pitt the Elder, the Earl of Chatham, the artist Thomas Gainsborough and Lord Robert Clive.

Diamond was still having doubts. "I keep asking myself

how I was shoehorned into this crazy situation. The head of CID dressed like this—it's a farce."

"You're wrong," Paloma said. "It does wonders for you. You look superb and everyone will respond."

"I know how my team would respond if they could see me."

"They'd respect you even more than they do already."

He went silent. He knew she was being positive. And how he needed the confidence she was trying to provide.

"Who suggested you came here—Georgina, wasn't it?"

"Suggested? She volunteered me. To be fair, she changed her mind later. She was thinking of sending someone else and that would have been pointless. I've got myself to blame for telling her so."

"That's to your credit, then. You're not a quitter. I think you're about to make a major breakthrough."

"I wish."

"If you find out who the skeleton must have been, you won't be complaining."

He nodded. Paloma's support was rock solid.

"And then you won't be far from naming his killer."

"Says you."

Suddenly his confidence-provider sounded a different note. "It could be one of the members."

"The murder was twenty years ago."

"They could still be around, couldn't they?"

"They could, but . . ."

"For God's sake be careful, Peter. You may be dressed up, but it's not a game. It's dangerous."

A large white minivan entered from Gay Street, glided around the central garden with its huge plane trees and came to a stop outside the house leased by the society. Like every other, this residence was fronted with twin Doric columns topped with a frieze decorated with serpents, nautical devices and emblems of the arts and sciences.

The van door slid aside and a woman in a huge hat looked out as if to make sure no one else was about. Self-conscious like me? Diamond speculated.

Her driver got out. He was in a modern suit.

Diamond recognised him. "That's Spearman, Sir Edward Paris's chauffeur. The woman must be Lady Paris."

"Watch this," Paloma said.

Lady Paris (if this was she) was having trouble getting through the door. She had to ease out by stages with the driver's help. He bent low and spread his arms and she giggled. The skirt was the problem. It had some kind of springy under-support.

"Is it a crinoline?" Diamond asked Paloma.

"No, they came later. It'll be a hoop dress, and difficult to manage. They were never made to travel in minivans."

Between them the lady and her chauffeur were coping, but dignity was difficult. The skirt swung up like a handbell when they finally pulled it free. Hoots of laughter. If this was indeed Lady Paris, she was no shrinking violet. At pavement level she spent some time rearranging the folds. Composed at last, she stepped up to the open door—fortunately as wide as any in Bath—and went inside.

"Okay, it's really happening. I believe you now." Diamond opened the car door.

"Walk tall, big man," Paloma said, "but keep your head down."

"Difficult—at the same time."

He braced himself and marched in.

His leather heels clattered on the stones of a black and white check stone floor that looked original. Loud voices were coming from ahead, so he moved on and found himself outside a room filled with chattering people in costume. One glimpse disposed of all doubts about the need for his wig, frock coat and breeches. Without the costume he would have been as out of place as a clown at a funeral.

"Do squeeze in if you can," someone said. She was in a hat shaped like a two-tier cakestand and he recognised her as the woman he'd just watched getting out of the minivan. Better start thinking of her as a lady if she was indeed Lady Paris. When she stepped back a little and pushed down on the hoops of her skirt to make room, he saw that the cakestand was topped with a round, stuffed fabric object made to look like a bun, with quite believable currants and flakes of sugar. A Bath bun, of course. These people didn't take themselves as seriously as he'd assumed.

"Thanks." But he was only able to take one step. Tube trains in the rush hour had more standing room.

She released the dress and the hidden hoop sprang up and lodged against his shins. "Don't back off," she said. "Touching is part of the fun."

"If you say so."

"You're new to this, aren't you? You must be Georgie's top detective. I was instructed to look out for you. I'm Sally, the Beau's ball and chain."

So this had to be Lady Paris. He managed a nod. "Peter Diamond."

"Gorgeous rug, Pete," Sally said, evidently meaning his wig. She was about his own age and already making him feel as if he should lighten up. "One like that gives a guy style. You could pass for George Washington. I wish my other half was allowed to sport a white one, but Beau Nash wore this long black shoulder-length thing that makes him look like Fred Basset, the cartoon dog. Don't laugh when you meet him. He'll bark if you do. He may bite."

Diamond felt sudden pressure on the backs of his knees. Someone else in a hoop dress was trying to enter the room.

Sally grabbed his arm and pulled him close. "It gets like this, I'm afraid. Every time anyone else comes into the room we all get more intimate, but you can relax. I defy anyone to go the whole way dressed like this."

Going the whole way hadn't crossed Diamond's mind. Right now he was trapped by whalebone digging into his lower limbs from front and back and it was uncomfortable. He edged sideways.

"Have I shocked you?" Sally said.

"No, ma'am. I'm trying for a better position."

A peal of laughter came from her. "If Ed hears that, it's pistols at dawn. You haven't met the old tosser, have you? I can't introduce you because he's way over the other side of the room."

"Actually I was told there are some senior members I ought to meet."

"You don't want to bother with them," she said. "Geriatrics. A man in his prime like you should be chatting up the girls."

A man in his prime? He enjoyed that, but he still had a job to do. "Seriously, that's why your husband invited me."

"You don't have to tell me, ducky. I was there. It's about the skeleton, isn't it? You think it could have been one of our members."

"That's only a theory," Diamond said. "It was wearing the clothes. And a long black wig. What happens when a new president takes over? Is the same costume handed on?"

"I've never heard that it is," Sally said. "No, that's ridiculous. Presidents come in all shapes and sizes. Orville Duff, the one Ed took over from, was a stick insect. Ed would never have got into his clothes."

"So they provide their own?"

"I suppose if the incoming Beau is short of a few pennies, he might enquire what happened to the last one's outfit, but that certainly didn't apply in Ed's case. Anyway, Orville died in office and you don't want to wear a dead man's clothes, do you?"

"Was he wearing them at the time?"

"That's not what I meant. And he didn't end up in a loft in Twerton."

"But the skeleton was dressed in a genuine eighteenth-century outfit."

"Really? Ed's was made in a sweatshop in Indonesia, far as I know."

"What about his wig?"

"Polyester. Take a look when you meet him." She shook with amusement. "It's far too shiny."

"So the wig doesn't get handed on either?"

"If I had my way it would get handed on to Oxfam. Yours is something else. Is it powdered?"

"It may be. Paloma—she's a friend—got it for me. She's quite an expert. Ouch." He felt more pressure on the backs of his calves. Someone else was trying to get into the room. He glanced over his shoulder and saw Estella. She winked and smiled.

"Sorry."

"Don't be," Diamond said. "Good to see you again."

"There you are," Sally said. "All the ladies want a piece of you, but I have you trapped."

He turned his head again. Estella was already talking to someone else. It was amusing listening to Sally, but he couldn't see any prospect of meeting the veterans he'd come to see. How did anyone get about in private houses in the eighteenth century when the women wore these vast skirts? The only movement possible was from fans being used by ladies. The air had become far too stuffy.

Like a mind reader, Sally answered his question. "This is the anteroom. We all transfer into the main reception room in a moment and then we can breathe again."

Already some movement at the other end was relieving the pressure. Soon he'd be able to look about and see if he recognised anyone.

"What happens in there?" he asked Sally.

"The meeting, hopefully short, and a chance to get a drink. You're not driving, are you?"

"No."

"Neither are we. Our chauffeur spends a boring evening waiting for us."

Some of the people behind them were now moving. Sally nudged him. "Come on. Use your elbows."

The main reception room had undergone some modern alterations, two fair-sized rooms opened up to become one, but whoever did the job had finished it in eighteenth-century style—a fine plastered ceiling and ormolu wall fittings with real lighted candles. The pictures were mostly copies, he guessed, several of people he recognised from the books he'd studied: Frederick, Prince of Wales, Princess Augusta, the Duchess of Marlborough, the Countess of Huntingdon, Ralph Allen, John Wood and of course Juliana Papjoy. The Beau himself wasn't on the wall. He was by the fireplace on a plinth in marble, a copy of the statue in the Pump Room.

"Grab a glass before the meeting starts," Sally told Diamond.

Footmen in blue and gold livery were circulating with trays of what looked like champagne, so he took her advice, moved about with glass in hand and got his first proper look at the membership. Difficult to recognise people in wigs and bonnets, but he spotted an ex-mayor, two headmasters, his own bank manager and two of the clergy from the Abbey.

Sally was in animated conversation, so he moved off to a distant corner where he could observe rather than socialise. A few chairs were provided along the walls, but it was clear that all but the old and infirm intended to remain standing. One thing he noticed had no possible bearing on the investigation. He'd thought it would be impossible for the women in their skirts to sit down, and then one managed it expertly by lifting the top hoop above her hips as she lowered herself on to the chair.

Near the fireplace someone thumped the wood floor with his stick to get attention and several of the company squeaked in surprise.

"Ladies and gentlemen, pray silence for the Beau."

An overweight man in a black wig waddled forward and one of the flunkeys helped him up to an antique footstool. Sir Edward Paris, ruddy-faced, double-chinned, full of his own importance. You needed to be self-assured in this company if your accent wasn't Oxbridge and his certainly wasn't.

"Everybody in? Right. Welcome one and all. We can get through this quick." He was speaking into a hand-held microphone, definitely not antique. "I'm going to start with a personal statement. I've been your Beau for the best part of twenty years now and I reckon it's time for some other mug to take over. That's a joke, about the mug. Don't take it personal."

No one laughed. The announcement had shocked everyone.

"But I'm not kidding about jacking it in."

Shock was turning to annoyance. It wasn't done for the Beau to quit.

"I know the last one died on the job, but there's nothing in the rules to say I have to go on till I drop dead."

"But there's a precedent." Someone spoke up in elegant vowel sounds obviously honed by generations of good breeding.

"A what?"

"A noteworthy precedent."

"I'm your noteworthy president in case you've forgotten."

A few polite laughs were heard. It was impossible to tell whether the pun had been intentional. Probably not, Diamond thought.

The well-bred man insisted on saying his piece. "The Beau, the original Beau, our revered Richard Nash, was still Master of Ceremonies when he departed this life. He collapsed over a card game in the Assembly Rooms. Four days later he was gone."

"So what's your point, Crispin?"

"Only, my dear Sir Edward, that nobody could possibly object if you chose to emulate the Beau and remain in office."

"My wife would. She wants her old man back."

This did earn some laughter.

Somebody else spoke from the back of the room. "Isn't there some question that Beau Nash was murdered? It was in all the papers the week before last."

"Rubbish," someone else shouted. "What do they know?"

"A skeleton wearing the Beau's clothes was found in a loft somewhere."

"Twerton," another voice said and caused more amusement.

"He'd been stabbed."

"How can they tell?"

"Regardless of how he met his death, my point stands," the well-bred man said. "He remained the Beau until the end of his life."

Ed was quick to say, "He would, wouldn't he? Nobody told me it was forever. I've got a life of my own and a business to run. I've done my bit and I want out, so I'm telling you now you'd better find someone to take over. Do I have a volunteer?"

Silence dropped like a capture net on the entire company.

Ed waited and asked, "Anyone up for it?"

Diamond was amused to see so many of the high-ups of Bath staring at the floor and plainly wishing they weren't high up at all and could fall straight through it.

The deadlock was ended only by one bold soul asking, "Does anyone know the latest on the skeleton?"

Ed said, "Hang on a bit. Are you lot deaf? You need a new Beau."

Then one of the clergy pointed out that it was customary in clubs and societies to invite nominations and have them proposed and seconded and then proceed to an election.

"It never happened when I got the job," Ed said. "Professor Plum went belly up and I was asked to take over next day, simple as that."

"Professor Plum?" someone queried.

Sally Paris spoke up. "He means Orville Duff, don't you, Ed?"

Ed wasn't there to talk about Duff. "How about you, vicar? You know how things are done. Do you want to be Beau?"

If the cleric had been asked to run naked up Milsom Street on a Saturday afternoon he couldn't have looked more horrified. "My ecclesiastical duties have to come first."

"Don't we have a constitution?" the well-bred man called Crispin asked. "We have our rules about dress and so forth. In fact, Beau Nash was famous for his rules."

"It's never arisen before," an older man said. "I suppose we're more feudal than democratic. We've always appointed a successor by invitation up to now."

"Because mugs like me stepped up to the plate," Ed said.

To which Lady Sally added, "Besides writing a large cheque to fund the building work when we took over this place."

"I don't want to give the wrong impression," Crispin said. "We're all immensely grateful for Sir Edward's generosity. Indeed the sheer scale of his largesse may account for our reluctance to volunteer."

Ed had misunderstood again, "My size has bog all to do with it." He looked round the room at all the uneasy faces. "Fair play, you weren't expecting me to give up. I sprang this on you. I'll do the honours one last time and you can decide among yourselves who stands on this soapbox next meeting, because it ain't going to be Ed Paris." He cleared his throat. "Next business, welcoming guests. Any takers?"

Some hands were raised and people were introduced.

The tension in the room had eased emphatically now that the prickly matter of the presidency was deferred.

Sally said something to her husband and he said, "Strewth. Almost forgot my own guest, Detective Dallymore from the Old Bill."

Sally was quick to correct him.

With some bluster, Ed resumed. "All right, all right. Now you see why you need a new Beau. I'm going soft in the head. My good lady tells me I should have said Detective Superintendent Diamond. Where *are* you, mate?"

Forced against all his instincts to break cover, Diamond raised his hand and said, "Peter will do."

"Peter it is. Welcome to the Beau Nash Society, Pete. And if some of you are asking yourselves how I come to be cosying up to the law all of a sudden, it's because he's the cop investigating the skeleton you was talking about just now. Ain't that the truth, Pete?"

The truth was that Diamond was in sudden danger of filling his breeches. He said, "Well, yes," and hoped the spotlight would shift.

It didn't. Some busybody said, "It sounds as if the Beau's guest is the ideal person to clear up the uncertainty about what actually happened at Twerton."

Oh no he wasn't.

Paloma's "Keep your head down" was a sick joke now.

To gain thinking time Diamond drained the champagne glass.

But Ed made a bad situation worse. "I'll hand you the mike, Pete. We'd all like to hear from you."

"There's nothing I can say," Diamond called across the room. "It's an ongoing investigation."

"Can't hear you," the busybody called out.

Ed had already stepped down from the stool and crossed the floor to where Diamond was. "Say something or they'll get stroppy."

Even the notoriously stubborn Peter Diamond wasn't proof against an audience of Bath's top people demanding a statement. He held the microphone to his mouth, "All I can tell you at this time is that the remains found in Twerton aren't those of Beau Nash. He's buried in the Abbey."

"The Abbey?" the man called Crispin said in disbelief. "I think you'll find the weight of opinion is against you. It's all over the internet that he ended up in a pauper's grave and no one seems to know exactly where."

Somebody who'd drunk too much shouted, "Twerton."

"You don't want to believe everything you read on the internet," Diamond said. "Go back to the original reports of the funeral as we did. They all say he was buried in the Abbey."

"Where does the story that he was a pauper come from, then?"

"I've no idea and I don't have the time or inclination to find out."

"It's not just the internet. I've seen it in books."

"I'm sorry, but the books are wrong. This is one of a number of myths about Nash that don't stand up to examination."

Ed was still at Diamond's side. He was rubbing his hands with anticipation. "What else is there? Now you've started, you'd better tell us."

Everything Diamond said was being amplified, seeming to lend authority to his statements. Ed was right. He couldn't really back down. So against all his best intentions he found himself giving the Beau Nash Society the truth about another bit of moonshine: the story that the Beau's former mistress Juliana Papjoy resurfaced when the Beau was old and infirm and came back to Bath to nurse him. "For the romantics among you, I'm sorry to spoil a happy ending," he said, "but in spite of what most of the biographies say, there's no evidence whatever that she came back.

We looked at original sources. For the last twenty years of his life he was under the thumb of a woman called Mrs. Hill, who by all accounts gave him a hard time. As for Juliana, she turned eccentric and lived out the rest of her life in the hollowed-out trunk of an oak tree."

Crispin hadn't been silenced. "You seem to be well informed, sir. 'No evidence whatever,' you say. How do you account for the notice outside the restaurant that was once the Beau's house stating—and I quote from memory—that 'they lived the whole of the latter part of their lives here until the Beau's death in 1761'?"

"It wasn't me who put it up."

"But the restaurant was known as Popjoy's until it changed hands."

"Yes, they spelt the name wrong as well," Diamond said. He was hitting raw nerves here. A few people smiled, but there were hostile faces out there as well.

Crispin said, "I don't know if you're aware that some of us are acknowledged experts on Nash."

Then a woman's voice cut in and this time it wasn't Sally's. "Mr. Diamond is right. Juliana never lived with him in the Sawclose house. He dumped her in 1743 when his fortune declined. She declared she'd never sleep in a bed again and went back to Warminster and lived in the tree and they never met again. You can read about that in the annual register for 1777."

Diamond looked to see where the unexpected support had come from.

Estella, bless her heart.

Considering she hadn't been in the society long, speaking out had required real courage.

"Are you sure of this?" Crispin demanded.

"I'm writing a new biography using primary sources," she said. "Believe me, I can endorse every word Mr. Diamond has spoken."

Ed took back the microphone and he was grinning. "Satisfied, Crispin? Some of us oldies can learn a few things from the younger generation."

Crispin wasn't done. "Perhaps she'd like to take over as Beau," he said in a sarcastic aside that caused some amusement.

"Good suggestion. Why not?" Ed said in all seriousness.

Crispin's voice shrilled in astonishment. "Because you can't have a female Beau. I was being facetious."

Sally Paris immediately took up the cause. "You can have a Belle instead. If none of the men are interested in stepping up, let's see how a woman manages, that is, if Estella is willing to stand."

Gasps came from some of the members. The pace of proceedings was more than they could cope with.

Ed looked towards Estella. "How about it, young lady? Would you care to be the Belle?"

"I don't know. Are you serious?" Estella said.

"Look at me. I'm not kidding."

"He means it, my dear," Sally said.

Ed said, "I can already see it on the cover of your book: Estella Rockingham, President of the Beau Nash Society."

Estella took a deep breath. "I'll need to think about it—and in fairness so should all of you. This would be a major change."

"A revolution," Sally said. "I'm all for it. If anyone wants to stand against you, we can have an election."

Estella was shaking her head at the speed of what was happening, but the mood of most members seemed to be positive.

Ed said, "We won't rush you. Take your time and let me know. And if anyone else thinks of putting up, we'll work out what happens next." He beamed at his audience and said in a blur of words that no one could interrupt, "Any other business? I thought not. In the absence of any other business I declare the meeting closed. That's the formal bit over. Let's get back to the fizz and fun."

Diamond went over to Estella and thanked her for the support. "Nobody believed what I was saying. The whole atmosphere changed after you said your piece. How do you feel about taking over from Sir Edward?"

"I can't believe it," she said. "I'm not at all sure they mean it."

"They do."

"Why didn't anyone else volunteer? Is it a poisoned chalice?"

"Looking at Ed, it isn't. How long has he held the post—almost twenty years? That's a long stint. I expect he made some useful contacts."

"This lot won't be easy to manage," she said. "There were a few discordant voices."

"You can boss them, I'm sure. You know more about Beau Nash than any of them. My guess is that this society isn't all it claims to be. A lot of them only come for the dressing-up and being seen here."

She smiled. "I'd already formed the same opinion."

"Go for it, then. And now I must have a word with Sir Edward."

He went over to where the Parises were chatting with friends.

Ed broke off in mid-conversation and became playful. "Ah, the law has caught up with us. You've got me bang to rights, officer. Loitering with intent to tell a dirty joke. If I plead guilty will I get off with a warning?"

"If it's one I haven't heard, you're in the clear," Diamond said. "But I'm ready to meet one or two of your long-serving members. You told my boss you'd fix it."

"'One or two' was an overestimate. I found the only one who was here before I joined and he's a basket case."

All the anticipation drained like water in sand. Had

this entire pantomime been a waste of time? "Can't he help?"

"We'll see."

Pausing only to take another glass of champagne from a passing footman, Ed carved a way through the throng to where an elderly man in a wheelchair seemed to be stranded inside a stockade of hooped skirts. The chair was a cumbersome contraption made of wicker with three metal wheels.

The basket case.

At least twice the length of a modern invalid chair, it had a capacious black canvas hood, fortunately folded.

"Is that an authentic bath chair?"

"Depends what you mean by authentic," Ed said. "It's a bath chair, yes, but they didn't have them in Nash's time. It's Victorian."

Diamond was impressed by Ed's bit of knowledge. Don't underestimate this guy, he told himself. "Does he know that?"

"Algy? You can bet your bottom dollar he does, but we turn a blind eye. He can't stand on his own two pins any more, poor old bugger, and the scooter he uses normally would look even more out of place. He's wearing the kosher costume, as you see."

"How did disabled people get around in those days?"

"Sedan chairs, but we don't have one here. The bath chair's old-fashioned and it does the job. No one is going to make an issue of it. We don't want to hurt his feelings, so it's kept here for him in a shed out the back." He called out to Algy, "Before you leave, old sport, can you spare a couple of minutes for my guest?"

Algy responded at once—and sounded normal. "Can he spare a couple of minutes for me?"

"Why? What's up?"

"I need to get to the accessible toilet. It's urgent."

"You've got it made." Ed winked at Diamond before

turning back to Algy. "Pete's your man. Trained for all emergencies, aren't you, Pete? First on the left through the far door."

"I'm obliged to you," Algy said.

Algy may have been obliged, but Diamond wasn't. The unwieldy chair on its iron wheels had to be tugged from the front rather than pushed, and its occupant was distinctly overweight.

"So I'll leave you fellows to it," Ed said and darted back to his friends.

The next minutes were ones Diamond would want to erase from his memory. The only way he could get the chair moving was by going backwards, bending double and dragging it, apologising each time his rear connected with someone. Having forced a passage through the crowded room and found the disabled toilet, he learned with relief that Algy could cope inside with the aid of the grab rails, so he stepped outside to stand guard. With the chair jammed inside, there was no way Algy could work the lock.

Diamond wasn't expecting the shout from inside that followed. Apprehensive of what he would be asked to do next, he opened the door a fraction.

"A certain item is missing in here."

The emergency could have been worse, but couldn't be ignored. The head of CID had faced many situations in his long experience. Stopping all comers to ask where the spare toilet rolls were kept was a first, made all the more odd with everyone in costume. Eventually he was directed to a bathroom upstairs.

"You're a credit to the force," Algy said from inside when Diamond returned with two spare rolls and handed them discreetly round the door. "I'm on the police authority for Avon and Somerset and I shall make a point of mentioning this at our next meeting."

"I'd rather you didn't," Diamond said.

"Perhaps you're right. It would take some explaining."

"Give me a shout when you're ready to move again."

"You don't mind waiting?"

After all this effort, Diamond wasn't going away. The spark of consolation from the episode was that Algy appeared to have his wits about him. But was he savvy enough to remember events from twenty years back?

"We can talk out here," Diamond said when he'd eventually tugged the chair and its occupant into the hallway.

"Are you tired of lugging me about?"

"It's not that. We'll hear each other better."

"Generally it takes two to haul me into the meeting in this contraption. I read somewhere that they used donkeys or ponies originally."

Diamond didn't want to know about the history of the bath chair. A far more urgent bit of history needed to be discussed.

"You've been a member for many years, I was told."

"At least a quarter of a century."

"So you've seen several presidents come and go."

"Not as many as you might imagine. Sir Edward has been Beau for most of my time in the society."

"And before him?"

"Professor Orville Duff, who was quite an expert on eighteenth-century Bath. A different character altogether than Ed, much more reserved. He died, unfortunately. He was about the age I am now, so I suppose he'd had a good innings. His health hadn't been good for some time. He wasn't our Beau for long. About eighteen months, no longer."

This checked with earlier information. Algy's memory seemed to be dependable.

Encouraged, Diamond asked, "Do you recall any earlier presidents?"

"Only one other. Before Orville we had Lord David Deganwy."

"Is that Welsh?"

"I suppose it might have been. I didn't know David well. He was another generation, well into his eighties when I joined and he'd lived in Bath most of his life and had been Beau for a number of years. Kindly as they come—too kind, as it turned out."

"Why?"

"Someone took advantage—and none of us saw it coming."

"What happened?"

"A fellow called Sidney Harrod came to one of our meetings out of the blue and announced he was keen to join, so we welcomed him on spec as we always do when a new person arrives. We don't ask for a subscription right away. A few spare costumes are kept in a wardrobe upstairs and Sidney borrowed one and settled into the society as if he'd been a member all his life. Extremely sociable, charming with the ladies and passably knowledgeable about Nash."

They were interrupted by a limping woman in a hoop dress looking for the disabled toilet, but too timid to ask. Algy turned in his chair and pointed. She nodded her thanks and scuttled in.

Diamond got back to business. "Do you remember what year this was?"

"Funnily enough, I do, because I had a special birthday that year: 1996. Sidney hadn't been coming long when he offered to teach us eighteenth-century dancing. Someone told me he was a former chorus boy. I don't know if it was true—or if anything he claimed was true—but he was supposed to have been in some of the big West End musicals in his youth. *The King and I, Half a Sixpence.* The dancing was his route into the society. He offered to teach us the minuet, which was by far the most popular dance in its day and quite terrifying because it was supposed to be performed by one couple in front of the entire company. Sidney did the research and taught us in a tumbledown community centre in Walcot. The idea was that we should become proficient enough to introduce dancing to the annual ball—and that's become a tradition now—so we can thank him for that, I suppose."

"Something went wrong?"

"Not at the start. Between ourselves, the society had become rather dull as David Deganwy got older. Up to that time we'd been mainly sedentary, with talks by experts on this and that, but no participation except for the dressing up. Sidney Harrod came in with new ideas that revitalised us. We learned posture and bowing and curtseying and some of the games they played in Nash's day. We had music. We went on visits. And the dancing lessons really took off when we progressed to country dancing. Very saucy, some of those country dances," Algy reminisced from his bath chair. "*Johnny Cock Thy Beaver, Cuckolds All in a Row, Rub Her Down with Straw.*"

Privately, Diamond was thinking he wouldn't have wanted to come within a mile of Sidney's dancing lessons, but then he would never have joined the society in the first place. "He knew his stuff, then?"

"We believed so. He must have had some background in dancing to carry it off as he did. Looking back, he may not have been the expert he claimed to be. I rather think he clued himself up on the dances and convinced us all by force of personality. He was extremely plausible."

A waiter with a silver tray loaded with sweetmeats came rushing towards the main reception room and almost tripped over the end of the bath chair. Algy put out a hand to steady him.

Diamond ignored the interruption. "What age would this Sidney have been?"

"Difficult to tell. Sixty to seventy, I'd say. He made a big thing out of being one of the Harrod family, as if he had some link with the department store, but his day clothes certainly weren't from Harrods. He was slightly shabby, in fact. But, oh boy, he talked like a millionaire, claimed to have gone through Harrow School and Oxford and was a member of several London clubs. A great name-dropper. Anyway, he was a dynamo compared to most of us. I don't think anyone would have objected if he'd become the next Beau."

Diamond was galvanised. "Was that ever a possibility?"

"It damned nearly happened. He befriended David."

"This is Lord David Deganwy?"

Algy nodded. "We should have seen it coming, but the blighter was so persuasive he took us all in and most of all he took in David."

"How?"

"We only learned about this later. He used to visit him in Widcombe Hall and take away items of antique furniture supposedly to get them cleaned or repaired. Of course, David never saw them again. The poor old lad was losing his memory as well as his furniture and Sidney took full advantage."

Diamond had come across parasites like Sidney Harrod many times before. People are so easily taken in.

"When did you find this out?"

"Too late, I'm sorry to say. At a meeting one evening— this would have been early in 1997—David announced to us all that he planned to hand over the presidency of the society at the end of the year because it was becoming a burden to him rather than a pleasure. He said he would be putting forward Sidney's name as the next Beau."

"Really? Someone as new as that?"

"To be candid, most of us were rather relieved that someone else's name was put forward. We weren't queuing up for the honour. We agreed it would be the best possible outcome."

"There were no suspicions about Sidney?"

"Not at that time. He'd made himself very agreeable, never missed a meeting and appeared to be a Beau Nash fanatic like the rest of us, but with a sense of fun. He once gave us a talk on the Beau's witty sayings—a book of them was published after Nash died—but to be brutally honest, eighteenth-century humour hasn't stood the test of time, so we were enjoying Sidney's wit rather than the Beau's. I do remember the session as hugely entertaining."

"So Sidney was all set to succeed Lord Deganwy as the Beau?"

"That was the intention and nobody objected, but it never happened. Between David's announcement and the meeting when we were supposed to welcome Sidney as our new president, he vanished."

"Sidney Harrod did?"

"Yes, without a word of explanation to David or any of us. Simply disappeared into thin air. We were all completely mystified. He wasn't answering phone calls and his landlady said he hadn't spoken to her about going. In fact, he owed six months' rent. Only later did it emerge that he'd been steadily disposing of David's furniture. He even took off with David's Beau Nash costume, which was genuine eighteenth-century and extremely valuable."

A genuine eighteenth-century costume stolen by a man who had gone missing more than twenty years ago? It ticked a lot of boxes.

"You just mentioned his landlady. Who was she?"

"I can't answer that. I only heard about it later, at third hand. I've no idea where his lodgings were."

"Didn't you report this swindler to the police?"

"Me?"

"All of you."

Algy shook his head. "There was this period of uncertainty that lasted several months. When he missed one meeting without explanation, we didn't think anything of it. David Deganwy was increasingly confused and when the next meeting came and David didn't turn up either, we asked Orville Duff to take over on a temporary basis. He was a good man, was Orville. He called on David and pieced together what had happened. That's how we learned about Sidney's appalling behaviour. Poor old David was succumbing to dementia. He couldn't be sure whether he'd voluntarily handed over the things to that thieving scoundrel. Anyway, the furniture went, the costume went, and so did Sidney."

"Was the wig taken as well?"

"The black Beau Nash wig? I believe it was," Algy said. "David was in poor health by then and died soon after."

Behind them the toilet door opened and the limping woman emerged and glided by without making eye contact.

"Was any more heard of Sidney Harrod?"

"Not a whisper. I suppose he did what conmen do and moved away to some other city to start up under a new identity."

Diamond didn't comment. He had his own opinion where Sidney had ended up. "Were his lodgings in Twerton, by any chance?"

"I already said I couldn't tell you."

"So the police were never informed?"

"Not to my knowledge."

"And Professor Duff took over?"

"He died in office, too, not long after. Lung cancer."

"Does anyone have pictures of these guys? Does the club keep a photo album of the annual balls?"

"I've never seen one. However, we do have the portraits of past presidents. Didn't you notice them in the anteroom?"

"It was such a crush in there I didn't see anything like that. I'll take a look presently. There won't be one of Sidney, I guess."

"Emphatically not. He's persona non grata."

"You said he was about seventy."

"Yes."

"Do you have any memory of his teeth?"

Algy blinked at the question. "Not particularly."

"Is it possible he had false teeth?"

He tapped his forehead as if it was a cash dispenser supplying memories rather than banknotes. "They may well have been false. He was a good-looking man for his age, I have to admit."

"Are you picturing him right now?"

"The smile. He was constantly smiling. Regular teeth certainly, but I couldn't say for sure whether they were artificial. That's the whole point of modern dentistry, isn't it, to make them appear real? I've had some implants myself."

"I'm not talking implants. I mean a complete set of dentures he could remove when he wished."

Algy plainly didn't know.

"Is there anyone else among the current members who was around at the time?"

After a moment's thought, Algy said, "I'm sorry. I believe I'm the only one left. Even Ed Paris wasn't in the society then. I expect you were hoping for someone sharper than me. I haven't been much help."

"You've been a fantastic help." Diamond hadn't given up on the possibility of finding a photo of Sidney Harrod. "Were the press invited to the annual ball?"

"The local press, you mean? I don't think we were reported in the *Bath Chronicle* but there was a glossy magazine called *Bath City Life* that covered all kinds of social events and sometimes we got into that. You might even find a picture of him there."

"We can try. He was probably smart enough to dodge the camera. What height was he?"

"Average."

"Did he have much hair?"

"I couldn't tell you. We all wore wigs for the meetings. I know exactly why you're interested and I wish I could tell you more. Tantalising, isn't it?"

"That's one way of putting it," Diamond said.

23

"**B**efore you say anything, guv, you'd better brace yourself," Ingeborg told him when he walked into the CID room next morning as chirpy as a sparrow at first light.

Then he saw the worry lines on Ingeborg's face.

"Why?"

"A call from Dr. Waghorn about the piece of bone John Leaman dug up at Twerton." She paused, looked into his suddenly hostile eyes and almost took a step away. "It's not human."

He'd tried to prepare for bad news as she'd suggested, and still the shock came like a kick in the stomach. "What is it, then?"

"Sheep."

"Get away."

"Really. It was from a sheep. Our theory about the wife being murdered and buried there isn't looking too good this morning."

"Hell."

"Apparently the bulbous bit at the head of the femur is roughly similar in size and shape although the shaft is longer in a human."

"Waghorn is certain?"

"You know him better than I do. He sounded very sure on the phone. And horribly smug."

"So you took the call yourself?"

"John wasn't in, so I got the full blast. What a smart-arse. He was going on about osteons, which evidently contain the channels or canals carrying the blood supply through the bone. Under the microscope he was able to make measurements proving that the bone wasn't human."

"Why would a sheep be buried in a garden?"

"The dog."

"Sheep, you said."

"I'm trying to answer your question," Ingeborg said through gritted teeth, showing she was feeling frayed herself. "Waghorn also said the femur showed signs of being chewed by a carnivore. I'm thinking of Tank's dog. Tank the squatter. His greyhound, remember? They were living in the Twerton house and dogs like nothing better than burying old bones. My guess is that the dog was given a mutton bone to chew on and it dug a hole and buried it at the bottom of the garden."

He made a sound deep in his throat not unlike a growl. "I knew that dog was trouble from the moment it slobbered over my trousers."

"You can't blame the dog for burying a bone," Ingeborg chided him. "If anyone is to blame, it's me. I was pushing the idea of the woman being murdered."

"My decision to dig up the garden. How is John Leaman taking it?"

"He doesn't know yet." Her face creased into a pained look. "I couldn't bring myself to phone him."

"Where is he?"

"He drove out to Twerton early to check on the crime scene people."

"Christ, are they still there?"

"John made sure they were. He was cracking the whip all of yesterday expecting more finds. All they dug up were fragments of bone." She sighed. "Poor old John. He's so excited to be in charge, like a dog with a—" She stopped in mid-sentence, angry with herself. "You know what I mean."

Her sympathy had to be deep-felt for the rivalries within the team to be set aside. Diamond, too, ached for his earnest colleague. "I'll go directly and see him. Is there anything else I should be told?"

"It can wait."

Leaman was in conversation with the senior crime scene specialist when Diamond ducked under the tape and picked a path through the heaps of excavated earth.

The man was cheerful, untypically, alarmingly, distressingly cheerful. "You should be in boots, guv. That's another pair of shoes you'll have to clean."

"Doesn't matter."

"We've almost cracked it now."

"Have we?"

"The house-to-house has brought a result. The lads found a retired newsagent living over one of the shops and he remembers Harry coming in sometimes for the *Daily Mail*. Our suspect was definitely called Harry, by the way, and the woman he was living with was Sarah."

"Okay," Diamond said wondering how on earth he could let the man down without too much hurt.

"Harry and Sarah, guv. The names are confirmed."

"Right."

Leaman gave him a puzzled look before resuming. "They didn't have much to say, either of them. The guy—Harry, I mean—was in his thirties, white, with dark hair, average height, always paid in cash rather than card, and didn't have much to say for himself. The woman was friendlier, quite a bit younger, nice-looking, with long reddish-brown hair, but she suddenly wasn't seen again and no one knew why. I didn't tell him we have our suspicions. This was in 1997, the year Labour were elected. Harry carried on living alone in the place for at least two more years before Jerzy the Pole took over the tenancy."

"Good. That could be helpful."

"I've asked for another check of the soil. If we can find some hair of the right colour, that will clinch it."

"Mm."

"You don't sound all that pleased. Is something up?"

"I wanted a few words, John."

The effect of the few words was pitiful to witness. Leaman turned deathly pale. He shook his head. His mouth shaped to say something and no words came.

It was left to the crime scene man to utter the obscenity the bombshell demanded.

"I look at it this way," Diamond tried to say in mitigation. "It's a violent death we all believed must have happened, but didn't. That's good news. Harry's woman isn't buried here. She must have left him of her own free will."

The crime scene man said in support, "It isn't the first time I've been called out to deal with an animal bone. Generally you can tell with a quick look. A complete femur from a sheep is going to be shorter, but of course this was just the end piece."

Diamond was moved to put his arm round Leaman's drooping shoulders. "My mistake, not yours. Don't take it personally."

Leaman stared ahead, still lost for words.

Diamond tried to bolster him. "I need you back at the office. We may have identified the skeleton."

His words made no impact at all.

"You're more likely than anyone to discover what the hell went on here."

The crime scene man said bitterly, "We re-dug every inch of the fucking garden."

"And it had to be done," Diamond said without sympathy. Right now he couldn't deal with a second malcontent.

"This is still the most likely crime scene, but the focus has shifted now."

Some of his earlier words had finally penetrated the avalanche of blighted hopes that had crushed his wretched colleague. "Have you put a name to the skeleton?"

"Kind of. We're not there yet." He was casting around for something to alleviate the pain and by some miracle he thought of it. "Which is why you're urgently needed. Shall we go?"

The task of locating a picture of the conman Sidney Harrod was high priority and well suited to Leaman's skills. A complete run of *Bath City Life* had been located in the Central Library. After Diamond had briefed him about Harrod's likely theft of the eighteenth-century costume owned by Lord Deganwy, Leaman drove to the library with a recovering sense of purpose to search every issue between 1990 and 2000. He would look for photos of Beau Nash Society events and scan them into his computer. With the stimulus of a new assignment, the hurt of losing his status as Senior Investigating Officer would ease a little. Once the file was complete he would return to Concorde House and produce an electronic rogues' gallery of likely candidates.

The result would be shown to Algy, the key witness.

That was the plan.

Meanwhile Diamond briefed the team.

"This man who called himself Sidney Harrod is by far the most likely individual yet to be our skeleton. He was a conman and his mark was an elderly man, Lord Deganwy, who seems to have been suffering from dementia. Harrod befriended the old man and allegedly took away a number of bits of antique furniture and we don't know what else apart from the genuine eighteenth-century suit and wig that we believe our skeleton was dressed in."

"How do we know it wasn't sold on?" Paul Gilbert asked. "The skeleton could be someone else."

"We don't until we can prove Harrod is our man. The age is about right, the height is similar and he may well have worn dentures."

"Is there a definite link to Twerton?"

There wasn't and everyone knew it. "That's something yet to be established. We need everything we can get on Harrod. It won't be easy. Algy has told me all he remembers. I'll be asking him to look at some old photos of the annual ball and see if he can pick Harrod out. John Leaman is assembling a file at this minute."

"Isn't there anyone else who may have known him?" Keith Halliwell asked.

"In the Beau Nash Society? No."

"His landlord?"

"From twenty years ago?" Ingeborg said. "Where do you start?"

"We definitely need a picture of the guy," Halliwell said. "Get it into the media for the public to see."

"If one exists," Diamond said. "A clever conman won't have stepped forward and said cheese when a photographer came by."

"And if there isn't a photo?"

"He was living in the city for the best part of two years and using the name of Sidney Harrod. There must be some trace of him."

"He won't have registered as an elector," Gilbert said.

"But he was sociable. He may have been known in clubs and pubs. You're going to groan, but we ask around. Another possibility is the public library."

"The *library*?" Halliwell said as if it was the townswomen's guild.

"This was a con artist aiming to crash the Beau Nash Society. Where would he have gone for his information?"

"The Internet?"

"Would that lot have had a website in 1996? Do they even have one now? I've never seen one. It's not that kind of organisation. I think he'd ask at the library, the ideal place to mug up on Nash. He had to be well in command to give them a lecture on the Beau's humour, as he did." Diamond's eyes fixed on DC Gilbert. "Paul."

"Guv?"

"There's a book called *The Jests of Beau Nash*. They should have a copy in the reference section, not for taking out."

"Would anyone bother to take it out?" Halliwell said.

"I know what you're saying," Diamond said. "It's not Peter Kay, but that's to our advantage. The book has a rarity value. The library would insist he signs for it, just to have a read. Ask to see their records."

Paul Gilbert didn't look convinced. He'd spent most of the previous day fruitlessly going through records at the university to see if Perry Morgan had been a student. He gave a nod.

Ingeborg started reading aloud from her iPhone. "'*The Jests of Beau Nash, late master of the ceremonies at Bath, consisting of a variety of humorous sallies, smart repartees and bon mots which passed between him and persons of the first distinction . . .*'" She paused before adding, "You can buy it as a reprint on Amazon for £13.99. In paperback."

Most of the team sniggered, if not chuckled. What had got into them this morning? Not one of them was showing the seriousness Diamond demanded. He could only suppose they were overworked dealing with two murders at once.

For an uncomfortable moment he had a return of that eerie sensation that Beau Nash himself had put the mockers on this investigation and was sitting at the back of the room in his white three-cornered hat and fancy frock coat with a grin spreading across his fat face.

Get a grip, Diamond told himself. "We're not wanting to read the bloody book. We only want to know if Harrod signed for it."

"If he did, he likely used another name," Halliwell said.

"We still check."

"It will be so much easier when we get a picture of the guy."

"Don't raise your hopes." This wasn't going well. He was out on a limb. After a pause, he said, "We also feed the name into the PNC. He may have used the same identity in some other place. Would you see to that, Inge?"

"If you don't mind me saying, guv, we're clutching at straws."

"It's either that, or drown."

"When you think about it," Ingeborg added, "this is the victim we're trying to identify. We haven't even started on the killer."

"Hold on," he said. "We're dealing in probabilities. We're ninety percent sure Sidney Harrod is the victim and Harry, the tenant in the Twerton house, is the killer. Nothing less than certainty will do, which is why I'm asking for more effort."

"Meanwhile," Ingeborg said, "we're working our butts off trying to find who shot Perry Morgan."

Diamond didn't say any more. He could have threatened them with DCI Charlie Crocker taking over the Morgan case. When he'd mentioned the possibility to Ingeborg before, she'd spooked. He wasn't sure if she'd alerted the others. But they *were* at full stretch and they didn't deserve more grief.

Before returning to his office he stared across the desks and computers and made quite sure no stranger in eighteenth-century costume had been listening in. He'd got the shakes. The team didn't know he was under more stress than any of them.

That afternoon he and John Leaman drove out to the house on the Warminster Road where Algy Sutton had a ground-floor flat. When the most senior member of the Beau Nash Society came to the door he was in a modern wheelchair called a Blazer, electrically powered, compact and capable of turning on a five-pence coin, a vast improvement on the bath chair. His clothes, too, were more suited to modern life: a turtleneck sweater and black cord pants.

"We'd like to show you some photos taken at the 1996 and 1997 balls," Diamond said after they had been invited into a small front room hung with souvenirs of travel in Africa and Asia. "We're hoping Sidney Harrod is there."

"Don't you worry," Algy said, taking reading glasses from his pocket. "I'll spot him if he is."

Leaman opened the laptop and accessed the file he'd prepared. "*Bath City Life* showed twelve shots of the event in 1996 and fourteen the following year. We know you were there because you're in both sets."

"Standing on my own two feet in those days," Algy said. "Do you want me to name people?"

"Only Harrod," Diamond said.

The first shot was on the screen, two women either side of a tall man in a white wig and frock coat. Regrettably the quality of the image was poor compared to modern high-resolution photography. The colour brown was dominant.

"He'd be wearing a wig like this, rather than a black one, I take it," Diamond said.

"Yes, indeed. He was never the Beau," Algy said. "But that's not him. That's Austen Carmichael, God rest his soul." He'd already forgotten that names weren't needed.

Leaman moved the picture aside. Another took its place, this time of two men facing each other and holding drinks.

"No," Algy said.

Quickly he rejected the next few.

"Wait." He leaned forward to examine a shot of six

men. "Did I really look like that twenty years ago? I was overweight even then."

"Say the word and I can zoom in on any of them," Leaman said.

"Don't zoom in on me, whatever you do. Actually I recognise them all and Sidney isn't among them." If nothing else, Algy's brain seemed to be up to the task.

Two more went through and Leaman said, "That's all there is from 1996."

"Onwards and upwards," Diamond said, trying to be positive.

The 1997 pictures featured several people familiar from the previous set. One group included an elderly man in a long black wig. "Now that's David Deganwy," Algy said. "He looks out of it already, poor old darling."

"Is this in focus?" Diamond said to Leaman. "Can you get it any clearer?"

"It's about as good as it gets, guv. The pictures in the magazine weren't the sharpest."

Squinting at the screen, Diamond tried masking the other figures with his hands to concentrate on Lord Deganwy. "The waistcoat he's wearing looks awfully like the one our skeleton had on, what you can see of it. Do those look like oak leaves to you?"

"Are you asking me?" Algy said.

"Either of you."

"I can zoom in a bit," Leaman offered, but the picture still wasn't all that clear. "Is that a button or an acorn?"

"Acorn," Algy said. "It's not in line with the other buttons."

"If we printed this out, I could look at it under magnification," Diamond said. He was trying to think of a circumstance in which Lord Deganwy could have been the skeleton in spite of all the evidence to the contrary.

"You'd do better looking at the original magazine

picture," Leaman said. "But I think you're right. They're oak leaves and acorns."

"I thought you were interested in Sidney Harrod," Algy said.

"We are," Diamond said, wrenching himself back to the real point of the exercise.

"And we're getting to the end," Leaman said.

Algy sighed. "I'm a dead loss as a witness."

"If he isn't among them, it's not your fault," Diamond said.

The final shot came on screen.

"Afraid not," Algy said. "Can I offer you a sherry?"

Diamond could almost hear John Leaman grinding his teeth. Another line of enquiry had come to nothing. "Run them through again, John. There are shadowy figures in the background of some. We were concentrating on the ones in focus."

The second run-through was slower. Leaman worked the zoom facility to feature sections they might have missed, but there were limits to the technology dealing with pictures scanned from a magazine and they soon went out of focus.

"Frustrating," Algy said. "He would have been there somewhere. He definitely attended the balls."

"Stay with it."

Another group from 1996 came up. "That's obviously a footman behind them," Algy said. "You can see the tray of drinks."

"How about the man in the foreground with his back to the camera?" Diamond asked.

"Impossible to tell. There isn't enough of him."

The only part of the figure properly in shot was the hand curled around a champagne glass. The head and wig were a blur in the top left of the screen.

Leaman dragged the next image across.

"Wait," Algy said. "Go back to the man holding the glass."

He whistled softly when it reappeared. "Look at the hand. Can you make it any larger?"

"We'll lose some definition," Leaman said.

"Hold it there, then," Algy said. "Would you mind handing me the laptop?"

Leaman did so.

Algy held the screen six inches from his face and then passed it to Diamond. "You have a look. Funny."

Diamond studied the screen and saw that something was indeed funny, but not laughable. It was funny in the sense of odd. Most of that right hand was obscured by the lace sleeve, yet the fingers clutching the glass were visible and one—the forefinger—was only a stump below the knuckle.

Algy said, "The things you forget over the years. If I'd had my wits about me I would have told you yesterday. It's only just come back to me that Sidney Harrod had most of his right forefinger missing. This must be him."

Diamond wasn't sure whether to hug him or thump him.

Here was the defining detail they needed—and it should have come so much more quickly.

In the autopsy, Dr. Waghorn had spoken about the forefinger of the right hand, telling his audience not to be deceived when they saw on screen that the skeleton was incomplete. He'd explained the absence of two sections of finger—calling them phalanxes—by saying they must have been lost when the skeleton was hoisted from the roof. Of far more interest, the anthropologist had said, was the left hand, and he'd gloried in pointing out the tiny nick he'd found, the proof of a defensive wound.

To be fair to Waghorn, the left hand *was* the more interesting. But in his keenness to show his discovery, he had made a wrong assumption about the other hand. The missing bones from the right hand hadn't been lost in the recovery operation. They were missing already.

"Have you got your phone with you, John?" Diamond asked.

Leaman produced it and tapped the screen.

"Can you find a picture of the skeleton?"

"This one?"

"Not that one, for pity's sake."

He'd brought up the infamous cherry-picker shot that had been in all the newspapers.

"Sorry. It's my wallpaper."

"Your *what*?"

Leaman didn't explain. He instantly replaced the offensive image with multiple tiny pictures and selected the skeleton seated in its chair in the partly demolished loft. "Will this one do?"

"Okay. Let's have a look. Can we zoom in on the right hand?"

No question: the hand bones resting on the faded wool of the breeches were incomplete. The forefinger ended at the first joint. And the shot had been taken before the skeleton was moved.

"This clinches it for me," Diamond said. "Sidney Harrod is our man."

24

Paul Gilbert drove to the Podium car park and rode the escalator to the Central Library, a place he rarely visited. Books didn't interest him much. In fact, he felt uncomfortable confronted by so many. He was only here because the boss had picked him for this. Much as he respected Peter Diamond, he didn't have any confidence that the conman who called himself Sidney Harrod had come here twenty-odd years ago, and he was willing to bet there wouldn't be any record of it.

The place was open plan and the reference section was at the far end, with rows of desks occupied mostly by students. He looked for a librarian his own age—which probably wasn't a wise decision. The young woman he approached must have been an infant when Harrod was supposed to have used the library, but she was friendly and willing to check. Unsurprisingly she found nothing on her computer. "We do keep paper records from that time," she told him, and insisted on going off to some storeroom to look for them.

He found a rack of magazines while he waited and was leafing through the latest *Autocar* when his help came back, pushing a trolley loaded with ring binders. Thirty years of written requests to consult rare books were all recorded in loose-leaf files.

"Are you going to leave me to it?" he asked with a bleak look.

"It's okay," she said. "It's my job to check these. Data protection. I brought them out here because I didn't want to spend an hour or more going through them and finding you'd got bored and gone away."

Would he have been so ill-mannered? He hoped not. He liked her. "Good thinking."

"So I'll get on. You'd know all about data protection in the police."

"Right. I suppose I do."

"What was the title of the book this man may have asked to read?"

Twenty minutes later, she'd done the job.

Only three people had asked for *The Jests of Beau Nash* in thirty years and none of them was called Harrod.

"Not much demand for Mr. Nash's jests, then," Gilbert said. "It must have been the way he told them."

The smile she gave him was nothing to do with library duties.

Gilbert made a snap decision that was nothing to do with police duties. He wouldn't leave without asking for a date.

"Do you mind if I take a look?"

He expected her to plead data protection again, but she gave a shrug and another smile. "I suppose it's all right. They were all filled in a long time ago."

She showed him the retrieval forms. They required a name, address, signature and details of the material to be consulted. Each recorded the issue and return of the material and was co-signed by a librarian. There were actually five entries for the Nash book because one person had asked for it on three occasions in 1996, which happened to be the year Sidney Harrod had been caught on camera—partially—at the Beau Nash Society ball. But the name on the forms was Mason. The other retrievals were dated 1991 and 1992.

"Mind if I take a picture?" he asked.

"Of the forms?"

For one exquisite moment he thought she was inviting him to get a shot of her. He couldn't be sure. Better not push my luck, he thought. "If photography isn't allowed, I can make a copy in my notebook, but I'd really like to show the handwriting to my boss."

She fingered her long hair nervously. "It's not flash, is it?"

"No."

"Go on, then."

"Thanks." He got busy with his iPhone. "This guy in 1996—Mr. Mason—seems to have come three days running. I don't recognise the address, do you? The Laurels, Victoria Street, Bath. Do we have a Victoria Street in Bath? I know Victoria Road in Oldfield Park, but Victoria Street is new on me."

She checked on her computer. "You're right," she said with admiration. "It doesn't exist."

"Then I don't suppose Mr. A. Mason existed either."

"Someone filled in the form."

"But with a made-up name and address."

"How peculiar," she said. "He returned the book."

"Certain people don't like giving personal information," Gilbert said with the air of a detective who has walked the mean streets all his life. "Me, I have no problem telling anyone my name. It's Paul Gilbert. What's yours?"

She turned an extra shade of pink and said after a moment's hesitation, "Tulip."

"Cool. How about a drink sometime soon, Tulip?" It wasn't the best pick-up line in the world and she didn't rise to it at once.

"Are you really a detective?"

"Of course. That's why I'm here."

"Honestly?"

"Want to see my warrant card?" He made it sound like seduction.

She smiled and shook her head. "I believe you."

Detective work at Gilbert's level was mostly plod, plod, but when a chance to make it work for you arrived you'd be a fool to back down. The date was fixed for Friday evening. By some miracle he also remembered to ask the boring question that would surely get him a grunt of approval from Peter Diamond. "Coming back to these forms, would you happen to recognise the initials of the librarian who issued the book in 1996? The letters look like M.S. and it's the same person each time."

She studied the form again. "I wish I could help, but I've not been here long."

"Maybe one of your colleagues would know."

"I can ask." Tulip got up and crossed the room and Gilbert watched her movement in perilously high heels and was even more delighted he'd fixed that date.

She spoke to one of her colleagues at a computer and soon returned. "M.S. is Mike Sealyham."

"You're a star. Is he about?"

"Not any more. He relocated to the records office late last year. He's an archivist now."

With reluctance Gilbert wrenched himself away. The library visit had confounded all his expectations. He'd made the date with Tulip and there might even be something worth investigating, as Diamond had predicted.

Feeling buoyant enough to act on his own initiative, he took the short walk from the Podium to the Guildhall, where he was directed to the search room. Mike Sealyham had to be the silver-haired man behind the enquiry desk.

"You've come to the right bloke," he said, after Gilbert had explained his mission. "I'm the old-stager here, one of the few who can remember working in that lovely building at eighteen Queen Square. I think it was 1993 when we all moved to the Podium."

"This was later. I'm interested in 1996, when the book was last borrowed," Gilbert said. "That would have been in the Podium."

"Correct."

"Would you happen to remember who requested it?"

"That's asking a lot." Mike Sealyham shook his head. "Valuable items like that were stored in the strong room. I would have collected it from there and returned it. More than twenty years ago? I'm sorry to tell you I don't have any memory of this."

"I'm thinking this guy may have been about seventy, good-looking, possibly with false teeth, charming, but not particularly well dressed. Gave his name as Mason, from Victoria Street."

"We saw a lot of retired men in the library."

"Missing a finger on his right hand."

"Him?" Sealyham was suddenly as alert as a meerkat. "I do remember him."

"You do?" Gilbert felt like giving him a hug.

"He was a regular in the library. I don't know where Victoria Street is, but he didn't live there and I don't suppose his name was Mason either."

"How do you know this?"

"Because I used to see him most mornings on my way to work and he always came out of a house in Moon Street."

"Moon Street?" Every police officer knew the notorious Moon Street estate, where drug busts were as regular as the postman.

"A turn off James Street West. Not the most salubrious street in Bath. I lived round the corner from him, in Mars Court. Couldn't afford any better on the salary I got."

"Did you challenge him about giving a false address?"

"I suppose I should have done, but no. I sympathised.

I wasn't proud of living there myself. He seemed all right. Didn't deface the books or anything."

"So you remember him pretty well?"

"When you mentioned the missing finger, yes. We had brief conversations about his researches. Nice man. He was writing something on eighteenth-century Bath, if I remember."

"Beau Nash?"

"Possibly. The Beau is unavoidable if you're studying that period. Oh, and it's coming back to me. He was knowledgeable about old furniture—Hepplewhite and so forth. Must have dealt in it at some time, I reckon."

Paul Gilbert was on a roll. A man with a missing finger who supplied a false name and address and was into antique furniture. This was looking awfully like the conman who had ended up as the skeleton in the loft.

"I don't suppose you remember the number of the house."

"Where he lived? Offhand, I couldn't tell you."

"Pity."

"But I can show it to you on Google Earth."

"Wicked."

In seconds, Sealyham was using the website to zoom in on Britain, on Bath, on Moon Street and on a particular house in a two-storey terrace that turned out to be number 8.

What next for Paul Gilbert? The right thing was to call Peter Diamond, report on his findings and get further instructions. But when you're really motoring, you don't want to stop. Except that this wasn't a motoring proposition. He was ten minutes' walk away, maximum. He would definitely walk. Park your car anywhere in the Moon Street estate and you might not see it again.

The buildings had been thrown up in the 1960s, replacing Victorian slums with twentieth-century slums said to be maisonettes when the word had some cachet. It was social housing on the cheap—built with that nauseous lemon-coloured reconstituted Bath stone—and now it screamed out for demolition.

Thanks to Google Earth, Gilbert knew precisely which house Mr. Mason—or Mr. Harrod—had occupied. The present tenant in number 8 wasn't likely to know who had lived there twenty years ago, but there is an unwritten law that in any estate there will be someone who has been around forever and is the collective memory. He found her at number 11, and she invited him in for tea. She'd been born in Moon Street, she said, and it had been going downhill ever since, but she still loved the place. Her name was Flossie and she was a bus-sized, jolly woman with a laugh so hearty you feared for her health.

The tea came up in Prince George mugs, with pictures of the royal baby against the Union flag.

Number 8, Flossie told him, was always changing hands—which wasn't what Gilbert wanted to hear. "It's a crack house now, as if you didn't know"—big laugh—"and before that it was a knocking shop for at least five years, but the girls were all right. They even hung a big flag from the bedroom window for the Diamond Jubilee. Didn't stop them working, though"—another peal of laughter—"and always open for business, it was."

"Going back a bit—" Gilbert started to say, but he was interrupted.

"Before them, we had an Indian family. They came the year Wills and Kate got hitched. I think they were Indian. Very quiet. Kept their children beautifully. Not like the little fiends next door to me, playing their so-called music at all hours."

"I'm interested in the people who were living there in 1996."

"1996. When was that? Princess Di was still alive, then. She went in 1997, poor lamb. I wept for a week."

He'd cottoned on. Everything Flossie remembered was measured by royal events. He'd have to think of something. Had a royal baby been born in 1996? The royal family wasn't his pet subject. He could have told you who finished top of the Premier League. No use here.

Happily Flossie came to his rescue herself. "It was the year Fergie's divorce came through," she said, with another chesty laugh. "That lass. You can't help liking her in spite of everything. I remember talking to Miss Bowman about it over a cup of tea. She was the lady in number 8 and she and I got on fine, but she liked to be known as Miss Bowman. Fur coat and no knickers, I called her. You know what I'm saying?"

He knew and he was practically twitching with anticipation. In the pause for mirth, he managed to say, "This was the tenant in 1996? Miss Bowman? Was she there right through the year?"

"Oh yes. She was there a long time. She arrived just after Windsor Castle went up in flames. Which year was that?"

Gilbert didn't know. "Did she live alone?"

The question brought a tsunami of laughter. "Now you're asking. She was the sole tenant as far as the benefits people was concerned, but she took in lodgers. My gentlemen, she called them. Gentlemen—in Moon Street. Mind you, I don't think there was any how's-your-father going on. They had their own room and she did a bit of cooking for them."

Gilbert's hopes had plunged at the words "sole tenant" and now they soared again. "Was one of the lodgers a Mr. Mason, by any chance?"

"I wouldn't know, dear."

"About seventy, with a missing finger?"

"That wasn't Mr. Mason. That was Mr. Fortnum."

"Mr. Fortnum?" Gilbert got it at once. Fortnum and Mason. The posh shop in Piccadilly. There was a pattern

to this conman's false identities. From Harrods to Fortnum and Mason. Names picked to impress. "So you
remember him?"

"Him and his little white van. Proper rogue, he was,
always with a twinkle in his eye and some saucy remark.
I used to tell him to act his age and he didn't like that."

"A white van?"

"Miss Bowman let him use her garage and added some
extra on the rent but most times he left the van outside,
the lazy blighter. We all have garages round the back and
can't afford cars. Mine's full of junk. Don't ask me what he
needed a van for. Something naughty, I expect."

"Did Miss Bowman have anything to say about him?"

"Not much. She was a bit hoity-toity, like I said. But
she nearly burst a blood vessel when he upped and left
without paying his rent. She told me he owed six months
and she couldn't do anything about it because she was
claiming the housing benefit and hadn't told them she
had a lodger."

"When you say 'left,' was it sudden?"

"He did a moonlight, didn't he? Buzzed off in his van
without a word and she never saw him again. She used a
few words of her own, I can tell you."

"Do you know when this was?"

"When did we say Fergie got divorced?"

"1996."

"Mr. Fortnum did his bunk the year after, in the
summer."

"1997, then?"

"Terrible year, that was. Are you old enough to remember, dear? All them flowers in front of Kensington Palace.
Heartbreaking. I went up to London specially to see them."

"Did Mr. Fortnum leave anything behind in his room?"

"After he left? Funnily enough, he did. A few clothes
and some bits and bobs. It was like he decided to get out

fast. She thought he was coming back, so she left them in the room for a couple of weeks. Then she put them in a plastic sack in her garage. In the end she got rid of them. I don't think she got anything for them."

"'Bits and bobs,' you said. Was there anything personal—like photos or letters?"

"You've got some hopes," Flossie said. "How would I know?"

"You seem to be well informed."

"Miss Bowman used to say he was her mystery man. Well, she did find a stack of magazines, but she knew about them already. She'd been nosing round his room a few times when he was out, but she never found nothing personal. She reckoned he kept any private stuff locked up in his van."

"What sort of magazines?"

"It wasn't *Homes and Gardens*, I can tell you." Pause for another outbreak of mirth. "Men's magazines, they call them, don't they? Tits and bums and other parts I won't mention to a young gentleman like you. I don't hold that against him. I know what you men are like. Well, we both knew what Mr. Fortnum was like."

"Really?"

"You know the one about the landlady who thought babies came from God? 'It weren't the Almighty that lifted her nightie, it was Roger the lodger, the sod.'" Yet another bout of chesty laughter followed this.

"What happened to Miss Bowman?"

"A bit of slap and tickle when they passed on the stairs. It never came to more than that. She wasn't the sort, even if he was."

"I didn't mean that," he said. "I was asking if she's still about."

"Miss Bowman? No, she's pushing up the daisies. She was gone before the Queen Mum went."

There might have been more a young man like Paul Gilbert could have learned from Flossie, but not of relevance to the case. Outside, he took a long look at number 8 and decided against knocking on the door. If it was indeed a crack house, the drug squad would know about it and the residents might not welcome a visitor from the police.

He had enough new information already to make Peter Diamond's day.

25

"All this?" Diamond said.

"That's why it took so long," Ingeborg told him. Knowing he was more comfortable working with paper than seeing it on a screen, she had handed him a printout of the contents of Perry Morgan's phone running to several hundred sheets. "Have you looked at his contacts? He's hit the upper limit of the app. That's ten thousand."

"How does anybody know that many people?"

"He was a professional schmoozer, guv. That was his business."

"He couldn't have known them all."

"But he had the means to reach them. He will have paid some marketing firm to get most of these."

"Talk about a needle in a haystack."

"You have to come at it from the opposite direction. Think of a name and see if it's there. The ACC is in it."

"Georgina? You're kidding."

"I can show you."

"Well, he did contact her, it's true."

"He doesn't have your number."

"He wouldn't. He was interested in the high and mighty." He paused as a new thought crossed his mind. "Makes me wonder what Beau Nash's contact list would have looked like. Pretty impressive, I reckon. Some of the royal family and a lot of the peerage. All the high command in Bath and Tunbridge Wells. I keep thinking these two had things in common."

"Except Beau Nash wasn't murdered."

That was still an open wound. Diamond continued leafing through the sheets. "Is anything here going to help us?"

"Loads of recent texts and emails connected with the fireworks. He worked hard to make a success of it."

"I know that. What about his drug habit? Any leads?"

"If there are, I haven't found them yet."

"His bank account might be instructive."

"Thought of that," Ingeborg said. "He banked with Santander. That much is easy, but of course getting into the account isn't."

"Apply for a production order."

"It's been done—on the grounds that he was involved in the drug trade."

"Shaky. He was a user, not a dealer."

"The magistrate gave it the nod. We should get access today."

He dropped the printed paper on his desk with a thump that seemed to say he wouldn't pick it up again in a hurry. "Thanks for this."

She eyed him with suspicion. "But . . . ?"

"I have a feeling this case is going to be solved by old-fashioned methods."

Understandably after all the trouble she'd taken, Ingeborg was scathing. "Beating the truth out of someone who knows?"

"Not *that* old-fashioned. I mean looking at motive, means and opportunity."

"Means and opportunity are obvious," she said. "The killer had a handgun and used it. That was the means. And the opportunity was the fireworks display when there were major distractions. Motive is all we have to work with."

"Yep, and it's a brute," Diamond agreed. "We know he

was a cokehead and drugs attract violent people, but I can't
see how his death was necessary. Even if he missed a payment, he was due a big profit from the fireworks contest
and would be able to settle up later."

"It was a free show."

"The finale was. The competition went on all week. The
ones at the Rec brought in gate money. Wasn't payment
discussed in the emails?"

She clicked her tongue, annoyed with herself. "I must
be blitzed from reading them. Now you mention it, there
was a down payment."

"This is stuff I rely on you to tell me." He was feeling
as frayed as she.

If he expected a show of contrition he didn't get it. She
folded her arms and stared him out.

"Anyhow," he went on, "dealers don't murder their users.
They want them alive and paying."

"Unless he'd threatened to name names."

"Unlikely. He had a reputation to keep up. He wouldn't
want it known he was on cocaine. The drugs may be a red
herring."

"What else is there? He didn't seem to have any rivals
putting on shows."

"He may have seriously upset someone with the kind of
thing he was doing."

"How do you mean?"

"Setting off the fireworks. Objections from the residents."

"The people living in the crescent? With *gunfire*? Come
off it, guv."

"They've had to endure displays before, but always set
off behind the terrace, not in front on their precious lawn.
I'm thinking some elderly army officer may have been so
incensed that he went out there with his service weapon
and shot the organiser. Simple as that."

Her eyes widened. "Are you kidding?"

He shook his head. "An Englishman's home is his castle. Never underrate an angry Bathonian."

"He would have shown himself by now. We've had a team knocking on doors at the terrace, haven't we?"

"For possible witnesses, not looking for Nimbys."

"Have you done a debrief?"

"To see if any of them spoke to a mad colonel? Actually, it wasn't mentioned as such. Seriously, we shouldn't discount the crazy person with a grudge against Perry. Anyone running big public events is going to ruffle feathers. There could be some nutcase with a grievance following the guy around with the idea of shooting him when the chance came."

She wasn't persuaded. "Did anything come back from ballistics?"

"You saw their report. No match with any known weapon, if that's what you're asking."

"I know that much. They were going to get back to us later with more findings."

He riffled through the paper stuffed into his in-tray. In the computer age most people had long ago dispensed with in-trays. Diamond had moved on, but only from wire to plastic. He found the document he wanted and handed it to Ingeborg. "This came in yesterday. Didn't excite me much or I'd have shared it with everyone."

She glanced through the summary of findings. "'Five bullets examined, but no casings . . . likely to have been a revolver.' Does anyone use revolvers now?"

"You mean in the services?"

"Army, police. It's all semi-automatic, isn't it? They stopped issuing service revolvers back in the 1960s."

"Still used in crimes," he said.

"But this one isn't on the database. It hasn't been fired in the course of a crime and certainly not a murder."

"What's the point you're making, Inge?"

"Our killer used an old-fashioned weapon not on the NABIS database. The chance is high that this was a one-off. Unprofessional."

The last time Ingeborg had made this point, he'd made some unkind remark about the killer keeping the weapon in his sock drawer. She'd stuck with her theory, and now he gave it more respect. "Okay. Where does that get us?"

"To somebody with a personal issue. It's unlikely to have been a contract killing or something to do with a drug war. I say we should home in on Perry's close circle, people he dealt with from day to day, family, friends."

"There weren't any."

"That was according to his landlady, Miss Divine, but how much did she know?"

"Quite a bit, I thought. 'I don't believe in prying,' she told us and clearly did the opposite. She had the combination and could enter the flat at will. Not much got past that lady."

"The cocaine in the cornflakes did."

He laughed. "You've got me there."

Ingeborg was in full flow. "Perry was smart enough to hide that part of his private life from Miss Divine, so why not the rest? He was born in Bath and lived here all his life. There must be people in this dozy town who know more about him than Miss Divine does. Got to be. He wasn't a recluse. He was a social animal, confident."

"We've been down this route before," he said. "What did we get from social media? Masses of flimflam about the shows he put on, but about the man, zilch. There's no family, no close friends, no obvious points of contact. All the press coverage brought in nothing we didn't have already. Paul Gilbert wasted most of a day checking the university registers."

"That was always a long shot," she said.

"All right, I'll put my hand up to that one. It was only

a hunch because we couldn't think where his confidence came from. I'd like to look at it from another angle—the low point in his life when his parents died, first his mother, from cancer, and then his dad in the car crash."

"Where does that lead us?"

"His dad was a taxi driver. They spend a lot of time sitting around waiting for fares. They all know each other, those guys. Haven't you seen them sitting in each other's cabs? They're the bush telegraph."

"It was a while ago."

"2007, the year Henry Morgan died. That's not the dark ages."

"I've no memory of it."

"CID weren't involved, that's why. It was an accident. Some of the older cabbies will remember. It must have been a big event in their lives, one of their number killed. And if they remember him, they'll remember Perry, how he took the shock and what happened after."

"I'll go." She was already halfway to the door. She said she'd try the rank at the railway station.

Paul Gilbert reported back shortly after Ingeborg had left.

"You took your time," Diamond said, still grouchy. "Chatting up the library staff, were you?"

He would never guess how close he came to the truth. Gilbert told the boss everything he needed to know. The date with Tulip wasn't included.

"And you got out of the Moon Street estate in one piece?" Diamond said with more admiration when he'd heard the story. "You're a legend. I only ever visit there with an armed back-up."

"It was quiet, guv."

"That's when I start worrying."

"Nothing happened."

"Brave man. The pieces are falling into place now.

Fortnum and Mason—I like that. I wonder which other names he went under."

"Flossie didn't mention any others."

"Mr. Harvey on the driving licence and Mr. Nichols on the bus pass?"

The joke passed Paul Gilbert by. His clothes came from T.K. Maxx.

Diamond went on, "He'd have to be careful what he called himself in Moon Street. Flossie sounds a sharp lady."

"Razor sharp."

"And you say the last she and Miss Bowman saw of him was 1997. Did she say precisely when?"

He shook his head. "The summer. He arrived in 1996 and left the next summer."

"It chimes in with what we heard from the Beau Nash Society. He surfaced there in 1996 and vanished suddenly the following year. And now we need to know why his body turned up in Twerton—eventually. Is there a connection with Moon Street?"

"It was another rundown place."

"But Sidney Harrod was all about aspiration, upwardly mobile, getting to know the cream of society, hobnobbing with them and fleecing them. He wouldn't find toffs living in a Twerton slum. He had no reason to be there. Have you looked at it on your map? It's across the river and a mile west of Moon Street."

"Are you thinking he was taken there by force?"

"By force? Who by? Harry, the Twerton tenant, and his woman? Why would they want to kill him? He wasn't rich pickings. It's become clear from your good work this morning that he was just a blagger living by his wits, but on a modest scale. He'd fastened on to that sad old gent on Widcombe Hill."

"Lord Deganwy?"

"Yes, and he was systematically stealing choice items of

furniture, but he'd have to fence them. He wouldn't get anything like their true value."

"Could the guy living in the Twerton house have been his fence?" Gilbert asked.

"Harry? That's a thought." Diamond became more interested. "That *is* a thought. We can check the records for known fences operating in that area at the time."

"What records, guv? Was it on computer then?"

He nodded. "But not all that efficient. As far as I can recall, we used HOLMES in those days, and the Criminal Records Bureau were still issuing paper certificates. The system was upgraded in 2000 and several times since. We may find out more from asking people who were around at the time."

"Like yourself?"

"Watch it, lad. You can soon run out of the goodwill you earned this morning. I used criminal records back then, but it was never my main job. There should be people in uniform who covered stolen goods."

"I'll ask," Gilbert said. "The thing that's really odd is that the skeleton was wearing the Beau Nash outfit."

"You don't have to remind me."

"Do you think he was killed for that?"

"They'd have stripped it off the body if that was what they were after."

"It was genuine eighteenth-century, wasn't it? How much would it be worth?"

"The real thing? A couple of grand or so, depending on the condition and the provenance. That's the problem for a thief—provenance. There aren't many of these costumes about. Any expert would know where it came from, in this case the Deganwy family. Anyhow, it was ripped and bloodstained."

"Not worth stealing?"

"Antique furniture is easier to fence because thousands of pieces were made and many have survived."

"Shame all this happened so long ago."

Diamond didn't think of it as long ago, but it was almost a lifetime to DC Gilbert.

The eager young man was off on another tack. "What happened to Lord Deganwy's house after his death? Did one of the family inherit?"

"He was the last of the line. The title died with him and Widcombe Hall was sold. It belongs to some company now. They hire out the house as a conference centre."

"Someone must have come into a small fortune from the sale. I could make some enquiries."

"Good man. Search the probate records and get a copy of the will. And Deganwy's death certificate while you're at it. I'd like to be sure he died naturally."

Ingeborg was glad to get out of the office. She had a high regard for Diamond's intellect but didn't enjoy his moods. It wasn't misogyny or she would have quit years ago. Actually he had an old-fashioned respect for women that bordered on the patronising and could be equally hard to take. He was complex, huffy one day and affable the next, well defended, a strong leader and a smart detective scarred by the tragedy of his wife's murder before Ingeborg even joined the police. She suspected there had always been this crossgrain of melancholy in his personality redeemed to some extent by a sharp sense of humour. And for all his faults, he was a good man.

On second thoughts, it was simpler than that. He was a man. They expected you to make allowances. Why the hell should you?

The taxi rank in front of the railway station looked promising in numbers, a double line of cars waiting for the next train from London. She knew better than to go to the front and raise hopes she was a fare, so she stood on the forecourt watching for a while, on the lookout for an older driver who might have a memory of the accident eleven years ago.

She settled on one towards the back of the line leaning against the passenger door of his cab. Poor choice. When she asked, he'd taken to driving taxis on retiring from teaching two years ago. He pointed to a much younger guy. "Tony's been driving longer than any of us. He's your man."

Hard to believe. Tony was the fresh-faced one she'd already decided couldn't possibly be any help.

Being near the front of the line, he wasn't keen to talk. "Soon as a fare turns up, I'm off, right? The train's overdue already."

Ingeborg toyed with the idea of hiring the taxi herself and then remembered she didn't have more than five pounds in her pocket. She had her warrant card and she showed that. "I'm asking about a driver called Henry Morgan."

"Never heard of him."

"Killed in an accident on the M4 in 2007."

"That was Harry."

"Harry, then. It amounts to the same thing, a nickname for Henry, isn't it?" Even as she spoke the obvious, Ingeborg had a lightbulb moment. The tenant of the Twerton house at the time the skeleton was killed had been called Harry. The thought hadn't entered her head until now.

So what? That was another case unconnected to the shooting of Perry Morgan. Harry wasn't an unusual first name.

Leave it, she thought. Concentrate on the Harry you've come to ask about, Perry's father.

Tony the taxi man glanced at his watch. "Supposed to be the fifty-nine."

"So you do remember Harry Morgan?"

"We had a proper cabby's funeral for him," he told her, eyes now fixed on the arched station entrance. "More than fifty of us stopped work and followed the hearse and when we got to his house in St. Saviour's Road we pulled up and sounded our horns for a minute. It was a tribute, like."

"St. Saviour's? Where's that?"

"Larkhall. Off the London Road. I remember when we took our hands off the horns, we'd started loads of dogs barking."

Larkhall was the other side of the city from Twerton.

"Obviously a popular guy if you gave him such a send-off." He still wasn't making eye contact and she tried not to get annoyed.

"I wouldn't say that, not specially. He was a cagy character. Never said much. We'd have done the same for any other driver we knew."

"And you all knew Harry Morgan?"

"I'll say this for him. He was a career driver, not like these oldies who do it in retirement to top up their pensions."

"Do you remember if he had any family?" she asked as if she didn't know already.

He had to think about that. "There was a kid, a boy. Harry was bringing him up on his own. The mother was dead. He was only a schoolkid, about fifteen or sixteen, and there was a lot of sympathy. I don't think Harry left much, so we had a whip-round for the boy and raised more than fifteen hundred quid."

"What became of him? Did you hear any more?"

"I'm trying to think. Can't even remember his name."

"Perry."

"You could be right about that."

This guy was *so* annoying.

"Some of the other drivers took an interest, made sure the money was put to good use. I think it covered his rent for a bit, until he found a job with the rugby club in their ticket office."

"This is Bath rugby club you're talking about?"

"They took him on as the office boy, I reckon, making the tea and posting the letters. I don't suppose they let him sell the tickets. He wasn't idle. There's a youth theatre company called Zenith that puts on shows at Kingswood School on Lansdown. Posh school. They've got their own theatre. Harry's boy joined and did a bit of acting and publicity for them."

The life history was coming together, making sense. The job in the ticket office, the acting and the publicity work. Through his link with the rugby club, Perry must have learned the basics about dealing with the public and how big events at the Rec were organised. All good grounding for a future impresario. Ingeborg had heard of Zenith and the shows at Kingswood. They were amateur only in the sense that they were run by and for volunteers. The shows were top class, mostly musicals.

There was movement at the station entrance. People were emerging in numbers.

"Train's in," Tony said. "That's your lot." He moved round to the driver's side. "You want to ask at the ticket office—on Pulteney Bridge."

Among the stream of passengers from London stepping into taxis she spotted Diamond's friend Paloma with a young black woman. Both were clutching designer carrier bags. The friend—who'd shopped at MaxMara in Bond Street—was likely to be Estella, the Beau Nash expert. Ingeborg had heard a lot about her from Diamond. The two women shared a cab and were driven away.

Taking Tony's advice, Ingeborg walked the short way up Manvers Street and Pierrepont reflecting on what she had learned. The two Harrys were a coincidence she should have picked up before today. Harry the Twerton tenant and Harry Morgan the taxi driver. Couldn't be the same man, surely? The murders under investigation were divided by twenty years, divided by everything she could think of except that both took place in Bath.

And yet Harry the tenant hadn't carried on living in Twerton forever. He'd moved elsewhere. Could it have been to Larkhall?

There had never been any mention of a child living in that Twerton house. Perry would have been six at the time of the murder.

On consideration, he wouldn't have lived there. His parents had separated and he was living with his mother.

Worth mentioning to Diamond. She didn't like to predict his reaction.

The Rugby Club ticket office is a shop on the iconic Pulteney Bridge over the Avon. Painted in Bath RFC blue and next to the club shop selling kit and souvenirs, it has the advantage of being no more than a fullback's kick away from the ground itself, the famous Rec.

"I'm hoping you can help," she said after showing her ID to the friendly woman behind the counter. "I'm wondering if anyone here recalls a young assistant called Perry Morgan."

"Perry who was shot at the fireworks?" the woman said immediately. "I was saying only yesterday that could have been our Perry."

And you didn't think to inform the police? Every media outlet howling for information and you stayed silent. Bloody typical of Bath's buttoned-up population.

Maybe the woman read the expression on Ingeborg's face because she added, "It was a long time ago."

"Were you working here at the time?"

"I've been here since January 2003, and the years just flashed by. I love it, all the regulars coming in. A lot of them know me by name."

"And what's that?"

"Isla. I was born in Scotland."

"So, Isla, you remember Perry first coming here? It would have been 2007."

"I do. He was a bit lost at first. His dad had died recently in a traffic accident and he didn't seem to have any family at all. One of the local cab drivers helped him get the job. That was because the father drove a taxi."

"You called him 'our Perry,' so he must have settled into the job."

"We did our best to make a fuss of him, knowing his story. Yes, he was a bright lad. He soon got to know how we do things here and made himself useful."

"Did he talk about his family situation?"

Isla shook her head. "Obviously, it was a painful subject, so we kept off it."

"While he was here did he make any friends?"

"In the shop, you mean?"

"Or outside?"

"Why do you want to know?"

"He got into bad company at some stage and we want to discover how soon it started."

"Bad company?"

"He used drugs."

"Not while he was here, he didn't. He wouldn't have stayed in the job five minutes."

"It isn't always obvious."

"A young kid like that?"

Ingeborg didn't see much point in enlightening Isla on drug use by adolescents. "How long was he working here?"

"Not all that long. A matter of months."

"What happened? Did he get another job?"

"He wasn't sacked. I know that," Isla said. "He was ambitious, I suppose. He found something that paid better. I have a faint memory of him working for one of the bus tour companies. Open-top, doing the commentary. I bet he was good at it. He was confident for his age."

It fitted the profile. "So you don't recall any friends he may have had, people who called here to see him or met up with him when he finished work?"

"No. He liked to be independent. He didn't welcome anyone getting too near. He made it very clear he didn't want mothering from any of us. There isn't much else I can tell you. Sorry."

Ingeborg had reached the same conclusion. She thanked Isla and walked back to where she had left the car.

26

Sleep had been difficult for Diamond after speaking to Ingeborg. Instead of phoning, she'd driven all the way back to Concorde House the evening before to make her report in person. She'd told him what she'd discovered at the taxi rank and the ticket office about the early career of Perry Morgan, vital background information that had fleshed out their knowledge of an unusually evasive young man.

But that hadn't kept the head of CID awake.

What had given him such a brute of a night wasn't Perry's life history. It was when Ingeborg fixed him with her you'd-better-be-listening look and said she'd been thinking outside the box and there was one more thing she wanted to get his opinion on. "I expect it's a red herring, guv, and I'm sure you thought of it yonks ago and kicked it straight into the long grass. Can you do that with a red herring? Anyway, for what it's worth, here goes. It's about Perry's father, Henry Morgan. We've been calling him Henry in all our talk about the case because that's how we know him—as Henry—in formal language from reports of his death and on his death certificate. But—here's what zoomed me out—the guy I met, the taxi driver on the rank, called him Harry. Fair enough, it's what people named Henry have been called for hundreds of years. Anyone who's read Shakespeare knows that. And then off the top of my head

I remembered Harry from our other case, the guy who was the tenant of the Twerton house at the time of the murder there. Am I totally out of order or is it remotely possible that the two Harrys were the same man?"

Simple as that.

Diamond's immediate response had been muted. Harry was a boringly common name. The phrase "every Tom, Dick or Harry" was proof of that. Out of consideration for Ingeborg, he'd offered to think about it. Once or twice lately he'd seen a look come into her eyes suggesting he wasn't open to debate about anything. He'd show her he didn't reject her ideas without weighing them carefully.

In the deep of the night, that so-called red herring swam into his thoughts and refused to leave. The little that was known about Harry the tenant didn't conflict with any of the facts about Harry the taxi driver. What if they *were* the same man? Harry the tenant had lived in Twerton with a woman called Sarah who had apparently left him in 1997. He'd carried on living at the same address for a couple more years until Jerzy the electrician took over the tenancy. He'd been described by the Twerton newsagent as in his thirties, white, with dark hair and not too talkative. He'd always paid in cash rather than by card. After he'd left the Twerton house the trail had gone cold.

Harry the taxi driver lived on the other side of town, in Larkhall, but nothing was known of his whereabouts before that. Could he have moved there from Twerton about 1999? His age at death had been forty-three, which fitted with Harry the tenant in his thirties in the late 1990s. Both had said little about themselves. The taxi driver was "a cagey character" and the tenant "didn't have much to say for himself."

How did this fusion of the two men fit the events they were involved in? Perry's father, the taxi driver, had formed a relationship with a woman called Fiona Glyn who gave birth to their child at Dolemeads in 1990. Both their names were on Perry's birth certificate. But Fiona had raised the child alone. Only after her death in 2002 did Harry take full responsibility. So there were these twelve years or so needing to be accounted for, years when the guy clearly hadn't left the area. Was he paying Fiona some form of maintenance and leading a double life?

Switch back to Harry in Twerton, living with another woman, called Sarah, until 1997, when she left him or was murdered, the same year a corpse in a Beau Nash costume was entombed in the loft of the terraced house they shared.

About 1999, Harry moved out of the house, leaving its gruesome secret so well concealed that the skeleton would not be found until the place was demolished. Nothing conflicted with him starting up again in Larkhall, taking on taxi work and providing a home for his young son in 2002 after Fiona died.

But then in 2007 came the fatal accident on the M4. Harry the taxi driver was killed and if he was also Harry the tenant he'd died with the secret of what really happened in the Twerton house in 1997.

Diamond heaved himself out of bed at four in the morning to make himself strong tea and see if it all made sense downstairs. He fed the cat and pondered the matter. He couldn't find a flaw in the reasoning. Each date, each event, slotted in. Ingeborg's red herring didn't smell fishy. It was the true explanation. Had to be.

Harry Morgan may have got away with murder. But the fates had dealt with him.

Case closed?

Not to the point of absolute proof. Even so, the match-up of the Harrys was a breakthrough. He felt like calling Ingeborg to tell her, but she might not appreciate a call at this hour. Texting was still a skill he had to learn.

He could now put all his effort into finding who had

murdered Perry. He returned to bed and fitted in two hours of untroubled sleep.

He was first in to work.

Ingeborg arrived at Concorde House soon after 8:30 and he called her into his office straight away. She stepped in apprehensively.

"Well done."

"What for, guv?"

"What you told me last night. The two Harrys being the same person. Everything fits. You've cracked it."

She actually blushed. Compliments from Diamond were as rare as rich uncles.

"Sorry I didn't show much excitement when you spoke of it last night," he said. "This hasn't been easy, dealing with two cases twenty years apart, and now to find a link between them is a shock to the system."

"If you're certain," Ingeborg said. "It was just an idea."

"An inspiration. Yesterday changed everything. We now know the name of the victim." He spoke on a rising note, as if testing her.

"Sidney Harrod."

"And who did it."

"Harry Morgan."

"Even better, we don't have to flog ourselves finding Harry because he's dead. We can focus on Perry."

"Good."

"That doesn't sound like a hundred percent good," he said. "What's bugging you?"

"Before we close the case," she said, "what was Harry's motive?"

"I thought you'd ask me that and the obvious answer is NOTS."

An acronym from Diamond, who despised them? He was in a heady mood today. "What's that?"

"Now open to suggestions. We already know Harrod was a conman, a particularly unpleasant individual who leeched on to a rich old man in the early stages of dementia and was stealing and selling items from his house."

"Did Harry know that?"

"Can't tell. What I'm saying is it's well possible Sidney Harrod became a threat to Harry."

"How come?"

"Harry was leading a double life, with a son he probably hadn't mentioned to Sarah, the woman he was living with in Twerton. Let's say Harrod got to know about his secret and demanded money in return for silence."

"Blackmail?" she said, frowning. "Do you have any evidence for that?"

"We know Sarah left."

"You think she got to know the truth?"

"That's my best guess. Either she quit because Harrod tipped her off about the other woman or it was after the murder and she legged it fast."

"If you're right, it may not have been murder," Ingeborg said. "The two men could have had a huge argument that turned violent."

"With a sharp implement?"

"The first thing that came to hand."

"Now you're talking like a defence lawyer," Diamond said. "They'd have a field day with this. Good thing the case will never come to court."

Paul Gilbert was waiting to see him after Ingeborg left his office. The young DC had just received copies of the documents Diamond had asked to see—Lord Deganwy's death certificate and will.

"So what do they say he died of?"

Gilbert passed the certificate across. "Vascular dementia and cardiac arrest."

"No surprise there." He glanced through the details. "This was April 1998, then. Not long after he gave up the presidency of the Beau Nash Society. Died at home, in Widcombe Hall . . . Funny."

"What's funny, guv?" Gilbert asked.

"Funny peculiar." Without saying any more he placed the certificate on his desk. "Give me the will."

Simple to dissect, a shorter document than he expected from a rich landowner. Basically, everything Lord Deganwy had owned, including Widcombe Hall, was to be sold. The proceeds were to go to the Electoral Reform Society, apart from a few legacies to his staff.

Electoral reform? The old peer's politics hadn't been discussed so far in this investigation. Evidently he'd espoused the cause of proportional representation and he must have been deeply committed to leave the bulk of his fortune to a society that after more than a century of existence was still a long way from achieving its aim. The two main parties in Britain had a vested interest in retaining the first-past-the-post system for the foreseeable future.

Diamond shook his head. The money was wasted, in his opinion. Personally, he didn't give a toss for politics and politicians even though he was at the sharp end of decisions made in parliament. He voted at elections and let them get on with it. The corruption scandals of recent years had hardened his cynicism.

The other legacies in Lord Deganwy's will were small beer compared to the millions destined for the ERS, but at least they would have gone to real people. Of those, one name stood out for Diamond.

"To my estate steward, James Spearman, I give ten thousand pounds free of duty, in recognition of his loyal service."

"Here's a thing," he said to Gilbert. "I know one of the beneficiaries and he's mentioned on the death certificate as well. Ask Keith Halliwell to join us, will you?"

Hearing the catch of urgency in Diamond's voice, Gilbert fairly scooted out and returned with Halliwell.

"It may be nothing," Diamond said as he handed his deputy the will, "but take a look."

Halliwell was quick. "Sir Ed Paris's chauffeur?"

"That's what I thought. His name is Jim, isn't it?"

"Certainly is, but we didn't know he once worked for Lord Deganwy. 'My estate steward,' it says here. Sounds a high-powered job."

"Very. He'd have his own office and a large budget for managing the place, hiring staff, buying equipment and materials, maintaining the upkeep. He'd be the top man on the staff. The Deganwy estate wasn't huge, but it was big enough to need someone like that."

"Can this be the same guy?"

"The name's not all that common," Diamond said, unsure if he could take yet another rise and plunge of the switchback.

"Yes, but this was a long time ago. What age is Spearman?"

"Around fifty, I'd say. He could have been thirty at the time."

"Young, for a position like that."

"Some people in their twenties are running business empires."

"True, but how come he ends up as a chauffeur? That's a comedown."

Diamond wouldn't let go. "As he was employed by one president of the Beau Nash Society, it's not impossible he was later offered a job by another. Ed Paris doesn't have an estate. It's a nice big garden, but he wouldn't need a steward for it. On the other hand, he needs someone to drive him around in the Bentley and the Range Rover."

"I guess estate steward jobs don't come up too often these days."

"We'll find out," Diamond said. "We'll ask him. There's

something else I haven't shown you." He picked up the death certificate and handed it to Halliwell. "Look at the name of the informant."

Halliwell read it aloud. "'James Spearman, present at the death.' Wasn't the doctor present?"

"Evidently not. The doctor certified the cause as dementia and cardiac arrest. He'd have been treating the old man, so he'd sign it off when he confirmed that life was extinct, but he wouldn't have needed to be there."

"And Spearman inherits ten grand. We'd definitely better see this guy."

Paul Gilbert had heard all this from two seasoned investigators and his eyes were the size of the spotlights above the desk.

Diamond picked up the phone and switched to speaker for the others to listen. "Get me Sir Edward Paris, will you?"

He was through straight away and reminded Paris who he was. "I'd like to come and see your chauffeur if he's with you."

"What's that about, then, my old chum? In some kind of trouble, is he?" As soon as the first words came out, the bluff, no-nonsense, twenty-first-century Beau materialised in Diamond's head like a pantomime genie.

"Not at all, Sir Edward. It's a routine enquiry."

"No big deal, then?"

"It's got to be done. We need to speak to him about something that's cropped up."

"And you're not saying what?"

"Not to anyone else. It concerns Mr. Spearman, nobody else."

"You'll have to try later, then. He's not here."

"Gone away, you mean?"

"Gone shopping. We're having a garden party here and this afternoon is going to be a belter, the weathermen say. Needed some last-minute items, extra sunshades, those super-sized beauties on stands. Spearman knows where to go for stuff like that. I can safely leave it up to him."

"So he's more than just your chauffeur?"

"Chauffeur, shopper, window cleaner, TV maintenance man. He can turn his hand to anything, just about."

"How long have you employed him?"

"Ten years, easy, and I'd be lost without him. He used to work for David Deganwy, who was the Beau when I joined the society."

Diamond glanced across at Halliwell. All uncertainty was removed. They needed to see this man of many parts—and soon. "We can be at Charlcombe in, say, an hour. He'll be back by then, won't he?"

The tone changed. "I don't want policemen at my party, for Christ's sake. It's a friendly get-together."

"Don't you worry about that," Diamond said. "I'm not a party animal. We can do this well away from your guests. Where does he go when he's off duty? Servants' quarters?"

"Lives in the gatehouse with his wife and kiddie."

"Ideal. We can speak to him there. This party—is it a special occasion?"

"Not really. Just a few of the Beau Nash mob. You was there the other night when I told them I'm stepping down. My wife had the good idea of putting on a bun-fight for the young lady taking over from me, to welcome her, like."

"Estella."

"D'you know her?"

"We've met."

"Well, there you go. Any excuse for a rave-up, eh? Shall I tip Jim off that you're coming?"

"Don't," Diamond said at once. "He might get the wrong idea."

"And do a runner? Is he in trouble?"

"I said before, it's a routine enquiry, Sir Edward. But people do sometimes get the wrong idea when the police come calling. If he does a runner, as you put it, that's no use to you or me."

"Too bloody true," Ed said. "I'll be up shit creek if he walks out now."

Diamond wiped some imaginary sweat from his brow. For a moment his whole operation had been at risk. "As soon as we get to Charlcombe I'll let you know by phone and you can tell him he's got visitors and send him to the lodge. Understood?"

"You won't keep him long? He's my barman for the afternoon."

"You'll get him back, Sir Edward."

He ended the call and tapped a finger drumroll on the edge of the desk. Alarming possibilities battered his brain. Over the past days he'd been diligently working towards completion of this crossword of a mystery. It hadn't been simple. Starting as the single challenge of the skeleton in the loft, one puzzle had become two after Perry was shot. Two sets of clues, two grids and two solutions. Then the strong suspicion that Harry had been both the Twerton tenant and Perry's father had changed the game. Evidently it was one grid after all, one diabolically difficult cryptic challenge, with the difference that the clues weren't conveniently listed and numbered. He had to find them first. If and when he got as far as that, he knew that in a cryptic crossword the obvious answer was likely to be a distraction. You had to spot the real meaning behind the words. He thought he'd been doing quite well, filling the gaps down and across with increasing confidence. The solution seemed to be achievable—until now. The demon who delights in tormenting detectives had struck a match and held the flame to the whole damned puzzle.

"Did you hear all that?"

Both colleagues nodded, cautious of saying anything. The surge in their boss's blood pressure was all too visible.

He was chuntering. "Ten years . . . ten years was what he said . . . ten years easily. But that isn't twenty. What was

Spearman doing for the other ten?" A direct question to Halliwell—as if he ought to know.

"We'd better ask him." A safe response, you would think.

"Feeble."

"Only a suggestion."

"I'd rather know in advance. I've got my suspicions, haven't you? An estate steward ends up doing shopping and cleaning windows? We check the PNC and see if he's got a record."

"When you say 'we' . . . ?"

"Do it now."

Halliwell took out his phone.

Diamond closed his eyes and shook his head like a poker player who has overcalled and lost a fortune.

Gilbert stared at his feet and wished he was anywhere else but here.

"Well?" Diamond's eyes opened.

Halliwell looked up from his screen. "James Walter Spearman was convicted at Bristol of theft and assault in February 2001, and sentenced to three years' imprisonment. You're right, guv."

Being right brought no satisfaction for Diamond at this stage. "He's got form, then. Anything else?"

"That's all."

"I don't have any memory of this. I want the details."

"There's only so much data they store, guv."

"If it got tried at Bristol it was local and must have been handled by uniform." He turned to DC Gilbert. "Run a check on our own records. The incident will have been sometime in 1997. These things take a while to come to trial. And ask John Leaman to look at the *Chronicle* archive. It will have made the papers for sure."

Halliwell said, "Do we have time for this?"

"Gilbert does. You and I don't. We're off to Charlcombe on the double."

27

When Georgina had boasted about hobnobbing with her titled friends in Charlcombe she'd said the house was ultra-modern. Did ultra-modern houses have lodges? The substantial brick building just inside the gate, with mullioned windows, a crop of moss on the gabled roof and two ornate chimneys, couldn't by any stretch of the imagination be called modern, let alone ultra-modern. The likely explanation was that Sir Edward Paris had bought the estate and left the original lodge untouched when he demolished the main house to build his own modern mansion.

Diamond sat in the passenger seat of Halliwell's Ford Fiesta parked on the turf just off the drive. He'd phoned Ed Paris to say they'd arrived and were ready to speak to Jim Spearman. They'd watched two expensive cars come through the main entrance and disappear in the direction of the main house.

"Partygoers, I suppose," he said, wanting to ease the tension that gripped him.

"All right for some," Halliwell said.

"You're not jealous, are you? Knowing you, Keith, if you had an invitation you wouldn't go."

"That's beside the point, guv. If I was one of the idle rich, I'd find better ways of filling my time."

"It's not all fun and games. If you're a high-flyer, you go to parties and make sure you meet the right people.

Georgina does it sometimes. She sees networking as an important part of her job."

"Nice work if you can get it."

"Networking, I said."

"Playtime."

"Networking," Diamond said for the third time. He was still on edge. His head turned as another car drove past. "I wonder if Georgina's invited. She claims to be friends with Lady Sally."

"Do they know she's a senior police officer?"

"It must have been discussed."

"Sir Edward said he didn't want police at his party."

"They might make an exception for assistant chief constables. Here's someone arriving by taxi. I doubt if it's her."

They both looked at the back window of the London-style black cab, in case. Definitely not Georgina. They had a glimpse of fluffy blond hair.

"Crumpet," Halliwell said.

"Not so. That was a bloke and I know him," Diamond said—and his usual unflappable front fell down like a fence in a hurricane. "Newburn, the drug-dealer. What's he doing here?"

"Is he one of the Beau Nash lot?"

"No, no. I can't believe that."

"Must be there to pep up the party, then."

The joke fell flat. "He's a bloody menace. Should be locked up. I took a gun off him."

Another vehicle was approaching.

"What the hell . . . ?" Diamond swung round in his seat. "That was Paloma's car, the Aston Martin. I'm sure of it. Did you see who was in it?"

The sleek yellow sports car had already zoomed past and up the drive.

"Two women, I thought," Halliwell said, "one of them black."

"That'll be Estella. Was Paloma at the wheel?"

"It did look rather like her."

"What the fuck is she up to?"

"Estella's got to be at the party, guv. She's the star guest. I expect she was told to bring a friend."

Diamond's hand went to his throat. "She didn't tell me. I'm not happy with this, not happy at all. In fact I'm bloody alarmed. There are dangerous people here. Why in Christ didn't she say?"

"I don't suppose she thought anything of it, a summer party with the Beau Nash set. There's nothing we can do about it, is there?"

The answer was obvious in what Diamond said next. "Get Ingeborg on your phone. I want her here fast. And Leaman and Gilbert. Tell them to park off the road nearby and await further instructions. We also need back-up. Same instruction. Do it now."

Halliwell did as instructed. A full-scale emergency was easier for him to handle than a playful dialogue about partying. He'd worked too long with the boss to doubt that he was dead serious now. And he knew better than to bombard him with questions. After a terse conversation with someone at Concorde House he said, "They're on the way."

"And so is Spearman, blast him."

The chauffeur was strolling along the drive towards them, confident, unhurried, staring ahead, deep-set eyes and high cheekbones accentuated by the midday sun. He was in a black waistcoat over a pale striped shirt that made Diamond the film buff think of the sinister gunslinger Wilson, played by Jack Palance in *Shane*.

Halliwell's thoughts must have run along similar lines because he asked, "Will he be armed?"

Anyone who had seen the film would be unlikely to forget Palance making a performance of fitting a black glove to his shooting hand prior to drawing his gun and killing a man, one of the most spine-chilling sequences in all westerns.

"Could be."

"Want me to frisk him?"

"No. Keep it civilised, but be alert."

They got out of the car and stood waiting. Spearman's step didn't quicken.

To fill the silence, Halliwell started talking. "He's been around from the start. Remember sending me over to speak to him at Twerton the day the skeleton was lifted out of the loft?"

"I do."

"And we had it confirmed that he worked for Lord Deganwy."

"Yes."

"He must have sussed what was going on, Sidney Harrod conning the old man and stealing his property. It would make anyone see red."

"You don't need to go over this," Diamond muttered.

Nothing was said by Spearman until he stopped almost toe to toe with Diamond and said, "You wanted to see me."

"Can we go indoors?"

"My house?"

"That's the plan."

"My wife and son are in there."

"It'll be less public than here, with people driving past."

Spearman appeared to decide this wasn't where he would make his stand. Without another word he led them towards the red front door of the lodge and took out a key.

A blond boy of about five was in the hallway. Superman sweatshirt and joggers. He turned and shouted, "Dad's home," and ran out of sight. They heard him speak to someone in another room, the shrill voice no longer understandable.

Spearman pushed open a door, stood back and tilted

his head. "You can go in." From the way he spoke, it was clear he wouldn't be joining them yet. Presumably he felt he should say something to his wife.

The way the interior was furnished didn't tell them much. Two fabric-covered armchairs and a sofa. A foxhunting print over a stone fireplace. A few nondescript vases. No dust, but the place still had an unused look, suggesting the Spearmans observed the outmoded British tradition that front rooms are kept for formal occasions.

Uneasy seconds passed.

Diamond looked at his watch. His thoughts were divided. He was mystified and deeply worried about Paloma being at the party.

Halliwell became suspicious that they'd been duped. "He hasn't done a bunk, has he?"

"Unlikely," Diamond said. "He needn't have come to meet us."

There was a movement at the door. It wasn't Spearman. The child walked in, hands in pockets, and his wide blue eyes assessed them.

This might be an opportunity. Diamond said, "Hi, Superman."

"Hi."

"What's your real name?"

After hesitation: "Rufus."

"Good name. I like it."

"My dad says you're policemen."

"We are."

"You're not dressed like policemen."

"We're plainclothes policemen."

"Like on the telly?"

"Just like that."

"Why have you come to our house?"

"To see your dad."

"Did he kill someone?"

Straight to it. Small kids don't mince their words.

Diamond couldn't allow himself to be so direct. "I haven't heard that he did. What makes you say that?"

"It's what policemen do, catch people who do killing."

"You think so?"

"Seen it on the telly."

"You don't want to believe everything you see on the telly, Rufus. It's mostly stories, made-up stuff."

"I saw a dead man. He wasn't a story. He was real."

"Where was this?" Diamond asked in the same even tone, trying to conceal his rocketing interest.

"Through the window in the fence. My dad held me up so I could see."

"See a dead man?"

"No, silly. See the houses being knocked down." He removed his right hand from his pocket, raised it high and swung it down so hard that he took a step forward. "Crrrrrrrash!"

"Got you." Diamond was on to it.

"The big ball crashed into the roof and made a hole. It's called a reh . . . reh . . ."

"Wrecking ball?"

"Yes, and there was dust and I saw the dead man in a chair."

"You were actually there watching?"

"I knew he was dead because he was a skeleton." The word came out as "skelington" but there was no doubt what the boy meant. "It was dressed in funny clothes. When my dad saw it, he said we'd got to go."

"Good thing, too."

"I wasn't scared."

"I believe you, Rufus."

The boards in the hallway creaked.

"That sounds like your dad now."

Spearman came in, saw the boy and saw red. "What the hell . . . ? Get out of here, Rufus. Go to your mother."

Rufus didn't stop to argue.

The full force of the father's anger was turned on Diamond. "Is that legal, questioning a kid? You have no right."

"He walked in and started chatting. As a matter of fact, Mr. Spearman, Rufus was asking the questions, not us. And why shouldn't he, two strange men in his home? He got us to admit we were policemen and wanted to know why we were here. They get ideas from the TV about what detectives do. These days it's part of growing up. But we're here to talk to you, not your boy. Sit down and let's make a start. We can't keep you too long from the party."

Diamond at his most urbane. He seemed to have persuaded Spearman that the issue wasn't worth pursuing. Shaking his head, the chauffeur did as he was asked, taking the sofa and leaving them to shift the armchairs to face him.

"Sir Edward told us you once had a high-powered job up at Widcombe Hall with Lord David Deganwy."

The dark eyes glinted some kind of assent.

"You were a younger man then, on the brink of a good career."

"For fuck's sake," Spearman said. "We all know what happened to me. I'd be a fool to think I paid my debt to society and the slate was wiped clean. It never is, as far as you lot are concerned."

"Do you want to tell us about it?"

"Why bother, when you obviously know already?"

"You're wrong, as it happens," Diamond said. "We didn't know you had a record until an hour or two ago, but we're catching up." He turned to Halliwell. "Anything yet from the oracle?"

Halliwell had his phone out and was studying Leaman's information from the newspaper files. "Assault on a security guard in the course of theft."

"A break-in?" Diamond said with interest. "Where?"

"It was never a break-in," Spearman said. "I had my own set of keys."

Halliwell said, "Widcombe Hall."

"Where you worked?" Diamond's eyebrows peaked.

"Where I used to work," Spearman corrected him.

"I get it now. The estate was sold after Lord Deganwy died and the new owners didn't change the locks and you didn't hand over your keys. Naughty."

"I was going through a bad time."

"But you came into money. I'd call that a good time. I've seen the will. The old man left you ten grand."

Spearman made a sound deep in his throat, a laugh like curdled milk going down a drain. "That's what the damned prosecutor said in court. He didn't tell them I was jobless and kicked out of my home."

"Your home?"

"The converted coach house at Widcombe Hall. Okay, I could afford to rent in Twerton, but it was a rubbish place."

"Not the house where the skeleton was found?"

"For Christ's sake, no. Give me a break, will you? That's South Twerton. I was the other side of the Lower Bristol Road. Moving from the Coach House at Widcombe Hall to that poky two-room flat was a shock."

"And you were unemployed?"

"Estate steward jobs are few and far between. I tried. Oh yes, I tried looking for work, calling in favours from people I'd known. All they could offer was sympathy. I went to the job centre. Nothing. It wasn't a downward spiral, it was a free fall."

"So you decided to make use of those keys?"

"When I reached desperation point. I knew Widcombe Hall was going to be converted into a conference centre. The sale had gone through. You say you've seen the will. Everything except a few legacies went to the Electoral Reform Society, the entire estate and the contents worth millions. They wanted the money so they sold it straight away and when I thought about making my visit no one was living there, or so I believed, but the place was still stuffed with antiques. I reckoned if I let myself in and picked up some items of value nobody would notice."

"You didn't know about the security man?"

"Should have realised, but didn't. I was naïve. I rented a van and drove in there bold as brass. I was shifting things into the van when the guy caught me red-handed. Came at me with a bloody great baton. In self-defence I hit him with a silver candlestick. Put him in hospital. Didn't think he would already have phoned the police. Your lot stopped me before I drove out the gate."

"And you got three years? I'd say that was lenient."

"In Shepton Mallet clink? No, officer. That wasn't lenient."

Diamond didn't argue. Shepton Mallet was the most depressing prison he'd visited. The oldest in Britain, dating from the seventeenth century, it had been closed in 1930 and then reopened during the war and brought into use again, finally decommissioned as recently as 2013. "Before we talk about your life since then, I'd like to hear about Lord Deganwy."

"David? We were on first-name terms. He didn't stand on ceremony. He was a sweet man, a real gent, but I saw the change in him as the Alzheimer's got a grip. It happened horribly fast. And he had no family to care for him. He brought in nurses. I didn't see much of him in the last months. I was left to my own devices, managing the estate. It wasn't huge, nothing like Longleat, or Prior Park, or even Widcombe Manor, but it was a full-time job. I didn't have a lot of experience when he took me on, so I was grateful to him. Still am."

"Did you come across a man by the name of Sidney Harrod, who befriended him in the last year of his life?"

The eyes glittered enmity. "I know a bit about Harrod, yes."

"Tell us."

"He arrived out of nowhere, and he seemed to know David. I'd see his rusty van parked on the drive, not much of a motor for a guy who behaved like he was family. First I thought he might be some distant cousin, but it turned out they'd met through the Beau Nash Society. They'd go to pubs together and come back late. I'd hear them drive in. He used to strut around as if he owned the place. I was introduced, but he had no interest in me. All his focus was on David."

"You didn't trust his motives?"

"Didn't trust his actions. I saw stuff go into his van. Chairs and a writing desk. They were Chippendale, worth thousands. I'm certain he was nicking them."

"Did you challenge him?"

"I asked where they were going and he said they needed expert repairs. I asked if he was a furniture expert and he grinned and said he knew a man who was. I never found out where he lived."

"He lodged on the Moon Street estate and had a lock-up garage there. It wasn't used for the van. Your theory about the furniture ties in with our information."

"Typical. He shifted quite a lot of David's property and got away with it. I tried it one time only and got sent down for three years. What happened to him?"

"Don't you know?"

"He cleared off while David was still alive, simply vanished as suddenly as he arrived. That's the way his sort operate. He's probably in another town right now, ripping off some millionaire. Losers like me are the ones who get caught."

Was this an attempt to deceive, or was the man truly ignorant about Harrod's fate? Diamond let it pass. "Did anyone else come visiting during those last weeks of Lord Deganwy's life?"

"Doctors and nurses mostly. I didn't see all the comings and goings." Spearman leaned back on the sofa and clasped his hands behind his head as if it would aid the memory. "There was a professor from the Beau Nash Society. He only visited the once. Can't remember his name."

"Professor Duff, I expect."

"That was him, yes. He came because they hadn't heard anything from David and he was still their president. They didn't know he was so far gone."

"Duff took over as the Beau. Dead now."

"Is he?" Spearman couldn't have sounded less interested in Duff's death.

Diamond had learned enough for the time being about the year of Lord Deganwy's decline. He was keen to move on. He had urgent personal concerns. "It's quite a coincidence, isn't it, that after you came out of prison you got a job with someone else from the Beau Nash Society?"

Spearman's cheeks flushed. "What are you saying? That I'm up to my old games? You're dead wrong there."

"I said no such thing."

He carried on as if he hadn't heard. He hadn't listened for sure. "I went straight. You can ask Sir Ed. No way am I going back to prison."

"So what happened after your release?"

He shifted awkwardly on the sofa. "I don't like the way this is going. I have a wife and son and a steady job now."

"And a roof over your head," Halliwell put in.

"That's no crime."

Diamond was impatient. "Tell it like it happened."

"It was bloody tough when I came out. I was almost two years on the social. Jobseekers' allowance. Did bits and pieces, couldn't get steady work. Slept rough for a time. Sold the *Big Issue* on the streets. Then I had the good luck to meet Astra. She was on the staff at the job centre."

"Astra?"

"My wife."

"Hang on. You married your advisor at the job centre?"

"Not right away. That's jumping ahead."

"Well, don't. We're trying to follow this."

"I was attending the centre for years and I got to know most of the staff in that time. Astra was the one I always hoped to get because she really cared. And she got me sorted at last."

"With the Parises?"

"Not immediately. Jobwise, she sorted me out quite soon. I did some work on building sites, but I wasn't up to it physically. Astra talked it over with me and we agreed an ex-con wouldn't find a post as estate steward anywhere, but she had the smart idea of offering me as a driver to one of the big estates. I was used to working for that class of people and I had my licence. Astra's mother happened to be a client of Lady Sally's."

"A client? In what way?"

"I don't know if she uses the word client. It's beauty therapy. Lady Sally looks after their faces. She's a sociable lady with tons of energy and she told me she's always worked with people. Just because she has a title, it doesn't mean she sits by the pool all day. So Astra knew from her mum about Sir Ed being the Beau. She's a big believer in making connections."

Halliwell said without looking at Diamond, "Networking."

"Spot on," Spearman said, nodding his approval. "She told the Parises everything about my conviction and Sir Ed still agreed to take me on as their chauffeur, especially when he knew I'd been estate steward to David Deganwy."

"The Beau Nash connection helped?"

"Certainly did. Sir Ed has been a member for a long time. He knew David and Professor Duff. Sometimes speaks about them in the car when we're driving. He must have known that scumbag Sidney Harrod as well."

"Has he ever mentioned Harrod?"

"No. I think he'd rather forget him."

"So how long have you had this job?"

"Since 2006. When I joined them they were living out at Monkton Combe. Nice house and garden, but they moved to a place near Bathampton and I went with them and then made the move here. They never settle for long, but they always make sure I'm comfortable as well. I'm almost family now."

"And when did you marry Astra?"

His eyes lit up. "Six years ago last June. The Parises were brilliant about it. They let me borrow the Bentley for the wedding and Lady Sally did Astra's make-up and made her dress. She's a top quality needlewoman as well as everything else. They gave us a week in Paris as their present."

"You're bloody lucky."

"You can say that again. While I was banged up in Shepton Mallet I'd never have believed how my life would change."

"Obviously they value what you do."

"I've always tried to be helpful. When they moved here and built the infinity pool I was able to give some advice because David Deganwy had one built when I was stewarding for him."

"They have an infinity pool?" He'd seen such things on TV commercials.

"Haven't you seen it?"

Diamond shook his head. "This is my first visit here. All I've seen is the lodge." He could have added that he was desperate to know what was going on at the main house.

Spearman was talking about infinity pools. "They're status symbols. People of their class get them built if they have the right kind of terrain. You need a really steep slope and that brings its own problems with the mechanics. They have to be anchored safely because they're incredibly heavy. It works like a weir. You need a second pool at a lower level to catch the water constantly overflowing and a system of pumps and balance tanks to circulate it. The engineering is quite complex."

"You're on the side of a valley here, aren't you?"

"Yes, with a great view. The pool is a feature, no question, but I'm the only one who uses it. Lady Sally sits beside it on a lounger sometimes, but Sir Ed doesn't bother much with it. To him, it raises the value of the property and he's happy with that."

"They'll be showing it off to their party guests." Diamond was still in two minds.

"You're right. They sent me out this morning to buy some better sunshades."

"Do you know who's been invited?"

"Beau Nash Society people, mostly. It's a sort of farewell do. He's stepping down as the Beau and he tells me he's pleased to be shot of it."

"His words?"

"He may have added something colourful. He can be down-to-earth when he chooses. He reckons he's done more than his share as chairman."

"President."

"Okay."

"Speaking of shots, does Sir Edward own a gun?"

Spearman looked startled by the question. "I've never seen him with one. There are no game birds here. The ground isn't suitable for shooting. Most of the property is a sixty-degree slope and even more sheer in places, perfect for the pool, but useless for anything else. They let the lower part grow wild and nobody ever goes there."

"Down in the valley—that's all part of the estate?"

"If you can call it that. There's a high wall to mark the limit of their land."

Diamond was thinking hard, making connections, networking inside his own head. "Do you have any idea whether

Sir Ed had an earlier marriage? Lady Sally is quite a bit younger than he is."

"Nothing wrong with that," Spearman said, straightening up on the sofa. "I'm nearly fifteen years older than my wife."

"It's a question, that's all."

"No idea."

"When they married, was he already the Beau?"

"Must have been. They hadn't been married long when I started work with them. He was already a big name locally. I expect he ploughed some of his money into the society." He looked at his watch. "I ought to be at the party handing out drinks. Can we draw a line under this?"

"Soon as possible," Diamond said, and meant it. "There's one more thing. Your boy Rufus was talking to us and if I understood him right you and he were at Twerton the morning the skeleton was discovered at the demolition site."

He reddened again. "Kids."

"It wasn't imagination. He said you lifted him up to one of the observation windows to see the wrecking ball at work. Is that right?"

"We happened to be there, yes."

"In Twerton?"

"I was having one of the cars serviced. There's a very reliable motor mechanic there I've used for years. I took the boy with me to give Astra a break. We were killing time."

"Killing time?"

"While the work was being done. He's at the age of asking endless questions and he noticed people at the windows and wanted to know what was going on. I lifted him up for a look and it was bad timing because that was when the ball ripped open the roof and exposed the skeleton."

"Was he frightened?"

"No, he took it in his stride. I got him away as soon as I saw the thing for myself."

"And you were there before we were called?"

368 ■ PETER LOVESEY ■

"Must have been."

"But two days later you were back with Sir Edward when the skeleton was lifted out. You'd managed to get inside the secure area. I remember seeing you both. I sent DCI Halliwell to speak to you."

Halliwell confirmed it with a murmur.

Diamond added, "You can't have forgotten. Sir Edward spoke to us later in the Archway café. Why the special journey for another look?"

Spearman didn't seem to think of their presence as guilty conduct. "The papers were full of the story, weren't they? Sir Ed wanted to see for himself so he asked me to drive him out there."

"Did he say anything to you about why he made the trip?"

"I just told you."

"He didn't make any link to the Beau Nash Society?"

"If he did, it was all in his head. Nothing was said to me."

This time it was Diamond who checked his watch. "You'd better get back to your duties serving the drinks. I'll follow shortly. Mine's a beer."

Spearman frowned and shook his head. "Sir Ed doesn't want you there. He made that very clear. That's why he sent me to see you."

"Obstructing the police is an arrestable offence. Tell him that, if you want. I'll have that beer in a tankard."

28

All the principal officers in CID together with a back-up of ten uniformed constables had gathered at a passing point along the lane not more than fifty yards from the front gate. Diamond stood on the bank opposite to brief them. Their objective was to seal off the grounds with a car and two officers blocking the front entrance and the others out of sight and marshalling the wild area along the escarpment immediately below the infinity pool. This, he explained, was the most obvious escape route for anyone trying to evade arrest. To be in place and remain unseen, the team would need to footslog their way along the rear of the property, climb the steep valley side as rapidly they could and space themselves at intervals out of sight along the margin.

Easily said. Peter Diamond was getting a reputation for commando-course missions. Some of these same officers had endured the rain-soaked dig at Twerton. This afternoon they had sweltering heat and a stiff climb to contend with. Yet if there was muttering in the ranks he didn't hear it.

He admitted he hadn't scouted the grounds for himself, but this was normal in police operations. Using Ingeborg's tablet he was able to show everyone a map and aerial photography of the terrain.

Halliwell, Leaman and Gilbert moved off with the constables towards a footpath descending to the valley floor. Ingeborg and one uniformed sergeant would set up the block at the main entrance. Diamond himself walked the short distance with them.

It was agreed that communication would be by phone. Nobody would contact Diamond, but he would alert the team to developments when an opportunity came. This could be the fatal flaw in the plan.

"Are you okay about making contact, guv?" Ingeborg asked as tactfully as she could.

Bloody technology. His nerves were at snapping point. "I'm not a total dumbo."

"Never said you were."

"It's a simple matter of pressing the right keys."

"Exactly."

"You'd better go over it with me."

The raised voices from the patio beside the infinity pool left Diamond in no doubt where to find most of the guests. Going by the shrieks of jollity no one had been deprived of drinks while Spearman was away being interviewed. Some of the forty or more were standing, glasses in hand, but a few had looked for shade and a place to sit at the tables. Lady Sally in a white dress flitted like a butterfly from group to group with a tray of canapés. More food and drink was served from an open marquee.

Diamond was quick to spot Paloma in a blue summer dress he hadn't seen before. Tie straps and billowy sleeves. She was looking relaxed in a group that included Estella, Sir Edward and several of the Beau Nash crowd including Crispin, the one who so enjoyed the sound of his own voice.

He decided not to go straight over. His plan was to merge inconspicuously, but this was already proving difficult. He was getting suspicious looks and he knew why. Leaving his suit jacket in the car and removing his tie hadn't done the trick. He didn't look the part of one of Bath's glitterati. The tankard of beer hadn't been such a good idea either.

He'd been desperate for a long drink because he was thirsty. Most of them were holding flute glasses.

The stunning effect of the blue water with its limitless edge projected against the soft scenery of the Charlcombe valley was almost lost on him, thinking of his hapless officers toiling up the slope.

Someone gripped his sleeve and he turned to find himself face to face with an unlikely vision in a straw boater and green maxi dress.

Georgina.

"What on earth are you up to?" she asked through the side of her mouth as if she didn't want to be seen talking to him.

"Going about my normal duties, ma'am."

"Did you get an invitation?"

"No, I'm a gatecrasher."

"What?"

"It's all downhill from here. I'm going to make an arrest."

"You can't."

"I must."

"These are my friends."

"Mine, too," he said. "Paloma's here, in case you hadn't noticed. My main concern is to avoid a shootout."

"Oh God."

"When the moment comes, I'd appreciate your assistance in controlling the situation, ma'am. If necessary tell them to throw themselves on the ground."

"I can't believe what I'm hearing. Look at my arms. They're covered in gooseflesh. Can't you wait for a better moment?"

He shook his head. "It's all set up. The place is surrounded."

Georgina had difficulty finding words. "Why wasn't I informed?"

"No time, unfortunately. I had to act fast."

"You'd better tell me who you're planning to arrest."

"I would, but . . ."

"But what?"

"We're about to be interrupted. Don't step to your right, whatever you do." He'd noticed an electrically powered wheelchair moving in rapidly from the rear. He pitched his voice higher to make the introduction. "This is my friend Algy, the most senior member of the Beau Nash Society."

"Don't know about that," Algy said, ready for a jovial chat. "I've never held office. I just go on and on."

"Georgina is my boss, the assistant chief constable."

"Making sure you behave yourself?"

"Too late for that," Diamond said and Georgina's look showed that for once they were in agreement.

Algy was looking dapper in a striped shirt and white chinos. "Peter is a hero as far as I'm concerned," he told Georgina. "A credit to the force. Rescued me at our last meeting from what I can only describe as an incommodious situation. I said I wanted to put him up for a commendation, but he wouldn't have it. Such modesty."

"'Secrecy' sums it up better," Georgina said. "He doesn't tell me anything."

Diamond's attention was elsewhere. "Tell me, Algy, is the small man with the fluffy blond hair and the purple kaftan one of your Beau Nash people?"

Algy had to crane for a look across the pool. "Him? No, no, he doesn't belong to us. That's Duncan Newburn, the owner of the Upmarket Gallery in Broad Street."

"I thought so. What's he doing here?"

"Top secret," Algy said. "My lips are sealed."

"A friend of the Parises?"

"Not that I've heard. All will become clear at some stage."

"He was definitely invited?"

"Certainly."

Georgina commented, "Which is more than one can say for everyone here."

"Speaking of which," Diamond said, "I'm going to circulate. That's what you do at cocktail parties, isn't it? I'll leave you two to get better acquainted." And he moved off before they could stop him.

Lady Sally was still offering canapés so he went over.

"Pete, how nice to see you," she said. "Did Georgie bring you?"

He had to think who Georgie was. "No, I'm a grown-up. I found my own way here."

She smiled. "These are nice. Try a mini quiche—or three. You look as if you could do with a bite to eat."

He didn't turn down the offer. "I was just saying I'm surprised to see one of your guests, Duncan Newburn, the gallery owner. He's nothing to do with the Beau Nash Society, is he?"

"Not to my knowledge," Lady Sally said. "I only met him for the first time a few minutes ago. But I do know what he's doing here and it's top secret, only not for much longer." She looked across the pool to where Newburn was telling some story with animated gestures. "He seems to be enjoying himself. Do you know him?"

"Our paths have crossed, yes."

She laughed. "I hope he doesn't have a criminal record."

"Speaking of which," he said, "I've been talking to your chauffeur."

"Jim? What about? Gossip? My failing marriage?"

The last remark caught him off guard and sounded as if it was a whole different story she might not wish to enlarge on, so he let it pass. "He had nice things to say about you and your husband—like the second chance you gave him when you offered him the job."

"That was years ago. He's more than justified our faith in him."

"He said you paid for their honeymoon."

"Did he? I'd almost forgotten. With Ed's money, we can afford it."

"Even more generously, you made Astra's wedding dress."

"And delighted to do it. Dressmaking can be awfully humdrum. A wedding dress is a joy to work on."

"But you've got to be experienced to take on a job like that."

"Actually, it's not the most difficult, provided that the bride knows what she wants and doesn't keep changing her mind. Astra was fine."

"Where did you learn?"

"Most women take up the needle at some point in their lives. I started young."

"But you don't do it professionally any more?"

The colour rose to her cheeks. "You're not an income tax inspector as well a policeman, are you? No, it's my hobby. Everything I do—the beauty therapy—is because I enjoy it. My clients pay a nominal fee, but that barely covers the materials. It's more for their peace of mind than mine."

They were interrupted by the sound of metal on glass, Jim Spearman striking an empty bottle with a large serving spoon to get attention. At his side was the host, Sir Edward Paris. People stopped their conversations and turned to hear the announcement.

"I know, I know, I know," a smiling Sir Ed wooed his audience with the confidence of a man who had paid for everything in sight and was on home territory among friends, "we told you it was just a bash by the pool. No speeches and no presents, but there's a reason why we're here—a very attractive reason—and she's gone all shy and trying not to be noticed, and that's difficult in a yellow trouser suit."

Estella was laughing.

Diamond looked to his left to see how Lady Sally was taking this. She wasn't sharing in the amusement. Evidence of the failing marriage? For all the banter between them, she and Ed had seemed a devoted couple until a moment ago.

Ed was saying, "Most of you know Estella is taking over from me as president of our esteemed Beau Nash Society—our new Beau—unless she decides to call herself the Belle. Does that have a good ring to it? Whatever it is, I want to congratulate her and wish her well, and if you'll just step forward, Estella . . ." He turned to Spearman. "Where are they, Jim?"

Spearman dipped behind a low wall and came up with a bouquet the size of Somerset. The mobile phones were out to take pictures but if a kiss was exchanged no one could tell behind the flowers as they passed from the Beau to the Belle. Estella had to return them to the ground straight away. She smiled and nodded her thanks and someone shouted, "Speech," and Sir Ed said, "No speeches. That's all, folks."

But somebody had other ideas. Who else but Crispin? He raised a hand and announced in beautifully articulated words, "Not quite all, Ed. After so many years as president you can't be allowed to walk into the sunset without some token of our affection. We have a small surprise for you in the main reception room of your house. Yes, it's come to that—you don't even know what's going on in your own home. If everyone would kindly move inside, we'll unveil our small tribute to Sir Edward in a few minutes."

"Was this the secret you mentioned just now?" Diamond asked Lady Sally.

"Yes. I had the job of distracting him while they got it ready."

"Something involving Newburn?"

"Indirectly, yes. I'd better go inside," she added. "They want me near the front."

Diamond was pleased to have a moment to himself—the chance to contact his back-up team by phone. He moved across the lawn to a shaded area under a willow.

Success at the first touch of the controls—and no one at his side to appreciate it.

"Guv?" Halliwell sounded pleased.

"How far away are you?"

"Some distance to go, I'm afraid. Maybe twenty minutes more climbing."

"As long as that?"

"It's bloody steep and overgrown in places. No one has come through here in years as far as I can tell. But we made a find."

"Oh?"

"Almost at the bottom of the steepest part, a gun."

Diamond pressed the phone harder to his ear. "Did I hear you right? A gun?"

"Handgun."

"Really?" His heart started pumping at a rate he could practically hear. "Amazing . . . What sort—a revolver?"

"A Smith and Wesson and what's more it says nine millimetres on the barrel. It's in good nick as far as I can see. Obviously hasn't been lying there long. Scarcely any dust and muck on it."

"Have any of you handled it?"

"It's okay. It won't get contaminated. John Leaman had a spare evidence bag in his pocket. He thinks of everything. But he wasn't the one who found it. That was one of the uniformed guys."

Diamond was silent for some seconds, processing this sensational new information. "You were just telling me no one had been through before."

"It must have been thrown from the top where you are. It's a sheer drop of maybe a hundred and fifty feet below the pool."

"Can you see the pool from where you are?"

"You're kidding. It's huge. From down here it looks like a multistorey car park built into the side of the hill. If someone stood where the water tips over and slung the gun as far as they could, it would land roughly where we found it."

He didn't have time to trade theories with Keith. They both knew the whopping significance of the find.

"Anyhow," Halliwell continued, "we marked the spot on the ground and moved on. Serious climbing in front of us and there's thick bracken here. A machete would be more use to us than a gun. How's it going with you?"

"Tough. I don't think I can manage another sausage roll."

"Still on for an arrest?"

"Definitely. I can't stand here talking. There's some kind of presentation underway. I'll call you again when I need you."

He pocketed the phone and stepped out towards the house. Most of the partygoers were already inside but a voice hailed him from behind. "What do you think of the building, then?"

He turned and saw Algy fast approaching in his scooter. A distraction he could do without.

"I haven't given it a proper look," he answered in all truth. "I got to the party late and came round the side without taking it in." Forced to take an interest in Ed's dream home, he wasn't over-impressed now he was facing the twisted steel and glass north aspect.

"Hideous, isn't it?" Algy said.

"Wouldn't be my choice, I have to say." Right now he didn't want to debate modern architecture.

"Nor mine. Frank Lloyd Wright, who knew a bit about designing buildings, once said something along the lines of a doctor can bury his mistakes, but an architect can only advise his client to plant vines."

"Nice one."

"And I don't think it's wheelchair-friendly. Ed ought to know better than that, being a builder. Will you help me up the steps?"

Diamond should have guessed Algy had been leading up to this. He meant the set of ten steps in front of the entrance. The house was sited on a steep slope.

Hard to refuse.

"We'll need a second person." Algy was already waving to recruit another helpmate. "When you're handicapped you soon learn it doesn't pay to be shy."

One of the Beau Nash regulars came over, a clergyman Diamond remembered from the meeting in the Circus and so thin that his dog collar gaped like a pouch. Surely capable of lifting hearts and minds, but a wheelchair containing the chunky Algy might be more of a test.

"The only way up is backwards," Algy told them both. "You take the handles, reverend, and Pete will provide the beef. He'll face me, hold on to the frame and do the lifting."

No point in suggesting Algy vacated the chair while they took it to the top. Diamond would end up trying to carry the overweight man upstairs in his arms. The wheels definitely had to be employed in this operation.

The two good Samaritans obeyed orders and with a bit of a struggle succeeded in raising the scooter step by step to the top. Diamond was on autopilot, absorbing the news he'd got from Halliwell. There was no proof yet that the revolver was the weapon that had murdered Perry Morgan, but everything suggested it was.

"Deeply obliged, gentlemen," Algy said. "Haven't delayed you much, I trust. I didn't want to skip the tribute after I helped pay for it. We won't have missed much. If Crispin's in charge, he's awfully long-winded." Free to go, he went—at some speed into the house.

The room was packed for the presentation. On this hot

afternoon no one in his right mind would want to be there long. People were making room for the wheelchair and Diamond followed far enough inside to get a reasonable view. At the front, Crispin was standing like an old-fashioned schoolmaster beside an easel, except that it wasn't supporting a blackboard but some substantial object draped in red velvet. Close by was Newburn, the drug-pusher and gallery owner. From his expression you would think he was an angel in a nativity play.

". . . and we decided at an early stage," Crispin was saying, "that we should look for something he could keep, a memento of his years as our Beau, and one of us happened to look into the window of a shop in Broad Street, the Upmarket Gallery, and see a rather novel work of art, a *trompe l'oeil*—is that the term, Mr. Newburn?"

Happy to be mentioned, the golden-haired cocaine-seller bestowed his blessing with a smile.

Crispin was in full flow. "This serendipitous event—the sighting of the object in the window—gave us the idea of commissioning a unique gift for Ed, something we believe he will enjoy for at least as many years as he has served as our president and, we hope, much longer than that. There wasn't a lot of time and there was research involved and official permission, questions of copyright and all manner of things Ed was blissfully unaware of. We took Lady Sally into our confidence and she has conspired with us to make sure the artist knew exactly what was required while Ed knew nothing."

On Crispin's other side, Lady Sally nodded. She was standing beside her new friend Georgina.

"So without more ado," Crispin said (and you could almost hear the sighs of relief), "I invite Sir Edward Paris, our respected Beau, to step forward and unveil his leaving present from the society."

To huge applause, the man of the moment appeared

from the front row, shaking his head in a way that was both gratified and baffled. He grasped the velvet cover and lifted it from a gold-framed picture of . . . who else but Beau Nash? Ed was getting a full-sized copy of the portrait in the Pump Room, the white tricorne, wavy black wig, pouched blue eyes, ruddy complexion and double chin—the fat old dandy in his dotage.

There is a famous film clip of Sir Winston Churchill on his eightieth birthday being presented with a gift from both houses of Parliament—his portrait by Graham Sutherland. The likeness was not flattering. Seated against a brown panelled background, Winston was depicted with chin thrust forward and brow foreshortened, eyes narrowed, nostrils flared and mouth downturned. He had seen the painting ahead of the unveiling in Westminster Hall and taken a firm dislike to it. After the curtains parted the old warrior took a theatrical look at the work before stepping up to the microphone. He was eloquent as always. This was "a remarkable example of modern art. It certainly combines force and candour." A moment of uneasy silence followed and then a wide grin from Churchill gave the audience the cue to laugh. The remarkable example of modern art was afterwards dumped in a cellar at Chartwell until it was taken out and burned on the instructions of Lady Churchill.

Ed's reaction to his gift from the Beau Nash Society was equally unappreciative, but far less polished than Churchill's. He glared at the old Beau as if he was the grim reaper making an appearance on Christmas morning. As he'd made clear several times, he'd "had it up to here" with Nash, who was "an old poser" and a "silly arse." He turned away from the offensive image, twisting the red velvet as if he was preparing to strangle someone and Crispin was the closest.

However, Crispin wasn't fazed. He stepped behind the portrait and shifted the angle a fraction and a remarkable thing happened. The image of Beau Nash underwent a change. It morphed into Sir Edward Paris himself, in the identical eighteenth-century costume, wig and hat. Gasps and cries came from the audience. Then they realised they were looking at a hologram and burst into applause.

Well and truly caught out, Ed was clapping harder than anyone.

29

Find Paloma first.

Diamond's planning was meant to avoid violence, but every plan is imperfect. He couldn't predict what would happen at the end. Faced with exposure, any criminal is a wounded tiger.

So his self-imposed duty as the guests streamed out of the house was to persuade Paloma to leave the party at once. If she remained, there was a real danger she would get caught up in the serious events to come. They hadn't spoken all afternoon, but she must have spotted him and she'd think it inexcusable to ignore him. It was sod's law that she would innocently pick the moment he was poised to make the arrest.

Find Paloma.

Before him was a civilised scene played out by decent people used to the conventions of the English garden party. Most were strolling towards the infinity pool and the view across the valley. A group was forming around a barbecue trolley in the marquee. Some were laying claim to the patio tables. A few more had found the circular tree seat surrounding a huge oak. All in a country garden on a perfect summer afternoon innocent of anything more dangerous than a few flying insects.

Or so it appeared.

Detached from it all, Diamond was increasingly concerned.

He shaded his eyes from the glare and scanned the entire panorama.

Mistakenly he'd assumed she would be with her friend, but Estella was at the foot of the steps surrounded by members of the society and Paloma wasn't among them. He trotted down the steps himself.

"Hi," Estella said.

When he asked, she shook her head.

"She wouldn't have left?"

She smiled at the possibility. "Better not. I'll need a lift home if she has."

"She was with you earlier."

"When I was given the flowers, yes."

"Was she at the presentation just now?"

"I didn't notice, but I wasn't looking for her. Is she still in the house, do you think?"

This was fast becoming one of those classic nightmares we have all experienced where you know of an imminent threat and need to warn people but can't make them understand. Typically the brain conjures up a social occasion like this where the guests, zombie-like, are unresponsive, intent only on interacting among themselves. Try as you might to communicate, everyone behaves as if you don't exist. You are the outsider.

He left Estella with her group and dashed up the steps to the house.

Inside the room where the presentation had taken place, Sir Edward Paris was still standing in front of his portrait, admiring it in conversation with the spindly clergyman.

From Diamond's angle all that was visible of the hologram was the gloating screw-you gaze of Beau Nash—the one-time King of Bath materialising once again to mock him. At each low point Nash found a way to show his malign presence.

He wouldn't allow it to mess with his brain.

"I'm looking for Paloma Kean."

"Come again," Ed said.

Diamond repeated the name and Ed said, "Can't say I know her. Do you?" he asked the cleric.

A shake of the head.

The hologram was grinning.

Merciless.

"She was with Estella," he told them, "but she isn't now."

"Oh yeah?"

"Blue dress and wearing a boater."

"I never notice what women are wearing," Ed said. "It all passes me by."

"I can't see her outside. Is anyone else in the house?"

"Only my wife. She went upstairs with someone."

"Which way?"

"Hold on, matey. It's Sally's private apartment. I don't go in there myself without knocking."

But Diamond was already through the door and mounting two stairs at a time.

He came to a short corridor with several doors. Another of those stock nightmare situations. He couldn't waste time. He thought voices were coming from behind one so he thrust it open.

Paloma was in there—but finding her was no comfort to Diamond, for she was held captive. The lady of the house, the charming Sally Paris, had grabbed her from behind, one hand around her chest and the other holding a pair of dressmaking scissors to her throat.

"Stand back, or she gets it."

30

They were in a fully equipped dressmaker's room with generous high windows for natural light; two sewing machines on tables; a long trestle table for cutting out; an adjustable tailor's dummy; an ironing board and steam iron; a glass-fronted cabinet filled with reels of thread in many colours; an open cupboard stacked high with rolls of fabric and storage boxes filled with patterns; several shelves of books on fashion; and three moveable racks of garments on hangers.

As a professional in the rag trade Paloma must have been thrilled by the invitation to see inside this amazing workplace. It was all as tidy as a barrack room ready for inspection except that on the floor at Paloma's feet was a large white hat she must have been admiring the instant before she was grabbed.

Diamond took in the scene at a glance, eagle-eyed for anything he might use to distract Sally Paris—but only if an opportunity came. Madness to try while the gleaming blades of the scissors were pressing into Paloma's flesh and the slightest movement could penetrate her skin and kill her.

Sally's eyes gaped wide. Behind them dangerous emotions spun like subatomic particles. In this state she was capable of anything.

Negotiate.

All he could think of doing right now was to take a small step back and make a calming movement with his hands, palms down as if he was warming them over a heater. This wasn't a moment for heroics.

Paloma said, "Pete—"

"Shut it." The scissors flashed as Sally's grip tightened.

Paloma cried out in pain, winced and closed her eyes. The two women were backed into a corner against the bookshelves, Sally almost hidden behind Paloma, looking over her right shoulder.

Briefly he locked eyes with Paloma. "For God's sake don't try anything, Paloma. We can resolve this."

Sally fixed Diamond with a glare that was more about him than her hostage. Her words were steeped in bitterness. "Damn you, I should have known you were on to me when you asked me about the wedding dress I made. 'You don't do it professionally any more,' you said—the killer phrase. I thought I'd closed off that part of my life."

She wanted dialogue and so did he.

"You did," he said. "You closed off your past, no question." The theory of negotiating with a hostage-taker starts with active listening, agreeing with everything, demonstrating empathy by picking up things they say and repeating them. Aim to achieve a rapport and treat their situation as a problem you both need to solve.

The theory—if you can hold your nerve enough to use it.

She asked him, "So where did I go wrong?"

"Go wrong? You didn't. Do you want to know how I found out?" he said, latching on to her curiosity while trying to think what the hell he would say next. The object was to keep her talking, get her confidence. He knew it shouldn't be rushed.

Excellent in theory. But this wasn't in the abstract. Across the room from him was Paloma with a lethal weapon to her throat and he was terrified of what might happen. Sally looked terrified, too, but terrified of him. "Put down the scissors," he told her, "and I'll tell you."

"I'm not that stupid."

The words burst out like machine-gun fire. He'd provoked her. As a negotiator he'd messed up already.

He could see Paloma's rapid breathing. He could practically hear her heartbeats.

This was all too personal to manage by the book. He was going to wing it.

Sally wouldn't have lured Paloma up here to attack her. She'd dropped her guard to share her interest in dressmaking. Both women must have felt relaxed until he came charging upstairs. Precisely what had been said between them he could not know. She was unlikely to know how important Paloma was in his life.

"Okay," he said. "I'll tell you what made me suspect you, but you'd better understand those scissors could be pressing on an artery. You don't want to take an innocent life."

Her slaughterhouse stare didn't change and neither did her grip.

"There were reasons for the other deaths," he said. "There's absolutely no reason to kill again."

It didn't seem to register.

"We dug up the garden at Twerton," he told her with a huge effort to keep his words from provoking her, "and we found various things that confused us, but one small item that got me thinking—a triangle of chalk."

Mistake. Far from taking the heat out of the revelation, the chalk came as a shock to her. She drew in her breath with such force that he thought she would stab the scissors into Paloma's neck.

He waited, uncertain whether to go on.

After a pause he decided he couldn't do anything but continue in as low key a delivery as possible. "Tailor's chalk is often shaped like that, isn't it? Made me think it must have belonged to someone who lived in the murder house at some stage. A tailor perhaps, or a seamstress. The tenant at the time we're talking about, 1997, wasn't a tailor. Harry Morgan drove taxis. But there was a woman called Sarah who lived with him and left suddenly after the killing and we didn't know much about her. Could she have used the chalk in her job? I asked myself. And now you're wondering how we discovered the woman in Twerton was you, the wife of a highly successful businessman."

At least she was listening. She hadn't denied a word of it.

"In any investigation it's a process of collecting information and it happens that one important clue is lying on the floor in front of you."

"Don't move," she warned him. "Don't you dare move."

"The hat," he said. "The nice big hat that you wore to the meeting. Beautifully made. Your own handiwork, I'm sure. For a long time you kept your dressmaking a secret, for obvious reasons. Your new husband knew nothing about it at the beginning. He had to make do with a ready-to-wear costume run up in some sweatshop in the Far East—even though you could have made one for him. But years later, when you felt safer and confident enough to equip this room and enjoy the needlework again as a hobby, you made the hat for yourself and your sense of humour came into play."

Her sense of humour was a memory now.

"You couldn't resist topping off the bonnet with a Bath bun made of fabric. I'm no dressmaker, but I think I know what that little item was originally—a pincushion."

She gave an impatient sigh that told him he was right.

"You came to the Beau Nash Society wearing a hat with a cloth Bath bun. Sarah the seamstress is Lady Sally the beautician. After all, the name Sally is a short form of Sarah."

She said, "Is that a crime?"

"On its own, no. Together with all the other evidence

stacking up it led me to speculate why the victim, the man who was finally reduced to a skeleton because his body was hidden in the loft for years and years, might have come to a humble house in Twerton."

"You don't know the half of it," she said.

"Care to tell me?"

"No. I'll hear your version." The scissors were still poised at Paloma's throat. Nothing he said was going to break Sally's concentration.

He kept talking. "The man who died wasn't a nice man at all. He was a con artist. He conned a rich old man out of some of his property, valuable items of furniture. More importantly, he took possession of an eighteenth-century costume the old man, Lord Deganwy, had worn because he was president of the Beau Nash Society. By then—I'm speaking of 1997—this con man known to most people as Sidney Harrod had so far insinuated himself into the society that he was being tipped as the next Beau. Lord Deganwy was suffering from dementia and it was inevitable they would need to find someone else. Harrod helped himself to the costume and wanted it altered so that he could wear it. He'd heard of a skilful seamstress in Twerton and he came to you. Am I making sense?"

She said nothing. Through all this he was trying not to look into Paloma's terrified eyes. Her ordeal had to continue.

"I'm guessing now," he told Sally, "and only you can say exactly what happened. There would have been more than one fitting. You and Sidney Harrod alone in that small ter-raced house. We know he had a reputation, fancied himself as a ladies' man even though he was getting on in years. You were young and attractive and the job of measuring and touching him, getting close, got him sexually excited. Is that the truth?"

A tightening of her mouth told him it was. The revulsion lingered, a stain that couldn't be removed.

"He made a pass at you, this grotesque old man, and you were shocked and tried to step away, but he grabbed or groped you and in panic you reached for your scissors in self-defence and thrust them towards his chest. We know they can be razor sharp. He put up his hand to defend himself and got cut to the bone in the process. But one more frenzied lunge from you got past, straight through his ribs. Fatal."

His depiction of the scene made such an impact on her that a sound more sob than threat came from her throat when he described the moment of death.

"Call it self-defence, unintentional, an involuntary act," he said. "Any decent lawyer would argue it wasn't murder. But you were there with a dead man, appalled at what you'd done. I can scarcely imagine the horrors you suffered in the hours that followed, the discussion you had with your partner Harry when he came home. You didn't report the death to the police for sure."

Her eyes slid upwards. She couldn't change anything now.

He persevered. "I get the feeling Harry came up with the plan to hide the body. Carried it up to the loft just as it was, in the Beau Nash costume, sat it in a chair and left it there to rot. Then he sealed the hatch and did some plasterwork, rendered the ceiling to make it appear there had never been access. You moved out. I can't say I blame you. Harry must have had nerves of steel to remain there another three years."

"He was a man in a million," she volunteered and if it didn't amount to a full confession, or even confirmation of everything Diamond had just said, it still told him plenty.

He continued to probe. "But Harry had a secret of his own, didn't he? When did you learn he already had a son by another woman?"

She said evenly, "Before I moved in with him. It was never a secret. He was always straight with me."

"About the year 2000, Harry moved out of Twerton and went to live in Larkhall. Two years later the mother of his child died of cancer and Harry offered his boy, Perry, a home. It didn't concern you because you and Harry had already gone your separate ways. You met someone else. Your life changed out of all recognition when you married Ed Paris."

"Why don't you tell me something I *don't* know?"

"I will in a minute. Perry was a bright lad, a born organiser, really going places. But of course he had a flaw. The cocaine. He spent nearly all his money funding his habit. It's never-ending."

"So . . . ?" Defiant, she still wasn't willing to admit anything.

"So when the demolition squad broke open the Twerton house and revealed the skeleton, Perry saw his opportunity. He knew his father had lived in that house with you and that you took in work as a seamstress and left suddenly in 1997. Exactly how much Harry had told him about the killing, I can't say. He may have referred to it obliquely as a bad time, a secret he preferred to forget. Or, being a man in a million, he may have felt he owed it to his son to tell him everything. Perry was smart enough to make the connection when the skeleton was discovered and all over the media. He knew what a catastrophe this was for you and he decided to cash in. Money for drugs in return for his silence."

Sally's expression underwent a total change. There was resignation in her look and her eyes had turned glossy with tears.

"He was an opportunist, but he met a better one in you," Diamond continued. "You found out what he did for a living and his role in the world fireworks competition. You possessed a revolver. I'm guessing here, but I expect you were in such a state of terror after what happened in Twerton that Harry Morgan obtained it for you to keep as self-protection. What is certain is that on the final night of the fireworks you shot Perry dead, knowing the gun blasts would be masked by all the bangers going off."

"You can't prove any of this," she said, but without conviction.

"Sorry to disillusion you, but I can. A moment ago you asked me to tell you something you don't know and this is it. A party of police officers is in the valley below your infinity pool and they found a gun that was obviously thrown into the wild part where nobody normally goes. Our ballistics people won't have any difficulty proving it was the Smith and Wesson revolver used in the murder."

The immediate reaction was a sound of despair, a strange primal moan from deep in Sally's chest. The scissors in her right hand twisted and gleamed and for one hideous moment Diamond thought she would plunge them into Paloma's flesh, but she loosened her grip and let them fall and clatter on the tiled floor.

Paloma wrestled herself free and took a step towards Diamond just as he moved to help her. She swayed, turned deathly white and collapsed into his arms.

Sally spotted her opportunity. She darted left and was out of the door and down the stairs.

31

Any first-aider will tell you that the correct procedure when someone faints in your arms from stress is to lower them gently to the floor and, after making sure they can breathe freely, raise their legs above the level of the heart to restore the flow of blood to the brain. Diamond knew the drill. He also knew he wouldn't be leaving Paloma's side. He was on his knees supporting her ankles.

Never mind that Sally had escaped. Let her go. He'd catch up with her eventually. For the present he was needed here.

The colour still hadn't returned to Paloma's face when her eyes opened after a matter of seconds. A fainting episode is usually over quickly, but the recovery can't be rushed.

She managed to say, "Where . . . ?"

"It's okay," he told her. "Keep still. You fainted."

"I never faint."

"I promise you, you did. What you went through was mind-blowing."

"I've gone cold, and yet I'm sweating."

"That's normal."

"It's coming back to me now." She raised her head off the floor. "Where is she?"

"Relax. She's gone."

She needed to make sense of the experience by

describing it to him. "I scarcely know the woman. We were talking, she and I, and she was charming. She asked what I do and I told her about my business and she offered to show me her needlework room. We were here, speaking normally, looking at the hat she'd made, and we heard footsteps running up the stairs—"

"That would be me."

"And the next thing she'd grabbed me and was holding the scissors to my neck."

"My stupid fault, blundering in," he said. "Shouldn't have alarmed her."

"Don't be daft, Pete. You're not responsible for her actions." She smiled and reached for his hand. "I'm not having it. You're my hero."

Cue the violins.

Paloma was recovering. Her brain had processed the events and now she understood enough to become calm and get back to normal. She propped herself on her elbows and then sat up, eyes clear and looking into his.

But this couldn't be the romantic ending. Diamond said, "Forgive me. I need to phone a couple of people."

He took out the mobile and spoke first to Ingeborg, warning her that Sally might attempt to drive through the gate.

"You mean Lady Sally?"

"I'll explain all later. Just stop her and make an arrest if she comes your way. I must update Keith now."

So much had happened since he'd last been in touch with Halliwell that he was shocked to hear his back-up team were still making the difficult ascent from the valley. Tempted to ask what had kept them, he bit back the question and instead asked how much farther they had to go.

"Five minutes max. There's a huge trough below the pool that catches the water tipping down and most of us are level with that."

"When you reach the top you can show yourselves. There's no need for secrecy any longer."

Who was he to be talking about secrecy after confiding so little? It was a bit rich coming up with a name and telling Halliwell who to arrest at this late stage, but suspicion, even strong suspicion, hadn't amounted to certainty when they'd spoken earlier. "It's unlikely she's armed," he added, "but be careful. She's on the run now."

More minutes needed to pass before he felt confident enough about Paloma's recovery to return downstairs with her. She seemed to sense where his thoughts were and offered to try and stand, but he insisted they waited.

When they finally managed the stairs, Paloma hanging on to his arm, and emerged from the house, he expected all the action to be over. Even so, an arrest at a garden party wouldn't have been easy. Nicking the hostess, a woman popular with just about everyone, was even more problematical, party-pooping with a vengeance.

Much as he'd anticipated, the conviviality was at an end. High spirits and excited voices had been supplanted by a sense of shock. The guests were huddled in small groups in near silence. Some had their hands to their mouths. Some were actually crying. He could see uniformed police down by the pool.

But something was wrong. Everyone was staring in the same direction, towards the infinity pool.

Now he saw why.

Sally Paris was still at liberty.

She was standing barefoot and precarious at the end of the infinity pool, right on the vanishing edge. She had found a way of stepping along the hidden narrow wall that contained the great mass of the water and she'd ventured as far as it was possible to go. She had her back to everyone and was poised like a high diver above the almost vertical drop.

A suicide bid.

Diamond muttered an apology to Paloma, paused only to point to a bench under a tree, and started running down the slope of the lawn, asking himself how this had been allowed to happen. Why had nobody stopped her?

She must have started her perilous walk along the edge before the police arrived: the only explanation. Her guests had no reason to think she was a fugitive from the law. If the lady of the house chose to perform a balancing act on the tiled side of her own pool, who were they to stop her?

The first familiar face he spotted in the crowd was Keith Halliwell's, creased in concern, sweaty, dusty and red-eyed, but so good to see.

"Sorry, guv. We took longer than I said. When we finally got to the top she was already out there."

"Is she saying anything?"

"Not much at all. Soon as anyone starts to move towards her, she turns her head and threatens to jump."

"What's the other side?"

"Immediately below her? A wall. If she goes over where she's standing, she's likely to break her spine on the rim of the catch basin. If she misses, she'll fall another hundred feet down the slope we came up, easily."

The sense of helplessness at the poolside was overwhelming.

Ed Paris was there, hands cupped to his mouth, appealing to his wife to come back.

She appeared indifferent. Actually she presented an amazing image. The artifice of the infinity pool suggested she was standing on water with her own reflection crystal clear beneath her.

"This is sheer bloody lunacy," Ed shouted across the pool. "What's got into you, Sally?"

He got no response.

Diamond needed a plan, and fast. He had all his back-up team available. Their reason for being here was to deal with a possible escape bid. In any other capture operation he'd be deploying the men, directing them to close in and make the arrest, but normal strategies wouldn't work here. Policemen in uniform weren't just superfluous, they were counter-productive.

Ed bellowed to his wife to see sense.

"We can't deal with it in front of this crowd," Diamond told Halliwell. "Get your men to move everyone away, right back and out of sight inside the house."

Ed Paris gave another despairing shout. "You'll kill your-self, Sal."

"Him, especially," Diamond said.

A familiar voice hailed him from behind. "Peter, this has got out of hand. Do something for pity's sake. Lady Sally is my friend."

Georgina.

This would not go down as the best afternoon of Diamond's life. Did the twelve labours of Hercules include a lecture from the assistant chief constable? He took a deep breath and said, "It's under control, ma'am."

"It doesn't look like it. What can I do to help?"

"You?"

"You heard me. Shall I step along the edge of the pool and speak to her?"

Amazing.

She meant it, too. Behind the officious manner was a brave woman.

"That's a fine offer, ma'am, but I can't allow it. We could lose both of you. There's something else you can do."

"Tell me, then."

"Set an example and move up to the house. We're in the process of clearing the poolside, taking some of the pressure off her."

"But can you save her from jumping?"

"That's my sincere hope, ma'am."

Georgina didn't act as if she was wholly confident, but others were already heeding the call and starting to move off. Sighing and shaking her head, she joined them.

Ed Paris was refusing to leave. John Leaman was with him and made the mistake of grasping his arm. Ed turned on him and all the stress exploded. "Don't you dare bloody touch me."

Diamond went over. "Leave it, John." With a tilt of his head he sent Leaman away and stepped closer to the troubled tycoon to speak in confidence. "Sir Edward, I've been talking to your wife. There's distressing stuff in her past that made her resort to this, things bottled up from before you ever knew her."

The already alarmed eyes widened even more. "What do you mean?"

"There isn't time to explain. She's obviously at desperation point and she's not going to be persuaded by anything you can say."

Ed's mouth tightened in disbelief, but he didn't answer.

"There's a chance, just a chance, I can get through to her. Will you let me try?"

For a second or two more, Ed wrestled with the suggestion. It must have been obvious to him he wasn't getting anywhere with Sally himself, but it was like a betrayal to give up. "She's my whole life," he blurted out. "I couldn't bear to lose her."

Diamond wouldn't give up. Ed, more than anyone, could ruin any chance of talking Sally down. He had to be persuaded to leave. "I'm asking everyone—that's everyone including you—to leave me here to reason with her." He added, almost in a whisper, "Trust me. I can save her."

Still the anguished husband lingered.

"Please."

"My God, man, you'd better be right." With that Ed turned away and followed the general movement towards the house.

Relieved that something was being done, most people had responded quickly once the police had started issuing instructions.

In the remaining time it took for Diamond to be sure he was alone with Sally, he thought about what he would do to make this succeed. Ed's words would haunt him for ever if this gamble ended in disaster.

Across the pool, nothing had changed. A faint breeze disturbed Sally's white dress, but her stance was rigid.

He stripped to his boxers, left his clothes where they fell on the marble flagstones and stepped down the tiled steps into the blue water. Success or failure and nothing between—he was committed now.

The sensation of the cool water on his skin after the heat of the afternoon should have been bracing. He scarcely registered the change, intent on what he needed to do. The depth was a little over four feet. He bent his knees, submerged his back and shoulders and started a silent breaststroke up the centre of the pool.

No heroics. He wouldn't be grabbing her legs and hoping she tipped backwards. She'd just as likely topple forward.

He swam to within ten feet of her and stopped. The depth was no different at this end, so he was able to stand with head and shoulders clear.

The next stage was steeped in danger, however he handled it. She would already be aware that the conversation behind her had stopped. Hearing his voice unexpectedly might startle her and that could be the end.

He said in little more than a murmur, "Sally, it's all right."

Plainly she didn't hear.

He repeated the words, still with scarcely any volume, and her calf muscles twitched.

She didn't change her stance or turn her back, but she rotated her head as far to the right as possible. It was the briefest of looks before she faced the front again and she couldn't possibly have seen him. He was way outside her angle of vision. At best she might appreciate that the poolside was deserted now.

"Everyone's gone except me," he told her. "Peter Diamond, in the water behind you. Turn right round and check if you want."

Too much to ask. She was facing death and she wouldn't budge.

So be it, he told himself. This will be a monologue.

How to start? Say something reassuring. "Your husband Ed pleaded with me that he should stay here, but I persuaded him to go up to the house with the others. He doesn't know what we discussed in the dressmaking room. Nobody knows, except you, me and Paloma, and I doubt if Paloma took much of it in."

Her clenched hands tightened. She was listening, for sure.

"I don't suppose you've thought it through, what will happen next, so I want to explain some things you may not appreciate. I've got a lot of sympathy for you, Sally, and I'm certain any court of law will be sympathetic, too."

The balance between empathy and harsh reality was so difficult to strike. In a sense, her footing was far more secure than his.

"Only you know precisely what happened in the Twerton house in 1997, how Sidney Harrod met his death. I'm assuming he got physical, coming on to you sexually, and you didn't intend to kill him. You acted in self-defence. If so, it wasn't murder. There was no premeditation. You picked up the scissors to defend yourself. At worst, it would count as manslaughter if the force you used was not reasonable, but any lawyer worth his salt would convince a judge and jury that you were under attack and the worst thing you did was to conceal a death and fail to report it and I'm guessing Harry Morgan was the instigator there. You wouldn't walk free without some sort of technical penalty, but judges have a lot of discretion and it's well possible you'd receive a deferred sentence."

He was trying to thought-read from watching her back. There was visible flexing in her shoulders while he was speaking. At least he was getting a hearing.

"Of course the other death, the shooting of Perry, is more serious in the eyes of the law because there was an element of planning. You took the gun with you to the fireworks show intending to shoot him, to kill him, in fact, and that's murder. A mandatory life sentence. But do you have any idea what that amounts to?"

He paused. He wasn't expecting her to reply. His best hope was to engage her in what he was saying. He waited and she turned her head a fraction as if she wanted to hear more and he took that as involvement.

He started over. "I shouldn't be saying this, but I've known cases where a life sentence meant less than six years in prison. These days a judge looks at all the circumstances and decides on the tariff, the term you actually serve. It can be as low as five years and once you've served that you can be considered for release on parole."

This was so difficult without seeing the reactions playing over her face.

"It's all about mitigating factors. Perry was trying to blackmail you. He needed the money to fund his drugs and it was obvious that if you paid him, the demands would go on indefinitely. An addict isn't reliable. You couldn't have any confidence he would keep your secret even if you paid him. Those are the mitigating factors your legal team would make clear to the judge. I can't predict what your minimum tariff would be, but it doesn't mean spending the rest of your life in prison, that's certain."

There wasn't any more he could usefully tell her. She'd need to plead guilty and that would be factored in by the judge, but he didn't want to inundate her with detail. He'd made the point about life sentences and, frustratingly, all he'd achieved were minimal signs of interest. She remained one short step from killing herself.

There was a last card he could play.

"Your husband's going through hell, Sally."

Unexpectedly, she turned her head again. And remarkably she had something to say.

"That's a prize porky if ever I heard one."

The first words she'd spoken in ten minutes were a rebuke, defiant and typical of the spirited woman he knew her to be.

She hadn't finished either. "Ed doesn't have the faintest. We've been married twelve years and I've told him diddley-squat about my past."

Her remark of much earlier, about the failing marriage, could be the clue to what was going on here.

But Diamond had got a different impression. Ed's desperation was fresher in his memory. "You misunderstood me. He's not going through hell because you killed two men. The poor guy's at the end of his tether. He can't understand why you're doing this. He loves you to bits—that's obvious. He's immensely proud of you. I've seen the look on his face when you're hosting an event like today, charming everybody, making sure it's a big success."

She'd gone silent again.

"Believe me, Sally, he'll be devastated if you jump. It won't just be your life that comes to an end. His world will collapse as well."

"Oh, fiddlesticks."

She exhaled, turned right about, stepped off the wall

and plopped into the water. A massive anticlimax. As a demonstration of love, it was unusual, but that was what it was, her commitment to Ed confirmed in one life-affirming drenching.

She surfaced and said, "Come on, squire, I'd better face the music."

After splashing towards him she linked her arm in his and together they waded the length of the pool. It was the strangest arrest Diamond would ever make. He didn't have the heart to speak the formal words required by law.

They made their way up the sloping lawn, she in her bare feet and wet, clinging dress, he in nothing except his striped boxer shorts. As they approached the ugly steel and glass house, the guests streamed out to meet them and formed an impromptu guard of honour and applauded. They didn't know Sally was a double-killer. She was their hostess who had come to her senses and chosen life over death.

The exhausted policemen who had spent most of the afternoon climbing the hill joined in the clapping. Even Georgina was celebrating the moment. The CID team were savouring it as well. Someone had collected Ingeborg and she was getting a photo.

Ed was waiting at the top of the steps with towels. He gave Sally a hug that seemed to last forever and then he turned to Diamond and hugged him as well. "Thanks, mate. I owe you a drink."

They moved into the reception room.

That wretched hologram was still on its stand facing them. Diamond couldn't be certain, but he thought he got a wink from Beau Nash.

A Note on Sources

Oliver Goldsmith's *Life of Richard Nash, of Bath, Esq* (1762), written a year after Nash's death, with the advantage of access to Nash's own fragments of autobiography, remains a fascinating work that can be read online. The other biographies consulted by the present author were *Bath under Beau Nash*, by Lewis Melville (Lewis S. Benjamin) (Eveleigh Nash, 1907); *Beau Nash: Monarch of Bath and Tunbridge Wells*, by Willard Connely (Werner Laurie, 1955); *Splendour and Scandal: the Reign of Beau Nash*, by John Walters (Jarrolds, 1968); and *The Imaginary Autocrat: Beau Nash and the Invention of Bath*, by John Eglin (Profile Books, 2005). Nash's entry in the *Dictionary of National Biography* was first written by Thomas Seccombe in 1894. The latest online version is by Philip Carter in 2009.

Of the sources mentioned in passing, the contemporary account of Nash's funeral was in the *Whitehall Evening Post or London Intelligencer*, 21 February 1761. The notice of Juliana Papjoy's death and strange living arrangements is in the *Annual Register* for March, 1777. George Scott's correspondence of 1761 concerning the formidable Mrs. Hill is discussed in Eglin's book and is held at the British Library in the Egerton collection. The details of Dr. Walsh's participation in the 1909 Bath Pageant can be found in *The Year of the Pageant*, by Andrew Swift and Kirsten Elliott (Akeman Press, 2009).

It only remains to be said that the Beau Nash Society and all its members, Widcombe Hall and the house at Charlcombe with the infinity pool were products of the author's imagination.

Other Titles in the Soho Crime Series

Sebastià Alzamora
(Spain)
Blood Crime

Stephanie Barron
(Jane Austen's England)
*Jane and the Twelve Days
of Christmas*
Jane and the Waterloo Map

F.H. Batacan
(Philippines)
Smaller and Smaller Circles

James R. Benn
(World War II Europe)
Billy Boyle
The First Wave
Blood Alone
Evil for Evil
Rag & Bone
A Mortal Terror
Death's Door
A Blind Goddess
The Rest Is Silence
The White Ghost
Blue Madonna
The Devouring

Cara Black
(Paris, France)
Murder in the Marais
Murder in Belleville
Murder in the Sentier
Murder in the Bastille
Murder in Clichy
Murder in Montmartre
*Murder on the
Ile Saint-Louis*
*Murder in the
Rue de Paradis*
Murder in the Latin Quarter
Murder in the Palais Royal
Murder in Passy
*Murder at the
Lanterne Rouge*
*Murder Below
Montparnasse*
Murder in Pigalle

Cara Black cont.
*Murder on the
Champ de Mars*
Murder on the Quai
Murder in Saint-Germain
Murder on the Left Bank

Lisa Brackmann
(China)
Rock Paper Tiger
Hour of the Rat
Dragon Day

Getaway
Go-Between

Henry Chang
(Chinatown)
Chinatown Beat
Year of the Dog
Red Jade
Death Money
Lucky

Barbara Cleverly
(England)
The Last Kashmiri Rose
Strange Images of Death
The Blood Royal
Not My Blood
A Spider in the Cup
Enter Pale Death
Diana's Altar
Fall of Angels

Gary Corby
(Ancient Greece)
The Pericles Commission
The Ionia Sanction
Sacred Games
The Marathon Conspiracy
Death Ex Machina
The Singer from Memphis
Death on Delos

Colin Cotterill
(Laos)
The Coroner's Lunch
Thirty-Three Teeth
Disco for the Departed

Colin Cotterill cont.
Anarchy and Old Dogs
Curse of the Pogo Stick
The Merry Misogynist
*Love Songs from
a Shallow Grave*
Slash and Burn
*The Woman Who
Wouldn't Die*
*Six and a
Half Deadly Sins*
I Shot the Buddha
The Rat Catchers' Olympics
Don't Eat Me

Garry Disher
(Australia)
The Dragon Man
Kittyhawk Down
Snapshot
Chain of Evidence
Blood Moon
Wyatt
Whispering Death
Port Vila Blues
Fallout
Hell to Pay
Signal Loss

David Downing
(World War II Germany)
Zoo Station
Silesian Station
Stettin Station
Potsdam Station
Lehrter Station
Masaryk Station

(World War I)
Jack of Spies
One Man's Flag
Lenin's Roller Coaster
The Dark Clouds Shining

Agnete Friis
(Denmark)
What My Body Remembers

Leighton Gage
(Brazil)
Blood of the Wicked
Buried Strangers
Dying Gasp
Every Bitter Thing
A Vine in the Blood
Perfect Hatred
The Ways of Evil Men

Michael Genelin
(Slovakia)
Siren of the Waters
Dark Dreams
The Magician's Accomplice
Requiem for a Gypsy

Timothy Hallinan
(Thailand)
The Fear Artist
For the Dead
The Hot Countries
Fools' River

(Los Angeles)
Crashed
Little Elvises
The Fame Thief
Herbie's Game
King Maybe
Fields Where They Lay

Karo Hämäläinen
(Finland)
Cruel Is the Night

Mette Ivie Harrison
(Mormon Utah)
The Bishop's Wife
His Right Hand
For Time and All Eternities

Mick Herron
(England)
Down Cemetery Road
The Last Voice You Hear
Reconstruction
Smoke and Whispers
Why We Die
Slow Horses
Dead Lions

Mick Herron cont.
Nobody Walks
Real Tigers
Spook Street
This Is What Happened
London Rules

**Lene Kaaberbøl &
Agnete Friis**
(Denmark)
The Boy in the Suitcase
Invisible Murder
Death of a Nightingale
The Considerate Killer

Heda Margolius Kovály
(1950s Prague)
Innocence

Martin Limón
(South Korea)
Jade Lady Burning
Slicky Boys
Buddha's Money
The Door to Bitterness
The Wandering Ghost
G.I. Bones
Mr. Kill
The Joy Brigade
Nightmare Range
The Iron Sickle
The Ville Rat
Ping-Pong Heart
The Nine-Tailed Fox

Ed Lin
(Taiwan)
Ghost Month
Incensed

Peter Lovesey
(England)
The Circle
The Headhunters
False Inspector Dew
Rough Cider
On the Edge
The Reaper

(Bath, England)
The Last Detective

Peter Lovesey cont.
Diamond Solitaire
The Summons
Bloodhounds
Upon a Dark Night
The Vault
Diamond Dust
The House Sitter
The Secret Hangman
Skeleton Hill
Stagestruck
Cop to Corpse
The Tooth Tattoo
The Stone Wife
*Down Among
the Dead Men*
Another One Goes Tonight
Beau Death

(London, England)
Wobble to Death
*The Detective Wore
Silk Drawers*
Abracadaver
Mad Hatter's Holiday
The Tick of Death
A Case of Spirits
Swing, Swing Together
Waxwork

Jassy Mackenzie
(South Africa)
Random Violence
Stolen Lives
The Fallen
Pale Horses
Bad Seeds

Sujata Massey
(1920s Bombay)
*The Widows of
Malabar Hill*

Francine Mathews
(Nantucket)
Death in the Off-Season
Death in Rough Water
Death in a Mood Indigo
Death in a Cold Hard Light
Death on Nantucket

Seichō Matsumoto
(Japan)
Inspector Imanishi
Investigates

Magdalen Nabb
(Italy)
Death of an Englishman
Death of a Dutchman
Death in Springtime
Death in Autumn
The Marshal and
the Murderer
The Marshal and
the Madwoman
The Marshal's Own Case
The Marshal Makes
His Report
The Marshal
at the Villa Torrini
Property of Blood
Some Bitter Taste
The Innocent
Vita Nuova
The Monster of Florence

Fuminori Nakamura
(Japan)
The Thief
Evil and the Mask
Last Winter, We Parted
The Kingdom
The Boy in the Earth
Cult X

Stuart Neville
(Northern Ireland)
The Ghosts of Belfast
Collusion
Stolen Souls
The Final Silence
Those We Left Behind
So Say the Fallen

(Dublin)
Ratlines

Rebecca Pawel
(1930s Spain)
Death of a Nationalist
Law of Return
The Watcher in the Pine
The Summer Snow

Kwei Quartey
(Ghana)
Murder at Cape
Three Points
Gold of Our Fathers
Death by His Grace

Qiu Xiaolong
(China)
Death of a Red Heroine
A Loyal Character Dancer
When Red Is Black

John Straley
(Sitka, Alaska)

The Woman Who Married
a Bear
The Curious Eat Themselves
The Music of What Happens
Death and the Language of
Happiness
The Angels Will Not Care
Cold Water Burning
Baby's First Felony

(Cold Storage, Alaska)
The Big Both Ways
Cold Storage, Alaska

Akimitsu Takagi
(Japan)
The Tattoo Murder Case
Honeymoon to Nowhere
The Informer

Helene Tursten
(Sweden)
Detective Inspector Huss
The Torso
The Glass Devil
Night Rounds

Helene Tursten cont.
The Golden Calf
The Fire Dance
The Beige Man
The Treacherous Net
Who Watcheth
Protected by the Shadows

Janwillem van de
Wetering
(Holland)
Outsider in Amsterdam
Tumbleweed
The Corpse on the Dike
Death of a Hawker
The Japanese Corpse
The Blond Baboon
The Maine Massacre
The Mind-Murders
The Streetbird
The Rattle-Rat
Hard Rain
Just a Corpse at Twilight
Hollow-Eyed Angel
The Perfidious Parrot
The Sergeant's Cat:
Collected Stories

Timothy Williams
(Guadeloupe)
Another Sun
The Honest Folk
of Guadeloupe

(Italy)
Converging Parallels
The Puppeteer
Persona Non Grata
Black August
Big Italy
The Second Day
of the Renaissance

Jacqueline Winspear
(1920s England)
Maisie Dobbs
Birds of a Feather